Praise for Emma Miller and her novels

"There is warmth to the characters that will leave readers looking forward to seeing more."
—*RT Book Reviews* on *A Match for Addy*

"[A] heart-warming romance."
—*RT Book Reviews* on *Courting Ruth*

"A captivating story."
—*RT Book Reviews* on *Miriam's Heart*

Praise for Alison Stone and her novels

"A captivating story full of exciting details and clever plotting."
—*RT Book Reviews* on *Plain Protector*

"Stone creates a great balance of action and romance, coupled with some interesting twists."
—*RT Book Reviews* on *Silver Lake Secrets*

"[A] well-researched tale with an engaging pace… it contains sweet romance, palpable suspense."
—*RT Book Reviews* on *Plain Peril*

Emma Miller lives quietly in her old farmhouse in rural Delaware. Fortunate enough to be born into a family of strong faith, she grew up on a dairy farm surrounded by loving parents, siblings, grandparents, aunts, uncles and cousins. Emma was educated in local schools and once taught in an Amish schoolhouse. When she's not caring for her large family, reading and writing are her favorite pastimes.

Alison Stone lives with her husband of more than twenty years and their four children in Western New York. Besides writing, Alison keeps busy volunteering at her children's schools, driving her girls to dance and watching her boys race motocross. Alison loves to hear from her readers at Alison@AlisonStone.com. For more information, please visit her website, alisonstone.com. She's also chatty on Twitter, @alison_stone. Find her on Facebook at Facebook.com/alisonstoneauthor.

EMMA MILLER
Johanna's Bridegroom

&

ALISON STONE
Plain Protector

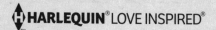

HARLEQUIN® LOVE INSPIRED®

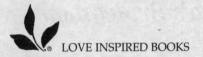 LOVE INSPIRED BOOKS

Recycling programs for this product may not exist in your area.

ISBN-13: 978-0-373-20973-6

Johanna's Bridegroom and Plain Protector

Copyright © 2017 by Harlequin Books S.A.

The publisher acknowledges the copyright holders of the individual works as follows:

Johanna's Bridegroom
Copyright © 2013 by Emma Miller

Plain Protector
Copyright © 2016 by Alison Stone

www.Harlequin.com

Printed in U.S.A.

CONTENTS

JOHANNA'S BRIDEGROOM

Emma Miller

Love is patient, love is kind. It does not envy,
it does not boast, it is not proud.
—*1 Corinthians* 13:4

Chapter One

Kent County, Delaware
June

Johanna kissed her sister's newborn and inhaled the infant's sweet baby scent before gently placing her into the antique walnut cradle. It was midafternoon, and Johanna, Anna, Rebecca and *Grossmama* were gathered on the screened-in back porch of the Mast farmhouse, enjoying cold lemonade and hulling a bounty of end-of-the-season strawberries to make jam.

Johanna stood over the cradle, gazing down at the baby's long thick lashes, her chubby, pink cheeks and the riot of red-gold curls peeping out from under her antique, white-lace bonnet. Tiny Rose sighed in her sleep, opened one perfect hand, pursed her perfectly formed lips and melted Johanna's heart. Tears blurred her vision. *She's so precious.*

It wasn't that she coveted Anna and Samuel's gift from God. She didn't. But it seemed so long since her own children had been newborns. Jonah, at five, was now old enough to be a real help in the garden and barnyard.

And, as he reminded her at least three times a day, he'd be starting school in the fall. Even her chatterbox, Katy, now three, had outgrown her baby smocks and become independent overnight. She was always eager to sweep the kitchen floor with her miniature broom, gather eggs and pick strawberries in the wake of the bigger children.

I want another baby, Johanna admitted to herself. *My arms ache for another child, but having one means marrying again.* And after her unhappy marriage to Wilmer Detweiler, and the tragedy of his suicide, she wasn't certain she had the strength to face that yet.

She knew that the children she had, especially Jonah, needed a father. She and Jonah had always been close, but there were so many things that only a man could teach him—how to plow and trim a horse's hooves, when to cut hay, how to mend a broken windmill. And while Wilmer had been kind to Katy, he'd shown only stern disapproval and constant criticism of Jonah. For all his energy and warm heart, Jonah desperately needed a loving father's guidance. Without it, Johanna feared that Jonah would never fully understand how to grow into a man. And she wasn't the only one who had come to that conclusion. It had been two years since Wilmer's death, and members of the community and her family had been hinting that it was time she remarry. Johanna prayed every night that she would know when the time was right and that God would bring a good man into her life.

"She's adorable, Anna." *Beautiful,* she thought, but she didn't say the word out loud. Physical beauty wasn't something the Old Order Amish were supposed to dwell on. Better a child or an adult have grace and a pure spirit within than a pleasing face.

"And such an easy baby," *Grossmama* said. "Like my

Jonas. A *gut* baby." She capped a large crimson strawberry and popped it in her mouth. Closing her eyes, she chewed contentedly, savoring the sweet flavor.

Anna looked up from the earthenware bowl in her lap and smiled with barely contained pride. "Rose is a good baby, isn't she? Poor Samuel can't believe it. He keeps getting out of bed at night to make certain she's still breathing."

Grossmama's eyes snapped open, and she nodded so hard her bonnet strings bounced. "Happy *mudder,* happy *kinner.* And such a quick delivery. Pray that Martha has such an easy birth when her time comes."

"It's Ruth who's expecting," Rebecca gently reminded her grandmother. "Not Aunt Martha. Our sister Ruth."

Johanna tried not to smile at the thought of Aunt Martha, older than her mother, having a new baby. *Grossmama's* physical health had been good, and she seemed happier since coming to live with Anna, but her memory continued to fail. Not only was she convinced that Anna's husband, Samuel, was her dead son, Jonas, but she mixed up names and people so often that one had to constantly think twice when one had a conversation with her. Only yesterday, *Grossmama* had been certain that Bishop Atlee was her new beau, come to take her to a frolic. Johanna couldn't help wondering what the English at the senior center, where *Grossmama* taught rug making several days a week, thought of their grandmother.

"Are these the last of them?" Rebecca asked. Two brimming dishpans of ripe strawberries stood on the table, waiting to be washed and crushed before being added to the bubbling kettles on the stove.

"No," Johanna said. "I think there's one more flat. I'll go—" She broke off as the pounding of a horse's hooves on the dirt lane caught her attention. "It's Irwin!"

She snatched open the screen door and hurried down the wooden steps, wondering why he was in such a hurry.

Blackie galloped into the yard with Irwin, hatless and white-faced, clinging to his bare back. Chickens squawked and flew in all directions as the teenager yanked the gelding up so hard that the horse began to buck, and Irwin nearly tumbled off.

"What's wrong?" Johanna cried. Irwin, the teen who Johanna's mother had adopted, never moved faster than molasses in January. "Ruth's not—"

"Not Ruth! It's Roland's J.J."

Roland. For an instant, Johanna felt paralyzed. *If Roland was in danger, she—* No, she told herself, *not Roland. J.J., Roland's little boy.* The moment passed and she regained her self-control. "What is it?" she demanded.

Irwin half slid, half jumped to the ground, letting the reins slip through his hands. Blackie made one more leap and blew flecks of foam from his mouth and nose. Neck and tail arched, the spirited horse trotted onto the lawn, where, after a few more antics, he began to snatch up mouthfuls of grass.

"You've got to come! *Schnell!*" Irwin steadied himself and ran toward Johanna. "Bees! A swarm! In Roland's tree. They're crawling all over J.J.! Roland says they could sting him to death!"

"Bees?" Johanna asked. "Roland doesn't keep bees." *If J.J. was in danger, she had to go, but how could she go? After everything that lay between them, knowing how she felt, how could Roland ask it of her?* "Are you certain they're honeybees?"

Irwin nodded. "H…honeybees!"

Johanna grabbed him by his thin shoulders and shook him. "Calm down!" she ordered. "Has J.J. been stung?"

"Ne." Irwin shook his head. "Roland doesn't know what to do. He says you have to come. You know bees."

"All right," Johanna agreed. J.J.'s little face, the image of his father, flashed through her thoughts, and she swallowed, trying to keep her voice from showing what she really felt. "You run to our farm," she instructed Irwin calmly. "Get my smoker and my bee suit and an empty nuc box and bring them to Roland's."

He knitted his eyebrows. "What kind of box?"

"A used hive body. A deep one. And don't forget my lemongrass oil. It's on the shelf beside my gloves. Bring them to Roland's." She took a deep breath and pressed her hands to her sides to keep anyone from seeing them tremble. "Can you remember all that?"

He nodded.

"Good. Now run, as quickly as you can!"

Anna and Rebecca had followed her into the yard. "What's happened?" Rebecca asked.

"Irwin says that there's a swarm of bees at Roland's."

"In the tree! By the pond. And…and J.J.'s up in the tree with them," Irwin said. For all his fourteen years, he looked as though he was about to burst into tears. Red patches stood out on his blotchy complexion, and his hay-thatch hair stuck up in tufts. Somewhere, he'd lost his hat, and one suspender sagged.

"Go now," Johanna told Irwin. "And don't stop for anything!"

Irwin took off.

"I've got to go see what I can do," Johanna said to Rebecca and Anna, taking care not to show how flustered she really was. She'd been an apiarist long enough to know that it was important to remain calm with bees. They seemed to be able to sense a person's mood and the best way to calm a hive—or a swarm—was to stay calm herself. *As if that's possible,* the warning voice in her head whispered, *when you have to go to Roland's house and pretend you're only friends.*

"Take one of our buggies," Anna offered. "We'll help you hitch—"

"Ne." Johanna glanced from her sisters to where the horse grazed on the lawn. "There's no time. I'll ride Blackie."

"Bareback?" Anna's eyes widened. "Are you sure? Blackie's—"

"Headstrong. Skittish. I know." Johanna grimaced. "It isn't as if we didn't get thrown off worse when we were kids." *How could she tell Anna that she was afraid? Not of Blackie or of being thrown, but of Roland...of the past she'd thought she'd put behind her years ago?*

"You're going to ride astride, like a man?" Rebecca shook her head. "It's against the *Ordnung.* Not fitting for women. Bishop Atlee will—"

"J.J.'s life might be in danger. The bishop will understand that this is an emergency," Johanna answered with more confidence than she felt. Her heart raced as she bent and ripped up a handful of grass and walked slowly toward Blackie. The animal rolled his eyes and backed up a few steps, ears pricked and muscles tensed.

"Easy," Johanna soothed. "Good boy. Just a little closer." She inched forward and grabbed a trailing rein. "Give me a boost up," she said to her sisters.

Rebecca shook her head. "You're going to be in *sooo* much trouble."

Ignoring Rebecca, Anna moved to Blackie's side and cupped her hands. Johanna thrust a bare foot into the makeshift stirrup and swung up onto the horse's back.

"Was is?" Grossmama shouted. *"Baremlich!"*

But Johanna had already pulled Blackie's head around, grabbed a handful of mane and dug her heels into the animal's sides. Blackie broke into a trot, and they galloped away.

Roland Byler's stomach did a flip-flop as he stood by the pond and stared up at his only child. J.J. had climbed into the branches of a Granny Smith apple tree and sat with his back against the trunk and his legs swinging down on either side of a branch. He was at least eight feet off the ground, but the distance ordinarily wouldn't have worried Roland too much. Although J.J. was only four, he was strong and agile, and climbed like a squirrel. He'd been scrambling up ladders and into trees almost since he'd learned to walk. What terrified Roland today was that his son was surrounded by thousands of honeybees.

"Please, God, protect him," Roland murmured under his breath. And louder, to J.J., he called, "Sit still, don't move. Don't do anything to startle them."

J.J. giggled. "Don't be scared, *Dat*. They won't hurt me. They like me." Bees surrounded him, walking on his bare feet, his arms and fingers. They buzzed around his head and face and crawled in his hair. And only inches from J.J.'s head, a wriggling cluster of the winged insects, thicker than the boy's body, swayed on a slender branch.

"Don't make any noise," Roland warned as J.J. began to hum the tune to an old hymn. Roland's heart thudded against his ribs, his skin was clammy-cold and his chest felt so tight that it was hard to breathe. "Do as I say!" he ordered.

When Roland was ten, he'd had a cousin in the Kishacoquillas Valley who'd attempted to rob a honey tree and had been stung to death. Roland shuddered, trying to shut out the memory of the dead boy's swollen and disfigured face as he lay in his coffin.

He couldn't dwell on his poor cousin or his grieving family. The bishop who'd delivered the sermon at his funeral had assured them that the boy was safe with God. Roland knew that was what the Bible taught. This world wasn't important. It was only a preparation for the next, but Roland's faith wasn't always as strong as he would like. His cousin's parents had had six living children remaining when they lost their son. J.J. was all he had. Roland had survived the death of his wife, Pauline, and the unborn babies she'd been carrying, but if he lost this precious son, his own life would be over.

"They tickle." J.J. giggled again. "Climb up, *Dat,* and see how nice they are."

"Hush. I told you not to move." All sorts of wild ideas surfaced in Roland's head. Maybe he could cut down the tree and J.J. could jump free. Or he could tell J.J. to jump into his arms. He'd leap into the pond—washing the bees off them both before they could sting them. But Roland knew that was foolishness. Neither of them could move fast enough. The bees were already crawling all over J.J.

Besides, if Roland startled the swarm, they might all attack both of them. He didn't care about himself, but his son was so small. The child could be stung hundreds of times in just a minute. Roland's only hope was prayer and the belief that Irwin would return soon with Johanna. She was a beekeeper. She worked with bees every day. If anyone could tell him what to do to save his child, it would be Johanna.

"Dat!" J.J. waved a bee-covered hand and pointed toward the meadow that bordered the road.

Roland looked up to see the Yoders' black horse coming fast across the pasture. But there was no gate along that fence line. Irwin would have to backtrack around by the farmyard to get to the pond. But the boy was galloping straight on toward—

Roland's stomach pitched. That wasn't Irwin on Blackie! The rider wore a blue dress and a white *Kapp*. *A girl? It couldn't be.* "Johanna?" Roland backed away from the tree and ran toward the fence waving his arms. *Was she blind? Couldn't she see there was no opening? Why hadn't she reined in the horse? Surely, she couldn't mean to...* "No!" he bellowed. "Don't try to jump that—"

But as the words came out of his mouth, Roland saw that it was too late. Blackie soared over the three-rail fence and came thundering down, Johanna clinging stubbornly to his back. She yanked back on the reins, but the horse had the bit between his teeth and didn't slacken his pace. When the gelding didn't respond, she pulled hard on one rein, forcing him to circle left. He dug in his front legs, then tried to rear, but she fought him to a trot and finally to a walk. Johanna pulled up ten feet from Roland and slid down off the horse's sweat-streaked back.

Johanna landed barefoot in the grass and straightened her *Kapp* as she hurried toward him. "Is J.J. all right?" she asked.

Speechless, Roland stared gape-mouthed at her. She was breathing hard but otherwise seemed no worse for her wild careen across the field. All he could think was that she had come. Johanna had come, and she'd find a way to save his son. But what he said was, "Are you crazy? You? A grown woman with two children? To ride that horse bareback like some madcap boy?"

Johanna...the woman who might have been his...who might have been J.J.'s mother if not for one stupid night of foolishness.

"Are you finished?" she asked, scolding him as if he was the one who'd just done something outrageous. Her chin went up and tiny lines of disapproval creased the corners of her beautiful eyes—eyes so piercingly blue and direct that for an instant, he didn't see a delicate woman standing there. In a flash, he saw, instead, Johanna's father, Jonas Yoder, as strong a man in faith and courage as Roland had ever known.

Johanna walked to the base of the tree, her gaze taking in J.J. and the writhing mass of bees above him. "Hi," she called.

"Hi." J.J. grinned at her, despite the two bees crawling over his chin. "Look at all the bees," he said. "Aren't they neat?"

"Very neat," she answered softly. She tilted her head back. "That's a lot of bees."

"A hundred, at least," J.J. agreed.

Roland stifled a groan. "There must be thousands of them," he whispered.

Johanna smiled, ignoring Roland. "You're a brave boy. Some people are afraid of honeybees."

J.J. nodded. "They're nice."

"I think so, too." Johanna glanced back at Roland. A bee lit on her *Kapp,* but she didn't seem to notice. "Do you have a stepladder?"

"In the shed."

"Could you go get it? Irwin should be coming anytime with my bee equipment. When he gets here, bring it to me. Keep Irwin away." She grimaced. "He makes the bees nervous."

"They make *me* nervous." Roland looked from her to J.J. and back at her again. "Are you going to smoke them? I've heard that calms them."

"It probably wouldn't hurt." She glanced back at the swarm. "They've left someone's bee box somewhere, or a hollow tree," she said to J.J. "Or maybe an abandoned building."

"Why did they do that?" the boy asked.

"Probably because their queen was old or the hive got too crowded. They're being so friendly because they don't have honey to protect." She shrugged. "They're just looking for a new home."

"Oh."

"Were they in the tree when you climbed up there?" she asked.

J.J. nodded. "I wanted to see what they were doing."

"He's been singing to them," Roland said, swallowing to try to dissolve his fear. "He just didn't understand how dangerous it was."

"The bees didn't sting me," J.J. said. "They like me."

"Do they like it when you sing?" Johanna asked. And when J.J. nodded, she added, "Then you can sing to them, if you want to. I sing to mine all the time."

J.J. giggled. "You do?"

"The ladder," she reminded Roland as she continued to watch J.J. in the tree.

Roland backed away slowly. He was still sweating and his hands and feet felt wooden, but some of the awful despair that had paralyzed him earlier had ebbed away. *Johanna didn't seem alarmed. Obviously, she had a plan.*

He turned and ran. "Don't leave him."

"Don't worry," she called after him. "We're fine, aren't we, J.J.?"

"Ya, Dat," he heard his son say. "We're fine."

Pray to God you are. Roland lengthened his stride, running with every ounce of strength in his body.

Chapter Two

"Honeybees are wonderful creatures," Johanna told J.J. He nodded, still seemingly unafraid of the dozens of insects crawling in his hair and over his body. J.J. was calm and happy, which was good. Far too many people feared bees, and she had always believed that they sensed when you were afraid. "Do you like honey on your biscuits?" she asked, trying to distract him while they waited for Roland to return with the ladder.

"My *grossmama* makes biscuits sometimes. And my aunt Mary. *Dat* doesn't know how." A mischievous grin spread across J.J.'s freckled face, and he blew a bee off his nose. "*Dat's* biscuits are yucky. He always burns them."

"Biscuits can be tricky if you don't watch them carefully," Johanna agreed. She glanced from the boy to where Blackie grazed. When Roland got back, she'd ask him to catch the horse and walk him until he cooled down. A horse that drank too much cold water when he was hot sometimes foundered.

Absentmindedly, Johanna rubbed her shoulder. It had been years since she'd ridden a horse, and tomorrow she'd feel every day of her twenty-seven years. Not that she'd admit it to Roland or anyone else, but jumping a three-rail fence bareback hadn't been her idea. It had been Blackie's. And by the time she realized that there was no opening in the fence and no gate, it was too late to keep the gelding from going over.

In spite of his high-spirited willfulness, Johanna was fond of Blackie. He had a sweet disposition and he never tried to bite or kick. Despite *Mam's* salary from teaching school, money from the farm, and the income from Johanna's bees, turkeys and quilts, money was always tight. If anything happened to the young driving horse, the family would find it difficult to replace him.

"Here comes *Dat,*" J.J. announced.

"Remember to think good thoughts," Johanna said aloud. In her head, she repeated the thought over and over.

"J.J., did you know that a community of bees thinks all together, like they have one brain?" she asked him, in an attempt to keep her composure, as well as help him keep his. "This swarm has drones and workers and, in the middle, a queen. The others all protect her, because without the queen, there can be no colony."

"Why did they land in this tree in a big ball?"

"They're looking for a new home. For some reason, and we don't know why, they couldn't live in their old house anymore. They won't stay here in the tree. They need to find a safe place where they can store their honey, protect the queen and safely raise baby bees."

"Uncle Charley said that when a honeybee stings you, it dies."

Johanna nodded. "Uncle Charley's right. But a bee won't sting unless it's afraid, afraid you'll hurt it or that you'll harm the hive. That's why we stay calm and think happy thoughts when we're near the bees."

"They like me to sing to them."

She smiled at J.J., wondering how so much wisdom lived in that small head. "Who taught you about bees?"

The little boy's forehead wrinkled in concentration, and Johanna's heart skipped a beat. She'd seen that exact expression a hundred times on Roland's face. *You think you can put the past behind you, but you can't.* All this time, she'd been telling herself that she didn't care anymore. And she'd been wrong. Her throat clenched. She'd loved Roland Byler for more than half her life, and in spite of everything he'd done to destroy that love, she was afraid that some part of her still cared.

"Nobody told me," J.J. said solemnly. "Bees are my friends."

Johanna nodded. "You know what I think, J.J.? I think God gave you a special gift. I think you're a bee charmer."

"I am?" He flashed another grin. "A bee charmer. That's me."

Roland halted behind Johanna with the ladder over his shoulder. "Where do you want this? I brought some old rags and matches, in case you want to try to smoke the swarm."

"No sign of Irwin?" Johanna looked back toward the house. "He should have been here by now."

"I saw your buggy coming up the road. He'll be here in a few minutes." Roland glanced up at his son. "Are you all right? No stings?"

"Ne, Dat." J.J. grinned. "I told you. Bees never sting me."

Roland frowned. "I don't know what possessed you

to climb up in that tree when you saw them. You should have better sense."

"*Atch,* Roland," Johanna said, as she put a proper mental distance between them. "He's a child. He's naturally curious. You don't see bees swarm every day."

"It would suit me if I never saw another one. I don't like bees. I never have."

"Then it's best if you stand back from the tree," she cautioned. "If you're afraid, they'll sense it. It might upset them."

"I can't see that bees have much sense about anything," Roland said. "How big can their brains be?"

"They're smart, *Dat.* Johanna said they pro...pro what the queen."

"Protect," Johanna supplied.

"Protect the queen," J.J. repeated with a grin.

"No need to fill the boy's head with *lecherich* nonsense." Roland used the Pennsylvania Dutch word for ridiculous. "Just get him down out of there safely."

Johanna rolled her eyes and reached for the ladder. "Let me do that. You might startle them."

"Don't you want to wait for your equipment?"

"I'm not going to need it," she said, eyeing the swarm. "J.J. and I are doing just fine. Give me the ladder."

Roland opened the wooden stepladder and set it on the ground. "It's too heavy for you to lift," he muttered.

Johanna bit back a quick retort. *Men! She might not be as tall and sturdy as her sister Anna, but she was strong for her size. Who did he think lifted the bales of hay and fifty-pound bags of sheep-and-turkey food? And who did he suppose moved her wooden beehives?*

She lifted the ladder onto her shoulder and carried it

slowly over to the apple tree. "Sing to the bees, J.J.," she said. "What do they like best?"

In a high, sweet voice, the child began an old German hymn. Johanna settled the legs of the ladder into the soft grass and put her foot on the bottom rung. She joined in J.J.'s song.

"Let me steady that for you," Roland offered.

She shook her head. "*Ne*. Let them get used to me." She began to sing again as she slowly, one step at a time, climbed the ladder. When she was almost at the top, she put out her arms. "Swing your leg over the branch," she murmured. "Slowly. Keep singing." J.J. did just as she instructed, and she nodded encouragement. "Easy. That's right."

As J.J. put his arms around her neck, she blew two bees off his left cheek.

He broke off in the middle of the hymn and giggled. "They tickle."

Instantly, the sound of the swarm's buzzing grew louder.

Behind her, Johanna could hear Roland's sharp intake of breath. "Come to me," she murmured. "Slowly. Keep singing." Another bee took flight, leaving the child's arm to join the main swarm. She caught J.J. by the waist, and the two of them waited, unmoving, as bees crawled out of his hair and flew into the branches above them. She brushed two more bees off his right arm. "Good. Now we'll start down. Slow and steady."

Sweat beaded on the back of Johanna's dress collar and trickled down her back. Step by step, the two of them inched down the ladder, and it seemed to Johanna that the tone and volume of the colony's buzzing grew softer.

As J.J.'s bare feet touched the earth, the last bee abandoned the child's mop of yellow-blond hair and buzzed away. "Go on," Johanna said to the boy. "It's safe now. Go to your *dat*."

She threw Roland an *I told you so* look, but her knees felt weak. She hadn't thought the boy was in real danger, but one could never be certain. And she knew that had anything bad happened to J.J., she would have felt responsible. She'd been frightened for the boy, nothing more, she told herself. And all those silly thoughts about Roland and what they'd once meant to each other could be forgotten. They could go on as they had, neighbors, members of the same church family, friends—nothing more.

A shout from the direction of the barnyard and the rattle of buggy wheels bumping over the field announced Irwin's arrival. "If you don't mind, Roland, I'll set up a catch-trap on the bench there. The water is what drew the swarm here in the first place. And if I can lure them into the nuc box, I can move the whole colony back to our place."

When he didn't answer, she glanced at him. No wonder he hadn't heard her. Roland's full attention was on his child. He was still hugging J.J. so hard that the boy could hardly catch his breath.

"Unless you'd like to keep the bees," Johanna added. "I've got an extra eight-frame hive that I'm not using. I could bring it over and teach you how to—"

"You take the heathen beasts and are welcome to them," Roland replied.

"If you're sure, I'll be glad to have them. But it'll take a few weeks for the colony to settle in to a new hive, before I can move them. Of course I have to lure them into it first."

"Whatever you want, Johanna." He dashed the back

of his hand across his eyes. "Thank you. What you did was…was brave. For a woman. For anyone, I mean. You saved J.J. and I won't forget it."

Johanna ruffled the boy's hair. "I think he would have been just fine," she said. "The bees like him."

J.J. grinned.

"But you'll keep well away from them in the future," Roland admonished.

"Obey your father," Johanna said.

"But I don't want to stay away from them," the child said. "I want to see the queen."

Roland gave him a stern look. "You go near them again and—"

"Mam! Mam!"

Johanna looked back to see Jonah, wearing his bee hat and protective veil netting, leaping out of their buggy. "I remembered the lemongrass oil, *Mam,*" he shouted. "Irwin forgot, but I remembered."

J.J. wiggled out of his father's grasp and stared in awe at Jonah's white helmet. Jonah saw the younger boy and positively strutted toward the tree.

It was all Johanna could do not to laugh at the two of them. She raised a palm in warning. "Thank you for the lemongrass oil, Jonah, but you won't need the hat. These bees have had enough excitement for one day." She gave her son *the look,* and his posturing came to a quick end.

"Hi, J.J.," Jonah said as he removed the helmet and tucked it under his arm. "Did you get stung? Where's the swarm?"

J.J. pointed, and the two children were drawn together as if they were magnets. Immediately, J.J., younger by nearly two years, switched from English to Pennsylvania

Dutch and excitedly began relating his adventure with the bees to Jonah in hushed whispers.

"Both of you stay away from the swarm," Johanna warned as she directed Irwin and Roland to carry the wooden hive to the bench beside the water. Irwin lifted off the top and she used the scented oil liberally on the floor of the box. "Hopefully, this will draw the bees," she explained to Roland as they all backed away. "Now we wait to see if they'll decide to move in. We'll know in a day or two."

"I brought your suit and the smoker stuff," Irwin said.

"*Danke,* but I don't think I'll need it," Johanna answered. "I didn't know what I'd find." She looked around and saw that Jonah and J.J. had caught the loose horse. "You can take Blackie for me, Irwin. Jonah and I can drive the buggy home."

She watched as the teenager used the buggy wheel to climb up on the horse's back and slowly rode toward the barnyard.

"Can I drive the buggy home, *Mam?*" Jonah asked.

Johanna laughed. "Down the busy road? I don't think so." Jonah's face fell. "But you can drive back to Roland's house, if you like." Nodding, Jonah scrambled back up into the buggy, followed closely by J.J.

"Don't worry," Johanna said to Roland. "They're perfectly safe with our mare Molly." It was easier now that the crisis had passed, easier to act as if she was just a neighbor who'd come to help…easier to be alone with Roland and act as if they had never been more than friends.

"*Dat,* I'm hungry," J.J. called from the buggy seat.

Jonah nodded. "Me, too."

"I guess you are," Roland said to J.J. as he and Johanna walked beside the buggy that was rolling slowly toward the barnyard. "We missed dinner, didn't we? I think we have bologna and cheese in the refrigerator. You boys go up to the house. Tie the mare to the hitching rail and you can make yourselves a sandwich."

J.J. made a face. "We're out of bread, *Dat*. Remember? The old bread got hard and you threw it to the chickens last night."

Roland's face flushed. "I'll find you something."

"How about some biscuits?" Johanna asked, walking beside Roland. "If you have flour, I could make you some."

"*Ya!* Biscuits!" J.J. cried.

Roland tugged at the brim of his hat. "I wouldn't want to put you out. You've already—"

"Don't be silly, Roland. What are neighbors for? I can't imagine how you and J.J. manage the house and the farm, plus your farrier work, just the two of you."

"Mary helps with the cleaning sometimes. I'll admit that I don't keep the house the way Pauline did."

"It won't be the first messy kitchen I've ever seen. Let me bake the biscuits," Johanna said, eager now to treat Roland as she would any neighbor in need of assistance. "And whatever else I can find to make a meal. If it makes you feel any better, Jonah and I will share it with you. It's the least I can do for your gift of a hive of bees."

"A gift you're more than welcome to." He offered her a shy smile, and the sight of it made a shiver pass down her spine. Roland Byler had always had a smile that would melt ice in a January snowstorm.

"The thought of homemade biscuits is tempting," he said. "There's a chicken, too, but it's not cooked."

She forced herself to return his smile. "You and the

boys do your chores and give me a little time to tend to the meal," she said briskly.

"Don't say I didn't warn you about the kitchen. I left dirty dishes from breakfast and—"

"Hush, Roland Byler. I think I can manage." Chuckling, she left him at the barn and walked toward the house.

An hour later, the smell of frying chicken, hot biscuits, green beans cooked with bacon and new potatoes drew Roland to the house like a crow to newly sprouting corn plants. The boys followed close on his heels as he stopped to wash his hands and splash cold pump water over his face at the sink on the back porch. Straw hat in hand, Roland stepped into the kitchen and was so shocked by its transformation that he nearly backed out the door.

This couldn't be the same kitchen he and J.J. had left only a few hours ago! Light streamed in through the windows, spilling across a still-damp and newly scrubbed floor. The round oak pedestal table that had belonged to his father's grandmother was no longer piled high with mail, paperwork, newspapers and breakfast dishes. Instead, the wood had been shined and set for dinner. In the center stood a blue pitcher filled with flowers and by each plate a spotless white cloth napkin. Where had Johanna found the napkins? In the year since Pauline's death, he hadn't seen them. But it wasn't flowers and pretty chinaware that drew him to the table.

"Biscuits!" J.J. said. "Look, Jonah! Biscuits!"

"Let me see your hands, boys," Johanna ordered.

Jonah and J.J. extended their palms obediently, and Roland had to check himself from doing the same. Self-consciously, he pulled out a ladder-back chair and took his place at the table. Both boys hurried to their chairs.

On the table was a platter of fried chicken, another of biscuits, an ivory-colored bowl of green beans and another of peaches.

"I thought it best just to put everything on the table and let us help ourselves," Johanna said. "It's the way we do it at home. I found the peaches and the green beans in the cellar. I hope you don't mind that I opened them."

"Fine with me." Roland's mouth was watering and his stomach growling. Breakfast had been cold cereal and hard-boiled eggs. Last night's supper had consisted of bologna and cheese without bread, tomato soup out of a can and slightly stale cookies to go with their milk. He hadn't sat down to a meal like this since he'd been invited to dinner at Charley and Miriam's house the previous week. Roland was just reaching for a biscuit when Johanna's husky voice broke through his thoughts.

"Bow your heads for the blessing, boys. We don't eat before grace."

"Ne," Roland chimed in, quick to change his reaching for a biscuit motion to folding his hands in silent prayer. *Lord, God, thank You for this food, and thank You for the hands that prepared it.* He opened one eye and saw that Johanna's head was still modestly lowered. He couldn't help noticing that the hair along her hairline was peeping out from under her *Kapp* and had curled into tight, damp ringlets. Seeing that and the way Johanna had tied up her bonnet strings at the nape of her neck made his throat tighten with emotion.

Refusing to consider how pretty she looked, he clamped his eyes shut and slowly repeated the Lord's Prayer. And this time, when he opened his eyes again, the others were waiting for him. Johanna had an amused look on her face, not exactly a smile, but definitely a pleased expression.

"Now we can eat," she said.

Roland reached for the platter of chicken and passed it to her. "You didn't need to clean my dirty kitchen, but we appreciate it."

"I did need to, if I was to cook a proper meal," she replied, accepting a chicken thigh. "It's no shame for you to leave housework undone when you have so much to do outside. I'm only sorry you haven't asked for help from the community."

"We manage, J.J. and I."

"Roland Byler. You were the first to help when Silas lost the roof on his hog pen. You must have the grace to accept help as well as give it. You can't be so stubborn."

"You think so?" he asked, stung by her criticism. Personally, he'd always thought that *she* was the stubborn one. True, he had wronged her and he'd embarrassed her with his behavior back when they'd been courting. He'd tried to apologize, more than once, but she'd never really accepted it. One night of bad choices, and she'd gone off and married another.

"Dat?" J.J. giggled. "You broke your biscuit."

Roland looked down to see that he'd unknowingly crushed the biscuit in his hand. "Like it that way," he mumbled as he dropped it onto his plate and stabbed a bite of chicken and a piece of biscuit with his fork.

"Gut chicken," J.J. said.

"If you don't eat all those biscuits, you can have one with peaches on it for dessert," Johanna told the boys. "If you aren't full, that is."

"We won't be, *Mam*," Jonah said. "I never get tired of your biscuits."

And I never get tired of watching you, Roland thought as he helped himself to more chicken. But he was building a barn out of straw, wishing for what he couldn't have, for what he'd thrown away with both hands in the foolishness of his youth.

Johanna's kind acts of cleaning his kitchen and cooking dinner for them had been the charitable act of one neighbor to another, nothing more. And all the wishing in the world wouldn't change that.

Chapter Three

At nine the following Saturday morning, Johanna stood in the combined kitchen-great room of the new farmhouse that her sisters Ruth and Miriam shared. Ruth and Eli had the downstairs. Miriam and Charley occupied an apartment on the second floor, but the two couples usually took their meals together and Ruth cooked. Miriam preferred outdoor work, and Ruth enjoyed the tasks of a homemaker. It was an odd arrangement for the Amish, one that Seven Poplars gossips found endlessly entertaining, but it worked for the four of them.

"Miriam?" Johanna called up the steps. "Are you ready? Charley has the horse hitched."

Today, *Mam,* most of Johanna's sisters and the small children were all off on an excursion to the Mennonite Strawberry Festival, a yearly event that everyone looked forward to. Their sister Grace, who still lived at home but attended the Mennonite Church, owned a car. She'd graciously offered to drive some of them, and *Mam,* Susanna, Rebecca, Katy and Aunt Jezzy had already gone ahead with her. But there were too many Yoders to fit in Grace's automobile, so Miriam was driving a buggyful, as well. Anna loved the Strawberry Festival, but since Rose was so tiny, Anna had decided to remain at home and keep Ruth company. Ruth was in the last stage of pregnancy with twins and preferred staying close to home and out of the heat.

"I feel bad going off and leaving the two of you," Johanna said. "We had such a good time last year."

Ruth settled into a comfortable chair and rubbed the front of her protruding apron. "Until these two are born, I don't have the energy to walk to the mailbox, let alone chase my nieces and nephews around the festival."

Anna smiled and switched small Rose, hidden modestly under a receiving blanket, to her other breast. The baby settled easily into her new position and began to nurse. "Don't worry about us," Anna said. "You're so sweet to take my girls. They've been talking about it all week."

"No problem. And your Naomi is such a big help with Katy." Johanna threw a longing glance at the baby. "First Leah, then you, and Ruth in a month. It will be Miriam next, I suppose."

"Miriam next for what?" Anna's twin sister came hurrying down the steps in a new rose-colored dress, her prayer cap askew and her apron strings dangling.

"Kapp," Ruth reminded.

Miriam rolled her eyes, straightened her head covering and tied her apron strings with a double knot behind her waist. "Satisfied?"

"Ya." Ruth, always the enforcer of proper behavior when out among the worldly English, nodded. "Much better."

"And what is it I'm next for?" Miriam asked, unwilling to have her question go unanswered.

Anna chuckled again. "A *boppli,* of course. A baby of your own. A little wood chopper for Charley or a kitchen helper."

Miriam shrugged. "In God's time. We haven't been married that long. And it took Ruth and Eli ages to get around to it." She glanced at Johanna with a gleam of mischief in her eyes. "How do you know it will be me? Maybe it will be *your* turn next. Look at you. You've got that look on your face when you hold Rose. You can't wait to be a mother again."

"She's right," Ruth agreed. "You've mourned Wilmer long enough. It's time you married again."

"To whom?"

Miriam laughed. "You know who. I've heard you've been at his place three times this week. And cleaned his house."

"Only the kitchen. And he was only there the first day, the day J.J. was up the tree with the bees. The other two times he was off shoeing horses. I had to go check on the new hive. The swarm moved into my nuc box, and I'm getting free bees." Johanna knew she was babbling on when she should have held her tongue. Arguing with Miriam always made things worse.

"I see," Miriam said. "You're going to *take care of the bees.*"

"Exactly. It doesn't have anything to do with Roland." Johanna sighed in exasperation. The trouble with being close to her sisters was that they knew everything. Nothing in her life was private, and all of them had an opinion they were all too willing to share. And the fact that they'd touched on a subject that had kept her awake late for the past few nights made her even more uncomfortable. First, she had to make up her own mind what she wanted. Then she would share her decision. "Who told you I went over to Roland's three times? Rebecca or Irwin?"

Ruth chuckled. "Just a little bird. But we're serious. It's not good for your children to be without a father. You know Roland would make a good *dat*. Even *Mam* says so. Roland owns his farm. No mortgage. And such a hard worker. He'll be a good provider. And don't forget he's got a motherless son. You two should just stop turning your backs on each other and get married."

"Before someone else snaps him up," Miriam quipped. "At Spence's, I saw one of those Lancaster girls giving him the once-over. At the Beachys' cheese stall. '*Atch*, Roland,'" she mimicked in a high, singsong voice. "'A man alone shouldn't eat so much cheddar and bologna in one week. Is not *gut* for your health. What you need is a wife to cook for you.'"

Johanna flushed. It was too warm in the house. She went to the door and opened it, letting the breeze calm her unease. In the yard, Grace's son, 'Kota, hung out the back door of Charley's buggy, and Anna's Mae bounced on the front seat. She couldn't see Anna's Lori Ann or Jonah, but she could hear Naomi telling them to settle down. "It's not as easy to know what to do as you think," Johanna said to her sisters. "People change."

"You haven't changed," Anna put in quietly. "What you felt for Roland years ago, that was real. It's not too late for the two of you."

Johanna looked back at Anna. "You think I should fling myself at him?"

Ruth folded her arms over her chest with determination. "It's plain as the nose on your face that he still cares for you. If you weren't so stubborn, you'd see it."

"What happened before…between you and him…it

hurt you," Anna continued. "I remember how you cried. But Roland was young then and sowing his oats. Can't you find it in your heart to forgive him?"

Not forgive, but forget. Could I ever trust him again?

"Miriam!" Charley shouted from outside. "Come take this horse! I don't trust these kids with this mare, and I can't stand here all day holding her. I've got work to do."

"Go. Have fun," Ruth said. "But promise me you'll think about what we said, Johanna."

"Please," Anna said. "We only want what's best for you and your children."

"So do I," Johanna admitted. "So do I."

The Mennonite school, where the festival was held, wasn't more than five miles away. *Mam* and Grace and the others were there when Johanna and her crew arrived. Jonah and 'Kota were fairly bursting out of their britches when Miriam turned the buggy into the parking lot, and Anna's girls appeared to be just as excited. A volunteer came to take the children's modest admittance fees and stamp the back of their hands with a red strawberry. That stamp would admit them to all the games, the rides, the petting zoo featuring baby farm animals, a straw-bale mountain and maze and a book fair where each child could choose a free book.

"There's Katy!" Jonah cried, waving to his little sister. Katy and Susanna were riding in a blue cart pulled by a huge, black-and-white Newfoundland dog. Following close behind trudged a smiling David King, his battered paper crown peeking out from under his straw hat. David was holding tight to a string. At the end of it bobbed a red strawberry balloon.

"I want a balloon!" Mae exclaimed. "Can I have a balloon?"

"If you like," Johanna said. "But your *Mam* gave you each two dollars to spend. Make sure that the balloon is what you really want before you buy it."

"I want a balloon, too," 'Kota declared. "A blue one."

"Strawberries aren't blue," Jonah said loftily.

"Uh-huh," 'Kota replied, pointing out a girl holding a blue strawberry balloon on a string.

Johanna smiled as she helped the children out of the buggy and sent them scurrying safely across the field that served as a parking lot. Despite his olive skin and piercing dark eyes, Grace's little boy looked as properly plain as Jonah. The two cousins, inseparable friends, were clad exactly alike in blue home-sewn shirts and trousers with snaps and ties instead of buttons, black suspenders and wide-brimmed straw hats. No one would recognize 'Kota as the thin, shy, undersized child who'd first appeared at *Mam's* back door on that rainy night last fall. *Another of God's gifts.* Life was full of surprises.

"Over here," *Mam* called. "Why don't you leave the girls with us? I imagine Lori Ann, Mae and Naomi would like to ride in the dog cart."

"There's J.J.," Jonah shouted. "Hey, J.J.! He's climbing the hay bales. Can we—"

"I promised Naomi we'd go to the book fair first," Miriam said, joining them. "Grace is working there all morning. Don't worry about the horse. Irwin's going to see that the mare gets water and is tied up in the shed. Do you mind if we go on ahead, inside?"

Quickly, the sisters made a plan to meet at the picnic tables in two hours. Children were divided; money was handed out and Johanna followed 'Kota and Jonah to the entrance to the straw-bale maze. From the top of a straw "mountain," J.J. waved and called to them. The area was fenced, so she didn't have to worry about losing track of her energetic charges. Johanna found a spot on a straw bale beside several other waiting mothers and sat down. Since J.J. was here, Johanna was all too aware that Roland couldn't be far away. She glanced around, but didn't see him.

Her sisters' advice about Roland echoed many of her own thoughts. Years ago, she and Roland… No, she wouldn't think about that. So many memories—some good, some bad—clouded her judgment. She had prayed over her indecision, but if God had a plan for her, she was too dense to hear His voice. Sometimes her inner voice whispered that she didn't need another husband, that she and the children were doing just fine. But at other times, she was assailed by the wisdom of hundreds of years of Amish women who'd lived before her.

Amish men and women were expected to marry and live together in a home centered on faith and family and community. Remaining single went against the unwritten rules of her church. Even a widow, like her mother, was supposed to remarry. Mourning too long was considered selfish. *Dat* and Wilmer, to put a fine point on it, had both left this earth. It was her duty and her mother's duty to continue on here on earth, following the *Ordnung* and remaining faithful to the community.

Johanna knew, in her heart of hearts, that it was time she found a new husband. She didn't need Anna or Ruth or even her mother to tell her that. Looking at it from the church's point of view, she had to first find a man of faith, a man who would help her to raise her children to be hardworking and devoted members of the community.

Second, as a mother, she should pick someone who would set a good example, and hopefully a man who could support her and her children—those she already had and those they might have together. She hadn't needed her sisters to offer that advice, either. She was very good at making logical decisions.

If she married Roland, she honestly believed that she wouldn't have to worry about struggling to feed and clothe her children. His farrier business was thriving. She knew that Roland, unlike Wilmer, would never raise his hand to her in anger. And she was certain that he didn't drink alcohol or use tobacco, both substances she abhorred. Johanna shivered as she remembered the last time Wilmer had struck her. She was not a violent woman, but it had taken every ounce of her willpower not to fight back. Instead, she'd waited until he fell into a drunken sleep, gathered her babies and fled the house.

She pushed those bad memories out of her head. With Roland, she would be safe. Her children would be safe. They wouldn't grow up under her mother's roof without a father's direction. And Roland, unlike Wilmer, would be a man both she and the children could respect.

Two English girls ran out of the maze together. The women beside Johanna stood and walked away with the laughing children. Johanna glanced back at the straw mountain, saw the boys and sank again into her thoughts.

Many Amish marriages were arranged ones. And many couples who came together for logical reasons, such as partnership, sharing a similar faith and pleasing their families, came to care deeply for each other. As far as she could tell, most of the English world married for romantic love and nearly half of those unions ended in divorce.

The Amish did not divorce. Had she been forced to leave Wilmer and return to her mother's home permanently, both of them would have been in danger of being cast out of the church—shunned. Under certain circumstances, she could have remained part of the community, but they would still have been married. As long as the two of them lived, there could be no dissolving the marriage.

Marrying a man for practical reasons would be a sensible plan. If each of them kept their part of the bargain, if they showed respect and worked hard, romantic love might not be necessary. She considered whether she would find Roland attractive if they had just met, if they hadn't played and worked and worshiped together since they were small children. How would she react if he wasn't Roland Byler, Charley and Mary's older brother, if she hadn't wept a butter churn full of tears over him? What would she do if a matchmaker told *Mam* that a widowed farmer named Jakey Coblentz wanted to court Johanna?

The answer was as plain as the *Kapp* on her head. She would agree to meet this Jakey, to walk out with him, to make an honest effort to discover if they were compatible. So why, when she valued her mother's and her sisters' opinions, had she been so reluctant to consider Roland? To forget what had happened? She closed her eyes and pictured his features in her mind.

"Don't go to sleep," a familiar male voice said.

Johanna's eyes flew open and she jumped so hard that she nearly fell off the bale of straw. Roland stood directly in front of her, holding two red snow cones. "Roland."

He laughed and handed her one of the treats. "It's strawberry. If I remember, you like snow cones. Any flavor but blue." He took a bite of his own.

She searched for something to say. In desperation, she grabbed the snow cone and took a bite. Instantly, the cold went straight to her brain and she felt a sharp pain. "Ow!"

He laughed at her, sat down beside her and reached over and wiped a granule of ice off her chin. "You always did do that," he reminded her.

"Let me pay you for this," she stammered.

"*Ne.* Enjoy. I bought it for J.J."

Johanna gasped. "I'm eating J.J.'s snow cone?"

Roland shrugged. "I'll buy him another one. Now that 'Kota and Jonah are up there..." Roland indicated the top of the straw slide. "With him, it would just go to waste. It would be a puddle of strawberry syrup by the time he got to eat it." He grinned. "So you're doing me a favor. Keeping me from wasting a dollar."

"Oh." She still felt flustered.

"That was smart—what you did with the bees. They went into the box you put out for them."

Bees were a safe subject. Tentatively, she took another nibble of the snow cone. It was delicious. She couldn't remember when she'd had one last. Whoever had made it had ground real strawberries into the juice. She fixed her gaze on the ground. Roland was wearing new leather high-top shoes. Black. His trousers were clean, but wrinkled. *Very* wrinkled. They needed a good pressing.

"I've always been afraid of bees," he said.

She licked at the flavored ice. "I know."

"J.J. seems fascinated by them. He asks me all kinds of questions—questions I can't answer."

She took another bite, chewed slowly and swallowed. "I think he's a bee charmer. They won't hurt him. You don't have to worry."

"I found the biscuits you left for us on the kitchen

table Thursday. And the potato soup. They were good, really good."

"I'm glad you liked them." A dribble of strawberry water ran down her hand onto her wrist. She passed the paper cone into her other hand and licked up the stray drop. "Messy," she murmured.

"Good stuff is."

Silence stretched between them. Shivers ran down her arms. Should she say something to him about what she'd been thinking? About the two of them? Normally, if a girl and a boy wanted to court, there was talk back and forth, between their friends at first, then between the girl and boy themselves. But she and Roland weren't teens anymore. They didn't need intermediaries, did they? She looked around. No one was within earshot. If she was going to say something, she had to do it now, before she lost her nerve.

"Roland?"

"Ya?"

"I want to talk to you about—"

"Johanna! Johanna! Did you see? King David and me! We rode in the blue cart." Johanna's sister Susanna appeared in front of them, laughing merrily. "No horse. A dog. A dog pulled the cart! Did you see us ride?"

David, glued to Susanna's side, smiled and pointed at Johanna's snow cone. "Ice cream? I like ice cream."

David, like Susanna, had Down's syndrome but was harder to understand. Johanna could usually follow what he was saying. He was a good-hearted boy, always smiling, and Johanna liked him.

"Ne," Susanna said. "Not a ice cream cone. A snow cone." She stared longingly at Johanna's. "Can we have one?"

"I don't like snow. To eat it," David said.

"You'll like it," Susanna assured him.

"I'll buy you snow cones." Roland reached into his pocket.

"You have money, Susanna," Johanna reminded her. "*Mam* gave you five dollars. Did you spend it all?"

Susanna shook her head.

"It's nice of Roland to offer, but you need to buy your own. And buy David one, too."

Rebecca joined them, with Katy in tow. Katy looked longingly at Johanna's snow cone.

"Here," Johanna said. "Have the rest of mine, Katy. Or get Susanna to buy you one. She and David were just headed to the snow cone booth."

Rebecca glanced from Johanna to Roland and back. Johanna could almost see the wheels turning in her sister's head.

"Ah," Rebecca said. "I think we need to find snow cones for Susanna and David. Can you help me, Katy?"

Johanna's fingertips tingled and her chest felt tight. Maybe this wasn't the time. Maybe Susanna and David's interruption had kept her from doing something she'd regret. "I'll come with you," she said.

Rebecca chuckled. "No need. You two *old* people sit here in the sun. I think I saw the snow cone stand by the school."

Roland pointed. "It's by the gym doors, but if you don't have enough—"

Susanna waved her five-dollar bill. "I have money," she said. "Come on, King David." She started off and, again, David followed.

Rebecca looked back at Johanna. "Have fun, you two,"

she teased. "Come on, Katy. Would you like to see the baby lambs?"

Roland watched the four of them walk away. "Smart, your sisters," he said. "All of them."

Johanna smiled at him. "*Ya.* All of them," she agreed. "Susanna, too."

He nodded. "I always thought so. A credit to your parents, that girl."

Johanna took a deep breath and clasped her hands so that Roland wouldn't see how they were shaking. "Roland?" she began.

In his gray eyes, color swirled and deepened. "Yes, Johanna?"

She took another breath and looked right at him. "Will you marry me?"

Chapter Four

Once, when he was eighteen and learning his trade as a farrier, Roland had been kicked by a stallion his uncle was shoeing. The blow had been so quick and hard that Roland was picking himself up off the ground almost before he'd realized that he'd been struck by a flying hoof. He hadn't lost consciousness, but for what seemed like an eternity, he hadn't been able to think straight.

Johanna's matter-of-fact question had much the same effect. He was stunned. "What did you say?" he stammered. Around him, the laughter and happy shrieks of the children, the red balloon that had come loose from its mooring and was floating skyward, and the sweet smell of ripe strawberries faded. For a long second, Roland's whole world narrowed to the woman sitting beside him.

Johanna rolled her eyes. "Are you listening to me? I asked if you would marry me."

He swallowed, opened his mouth to speak and then took a big gulp of air. "Did you just ask me to marry you?" he managed.

She folded her hands gracefully over her starched

black apron. "It's the logical thing for us to do," she answered.

He heard what she said, but his attention was fixed on the red-gold curls that had come loose from her severe bun and framed her heart-shaped face, a face so fresh and youthful that it might have belonged to a teenage girl instead of a widow and mother in her late twenties. Johanna's skin was fair and pink, dusted with a faint trail of golden freckles over the bridge of her nose and across her cheeks. Her eyes were the exact shade of bluebells, and her mouth was... Roland swallowed again. He'd always thought that Johanna Yoder had the prettiest mouth—even when she'd been admonishing him for something he'd done wrong.

They had a long history, he and Johanna...a history that he'd hoped and prayed would become a future. In the deepest part of his heart, he'd wanted to ask her the very question that she'd just asked him. But now that she'd spoken it first, he was poleaxed.

"Do I take that as a *no?*" she asked, as a flush started at her slender throat and spread up over her face. "You don't want to marry me?"

He could hear the hurt in her voice, and his stomach clenched. Johanna's voice wasn't high, like most young women's. It was low, husky and rich. She had a beautiful singing voice. And when she raised that voice in hymns during Sunday worship service, the sound was so sweet it almost brought tears to his eyes.

Abruptly, she stood.

"*Ne,* Johanna. Don't!" He caught her hand. "Sit. Please."

Clearly flustered, she jerked her hand away, but not before he felt the warmth of her flesh and an invisible rush of energy that leaped between them. The shock of

that touch jolted him in the same way that his skin prickled when a bolt of lightning struck nearby in a thunder-
storm. He'd never understood that, and he still didn't,
but he felt it now.

"You know I want to marry you," he said, all in a rush,
before he lost his nerve. "I've been waiting for the right
time...when I thought you were—"

"Through mourning Wilmer?" Johanna's blue eyes
clouded with deep violet. She lowered her voice and
glanced around to see if anyone was staring at them.

Roland found himself doing the same. But the children were busy climbing the mountain of straw, and no
one else seemed to have noticed that the ground under
his feet was no longer solid and his brain had turned to
mush. He returned his gaze to her. "To show decent respect for my Pauline and your—"

"Deceased husband?" She made a tiny shrug and her
lips firmed into a thin line. "Wilmer was my husband
and the father of my children. We took marriage vows
together, and if..." She took a deep breath. "If he hadn't
passed, I would have remained his wife." She shook her
head. "I'd be speaking an untruth if I told you that there
was love or respect left in my heart for him when he
died—if there wasn't the smallest part of relief when I
knew he'd gone into the Lord's care. I know it's a sin to
feel that way, but I—"

"Johanna, you don't have to—" he began, but she cut
him off with a raised palm.

"*Ne,* Roland. Let me finish, please. I'll say this, and
then we'll speak of it no more. Wilmer was not a well
man. His mind was troubled. But the fault in our marriage was not his alone. I've spent hours on my knees

asking for God's forgiveness. I should have tried harder to help him…to find help for him."

One of Johanna's small hands rested on the straw bale between them, and he covered it with his own and squeezed it, out of sympathy for her pain. This time, she didn't pull away. He waited, and she went on.

"You know I was no longer living under Wilmer's roof when he died. His sickness and his drinking of spirits made it impossible for me to remain there with my children." Johanna raised her eyes to meet his gaze, and Roland saw the tears that her pride would not allow to fall.

A tightness gathered in Roland's chest. "Did he… Was Wilmer…" A rising anger against the dead man threatened to make him say things he might later regret. As Johanna had said…as Bishop Atlee had said, Wilmer's illness had robbed him of reason. He was not responsible for what he did, and it was not for any of them to judge him. But Roland had to ask. "Did he ever hit you?"

Johanna turned her face away.

It was all the answer he needed. Roland wasn't a violent man, but he did have a temper that needed careful tending. If Wilmer had appeared in front of them now, alive and well, Roland wasn't certain he could have refrained from giving him a sound thumping.

Johanna's voice was a thin whisper. "It was Jonah's safety that worried me most. When Wilmer…" A shudder passed through her tensed frame. "When he began to take out his anger on our son, I couldn't take it any longer. I know that it's the right of a father to discipline his children, but this was more than discipline." She looked back, meeting Roland's level gaze. "Wilmer got it into his head that Jonah wasn't his son, but yours."

"Mine?" Roland's mouth gaped. "But we never...you never..."

Johanna sighed. "Exactly. I've been accused of being outspoken, too stubborn for a woman and willful—all true, to my shame. But, you, above all men, should know that I—"

"Would never break your marriage vows," he said. "Could never do anything to compromise your honor or that of your husband." He fought to control the anger churning in his gut. "In all the time we courted, we never did anything more than hold hands and—"

"We kissed once," she reminded him. "At the bishop's husking bee. When you found the red ear of corn?"

"We were what? Fifteen?"

"I was fifteen," Johanna said. Her expression softened, and some of the regret faded from her clear blue eyes. "You were sixteen."

"And as I remember, you nearly knocked me on my—"

"I didn't strike you." The corners of her mouth curled into a smile. "I just gave you a gentle nudge, to make you stop kissing me."

"You shoved me so hard that I fell backward and landed in a pile of corncobs. Charley told on me, and I was the butt of everyone's jokes for months." He squeezed her hand again. "It wasn't much of a kiss for all that fuss, but I still remember how sweet your lips tasted."

"Don't be fresh, Roland Byler," she admonished, once again becoming the no-nonsense Johanna he knew and loved. "Remember you are a grown man, a father and a baptized member of the church. Talk of foolishness between teenagers isn't seemly."

"I suppose not," he said grudgingly. "But I never forgot that kiss."

She pulled her hand free and tucked it behind her back. "Enough of that. We have a decision to make, you and I. I've thought about it and prayed about it. I've listened to my sisters chatter on the subject until I'm sick of it. You are a widower with a young son, and I'm a widow with two small, fatherless children, and it's time we both remarried. We belong to the same church, we have the same values, and you have a farm and a good job. That we should marry and join our families is the logical solution."

Logical? He waited for her to speak of love…or at least to say how she'd always cared for him…to say that she'd never gotten over their teenage romance.

"What?" she demanded. "Haven't I put it plainly? We both have to marry someone. And you live close by. We're already almost family, with your brother Charley and my sister Miriam already husband and wife. You have plenty of room for my sheep and bees. I think that empty shed would be perfect for my turkey poults."

"Turkeys? Bees?" He stood, backed away, and planted his feet solidly. "I'd hoped there'd be a better reason for us to exchange vows. What of affection, Johanna? Aren't a husband and wife supposed to—"

Her eyes narrowed, and a thin crease marred her smooth forehead. "If you're looking for me to speak of romance, I'm afraid you'll be disappointed. We're past that, Roland. We're too old, and we've seen too much of life. Don't you remember what the visiting preacher said at Barbara and Tobias's wedding? Marriage is to establish a family and strengthen the bonds of community and church."

Pain knifed through him. All this time, he'd been certain that Johanna felt the same way about him that he felt about her. Not that he'd ever betrayed his late wife—not in deed and not in thought. He'd kept Johanna in a quiet corner of his heart. But now he'd thought that they'd have a second chance. "It was my fault, what happened between us. What went wrong… I've never denied it. I know how badly I hurt you, and I'm sorry. I've been sorry ever since—"

"Roland. What are you talking about? We were kids when we walked out together. Neither of us had joined the church. That's the past. I'm not clinging to it, and you can't, either. It's time to look to our future. What we have to do is decide if we would be good for each other. We're both hard workers and we're both dedicated to our children. It seems silly for me to look elsewhere for a husband when you live so close to my mother's farm."

"So we're to decide on the rest of our lives because my land lies near your mother's?" He hesitated, realizing his words were going to get him into trouble. But he couldn't help how he felt and he wouldn't be able to sleep tonight if he didn't express those feelings. "I take it that you'd want to have the banns read at the next worship service. Since you've already made up your mind, why wait? Widows and widowers may marry when they choose. Why waste time with courting when you could be cleaning my house and your sheep could be grazing in my meadow?"

"Are you being sarcastic?"

"Answer me one question, Johanna. Do you love me?"

She averted her eyes. "I'm too old and too sensible for that. I respect you, and I think you respect me. Isn't that enough?"

"No." He shook his head. "No, it isn't." Where had this gone so wrong? He had pictured the two of them riding out together in his two-seater behind his new trotter, imagined them taking the children to the beach, going to the State Fair together this summer. He badly wanted to court Johanna properly, and she'd shattered all his hopes and dreams by her emotionless proposal. "It's not enough for me. And it shouldn't be enough for you."

She pursed her lips. "Well, that's clear enough. I'm sorry to have troubled you, Roland. It's plain that we can't—"

"Can't what? Can't find what we had and lost? Pauline was a sensible match that suited both our families. In time, when J.J. came, love came and filled our house. When I lost her, part of my heart went with her. But I won't marry for convenience, not again. If the feelings you have for me aren't deep and strong, you'd be better to find some other candidate, some prosperous farmer or tradesmen who would be satisfied with a sensible wife. Because…because I'm looking for more."

Red spots flared on Johanna's cheeks. "It's good we had this talk. Otherwise, who knows how much time we would have wasted when we should be looking for—"

"I hope you find what you're searching for," Roland said. "And when you find a man willing to settle for a partnership, I hope you're happy."

She folded her arms over her chest. "You don't find happiness in others. You find it in yourself and in service to family and community."

"So you're saying I'm selfish?"

"I didn't mean it that way."

"It sounds as if that's exactly what you meant." With a nod, he turned to search for his son and walked away. There was nothing more to say, nothing more he wanted to hear. He wanted to make Johanna his wife. He could think of no one who would be a more loving mother to J.J., but not under these circumstances…never under these circumstances.

"I'm glad we got this straightened out," she called after him. "Because it's clear to me that the two of us would never work out."

Johanna's temper was out of the box now. She was mad, but he didn't care. Better to have her angry at him than to feel nothing at all.

Later that evening, at the forge beside his barn, Roland shaped a horseshoe on his anvil, with powerful swings of his hammer. Sparks flew, and his brother Charley chuckled.

"Just make it fit, Roland," Charley teased. "Don't beat it to death."

It was after supper, but Roland hadn't taken time to eat. He'd been hard at work since he'd left the festival. Not wanting to spoil J.J.'s day, he'd given permission for Grace to keep him with her boy, 'Kota, and bring him home in the morning. Since tomorrow wasn't a church Sunday, it would be a leisurely day for visiting. Hannah Yoder, Johanna's *mam,* had invited him to join them for supper tonight, but after the heated words he and Johanna had exchanged, her table was the last place he wanted to be.

Besides, Roland was in no mood to be a patient father this evening.

Charley had apologized for bringing his mare to be shod so late in the day. "I wouldn't have bothered you, but I promised Miriam we'd drive over to attend services in her friend Polly's district. You know Polly and Evan, don't you? They moved here from Virginia last summer."

Roland did know Evan Beachy. The newcomer had brought a roan gelding to be shod just after Christmas. Evan was a tall, quiet man with a gentle hand for his horses. Roland liked him, but he didn't want to make small talk about the Beachys from Virginia. He wanted to get Charley's opinion on what had gone wrong between Johanna and him.

Charley was always quick with a joke, but he and his brother were close. Under his breezy manner, Charley hid a smart, sensible mind and a caring heart. Roland had to talk to somebody, and Charley and he had shared their successes and disappointments since they were old enough to confide in each other.

"Brought you some lamb stew," Charley said. "And some biscuits. Figured you wouldn't bother to make your own supper. You never did have the sense to eat regular."

"If I ate as much as you, I'd be the size of LeRoy Zook."

Charley pulled a face. "Don't try to deny it. You don't eat right. What did you have for breakfast?"

"An egg-and-bologna sandwich with cheese."

"And dinner? Did you even have dinner today?"

Roland didn't answer. He'd had the strawberry snow cone. He'd had every intention of asking Johanna if she'd join him for the chicken-and-dumpling special that the Mennonite ladies were offering, but after their disagreement, he'd lost his appetite.

"So, no dinner and no supper. You're a pitiful case, brother. Good thing that I remembered to bring you Ruth's lamb stew. She made enough for half the church."

"I appreciate the stew and biscuits, but I can do without your sass," Roland answered.

When the shoe was shaped to suit him, Roland pressed

it to the mare's front left hoof to make certain of the fit, then heated it and hammered it into place. Last, he checked the hoof for any ragged edges and pronounced the work sound. He released the animal's leg, patted her neck, and glanced back at his brother.

"I've ruined it all between Johanna and me," he said. And then, quickly, before he regretted his confession, he told Charley what had happened earlier in the day. "She asked me to marry her," he said when he was done with his sad tale. "And fool that I am, I refused her." He raised his gaze to meet his brother's. "I don't want a partner," he said. "I couldn't go into a marriage with a woman who didn't love me—not a second time. Pauline was a good woman. We never exchanged a harsh word in all the years we were married, but I was hoping for more."

Charley removed the sprig of new clover he'd been nibbling on. "You love Johanna, and you want her to love you back."

Roland nodded. "I do." He swallowed, but the lump in his throat wouldn't dissolve. He turned away, went to the old well, slid aside the heavy wooden cover and cranked up a bucket of cold water. Taking a deep breath, he dumped the bucket over his head and sweat-soaked undershirt. The icy water sluiced over him, but it didn't wash away the hurt or the pain of the threat of losing Johanna a second time. "Was I wrong to turn her down, Charley? Am I cutting off my nose to spite my face? Maybe I would be happier having her as a wife who respects me, but doesn't love me, instead of not having her at all."

Charley tugged at his close-cropped beard, a beard that Preacher Reuben disapproved of and even Samuel had rolled his eyes at, a beard that some might think was too short for a married man. "You want my honest opinion? Or do you just want to whine and have someone listen?"

"You think I've made a terrible mistake, don't you? Say it, if that's what you think. I can take it."

Charley came to the well, cranked up a second bucket of water and used an enamel dipper to take a drink. Then he poured the rest of the bucket into a pail for the mare. She dipped her velvety nose in the water and slurped noisily.

Roland wanted to shake his brother. In typical fashion, Charley was taking his good old time in applying the heat, letting Roland suffer as he waited to hear the words. Finally, when he'd nearly lost the last of his patience, Charley nodded and glanced back from the mare.

"You're working yourself into a lather for nothing, brother. Don't you remember what a chase Miriam gave me? 'We're friends, Charley,'" he mimicked. "'You're just like a brother.' Do you think I wanted to be Miriam's friend? I loved her since she was in leading strings, since we slept in the same cradle as nurslings. Miriam was the sun and moon for me. It's not right for a Christian man to say such things, but sinner that I am, it's how I feel about her. But you know what men say about the Yoder girls."

Roland nodded. "They're a handful."

"It's true," Charley agreed. "From Hannah right down to Rebecca. Even Susanna, one of God's sweetest children, has her stubborn streak."

"But they're true as rain." Roland ran his fingers through his wet hair. "Strong and good as any woman I've ever met, and that includes our sister Mary."

"Exactly. Worth the trouble, and worth the wait." He smiled. "You know I've never been a betting man. The preachers say the Good Book warns against wagering, and I take that as gospel. But if I was an Englishman without a care for his soul, I'd risk my new Lancaster buggy against a pair of cart wheels that you and Johanna will be married by Christmas next. Mark my words, brother. Everyone in the family knows it. The two of you will come to your senses and work this out. And if you don't, I'll grow my beard out as long and full as Bishop Atlee's himself."

Chapter Five

At nine-thirty on Tuesday morning, Johanna tied Blackie to a hitching rail under a shady tree at the back of one of the buildings at Spence's Auction and Bazaar. Some people didn't bother to remove the bridles of their animals at market, but *Dat* had taught her differently. If a horse had to stand for hours, he didn't need a bit in his mouth. The halter was just as secure and more comfortable for the horse. Any animal deserved respect and loving care, especially one who served so faithfully in pulling the carriage and helping with farm work.

After Johanna had watered Blackie and double-checked his tie rope, she took her split-oak market basket, containing a dozen jars of clover honey, and carried it through the milling shoppers to the family booth.

This spring, the Yoders had had been blessed to take over the space of another Amish family, who was moving to Iowa. The stand was inside a three-sided shed, a little smaller than what they'd had outside, but in an excellent location and sheltered from the weather. Sometimes they sold vegetables from *Mam's* garden, and—depending on the season—they offered honey, homemade jams

and preserves, pickles and relishes, and holiday wreaths.
And since they'd acquired the new, shaded booth, Aunt
Jezzy had taken over running the table with help from
whichever Yoder sister was available.

Going to Spence's two days a week and selling to
strangers was a big step for Aunt Jezzy because she was
naturally shy around the English. *Mam* had secretly wondered if it wasn't too much to expect of her, but after a
few weeks, Aunt Jezzy had really taken to the job and
had proved to be an excellent businesswoman. Her cash-
box always balanced out to the penny, and she quickly
became popular with customers and other sellers.

Grace had dropped Aunt Jezzy and Rebecca off early
that morning on her way to the local community college,
where she was studying to be a veterinary technician, but
her classes didn't let out until five today. Johanna would
have to remain until afternoon to drive her aunt and sister home when they closed the booth. Usually, Johanna
brought Katy or Jonah or both with her, but since they'd
gone to spend the day at Anna's, she was alone.

The weather was warm and sunny, and there seemed
to be a lot of people at Spence's that morning. As Johanna entered the open building with her heavy basket,
she was pleased to see several regular customers standing at the table, and her display of honey and beeswax
lip salve and soap nearly gone. Aunt Jezzy was counting out change to an older man, and Rebecca was bag-
ging the last pint of strawberries, berries that Susanna
had picked before breakfast.

How pleased her little sister would be to add to the
savings she kept in a hen-shaped crockery jar under her
bed. This morning, Susanna had whispered that she was
going to buy *Mam* a birthday present. Of course, last

week, she'd wanted Charley to buy her a pink pig with black spots, and at supper last night, she'd announced that she wanted a big dog and a cart, so she and King David could drive it to Dover every day. Susanna always had plans, but no matter how they turned out, she was always happy.

Susanna is truly blessed with a loving spirit, Johanna thought. *She was born with the grace I've always struggled to find.*

Rebecca glanced up and smiled. "Hi. We were wondering where you were. Your bee-tending took longer at Roland's than you expected?" she said in Pennsylvania *Deutch.*

Johanna ignored her sister's teasing remark. "It was a busy morning," she said, once the customers had been waited on and moved on. "You've sold a lot."

"Ya," Aunt Jezzy agreed as she spun the closed moneybox exactly three complete rotations before stashing it safely under the table. "Most of Susanna's strawberries went right away," she said, continuing on in the same dialect. Aunt Jezzy's English was excellent, but she always preferred Pennsylvania Dutch when they were alone or with other Amish. "Without Rebecca's help, I would have been hard-pressed. She is a good girl, your sister. Always kind to me and your *grossmama,* Lovina, when she and Leah stayed with us in Ohio."

"I think we did so well because a tourist bus from Washington stopped," Rebecca explained, switching the conversation back to English. "Some of the people started staring and asked silly questions, but then Leah's husband's aunt Joyce came over. She spoke up, saying how the salve was organic. One lady bought a lip balm and tried it right away. And then the others started buying."

"They snapped up those fancy half-pint jars of honey, too," Aunt Jezzy said. "And never argued about the price." She chuckled. "But they talked loud, like I was deaf."

"You handled them perfectly," Rebecca said. "You should have seen her, Johanna. *Schmaert*. Smiling, and so quaint." Rebecca giggled. "*Vit* a heavy *Deutch* accent. And when one Englisher whipped out her cell phone to take a photograph of her, Aunt Jezzy turned her back. She refused to wait on anyone else. Then the bus driver blew his horn to leave, and the other tourists made the woman put her cell away so they could buy before they had to go."

Aunt Jezzy's cheeks glowed rosy with pleasure at the praise. "Maybe it's not this *narrisch* old woman. Maybe your sister Rebecca is why you sold so many of those salves and soaps. She made those pretty labels with her good handwriting. And it's good that she can talk so easily to the English."

Rebecca beamed. "It's wonderful honey," she said. "It sells itself. Johanna does all the work."

"I think the bees do most of it," Aunt Jezzy said.

"God's handiwork." Rebecca smiled. "You're right to remind us, Aunt Jezzy. We receive so many blessings from Him every day."

Johanna nodded and busied herself arranging the jars of honey she'd brought with her. She could always trust Rebecca to remember what was important. The two of them hadn't been as close as they might have been when they were growing up. Rebecca had been younger and unwilling to listen to a bossy older sister, and Johanna feared she'd underestimated Rebecca.

But since Leah had married Daniel and gone away to South America to be a Mennonite missionary, Rebecca had stepped in to fill the empty place in Johanna's heart. Why had she never realized how wise Rebecca was? Strong in her faith and always willing to turn a hand to what needed doing, Rebecca reminded Johanna so much of their mother.

But Rebecca would marry soon and start her own family, Johanna thought. She might move away, as well. Johanna didn't want to dwell on that. She'd never liked change, and she needed her family around her, all of them, even Aunt Jezzy, *Grossmama* and their new sister, Grace, and 'Kota. *If only I could keep them all close to me.*

Rebecca brushed Johanna's hand with her own. "The past few years have been difficult for you, I know," she murmured. "But the Lord never deserted you, even in your darkest hour."

Johanna nodded, too full of emotion to speak. Her sister's words were true. Her own life might be in turmoil, but she had never felt deserted by His mercy. He had kept her and her children safe from Wilmer's rage, and He had provided a refuge for them in the arms of her family.

Johanna couldn't imagine what she would have done if her mother hadn't welcomed her and her children into her home. Sometimes, Johanna thought that the easiest thing to do would be to remain there under her mother's roof, supporting Jonah and Katy by selling her quilts, her wool, her turkeys and her honey.

Aunt Jezzy had never married, and she never seemed to mind. She went her own way, tapping on wood, spinning her coffee cup three times before she added her sugar, talking to herself when she was alone and always wearing violet-colored dresses. In spite of her nonconformity, she seemed unconcerned by what others thought of her and was always smiling. Maybe some of the Yoder women were meant to follow a different path.

"Rebecca didn't have time to get her breakfast," Aunt Jezzy said, tugging Johanna from her thoughts. "You two go along and have a good chat. It's slower now. I'll be fine until you get back."

"Are you sure?" Rebecca asked, but she tucked her pencil and small notepad into her apron pocket.

For years, Rebecca had been a faithful correspondent, submitting Kent County happenings to the *Budget,* the paper subscribed to and read by Amish and Mennonites all over the world. Her sister had never signed her name, simply putting *Your Delaware Neighbor* at the bottom of her submissions. The *Budget* shared news of new neighbors, farms sold, visitors, births, illnesses, weddings and deaths. It was a way for those apart from the world to remain connected to each other and, in her small way, Rebecca helped to hold the larger Amish community together.

"We won't be long," Johanna promised her aunt. "I came to help, not to sit and visit and drink iced tea."

"Take your time," Aunt Jezzy urged with a wave. "You work too hard, both of you. You're young. Enjoy yourself for once."

As soon as they were out of their aunt's earshot, Rebecca asked, "So, was he there this morning when you went to tend your bees?"

"Ne." Johanna shook her head. "His sister Mary was there with J.J. Did you know that she's walking out with Donald Troyer? They rode home from the Kings' last Sunday night."

"I hadn't heard." Rebecca's eyes sparkled with mischief. "But you know Mary. She never stays long with one boy. She told me she doesn't want to marry for years yet. She's having too much fun."

Johanna waited, knowing Rebecca would ask.

"So, Roland hasn't spoken to you since he turned you down on Saturday?"

"I'd rather not talk about Roland Byler."

Rebecca made a face. "You want to talk about him. You know you do."

Johanna shook her head again. She did, she supposed, but Rebecca shouldn't be able to see through her so easily. "It was mortifying. I never would have asked him to marry me, if I thought he'd refuse. I was so sure that he…that he cared for me."

"It must have been awful for you." Rebecca stopped to look at a pewter sugar bowl and pitcher for sale. "Pretty, aren't they?"

"You could buy them for your hope chest." Johanna checked the bottom. There was no price marked. "How much for the set?" she asked the woman behind the table. The shape was graceful but simple, perfect. An Amish kitchen was plain, but there were no rules on dishes or tableware. It was a set that Johanna would have loved on her own counter.

When the clerk quoted a price, Rebecca nodded. "I'll think about it."

"It might be gone when you come back," the seller, a pleasant Asian-American woman in a red straw hat and sunglasses, said.

"I know," Rebecca answered. "But I need to decide if I want them." She walked on and Johanna followed.

"If you like the creamer and sugar bowl, you should make an offer," Johanna urged. "Nice things don't last long, not when the sale is so busy."

Rebecca arched an eyebrow. "Could it be the same with good men? If you wait too long to decide, does someone else snap them up?"

"Roland. You're talking about Roland." Johanna's mouth firmed. "I asked him to marry me. What else can I do?"

Rebecca stopped and looked at her. "Maybe you didn't ask him the right way." She gestured to an open doorway, and Johanna followed her outside, into an alley that ran between two buildings. Rebecca glanced both ways, and—when she saw that they were alone—said, "Everyone thinks you're the sensible Yoder girl, the one with the good head on your shoulders. Practical Johanna. They don't know you the way your family does. You're smart, but sometimes you come off too strong, too unemotional. It makes people think you don't feel things. In here." She touched the place over her heart. "Maybe Roland wants a courtship. Maybe he's not so practical. Maybe he wants romance."

"Romance? At our age?"

"Don't be so quick to knock romance," Rebecca said. "Even men can be sentimental."

Johanna frowned. "Could it be that *my* asking *him* upset him? That he thinks I'm too forward for a woman?"

"I doubt that. He's known you all your life. He knows you speak your mind." Rebecca considered. "Did you ever think that Roland might be as scared as you of remarrying? He lost his wife, and he's been hurt, maybe more than you have, because she never hurt him like…"

"Like Wilmer," Johanna supplied. "It's all right. We can be honest with each other."

"*Ya,* we know what Wilmer was like before he passed. Some of it, but you didn't share everything that happened."

"I couldn't. I was ashamed."

"I understand," Rebecca agreed. "But Roland isn't Wilmer. Roland is sweet like Charley. You know how Charley feels about Miriam. Can you blame Roland for wanting to be sure? For wanting the kind of love match his brother has?"

Johanna swallowed. For a moment, all her fears rose inside her.

Rebecca gripped her arm. "And what about you? Are you certain you're ready to remarry? Can you turn your life over to another man? To accept him as head of your family? To obey him?"

"It's the right thing to do…the sensible thing for our children."

"And you always have to be *sensible,* don't you?" Rebecca asked.

"I don't know." Johanna clenched her damp hands. "I suppose it's in my nature. And Ruth and Miriam and Anna are sure Roland and I would make a good marriage. Even *Mam* thinks—"

"*Mam* isn't marrying him. It has to be you," Rebecca said. "Maybe when you're sure…with your heart—not just your head—maybe then, Roland would say yes."

"And if he doesn't?"

Rebecca's eyes brimmed with compassion. "Then you wait until God sends you another opportunity."

"How long?"

Rebecca shrugged. "I don't know. Maybe until the cows come home or you're as old as Aunt Jezzy." She motioned toward the lunchroom. "Now let's eat. I'm starving."

Johanna nodded again. Another moment, and she'd have been in tears. And she didn't want to go back to

Aunt Jezzy with red eyes, because their aunt would want to know what was wrong.

Together they went into the noisy food building. It was filled with mingling strangers and at least a dozen Amish. They were lucky enough to find a couple leaving a table and sat down. Rebecca opted for a soda and a roast-beef-and-cheese sandwich.

"That's breakfast?" Johanna teased. She was sticking to iced tea, heavy on the sugar.

Rebecca laughed. "This is what the English call brunch. I ordered cheese fries for Aunt Jezzy. You know how she loves them."

"Guder mariye!" Lydia Beachy waved and came toward them, three children in tow. "How is your mother?"

Johanna found a chair for her mother's friend and they each took a little one on their laps while the adults shared news of the past week. After a few moments, Johanna suggested that they'd better get back to help Aunt Jezzy with the stand.

"I just saw her," Lydia said. One of her older children joined them, and Lydia doled out money for pizza and lemonade. "She was talking to Nip Hilty. You know Nip, don't you? He has the harness shop on Peach Basket Road." Lydia rolled her eyes. "Saw them talking last Friday, too."

"Nip Hilty?" Rebecca asked. "Didn't his wife die last fall?"

"Ne." Lydia leaned closer to Johanna. "Two years ago, Bethany passed. A good woman. Came to our quiltings sometimes. Her heart, I think, but Bethany carried some weight on her. Like me." Lydia patted her rounded abdomen.

Lydia herself was tall and thin with a wide, smiling

mouth and a prominent nose. Lydia was definitely not and probably never would be a fat woman, Johanna thought. And if Lydia was gaining weight in the middle, it probably meant that she was expecting another baby. But there wasn't a woman in Kent County with a better heart, unless it was Anna or *Mam*. Lydia was so sweet that people naturally told her everything about everyone. Lydia sifted through the gossip and only passed on what was good and what she believed was true. And if Lydia was hinting at something between Aunt Jezzy and this Nip Hilty, it must have been commonly talked about in the Amish community and generally approved of.

"I've always thought the world of your aunt," Lydia said. "Since your *grossmama* went to live with Anna and Samuel, Jezebel has really perked up. Wouldn't it be something if she found herself a beau at her age?"

Rebecca exchanged glances with Johanna. "Maybe we should get back to work."

"You go on," Lydia urged. "You take a look and see if I'm not right. Like as not, Nip will still be there. Last week, he stood there the better part of an hour, talking her ear off. And Jezzy didn't seem to mind, not one bit."

"What do you think?" Rebecca asked when they were far enough from the lunch area that Lydia could no longer hear them. "She'd never... Not Aunt Jezzy. I just can't imagine..."

Johanna kept walking. She'd make no judgment until she saw them together with her own eyes. It didn't seem possible. Aunt Jezzy was even shyer around Amish men than she was around the English, in general. Johanna had rarely heard her speak to Anna's husband, Samuel, and he certainly wasn't a stranger in the Yoder house. The only male she regularly spoke to was Irwin.

"I don't know what started that talk," Rebecca continued, "but I don't think that she would…would…"

Johanna stopped so quickly that Rebecca nearly bumped into her. There, behind the table, was Aunt Jezzy, and leaning against a post, eating an ice cream cone, was Nip Hilty. Aunty Jezzy's cheeks were pink and her eyes were sparkling. She was talking up a storm, and Nip Hilty was laughing. And in Aunt Jezzy's hand was a half-eaten double-dip strawberry ice cream cone—a treat she certainly hadn't bought herself.

Chapter Six

"Have you heard anything about Aunt Jezzy and Nip Hilty?" Johanna asked her mother. The two of them were in the kitchen, just finishing preparing supper. Since she, Rebecca and Aunt Jezzy had been at Spence's during the midday meal, *Mam* had gone to more trouble than usual tonight. She'd roasted three fat hens and had made fresh peas and dumplings to go with loaves of dark rye bread, German potato salad, garden salad and a counter full of peach pies. Susanna had already set the table, with Katy's help, and the two of them had gone out to call Irwin, Jonah and 'Kota in to wash up.

"I've met Nip," *Mam* answered, "but I think you and Rebecca must be hatching chickens out of turnips. I can't imagine that Aunt Jezzy would like him in any way other than someone to exchange neighborly talk with."

Johanna glanced toward the door to see Rebecca, her arms full of wildflowers, push open the screen door and enter the kitchen. Once they'd returned home from the sale, Rebecca had changed out of her good dress and had exchanged her *Kapp* for a blue kerchief. Her eyes were shining, her bare feet were dusty and bits of leaves were caught in her hair.

"The flowers are beautiful," Johanna said, admiring the bouquet of yellow oxeye daisies, evening primrose and marsh marigold mixed with the vivid blues of wild lupine and Jacob's ladder. "But you look like you lost a tussle with a banty hen."

Rebecca laughed. "They don't call them wildflowers for nothing. Some are pretty tough."

Mam joined in the easy laughter. "Here, you can put them in this tin pitcher. They'll look nice on the supper table."

Rebecca dumped the flowers and greenery in the sink and began to cut the stems to fit the flowers in the tin pitcher. Of all of them, Rebecca had the greatest gift for growing and arranging flowers. She'd gathered the blooms in less than half an hour.

"I haven't seen the lupine yet this year," Johanna said. "The blue looks so pretty against the yellow of the daisies. Where did you find them?"

"The usual places—the edge of the orchard, behind the barn," Rebecca replied. "But don't change the subject. I heard you say something about me, and I want to know what."

"Nothing bad," *Mam* assured her.

Johanna chuckled. "I was telling *Mam* about Aunt Jezzy and Nip Hilty—about how we were sure he bought her that ice cream cone."

Rebecca glanced at their mother. "If you'd been there, *Mam,* you would think the same thing. She was so relaxed with him, not shy the way she usually is, but all giggly and rosy-cheeked. I'm telling you, Aunt Jezzy has a beau."

Mam folded her arms and shook her head. "You two.

You're worse than Martha for gossip. If Jezzy hasn't found a match to suit her in all these years, I doubt she'll change her mind now."

"I'm just saying, it looked suspicious." Rebecca added water to the pitcher and set the arrangement in the center of the white tablecloth. "In a good way," she added. "It would be wonderful if Aunt Jezzy did find a husband, don't you think? She's never had her own home. She's such a good person. She deserves to be happy."

Mam looked from one of them to the other and pursed her lips. "Better the two of you concern yourselves with finding your own husbands." Johanna knew her mother was teasing them, but there was always a thread of truth in *Mam's* jests.

"Not me," Rebecca protested. "I'm too young to get married."

The sound of a car engine caught Johanna's attention. She went to the window to see Grace drive cautiously across the barnyard and park her automobile in the shed. "I can't get used to that motor vehicle coming and going," Johanna remarked. "But I suppose Grace needs it to get to school."

"It will only be here a few more months," *Mam* said, "until her wedding. And I'm sure you'll miss her when she's gone."

"We all will," Rebecca agreed. "We all love her, but it's awkward sometimes, explaining to other Amish why we have a car in our shed and an Englisher living in our house."

"She isn't an Englisher," *Mam* corrected gently. "Grace is a Yoder, and she and her son have as much right to be in your father's house as any of us."

Rebecca's expression grew instantly contrite. "I was lacking in charity to say that, wasn't I?"

"It's no more than what I've thought a hundred times."
Johanna sliced the still-warm loaves of bread with a ser-
rated knife. "But *Mam* is right. Grace is our sister, and
she belongs here. I didn't mean to be unkind. It's just…"

"Just that change comes hard…for all of us," *Mam*
agreed. "I agree that our life was simpler before Grace
came, but maybe simple isn't God's plan for us. Maybe
loving one another when it isn't easy makes us grow."

Mam removed her work apron and replaced it with a
freshly ironed one as white as her starched *Kapp*. She
went to the door and opened it wide. "Come in, child,"
she called. "You're late tonight, but just in time for the
evening meal."

From across the yard, Johanna heard the laughter of
her daughter and the noisy chatter of Grace's 'Kota and
her Jonah. Irwin was a few yards behind them, strolling
along in his awkward long-legged gait, but keeping pace
with a smiling Susanna.

*How could I think of leaving this happy house? Of
risking my children's happiness to marry Roland, or any
man for that matter?* Her years with Wilmer had been
tumultuous, and despite her efforts and her tears, she'd
never been able to provide the warmth and security her
mother's home provided for them all. Jonah and Katy had
both blossomed here in this big house. The once-quiet
Katy never stopped chattering, and Jonah had changed
from a sad child to a bundle of energy.

*I should be more like Mam. I have a good enough
example. It wasn't enough that Mam was widowed with
seven daughters to raise. She not only managed with us
and the farm, but she'd opened her arms to Irwin and
Grace and 'Kota. She opened her arms to me….*

Katy came running into the kitchen. "I found a duck

egg!" she cried. "Look, *Grossmama!* And I carried it my-self!" She thrust the egg out. "Aunt Susanna says I can have it for breakfast tomorrow!"

"Better you let me beat your egg into pancakes," Re-becca suggested. "Duck eggs are rich and make nice batter."

The two boys spilled into the room on Katy's heels, and Johanna sent them along to wash their hands. She greeted Grace, heard Irwin's tale of an escaped pig and agreed with Susanna that more people were coming every day to borrow books from the tiny lending library that she managed in the old milk house. And in the familiar bustle and routine of the supper hour, Johanna was able to forget her worries about the future and lose herself in the here and now.

Soon the family gathered around the table and low-ered their heads for silent prayer. Even Katy and the two boys understood the need to give thanks to God for all the blessings He had bestowed on them. A sense of peace flowed though Johanna. The cares of the world seemed far away.

Once grace was over, everyone began to help them-selves to the delicious food. "Wonderful bread," Aunt Jezzy proclaimed. "And your dumplings are light enough to float up to the ceiling."

"Why would they do that?" Susanna asked, poking at a dumpling with her fork. "I want them to stay on my plate so that I can eat them." Everyone smiled at that, and Susanna laughed.

I am truly blessed, Johanna thought. *To be born into this family and faith.* She promised herself that she would try harder to be worthy of them.

"So," *Mam* said to Aunt Jezzy, "the girls say you have an admirer. Nip Hilty. Isn't he a bachelor?"

Aunt Jezzy flushed a bright pink and giggled like a teenager.

"Maybe he's the reason you're so eager to tend the table on sale days," *Mam* suggested.

Aunt Jezzy peeked up through her lashes and spun her water glass exactly three rotations. "He bought me ice cream," she said. "Strawberry." She smiled. "And that's all I'll say about Nip tonight."

The following morning, Johanna and Katy followed the winding path that led across the field from *Mam's* house to Ruth and Eli's. It was a beautiful morning. The sun was shining and last night's shower made the world smell new and fresh in a way that brought tears to Johanna's eyes. *I couldn't imagine not living close to the earth. How do people in cities breathe, let alone thrive?*

Bees buzzed around the honeysuckle in the hedgerow, and the clover was soft under their bare feet. Johanna paused and knelt down to catch Katy in her arms and hug her tightly. "I love you," she murmured. "I love you so much."

"I love you, too, *Mam,*" the child echoed in her sweet voice. "I love you more than the moon."

Off to her left she saw Charley digging post holes for his new fence line. "Morning, sister," he called to her. Johanna waved back. Secretly, she was glad that Charley was busy and wasn't at the house. Charley was as close as a brother to her, and it certainly wasn't his fault that Roland had proven to be so difficult, but making small talk with him this morning would have been awkward.

Since Ruth had gotten so large with the coming twins, Johanna and Rebecca tried to come over at least one day a week to help her with the housework. Miriam and her husband, Charley, lived upstairs, but Miriam—always happier outside than in—spent her days working the farm beside her husband.

As they entered the house, Johanna could smell Ruth's coffee. Katy ran to her and gave her a hug. "Wait until you see what I have," Ruth said. She opened the pantry door, and there in a laundry basket, Johanna saw her sister's orange tabby with three tiny kittens.

"Ooh," Katy said. "Can I hold one?"

Ruth squatted awkwardly and picked up a fuzzy black kitten with white paws and a white spot on its chest. "You can touch it. Gently," she instructed. "But they are too young for you to hold yet. Next week you can hold them." Ruth glanced back. Johanna nodded. "And, if you do just as I tell you, if you are very, very responsible, you can have one of the kittens as soon as it's old enough to leave the mother."

"I can? For my own?" Katy wiggled with joy. "*Mam?* Can I?"

"You heard your aunt Ruth. You must show her that you know how to take care of a *bussli.* A kitten is a big responsibility. You must feed it and take it outside and keep it safe until it's large enough to take care of itself."

"She's a sensible child," Ruth said after they'd left Katy to admire the kittens and gone out to sit on Ruth's screened-in porch with their coffee. "You've done a wonderful job with her. You're a fine mother. I only hope I can do as well."

"You?" Johanna chuckled. "You'll be a far better mother than me."

Ruth rubbed the front of her apron. "I can't wait. It doesn't seem possible. Eli and I...after we lost..." She sighed. "I worry that everything will be all right, Johanna. I don't know how I'd bear it if something went wrong."

"We must trust in God. You're healthy. The babies have strong heartbeats." Johanna had gone to the midwife with Ruth on her last checkup and heard the heartbeats herself. "There's no reason to be afraid. Enjoy your last days of peace and quiet. With twins, you and Eli won't get a full night's sleep for at least two years."

Ruth laughed. "If I ever complain, remind me that I prayed for this." For a few moments, they sat in silence, listening to a Carolina wren scolding a jay that approached too close to the wren's nest under the porch eaves. They watched the sunshine sparkle on the dew-drops that lingered on the hollyhocks, savoring the quiet companionship of sisters who were best friends.

And then Ruth broke the comfortable solitude by saying, "Dorcas came by yesterday afternoon. She told me that Roland asked you to marry him and you turned him down flat."

Johanna nearly choked on her mouthful of coffee. "What?" she sputtered. "Who told her that?" Their cousin Dorcas could be a bit of a gossip.

The expression in Ruth's nutmeg-brown eyes grew serious. "Is it true? Did you turn him down?"

Anger flared in Johanna's chest. *How could Roland betray her by spreading such gossip? By telling an outright untruth?* "No," she said. "That's not the way it happened. *I* asked Roland to marry me, and *he* refused."

"Verhuddelt." Ruth shook her head. "I thought it was *lecherich*—ridiculous—but you know Dorcas. I thought it was best to ask you to your face. By now Aunt Martha has probably spread the rumor over half the county."

"And all the way up to Lancaster. By next week,

they'll be talking about it in Oregon." Johanna felt sick. *What could make Roland say such a thing? Was he so ashamed of his reaction to her proposal that he had to make it seem as if everything was her fault?* "If Roland's that low to spread such gossip, maybe it's better that he did refuse me."

"I've hurt you," Ruth said. "I didn't mean to. But I thought it best you hear it from family, rather than at church or at the market. And I won't ask you what happened. You can tell me when you're ready. If you want to tell me at all."

Johanna wasn't up for retelling the whole story, at least not right now. "Did Dorcas say where her mother heard it?"

"I think she said it came from Roland and Charley's sister Mary, but…" Ruth looked heavenward. "Dorcas never gets anything right. It could have been Rebecca or Miriam or even Anna. Roland is close to Charley. They confide in each other, and Charley can't keep anything from Miriam." She chuckled. "He's mad for her. You'd think they were still courting, rather than an old married couple."

"Aunt Ruth?" Katy peered through the open door to the porch. "Why can't the *bussli* open its eyes?"

"The light is too bright for such a young kitten. All in God's time, precious. Have you decided which one you want?"

"The black one with the white mittens. I'm going to call her Mittens."

Ruth laughed. "Mittens is a good name, but it isn't a girl. The black *bussli* is a boy."

Johanna stood up, grateful that Katy had interrupted their conversation. She didn't want to think about Roland or the stupid rumor that he'd started. She wanted to clean something. She wanted to scrub floors and wash windows, anything requiring physical effort…anything to stop the hurt gathering in the hollow place inside her. "Time I got to work," she said lightly. "Shall I start on this porch? I think the floor needs a good scrubbing."

Two hours, three floors and nine windows later, Johanna's temper flared just as hot. She knew she should just let it go, but she couldn't. She just couldn't.

"Would you watch Katy for me?" she asked Ruth. "I'm going over to Roland's and straighten this out with him."

"Now?" Ruth asked. "Of course. You know I love having Katy anytime." She grimaced. "I don't think I'd want to be Roland Byler just now."

"I'm not going to argue with him. I just want to know if he did tell anyone that I was the one who rejected him and why he did it—if it's true. I wouldn't want to jump to conclusions. Just because Dorcas said it, doesn't mean that it's so."

Ruth stirred sugar into her pitcher of iced tea. "It's probably right that you two have this out now. But…"

"But what?"

Ruth grimaced. "Don't do or say anything that will make things worse."

"What could possibly make things worse? I made a fool out of myself by asking a man to marry me, and now the story, or at least *a* story, is spreading. I'll be a laughingstock, and so will my family."

Ruth hugged her. "I'm so sorry, Johanna. I'll admit, I wanted you and Roland to marry. I thought he'd be perfect for you."

So did I, Johanna thought. *So did I. But it's clear that I was badly mistaken.*

* * *

Roland drove the ax deep into the upright section of log and it split with a satisfying crack. He'd been at it since before noon, and the woodpile beside the corn-crib was growing steadily. This was applewood, rescued from an English neighbor who had planned on having a bonfire after he cleared an old orchard. Apple burned clean and hot and gave off a wonderful smell. Burning applewood as trash was a terrible waste, but when he'd offered to buy the uprooted trees, Paul had suggested a trade. Two days' labor at harvest time in exchange for the applewood, an offer that Roland had been more than willing to accept.

There was an old saying, "Firewood heats twice, once when you chop it, and again when you burn it." That was true enough, but he'd be glad to have the cured logs when cold weather came. And splitting wood took a lot of ef-fort. It kept a man's body in good shape, and prevented him from thinking too much about things that troubled him. At least, he'd hoped it might. Johanna had been worrying him like a stone wedged under a horse's shoe.

He couldn't help going over and over that last conver-sation they'd had at the Mennonite festival, when she'd suggested they marry, saying it as plainly as if she had asked him to pass the salt—and with as little emotion.

When he'd lost Pauline and the babes she was car-rying, he'd felt for months as if he was dead inside. But then, when Johanna's husband had passed away, a small seed of hope had begun to sprout. Maybe there was a chance that he and Johanna could find what they'd both felt for each other once, and nourish it again. Maybe they could have a second chance.

Years ago, when Johanna had thrown him over, she'd

been right to do it. He wasn't worthy of her, wasn't the man his mother and father had raised him to be. He'd paid the penalty for his reckless behavior. But later, he'd truly repented for his acts, and he'd returned to his faith. He'd been honest with Pauline, and she'd been willing to believe in him. He would have loved her for that, if for nothing else.

But when he began to live again, when his mourning for Pauline had grown bearable, he began to long for Johanna Yoder. He'd pictured her at his table, in his garden and in his orchard. He'd imagined walking to church with her and watching her face when she sang the old hymns. But in that dream, she loved him as much as he loved her. And if she didn't love him…if she couldn't, how could he go through with a farce? How could he marry a woman who wanted him because he had a good sheep meadow and a farm without a mortgage? Better to live alone than live a lie…. So why did it ache so much?

"Roland?"

He sank the blade of the ax into the chopping block and turned, expecting to see his sister Mary. She'd taken J.J. for the morning and promised to bring him back on her way to her afternoon cleaning job at an English-woman's house. But it wasn't Mary, and it wasn't J.J. Roland's pulse quickened at the sight of Johanna walking toward him.

"We need to talk," she said.

Chapter Seven

Roland stepped away from the woodpile, pulled off his leather work gloves and inhaled deeply. He was filthy and sweating heavily, no fit sight for a woman he'd hoped to court. But here she was and here he was, and it was face her or run, and he'd never been a coward.

"I'm listening," Roland said. His chest tightened, and he felt as if the earth was unsteady under his feet. Why was it that Johanna always made him feel unsure of himself? It wasn't just that her big blue eyes radiated strength, and it wasn't the unusual color of her red-gold hair, or her beautiful, heart-shaped face. A man would have to be blind not to see the neat waist or her tidy figure. But Johanna was a woman who had more that just beauty.

For him, she had always brought joy into his life. When he caught sight of her, his heart always beat a little faster and the sky seemed bluer. Johanna wasn't shy and retiring, like so many Amish girls, and she never hesitated to speak her mind. She didn't say the first thing that popped into her head, though, and she had a dry sense of humor that matched his own.

"Roland?" The sound of her voice was as soothing as rain on a tin roof after a drought.

He straightened his shoulders, shaking off the ache of hard-used muscles and the cramping at the back of his neck that came from swinging an ax for hours on end. "I'm sorry for the way we parted last," he said with what he hoped was quiet dignity.

"Did you tell anyone about what passed between us on Saturday?" Her tone came firm, without being strident, and her bright blue eyes demanded honesty.

Regret flooded him. Charley had a big mouth, and from the look on Johanna's face he'd obviously shared their conversation, at the very least with his wife. "I did," Roland admitted, trying not to sound defensive. "It troubled me that you and I should argue over something so important as marriage. I talked it out with my brother."

"I see." Johanna's lower lip trembled, and her face paled so that her freckles stood out against her creamy skin. She looked as if she might cry.

Roland swallowed. He never could abide a woman's tears, and the thought that he might hurt Johanna enough to make her weep hit him like a horse's kick to his midsection.

She came closer and lowered her voice, although there was no one but God and the two of them to hear. "I ask because there's talk. Yesterday, Dorcas told my sister Ruth that you asked me to marry you and I wouldn't have you."

"What?" He blinked. "I never said that. I told Charley... I didn't repeat everything that passed between us, but I would never lie. I told Charley that it was me who said no."

"So Dorcas had it wrong?"

He nodded. "Dorcas had it wrong."

Johanna took a deep breath and glanced away, them back at him. "I'm glad." She looked… She looked vulnerable, and that made him feel even worse. He'd always thought of her as tough…but she wasn't. Not really. She just did a good job of hiding her weaknesses.

She took a step closer. "Despite our quarrel, Roland, I never thought you'd be one to go behind my back with an untruth. I thought it fair to come and ask you, face-to-face—not to just believe rumors."

"I appreciate that."

She nibbled at her bottom lip, and he saw that she was as nervous as he was. "But you told Charley."

He nodded. "I did. I thought I needed advice."

"And what did Charley say?"

Roland shrugged. "That the community…the family…think we should marry. They expect us to come to an agreement."

Johanna took another step toward him. Roland felt like a weather vane on top of a barn, gusts of wind catching it and blowing it first one way and then the other.

"And…do you still feel the same as when we talked last?" she asked. "About wanting romantic love? You don't think we should listen to those who know us best— if we shouldn't just make the match…for the sake of our children?"

He hesitated. This was his opportunity to make everything right. All he had to do was swallow his pride. He could have Johanna as his wife, as long as he didn't ask for her pledge of love. But he couldn't do it, because there could be no real marriage between a man and woman without honesty. "I do," he said. "My thoughts on that haven't changed."

"All right," she agreed. "That's fair. I still stand by my words, as well."

Disappointment made him bold. Or maybe it was the thread of hope he still held in his heart. "Is it because of what happened between us when we were walking out?" he asked. "How I failed you? Or is the problem because of Wilmer?"

She looked unsure. Maybe a little afraid. Not of him… but of herself. "I don't know," she said. "Maybe both."

He knew how close he was to pushing too far with this honesty, but he had to take the chance. "And is this something that could change, or is there no chance of… of love between us?"

She covered her mouth with that slender hand and shook her head. Slowly, she lowered her hand. "I don't know, Roland."

He exhaled, letting out a breath he hadn't realized he had been holding. Did she mean there *was* a chance?

"We're agreed, then," she said. "The question is, what do we do about the gossip?"

Agreed? There had been no agreement. They were like two hardheaded goats with their horns locked together. "Why do we have to do anything? It's what we know that matters. Next week they'll be talking about somebody else."

"It *does* matter," Johanna said. "These are our friends, our neighbors…our family. How did the story get twisted from what you told Charley to what Dorcas told Ruth?"

"I'm sure you have more important things to worry about than what Dorcas says."

"So I'm to go to each person who's heard this tale and straighten them out?"

He shrugged. "I'd let it lie. If you talk to Ruth, she'll tell Eli and Miriam. Miriam will tell Charley and—"

"I thought Charley had it straight."

"He did, from me." Roland flushed. "I suppose, I shouldn't have said anything to him but—"

"*Ne.* You shouldn't have. It wasn't Charley's business. It was private, between us." Her mouth firmed. "I wish you'd left it that way."

"So I shouldn't talk to my brother about what's bothering me, but it's all right for you to share what passes between us with your sisters?"

She folded her arms. "I didn't come here to argue with you, Roland."

"I suppose I should be grateful for that."

"You should." She looked down at her bare feet and surprised him with a chuckle. "Listen to us, arguing like an old married couple. "I'm sorry. I came to get an explanation, but I never doubted you. You can be thickheaded, but you're…"

"A decent person?" He forced a wry smile. "While you're here, you might as well tend your bees, and I'll finish chopping my wood. I think we've both said enough on this subject to last a week or two."

"If it bothers you, my coming here to look after the hive, I can move it. I think they're settled enough now. If I come at night and—"

"Keep your bees here as long as you like. They're no trouble to me, and it seems they like my garden. I see them everywhere. Even I know that it's safer to move them in cool weather. I wouldn't want to see you lose them after all your hard work."

She nodded. "There's sense in that. But I'll tell you

plainly, I mean to find out what Charley said and who he said it to."

"That again, is it?" Roland shrugged again. "Go to it, if it pleases you, but I'll have no part of your detective game." She turned to walk away, and he couldn't resist saying, "There's a work frolic at the Stutzman brothers'—you know the Lancaster Amish who bought the Englisher farm next to Norman and Lydia's. On Saturday the twenty-first. Not this Saturday but the following. Some of us are going to build a dog-proof pasture fence and a shed for their dairy-goat herd."

"Lydia said they were camping in a tent on the property, but I haven't met them."

"Thomas and Will Stutzman, brothers. Big lot of their friends and family coming down from Pennsylvania in July to put up a house, but they needed help to get their herd settled in."

Johanna relaxed her arms and tilted her head, obviously curious. "*Mam* said that she'd heard they were cheese makers."

"It's mostly young married couples and those walking out going. Charley and Miriam are going, and so are Mary and Little Joe King. We're having food and a bonfire after dark. Maybe you'd like to come with me?"

She hesitated. "I don't think so. Not with things the way they stand with us."

"So this time, you're refusing me," he said quietly.

"I'm afraid so." She averted her eyes. "I don't mind going to help out our new neighbors, but I'll drive myself or come with Charley and Miriam. There's no sense in causing more talk about us.… Or in pretending we're courting, when we're not."

"We wouldn't want that," he said, trying to keep the edge from his voice. "Especially since there's no *us* to feed the gossip."

The following afternoon, Johanna, Jonah and 'Kota were driving Johanna's flock of sheep from one pasture into the low meadow with the aid of *Mam's* Shetland sheepdog Flora. Nine of the cheviot ewes and their lambs were obediently following the dominant cheviot ewe, but two didn't want to cooperate. The troublemaker, as usual, was Snowball—the only Cormo. She managed to squeeze under the fence, followed by a straggler, and trot toward the cornfield.

"Abatz dummkopf!" 'Kota cried, pointing at the escapees. "Stop, stupid heads!"

"They're going into the corn!" Jonah shouted.

"You two keep the flock moving toward the meadow, and when they're all in, close the gate. But wait there until I chase the other two back, and let them in."

"And lock the gate!" 'Kota jumped from one foot to the other with excitement.

Since he'd come to live at *Mam's* farm last fall, he'd fallen in love with barnyard animals, but the sheep were his favorite. He was fascinated by every aspect of caring for them, including the lambing and the shearing of their fleece. Jonah, in contrast, liked the sheep well enough, but he favored the larger animals. He loved nothing more than trailing after his uncle Charley and helping to tend the horses and cows.

Johanna hitched up her skirt and climbed over the fence. The two sheep had found a row of corn and were busily munching on the six-inch-high plants. "Shoo! Shoo!" Johanna said.

Charley came out of the orchard on a three-year-old gelding that he was breaking to saddle for an English-woman and spotted the runaway sheep. He shouted to Johanna. "I'll give you a hand!"

She waved her apron and ran at the two sheep. The cheviot ewe went one way, and Snowball went in the op-posite direction, a mouthful of corn leaves dangling from her mouth. Johanna took off after Snowball, leaving the other ewe for Charlie to corral.

The silly creature trotted down the rows of corn just as Aunt Martha and *Mam* came into the yard in her hus-band's, Uncle Reuben's, buggy. The two women climbed down and made an attempt to chase Snowball into an open shed. Hearing the shouting, Susanna and Rebecca left the side yard, where they'd been hanging clothes, and joined in the pursuit. Susanna caught hold of Snow-ball's collar, but the sheep yanked free and made for the garden gate with Aunt Martha and *Mam* hot on the ani-mal's heels.

Johanna tripped over a clod of dirt and fell on her bottom. Then she began to laugh. Seeing her mother and Aunt Martha running after the ewe was the funni-est thing she'd seen in weeks. She laughed until she was breathless and tears of laughter ran down her cheeks. She was still laughing when Charley rode up on the gelding.

"I got mine," he said. "Chased it back through the fence. The boys turned it in with the others."

"I didn't get mine," she admitted between chuckles. "For all I know, it's halfway to Dover. That one sheep is more trouble than the whole flock." She got to her feet and brushed the dirt off her hands and skirt.

Charley took off his hat and wiped the sweat off his forehead. The horse danced nervously and twitched its ears. Charley stroked the animal's neck and spoke sooth-ingly to it. "Easy, easy, boy." He looked back at her. "If it's so much trouble, why keep it? Send it to the sale."

Johanna sighed. "Snowball doesn't belong to me. Wilmer brought it home for Katy, just before he died. The man he worked for couldn't pay his wages and gave Wilmer the ewe instead. She's worth a lot of money. She's a Cormo, and their wool is greatly sought after. I hoped to improve my flock with her and we could always use the extra money."

"And meanwhile, you put up with the monster."

"I suppose I do." She rolled her eyes. "Aunt Martha may have killed her by now. She nearly ran Aunt Martha and *Mam* over, and I think they chased her through the garden."

Charley tugged his hat down. "Sorry I missed that."

"Me, too." She surveyed the damaged corn. "At least they didn't have time to eat enough to make themselves sick or to destroy too much of the crop."

"The flock could do some damage here," Charley re-marked.

Johanna nodded. *Mam* was coming to depend more and more on him to do the heavy farming. With the girls marrying off, one by one, it was a blessing that they had Charley and that he and Miriam would continue to work *Dat's* land in the future.

He shifted in the saddle. "You and my brother still butting heads?"

Johanna frowned. "I've been wanting to talk to you. I understand that Roland told you about something that happened between us—that I said it made sense for us to marry. And he turned me down. Is that what he said?"

Charley nodded. "That's what he said."

"Well, there's a rumor going around. And it seems people have it all wrong. What did you tell Miriam?"

Charley's brow wrinkled. "Nothing. I didn't say anything to her. I thought that you'd tell her yourself—if you wanted her to know."

Johanna gazed up at him. "But if you didn't tell Miriam, who did you tell?"

Charley's face reddened. "Mary. I didn't mean to. It just slipped out. She was asking about Roland, and…"

"Did you tell anyone else that he'd refused to marry me?"

"Ne." Charley shook his head. "Nobody. Just Mary."

"So I'll have to find out who Mary confided in, because Ruth heard a completely different story from Dorcas. Her mother told her that I didn't want to marry Roland." Johanna grimaced. "Now the neighborhood is talking about us, and they don't even have the story right."

"I'm sorry, Johanna. I feel awful. I should have kept my mouth shut." The horse pawed the ground, and Charley reined him in a tight circle. "Hope you aren't too mad at me."

Johanna shook her head. "No, not mad. Of course, if Roland hadn't said anything to you, none of this would have happened."

He sat there for a moment. "Oh, Miriam wanted me to ask you if you wanted to go fishing with us on Saturday. We bought tickets to go out on a charter boat in the Delaware Bay. For trout. Eli was going to go, but now he can't. Miriam knows how much you like fishing, and Eli's giving away the ticket. Anna said she'd be glad to watch Katy and Jonah for you."

"I haven't been fishing in the bay for years, not since Katy was born. I'd like that."

"We've got a driver. Be ready at five. And pack a big lunch. They have water and soft drinks on the boat."

Johanna heard someone call her name and turned to see *Mam* and Aunt Martha coming toward her, dragging Snowball behind them on a length of clothesline. "Did you lose something?" *Mam* asked.

"You caught her. I hope she didn't tear up too much of the garden."

"No sheep born that can get away from me," Aunt Martha proclaimed proudly. "You've just got to show an animal who's boss."

It was all Johanna could do to not start laughing again. Aunt Martha had dirt and bits of wool stuck to the front of her dress and apron. Her shoes were caked with dirt, her *Kapp* was wrinkled and nearly falling off the back of her head, and there was a big smudge on her cheek and another on her nose.

Charley choked and began coughing, said a hasty goodbye and rode off, leaving Johanna struggling to maintain her dignity.

"I almost had her in the lettuce," *Mam* said, "but she broke loose and ran through the beans. I don't know where she'd be if Martha hadn't dove on her back and rode her to a standstill."

Johanna's eyes widened. "You did that, Aunt Martha?"

Aunt Martha nodded vigorously. "That beast deserves nothing better than to be carved up and served with new potatoes and baby beets. She's a danger to life and limb."

Mam's smile spread across her face and her eyes twinkled. "You're just lucky that Martha was here when you needed her, Johanna," she said. "Otherwise, it would have been a real disaster."

Aunt Martha beamed. "I always did have a hand with sheep," she boasted as she glanced at *Mam* and began to chuckle. "And just between us women, I haven't had so much fun in a month of Sundays."

Chapter Eight

Ribbons of lavender and peach uncoiled on the eastern horizon as Johanna, Miriam, Charley and three other Amish men climbed onto the deck of the charter boat *Gone Fishin' IV.* Overhead, Johanna heard the screech of seagulls and, below, the lap of gray-green waves against the weathered dock. The tangy air smelled of salt marsh and bay, and even though it was early, the night dampness was already evaporating from the shore, leaving a promise of a glorious day.

Bowers Beach, the small bayside fishing village, teemed with pickup trucks and boat trailers. Excited sportsmen and commercial fishermen rushed to stock up on bait and ice and launch their vessels. Off the stern of the charter boat, seemingly oblivious to the commotion, a mallard hen bobbed on the choppy waves, trailed by seven tiny yellow-and-brown ducklings. Gulls shrieked and dove for scraps in the shallows, and Johanna caught sight of a huge horseshoe crab lurking in the shadows of the dock. She leaned so far over the gunnel to watch it that, for a moment, she struggled to keep her balance.

Then, out of nowhere, someone snatched her back from the edge of the boat.

"Careful," a familiar male voice warned. "Don't want to have you fall overboard. That water's too cold to suit me, and I'd have to dive in and pull you out."

Johanna's eyes widened in surprise as she turned to him. "Roland! What are you doing here?" She took a step back from him, planting her hand on her hip. "And, if you recall, the last time one of us fell into the pond, *I* had to rescue *you*."

A shy grin lifted the corners of his mouth and added sparkle to his eyes. "I was nine, and I didn't know how to swim yet."

"I was younger than you, but my *dat* made certain his girls all knew how to swim."

Roland grimaced. "You're never going to let me forget that, are you?"

Johanna turned away, glancing at the water. There was no way this was coincidence, she and Roland being on the same charter boat. It had to be a plot cooked up by her sister and brother-in-law, but Roland was obviously in on it, too. She supposed that she should be angry, but she couldn't help finding it just a little funny. The horseshoe crab she'd been watching had vanished into the dark depths under the dock.

One of the reasons she'd agreed to come on this fishing trip was to get away from thinking about Roland, and trying to explain to family and friends what had and hadn't happened between them. But instead of leaving her trouble back at Seven Poplars, she was trapped on this fishing boat with him for the entire day.

Can't run away from stuff you fear, Johanna heard her father whisper from the shadows of her mind. *Be it a rotten tooth or a bad mule, may as well face it down,* he'd always advised. And *Dat* was right. She couldn't run from Roland…didn't know if she wanted to. That was the trouble…she didn't know what she wanted, and just being near him made her common sense fly out the window.

"You didn't answer my question," she said, turning back to Roland. "What are you doing here?"

"I'm on this boat to catch fish—same as you."

What Roland said was mild enough, but the expression on his face—when she turned to face him—was smug. And they both knew that fishing wasn't his entire reason for being there.

For just an instant, she had the most wicked urge to give him a good shove overboard. She imagined what a big splash he would make. But she couldn't do that, no matter how much satisfaction it might give her. Charley and Miriam were probably watching, waiting to see what she would do. They were hoping for a show, and she was determined not to give them one.

It was too late to chicken out and just go home. The captain had already started the boat's engines, and they were pulling away from the dock. Besides, the driver who'd brought them in his van had already left, and wouldn't return until five o'clock. She would have to deal with Roland, no matter what his ulterior motive. She had come here to go fishing. She wouldn't let Roland ruin her day.

After a moment's thought, she offered her hand. "Truce?"

He returned her smile and shook on it. "As I said, just wanted to go fishing."

Why did she doubt that? And why did the sight of him, standing there, so tall and appealing, make her heart beat just a little faster? *You're too old for this nonsense,* she told herself. Her head had been filled with ideas of romance once, and life had taught her differently. But why did her hand tingle from the touch of his? And why did her chest tighten and her stomach feel as if she'd swallowed a handful of goose down?

"And maybe I came so I could see you," he admitted. "Just as a bonus."

She leaned against the cabin, enjoying the feel of the boat rocking gently under her. "I thought we'd agreed that this was a mistake...looking for a match between us."

His eyes were shaded under the brim of his straw hat. Oddly, it disappointed her that she couldn't see the expression in them. Roland had never been good at hiding from her what he was thinking. He didn't answer.

"Whose idea was it for you to come?" she asked softly. She wondered what had ever possessed her to propose marriage to Roland in the first place. That was what had caused all this upset. It would have been better for her and Roland both if she had just let things remain as they were, rather than stirring up feelings from long ago.

Her life with *Mam,* her children, her sisters and her faith were all fine just the way they were. Seeking out Roland had been a mistake that just made things more complicated. "Whose idea was it," she repeated, "for you to come on the boat and not tell me?"

"Charley's."

Johanna's eyes narrowed. "And Miriam's? She had to be in on it." Wait until she got her sister alone. She'd give her a good piece of her mind. Johanna sighed. "Nothing has changed, Roland," she said. She looked up at him again. "But we used to be friends...a long time ago. Maybe we could just be friends again...for today."

He stepped close to her, steady despite the rocking

of the boat as it sliced through the waves. "You know I want to be more than friends, Johanna."

She folded her arms over her chest. "If we're going to have a truce today, you have to promise not to talk about that anymore."

"You're tough," he murmured, switching to Pennsylvania Dutch.

"Tough enough to catch more fish than you," she answered in the same dialect.

"I guess we'll just have to see about that." He didn't move away, and they stood there, watching as the dock grew smaller and smaller in the wake of the *Gone Fishin' IV.*

Three middle-aged Amish men from one of the other church districts had taken spots on the deck a few yards away. She knew them by name, but not well. One man owned a greenhouse, and the other two, she thought, worked as masons. Johanna couldn't see her sister or Charley. They were probably hiding out on the other side of the boat, as well they should.

A black-and-white osprey soared overhead on powerful wings, with a fish caught in its talons. She watched it until the beautiful bird was out of sight. Already, the sky was growing much brighter, and the rising sun painted a wide swath of the rippling water orange-gold. Other boats passed them, motors roaring, and a buoy bobbed as the *Gone Fishin's* captain went around it. A family on a pontoon boat in the distance had already anchored, and Johanna could see a boy Jonah's age lowering a crab line over the side while a woman dipped a long-handled net into the waves.

Johanna stared at the churning surface of the water, inhaling deeply. She'd always loved the smell of the salt air. It took her back to all the times *Dat* had taken them fishing, crabbing and wading in the ocean when she was a child. They'd gone every summer since she'd been born… until he died. Her father had been a good swimmer, and he'd taught them all to swim, including *Mam* and Susanna. Susanna was still awkward, but she'd become an expert at floating and could keep her head above water as well as any of them.

It had been important to *Dat* that they all learned to swim because of a boating tragedy that happened when he was a teenager. An Amish youth group had gone out on an excursion boat somewhere on one of the Great Lakes. There had been an accident, and the boat had gone down, taking far too many of the children with it because none of them could swim. *Dat* had promised himself that it would never happen to his family, if he could prevent it. *Have faith in God,* he would say. *But God doesn't expect us to be foolish servants.*

It hit Johanna that her father would be upset with her if he knew that she hadn't yet taught Katy and Jonah to swim. This summer, she'd have to do something about that.

Wilmer hadn't been able to swim a lick, and he had forbidden her to teach their children. He hadn't liked boats or the beach, and he had never eaten fish or seafood of any kind. It troubled Johanna that her own little ones had missed the joys of hunting for seashells, digging clams and watching long-legged water birds foraging in the marsh grass. Wilmer had forbidden her to even wade in the water, saying that it wasn't decent for a woman.

But Wilmer was gone. She couldn't use him as an excuse for neglecting her children's safety anymore. She was the one to decide what was best for her children. "Have you taught J.J. to swim?" she asked Roland.

He nodded solemnly. "I have. I wasn't satisfied until

he could jump into our pond fully clothed with his shoes on and swim from one end to the other."

She considered that. "Maybe," she ventured, "if it wouldn't be too much trouble, you could find time to teach my Jonah this summer."

"I would be pleased to," Roland said. "And what of Katy?"

"*Ne*," she said. "You know how shy she is. I can give her lessons myself." Roland wasn't her father...wasn't her uncle or brother. It wouldn't be fitting for her to ask him to perform such an intimate thing for her little girl. Of course he could, she thought. If they married and Roland became her children's father. If only things weren't so complicated between them.

Maybe Roland wasn't really the problem. Maybe the problem was her. Maybe it was the thought of giving herself and her children over to any man that frightened her. Was that why she told him she could never love him?

Among the Old Order Amish, the man was the head of the family and his was the final say. He could decide to leave one church group and attend another, and his wife would have to do as he wished. Roland, or any husband she might choose, could—if he wished—move them to Wisconsin or Colorado or even to Canada, as some of the faith had done. A husband would have the right and the power to turn her life upside down, and there would be nothing she could do or say to prevent it...nothing but remain single.

Maybe she was too attached to her mother and her sisters.... But the truth was, she still didn't want to leave Seven Poplars...she still needed her family around her. And to do that...to make certain that her life remained as it was, she would have to remain single, like her mother.

It was so much safer this way. Immediately, relief flooded through her. She didn't have to chance their future. She could keep things just as they were until her children were grown. It wasn't as if she didn't have a home, didn't have a place to raise Katy and Jonah. She had her bees and her sheep and her quilts. Her desire for a baby would pass, wouldn't it? She didn't need a man... not really. And she didn't need Roland.

Well...maybe she did, but as a friend...as they had been when they were children. She'd thought of Roland then as a brother or maybe a cousin. It wasn't until things changed... until she'd allowed him to take her home from frolics and singings that he'd become something more. It wasn't until they'd walked out together and she'd allowed him to hold her hand when they walked through the orchard that she'd begun to think of what it would be like to be his wife.

She and Roland had shared a time of fun and laughter and dreams...until he had betrayed her and everything had gone wrong between them. Then she'd married Wilmer, on impulse for certain.

She'd thought she was so grown-up when she and Wilmer had taken their vows before God and Bishop Atlee, when they'd sat at the bride and groom's table with family and friends around them. But she'd had so much to learn. She'd not always been wise and she'd not always had charity in her heart for Wilmer's weaknesses. But she'd never realized just how lost he was... until it was too late.

"Johanna, look!"

Roland's words brought her back to the present and she glanced in the direction he pointed. A smooth, dark head cut the water, and as she watched, a beautiful bottlenose dolphin dove out of the water, followed by a second, a third and a fourth.

"One of God's wonders," Roland remarked.

Johanna exhaled softly, caught in the excitement of the moment as the dolphins raced beside the boat, diving and leaping and diving again, seemingly just for the joy of being alive. *I wish I'd brought Jonah with me. Maybe if Roland teaches him to swim, I can take him on a fishing boat next year. Jonah would love to see the dolphins and the other boats and the seabirds, and he would love trying to catch fish.* Katy was too young to come out on the bay yet, but someday, Johanna promised herself, someday, she would bring Katy, too.

"I've got a bite!" Johanna called.

Another one? Roland bit back the words. It was mean-spirited to resent Johanna's prowess, and he didn't really feel that way. Still, in the hour since the captain had anchored at Fourteen Foot Lighthouse, Johanna had already caught a nice-size trout and a croaker. The only thing that he'd managed to land was one toadfish and a sea bass too small to keep.

Charley had three trout, and Miriam had caught a flounder. If things didn't improve, Johanna would never let him hear the end of it. It wasn't that he was a terrible fisherman. He was using the same bait as everyone else, and he was just as capable of catching fish. The trouble was, nothing was biting on his hook.

But his day wasn't all bad. Johanna was actually speaking to him, and they were having a good time. Once she'd gotten over her annoyance that they were spending the day together, she'd begun to act more like her old self. It was good to see her laugh. They'd always found things to talk about, and today was no exception. Johanna never hesitated to give her opinion, but she wasn't one of those women who always had to dominate the conversation. She was a good listener, and when she listened to him, he felt as if she really paid attention to what he said.

Roland kept coming back to the same conclusion—that if he and Johanna ever could work out their differences, she would make a good partner. She was the kind of woman who could hold up her end of the marriage, a strong woman, a woman who wouldn't fall to pieces if misfortune came. She was the kind of woman he was looking for.

He'd loved Pauline; he really had. She'd been a good wife, but her poor health had often made her sad or worried. She'd become fearful for J.J. in the last year before her death, so much so that at times they knocked heads over what was best for the boy. She'd wanted to protect J.J. so badly that Roland often felt shut out of his own son's life. Still, Pauline's passing had hit them both hard. Never a night did he lay his head on the pillow to sleep that he didn't remember to pray for her, and to hope that she and the children that she'd miscarried were safe in God's care.

But Pauline was in heaven and he was here. A decent time had passed since her death, and he'd felt that it was time to move on with his life…time to give J.J. a new mother and time for him to have a wife and, God willing, more children. He wanted Johanna Yoder to be that wife. He couldn't picture any other woman walking beside him in the garden or sitting across the supper table and sharing evening grace. He could see Johanna there, her sweet heart-shaped face, those wide blue eyes so full of wisdom, and the soft curve of her mouth when she smiled.

Was it so wrong of him to want her to love him? To want to put the mistakes he'd made in the past? To want more than an arranged marriage as his parents' had been? His *mam* and *dat* respected each other and worked well together. He could never remember his mother raising her voice in anger to his father. They had reared three children and buried two more. *Dat's* farm was a well-maintained one, and the family had never suffered real want. His parents were faithful to church and were good neighbors, never ones to cause trouble or dissension in the community. But Roland had never felt that there was a powerful man's and woman's love between his mother and father. And, selfishly, he wanted that. He wanted Johanna to love him so badly that if she couldn't, he was pretty sure he would walk away.

But was he thinking wrongly? According to the way he'd been raised, a marriage was supposed to be for family, for community, for carrying on God's work and raising children in the faith. A marriage was not to fulfill the selfish desires of a man and a woman, so a marriage of convenience was as good a way to form a family as a romantic attraction between couples. Young people were expected to listen to their parents and the elders of the church. Mature friends and relatives who knew the prospective couple were often in a better position to provide sound advice on the suitability of the match than the girl and boy themselves.

Roland couldn't accept that. Marriage was for life. If he didn't choose well, if he picked a woman he found difficult to live with, he wanted to be solely responsible. *Be honest.* He wanted desperately for Johanna Yoder to love him.

Another trout flopped wildly on the deck between him and Johanna. "You can have that one," she teased. "I wouldn't want you to go home without anything to cook for J.J.'s supper."

He chuckled. "Thanks, but the truth is, if I fried it, it wouldn't be fit for J.J. or me to eat."

The mate removed Johanna's fish from her hook and carried it to the fish box. "Maybe Cap'n should hire you to show the others how to catch fish," he said.

Johanna laughed and glanced at Roland as the mate walked away. "You have an oven. Frying isn't the only way to cook fish. You could bake it, or even make a fish stew."

"But fried fish sounds good." Roland caught her line and carefully baited her hook with a fresh piece of squid. "*Mam* always served it with johnnycake or corn bread. Maybe you could come over and cook it for me."

She arched an eyebrow. "And why would I want to do that?"

"Charity." He thrust out his upper lip, pretending to look forlorn. "Pity on a poor widower who needs a decent meal. And his young, undernourished son," he added.

She tried not to smile, but she couldn't help herself. "Roland. I don't think my making suppers for you is such a good—"

"Truce, right?"

She was laughing now. *"Ya,"* she agreed.

"And we're friends again?" he urged.

"Ya, I suppose we are friends."

"Then, as a friend, I could ask you to cook for me the fish that you have so graciously offered to share."

She cast her baited line over the edge of the boat, and the lead sinker pulled it down. She kept her eyes on the line where it disappeared into the water, but he knew he had her attention.

"Come on, Johanna." He could tell by the look on her face that she was about to give in. "There's nothing wrong with friends sharing a meal, is there? And three children should be chaperone enough to spare either of our reputations."

"Maybe I could whip you up some fried fish tonight," she said. "It wouldn't take long to make."

"I've got cornmeal."

"I'd need flour and shortening and milk."

"Got them."

"And we'd have to pick up my children first. I'll not come to your house alone and be the subject of loose talk."

"Fair enough," he said.

The tip of her fishing pole dipped. She let it go, then yanked back hard when it dipped again. The resulting tug was so hard that she nearly lost her balance. Roland dropped his own pole, threw his arms around her and gripped her fishing rod. There was a fierce pull and then the line snapped.

Roland stood where he was, holding Johanna in his arms for a few seconds. "Roland!" she protested. From somewhere, he heard Charley's laughter.

"Sorry." Reluctantly, Roland released her. "I was afraid that fish might pull you in."

She gave him a look as if he was up to no good, but she was onto him. "I doubt that."

"It was huge. Might have been anything. A shark— even a whale."

"A whale?" She began to laugh. "You're impossible."

He laughed with her, and it felt good to be standing on the deck of a rocking boat in the June sunshine, but not nearly as good as holding her for that brief scrap of time.

Chapter Nine

By the time Johanna and the others arrived home from the fishing trip, it was too late to bring her children to Roland's farm for a fish supper. They'd had a busy day and were already sitting down to a cold supper. Instead, when her mother offered to keep Katy and Jonah, Johanna invited Susanna and Aunt Jezzy to come as chaperones. It was a good decision because it was after eight o'clock when Johanna and Susanna got the promised meal on Roland's table.

Aunt Jezzy contributed her famous wild dandelion and lettuce salad, rich with hard-cooked eggs and Swiss cheese, and a loaf of her delicious potato sponge bread. All Johanna had to do was roll the fish filets in egg, flour and cornmeal and fry to a golden brown. *Mam* sent along a Dutch apple tart for a sweet, and Susanna's contribution was a plate of anise cookies that she'd baked that afternoon.

"I made them for King David," Susanna said, proudly showing Johanna the plate of cookies as they set the food on the table. "Me. For King David. For after church. But you…you can have some."

"They look wonderful," Johanna said as she set the platter of crispy fish on the table with the other dishes.

Roland and his sister Mary came downstairs from tucking J.J. into bed and joined them in the kitchen. Mary had spent the day with J.J. and had given him his supper earlier. She would be sharing the fish fry with them.

Mary lived with her and Roland's parents about four miles away in another church district, one that held Sunday services on a different schedule than the Seven Poplars community. Since tomorrow was a Visiting Sunday for her, Charley had invited her to spend the night and attend church service in Seven Poplars. Afterward, he could drive her home in his buggy.

When Mary protested that she hadn't brought her Sunday-go-to-church dress and bonnet, Johanna assured her that she could loan her something suitable. So, instead of spending the night with Roland, it was arranged that Mary would sleep over at the Yoder farm.

Johanna was pleased. She and Mary had been friends since they were children, and she knew her whole family would enjoy visiting with her. Besides, Johanna welcomed the opportunity to get Mary alone so that she could ask her exactly what Charley had told her about Roland's refusal to marry her. Johanna also was eager to find out to whom Mary had passed on the tale.

Roland had made it clear that he didn't care what other people might believe, but it mattered to Johanna, and she wouldn't be satisfied until she tracked the false gossip to its source. She didn't believe for a moment that Roland would be dishonest about what he told Charley, but she would feel better once she found out who had become confused and was spreading false information about her.

Everyone gathered at Roland's table and lowered their

heads for silent grace. Johanna had to remind herself that these sacred moments were for being thankful to God for his blessings, not for remembering how much fun she'd had today, or for wondering if the fish had cooked through. Frying fish was an art. She had her own secret for the coating, but if the fish was overdone, it would be a shame.

Chastising herself for failing in grace, she allowed a quiet moment to flow through her, and her unspoken words of thankful praise poured out in truly heartfelt passion. She had so much to be grateful for, and those around her were a large part of her life—even Roland, as much as she hated to admit it.

"Johanna."

Susanna's merry voice cut through her thoughts. Johanna opened her eyes to see everyone looking at her expectantly.

Susanna's mouth puckered with impatience. "Can we eat *now?*" she begged. "I'm hungry…an' the fish…the fish smells so *gut.*"

"Of course." Johanna smiled in spite of her discomfort that she'd kept everyone waiting. *Dear, dear Susanna. Trust her to bring me back from my self-absorption.* Cheeks glowing with embarrassment, Johanna passed the heaping plate of fish to Roland. As he accepted the platter, their gazes met and warm pleasure made her want to giggle as lightheartedly as Susanna.

Aunt Jezzy passed the salad, and soon everyone was laughing and talking. There was something about Roland's house that made them all feel comfortable. It wasn't as large as *Mam's,* and the kitchen had lower ceilings and open chestnut beams overhead, but Johanna found it charming. *People have been happy here.*

And from deep inside came the disquieting thought, *Maybe I could be happy here, too.*

Johanna banished the wispy dream. Best to enjoy the moment…the evening of family and friends. With Mary, Susanna and Aunt Jezzy here, she quickly shed the awkwardness that being alone with Roland so often brought on. She could relax and be herself. And she could delight in Roland's exaggerated stories about the huge fish that bit on his line but somehow managed to escape after prolonged battles, fabrications that they all knew were just for fun.

To her delight, the fish was perfect, bursting with flavor, crunchy on the outside and succulent on the inside. The preachers taught that pride was contrary to plain living, but she couldn't help taking secret satisfaction from Roland's compliments on the supper.

He'd always made her laugh, and tonight was no exception. The friendship between them made conversation so easy and the meal so much fun. Johanna was just sorry that it had been too late in the day for Katy and Jonah to join them. It seemed strange not to have their sweet faces looking back at her across the table. Next time, she would make certain that all three children could share the meal with them. Next time…

Don't be foolish. Why would there be more suppers at Roland's house?

"What I want to know, Johanna," Roland said as he reached for another slice of Aunt Jezzy's sponge bread, "is how you caught so many more fish than me?" He made such a sad face that Susanna giggled. "We used the same bait and we were fishing in the same spot. What's your secret?"

Johanna chuckled. "You really want to know?" And

when he nodded, she shrugged. "It's simple, Roland. Every time I bait my hook and drop it overboard, I pray."

"I didn't tell anyone but my mother that you and Roland had discussed marriage," Mary confided the next morning as she and Johanna walked down the farm lane to the main road. Katy and Jonah trailed behind them, chattering to each other. Roman and Fannie's chair shop, where church would be held today, stood at the intersection of Seven Poplars Road and School Lane, just down the street.

Mary lowered her voice. "And I told her what Roland told me…that he had not consented," she said, putting it delicately. "At least for now."

"I just can't understand it," Johanna said. She tried to focus on the purpose of the conversation and not the confusing emotions that kept popping up. "Somehow the story got turned around."

She and Mary wore identical dark blue dresses and aprons, black bonnets and black leather shoes. Small Katy's dress was a pale robin's-egg blue, but her prayer *Kapp* was white and her apron crackly-stiff with starch. Jonah wore a white shirt, black trousers and a black vest over his new high-top leather boots. His straw hat was new as well, because he'd outgrown his last hat. This one had just arrived Friday from the mail-order house where *Mam* had always purchased the items of clothing that they couldn't make.

"It was kind of your mother to lend me your sister's dress and bonnet," Mary said. "I've been wanting to attend your services. I should have thought to bring my good clothes when I came to watch J.J."

"*Ne.* It's no problem. With so many women in our house, there are always extra dresses," Johanna assured her.

Mary was closer to Leah's size than Johanna's, so *Mam* had fetched Leah's church dress out of her Old German marriage chest. "I know Leah wouldn't mind," Johanna continued. Since her sister had turned Mennonite and gone to Brazil as a missionary with her new husband, the dress had lain unused. *Mam* kept it carefully wrapped in tissue paper and sprinkled with dried basil and rosemary to ward off moths.

"But it was still nice of your *mam,*" Mary said. They walked on a little farther, waited until no cars were passing and crossed the road, the children still a few steps behind them. "About what you asked me before…about the talk. Maybe it's best to let it all drop."

"But I need to get to the bottom of this," Johanna said.

"No, you don't. You need to just let it go. It's not important."

Johanna's first impulse was to disagree, but she knew there was truth to what Mary was saying.

"The gossip about you and Roland will die down on its own," Mary suggested. "If you two aren't going to walk out together, word will get around."

Johanna knew that Mary was disappointed that things hadn't worked out between the two of them. She'd been as eager as Ruth and Anna for the match. *Roland's mother, Deborah, probably not as much.*

Deborah Byler had been born and raised in Kentucky in a very strict community and made it clear that she didn't approve of the Yoder girls—or of Widow Hannah Yoder, for that matter. *Mam's* choice to remain single and teach school instead of remarrying was still something of a scandal in the other Kent County church districts.

Their own church community here in Seven Poplars and Bishop Atlee, thankfully, accepted *Mam* for the blessing she was.

When Charley and Miriam had been courting, Mary had told Johanna that their mother expressed doubt that Miriam was right for her son.

Apparently, Deborah was shocked at Miriam's doing fieldwork and seeing to the livestock, rather than tending to traditional women's chores in the house. In Deborah's opinion, all the Yoder women showed a lack of superior values and were altogether too headstrong to make proper wives. But *Mam* said that she would rather her girls be outspoken than to make judgments about people they'd never taken the effort to get to know.

"There's the bench wagon!" Jonah cried, pointing to a low, enclosed vehicle parked in the side yard of the chair shop. "Look, *Mam!* I helped Uncle Charley bring it from the Beachys'. He let me drive the team."

Johanna arched an eyebrow. "Uncle Charley let you drive? On the road?"

No family had enough chairs for the entire church. Instead, each community had their own collection of folding benches that they carried from house to house every two weeks. When Roman and Fannie hosted church, service was held in the large workshop, rather than in their home, because the house was too small to accommodate the congregation. The previous day, Charley, Eli, Roman and Irwin had cleaned the woodshop and set up the benches and chairs. Preparations for church were always done the previous day because no work could be done on Sunday. Johanna was pleased that Charley and Eli had thought to include Jonah. Without a father, it was important that he learn from other men how to be helpful.

Jonah's cheeks flushed cherry-red under his wide-brimmed straw hat. "*Ne.* I didn't really drive…but I held the reins," he added quickly. "And I helped Uncle Eli sweep the workshop, too."

"Irwin said you did," Johanna agreed. "He told me that you were a big help."

Jonah grinned. "I was."

"I hear Eli's a partner in Roman's chair shop now," Mary said as they drew closer to the chair shop.

Johanna nodded. "You probably know that it was my father who started the business. It did so well that he needed a partner, so he asked his friend Roman to move down from Pennsylvania. Roman hired Eli, and after Eli and Ruth married, *Mam* gave her interest in the chair shop to them as a wedding gift. It would please *Dat,* I know. Eli's a fine craftsman."

"And a good businessman, I hear," Mary said. "So my father says. We heard he just got a contract for building reproduction furniture for some English museum."

"It works out well that Eli and Ruth got *Mam's* share of the shop," Johanna said. "Because she means for Charley and Miriam to take over the farm someday. Charley is a hard worker, and he'll care for the land."

"Both my brothers are good farmers," Mary said, quickly defending Roland. "They're both hard workers."

"Everyone says Roland has done wonders with that farm," Johanna agreed.

A horse and buggy passed them and turned into the parking lot at the front of the shop. A small boy's face, framed in a straw hat, was pressed against the back window.

Jonah squealed and waved. "*Mam,* it's Benjy! Can I go talk to him?"

"Run on," Johanna said, "but stay out from under the horses' hooves. Don't get dirty, and don't you dare come into service late."

"Me, too," Katy echoed. "I can go, too."

"Ne." Johanna took a firm grip on Katy's hand. "You stay with me."

"There's Lydia." Mary looked to Johanna. "Do you mind if I say hello before service?"

"Of course not. We'll see you inside."

Buggies were lined up on the far side of the parking lot, and women were carrying baskets and covered dishes around the building. Mary called to Lydia Beachy and hurried to help her carry one of the two baskets in her hands. Since it was a fair June day with no sign of rain, they would take the communal after-services meal outside at long tables.

Mam would be coming soon with Susanna, Rebecca and Aunt Jezz. There would be coolers full of ham sandwiches, potato salad, coleslaw, pickled beets and fruit pies. Since no cooking could be done on Church Sunday, all the food for the midday dinner had been prepared the previous day or earlier in the week. *Mam* was bringing a large wedge of cheddar, a three-bean salad, a basket of whoopee pies and—of course—Susanna's anise cookies.

Johanna loved Visiting Sundays, but she also cherished the peace and inner joy of Church Sundays. *Food for the soul.* Singing the old hymns, joining together in prayer with her friends and neighbors, listening to the preachers' sermons—those treasures of the heart gave her the strength to carry on through all the days in between.

Johanna was suddenly filled with thankfulness that she'd been born into the Amish faith and community. *We are a people apart.* People who try to spend each day and each hour serving Him and doing His work on earth in hopes of greater reward in heaven.

"I like church," Katy said, smiling up at her.

"So do I, sweetie," Johanna replied. "So do I."

That day, Uncle Reuben preached on the Good Samaritan, a story from the New Testament that he often chose for his message and one that he could speak on at great length. It was one of Johanna's favorite passages, and she enjoyed his words for the first hour, but as the minutes ticked away and Katy began to wiggle in her lap, Johanna found her attention wandering.

She had chosen a seat near an open window, beside Anna and Mary. Anna's baby, Rose, had fallen asleep, and Johanna couldn't help glancing over at her. Rose was such a precious child, and she brought so much joy to her parents. Johanna loved her dearly—the entire family cherished the little girl—but Johanna couldn't help comparing her to Katy. Next to Rose, Katy seemed so big, no longer a baby, but an adorable little girl. Johanna longed for the baby that Katy had once been, and she longed to cradle another infant—her infant—in her arms.

Uncle Reuben's voice thundered out, echoing off the rafters as he warmed to his subject and began to repeat himself for the third time. Johanna tore her attention from the sleeping babe and tried to focus on her uncle's words. But as her gaze swept the room, she spotted Roland. He wasn't watching Uncle Reuben, either. He was staring directly at her. And when their gazes met, Roland grinned at her.

Startled, Johanna averted her eyes, but when she glanced back from under her lashes, Roland was still watching her. She should have felt disapproval, and she should have let him know that she didn't appreciate his levity during worship, but the truth was, she was secretly pleased. Worse, when Uncle Reuben finally wound up his sermon and the congregation rose to offer the final hymn, she looked at Roland and found him looking at her again, instead of his hymn book.

Anna elbowed her. "Johanna," she whispered as voices raised in praise around them. "Stop flirting and pay attention to service," she admonished. Mischief danced in her eyes. "Stop watching Roland."

"I'm not," Johanna protested, but then she had to stifle a giggle. What was wrong with her? She was acting like a giddy teenager, and it was all Roland Byler's fault.

The hymn ended. Everyone sat down, and Bishop Atlee offered a traditional prayer in High German before dismissing the congregation for the midday break. There would be a short service after the communal meal, but that would consist of prayers, a few more hymns, and everyone would leave by four to head home. As in the morning, the only chores that would be done would be those that were absolutely necessary, mostly involving caring for the children and farm animals.

"*Mam* will have your head," Anna teased as service ended and families rose and gathered their children and belongings.

"She will not. I didn't do anything," Johanna murmured in her sister's ear. "He was staring at me." She reached out for Rose. "Here, let me take her. Your arms must be tired."

Anna passed the sleeping baby, and Johanna cradled her against her chest. Rose never stirred. "She's such a good baby," Anna said. "She slept through Uncle Reuben's entire sermon."

Katy scrambled up on the bench. "Can I hold Rose, *Mam?*" she begged. "Can I?"

"Later, when she's awake," Anna said, stepping around Johanna and sweeping Katy off the bench to safety. "Now I need you to come with me and help me take bread to the tables."

Johanna followed Mary, Anna and Katy. As she passed through the crowded workshop, neighbors stopped her to admire Rose and to exchange news of the past two weeks' doings. There was a crowd of elders at the back of the spacious room, so she turned left to leave by the door that led to the showroom. When she reached the hallway, however, she found Roland alone, arms folded, blocking her way.

"For a woman who isn't interested in me, you spent a lot of time staring at me during service."

Chapter Ten

"I was not staring at you during worship," Johanna said.

"Were, too."

"Was not." She pressed her lips together tightly to stifle a giggle and glanced over her shoulder to be certain no one was too near. She looked back at him. "And I suppose you weren't staring back at me?"

"Me?" Roland smiled that sweet mischievous smile of his, and for a moment, the years fell away and she was looking into the dirty face of the eight-year-old hero who'd chased two bigger English boys at the Delaware State Fair and rescued her *Kapp* from them. "Not me," he teased. "I was watching Preacher Reuben the whole time. I think he preached on the Barren Fig Tree."

"He did not." She could hardly keep from laughing. "Shame on you. You know his sermon was the Good Samaritan."

"Again," they both said together.

Still chuckling, she tried to duck past him, but Roland stretched out both arms and suddenly she was very close to him, with only the still-sleeping Rose between them.

The game was no longer innocent fun. Her heart raced

and, for an instant, she thought Roland was going to kiss her. "Please let me go," she whispered. "Someone will see us."

"And what if they do? Why shouldn't we talk to each other? I want to court you, Johanna. I know that if you give yourself the opportunity, you'll fall in love with me all over again."

A whisper of fear raised goose bumps on the nape of her neck. Not fear of Roland, but fear of herself—fear that she wanted him to kiss her. She tightened her grip on Rose. "Don't you think we're too old for courting? I said I was willing to be your wife, but you turned me down. You said you didn't want to marry me." She felt her lower lip tremble and for a moment she feared she'd embarrass herself with tears. "Courting is for couples intending on marrying."

He shook his head. "I didn't say I didn't want to marry you. I never said that. I said I wouldn't marry you for convenience's sake…or because our families think we should marry."

"Roland," she sighed. "I'm not the innocent girl I used to be…the one you want me to be now."

"Excuses. Fears."

The intensity of his gaze made her tremble.

"You're stubborn," he said softly. "You know that we're meant for each other. You're letting that stubbornness stand in the way of real happiness. Happiness for both of us."

A flush of heat shimmered under her skin, and her eyes teared up. *God help me.* And aloud she whispered, "Why can't we just go on being friends?"

Tenderly, Roland brushed a single tear from her cheek. "I can't settle for that. Not with you."

"Why?"

"Because I want you to be my wife…because I want to stand before the bishop…before God… I want us to be a real family, Johanna."

She forced herself to meet his gaze. "I don't know if I even want a husband," she admitted. He was standing so close that she could smell the starch in his shirt. It was a good, clean scent, and it made her even more uncertain…more afraid. If he frightened her now, how much worse would it be if they married?

"Is it taking another husband? Or is it me?"

She tried to think how to answer, but her thoughts were all aflutter. Rose stirred in her arms, and Johanna seized on the excuse. "Let me go," she said. "You'll wake the baby."

"And if I do, you'll soothe her. You were born to be a mother. I want more children, and I think you do, too. We could have them together, if you'd marry me."

Another baby. The sweet thought of carrying another child in her body—of bringing new life into the world—made her weak. "Don't." Tears clouded her vision as she turned her face away.

"Are you afraid of me?"

"*Ne.* That's *lecherich.* Foolishness. How could I be? It's me…"

"What did your *dat* say?" Roland demanded. "You can't have forgotten. Didn't he tell you to face what frightened you the most? It's what he told me when he taught me to swim."

He moved a step closer, and her breath caught in her throat.

"Let me court you," he said. "If love doesn't grow between us, I'll trouble you no more. But if I'm right, and it's your own stubborn nature keeping us apart, you'll thank me for it."

"Will I?"

Door hinges creaked behind Johanna, and someone cleared her throat. Roland stepped back a decent distance, and Johanna heard her mother say, "There you two are."

"I was just…" Johanna said. *Just what?*

"Roland, they've called you to the first seating for dinner. Bishop Atlee himself asked for you."

Roland nodded. "We'll talk later, Johanna," he said as he strode away.

Her mother eyed her suspiciously. "Is this what I think it is?"

Johanna shook her head. "I didn't meet Roland on purpose, if that's what you're asking. He wants to court me, but I don't know what to do. I'm not sure I want to marry again."

Women's chatter, followed by laughter, drifted through the doorway. *Mam* motioned toward a small room that Eli and Roman used as an office. Johanna followed her in and nudged the door closed behind them. A rainbow of sunlight spilled through a single window and the skylight. Her mother reached for Rose and settled into a rocker, one of the fine spindle-back chairs that Eli designed. Rose slept on.

"You haven't remarried," Johanna said. "You've made a life for yourself without a husband. Why can't I?"

"What is right for me may not be best for you."

"Why not? I've proved I can support myself and my children."

"You're still a young woman. I'm nearly fifty, child. I have eight daughters, counting Grace, an adopted son, four good sons-in-law and a bevy of grandchildren. Your father and I had a strong marriage, a loving marriage. My life is full to overflowing with God's bounty, but you…you, my precious daughter…you have yet to know that blessing."

"I have a family. Katy and Jonah. You and my sisters and their children. Why do I have to marry again and have a man…" Words failed her.

"Marriage to Wilmer was difficult."

Johanna nodded. Even now, pride kept her from telling her mother just how difficult. What went on between a husband and wife was private, not to be discussed, not even with a mother. "Wilmer called me hardheaded, said that I was an unnatural woman…that I couldn't accept that my husband was God's appointed head of the family."

"Do you believe that you are unnatural?"

"I don't know. Sometimes, maybe." Johanna sat on the floor by her mother's feet and rested her head against her mother's knee. "What if he was right, *Mam?* What if I don't know how to be a proper wife? What if I were to marry Roland and make him as unhappy as I made Wilmer?"

"Roland is a better man than Wilmer ever was. Do you think Roland would ever raise a hand to you in anger?"

"Ne."

"Is he an abuser of alcohol?"

Johanna sighed as her mother's hand rested on her cheek. *"Ne,"* she managed. "Never."

"And you believe him to be a good father—that he would be a good father to Katy and Jonah as well as his own son?"

"I think… I'm sure he would be." She squeezed her mother's hand, and then got to her feet.

"You loved him once, didn't you?"

Johanna didn't answer…couldn't answer. The truth was too painful to share even with her dear mother.

"All I can tell you is to pray to the Lord for guidance and search your own heart for the answer," *Mam* said. "You're right to be cautious, but know this… With all the love I have from my family, my friends and my church, there are times when I'm lonely. I miss having a partner to care for and to care for me…a man's hand to hold mine when we walk through the orchard after a long day's work. I miss the looks that pass between a husband and wife and the quiet laughter. I'll always love and remember your father. But, I tell you, Johanna, I still have a lot of life left in me. If the right man came along, I would marry again."

Johanna lifted her head and stared at her mother. "You'd take the risk to love again? After *Dat?*"

Her mother laughed. "Life *is* risk, Johanna. Be cautious, follow your conscience, but never stop taking risks. If you do, part of your spirit will wither and die as surely as a garden without rain."

Monday was so busy that Johanna hardly had time to worry about Roland or the possibility of their marriage. On top of her normal chores—caring for Katy and Jonah, helping Susanna with 'Kota while Grace was at work and school, feeding and looking after her turkeys, bees and sheep—Johanna spent the day helping Ruth. She did her wash and stitched up another two dozen cloth diapers for the expected twins.

On Tuesday morning, she and Rebecca finished a queen-size rose-of-Sharon quilt for an Englisher lady in Salisbury. Then they spent the afternoon making kettles of strawberry-rhubarb jam and mulberry jelly in *Mam's* summer kitchen.

Rebecca, always clever with pen and paint, fashioned hand-printed labels and topped each half-pint jar with a checked cloth cap that fit over the sealed lids. Aunt Jezzy insisted that fancy jars sold for more money and went faster at Spence's than plain ones. If the jams went as well as Aunt Jezzy promised, Johanna decided that she and Rebecca would come up with something equally clever to dress up the honey containers, as well.

Normally, on Tuesdays, Johanna would walk to Roland's to check on the new bee colony, but not this week. The bees at his farm were doing well, and there were plenty of wildflowers and blossoming vegetables and clover to keep them happy. After Sunday's encounter, she was determined to keep far away from Roland until she made up her mind as to what she wanted to do.

Wednesday, she, Rebecca, Miriam, Susanna and *Mam* scrubbed floors, washed windows, polished woodwork in the entire downstairs of the farmhouse, and washed and ironed all the window curtains. Thursday, she and Katy helped Miriam and Susanna in the garden, planting lima beans, green beans and corn, cutting the last of the spinach, and setting out the eggplant, peppers and late tomatoes that Miriam had started in the greenhouse.

Friday, Johanna packed produce and jam, honey and jellies for Aunt Jezzy's table at the sale and spent the rest of the day cleaning the front and back porch, raking the yard and helping her sisters clean the second floor as thoroughly as they had the first. Since no cooking could be done on Sunday, the Yoder girls worked in the kitchen all day Saturday, baking, churning butter, stirring up a huge kettle of chicken and dumplings, roasting a turkey, and making salads and desserts.

Saturday night, when Johanna knelt beside her bed for her evening prayers, she was tired but pleased at the work she'd managed to do that week. The following day would be a day of rest, a day for laughter and talk, playing quiet games with her children and welcoming friends and relatives.

Sunday began with family prayers around the kitchen table. It was a beautiful morning, with low humidity and glorious sunshine. Anna and Samuel and the children were coming for supper, and the whole day of fun and visiting stretched before them. As a special treat, Johanna planned to take picnic baskets full of fresh fruit, yogurt, deviled eggs and blueberry muffins to Ruth's house so that they could all share breakfast together—all but Grace and her son. Grace and 'Kota had left early with John to attend the Mennonite church service. Afterward, they were planning to visit John's mother in Pennsylvania, so they wouldn't be back until evening.

Irwin had gone to spend the day with his Beachy cousins, which left *Mam,* Aunt Jezzy, Rebecca, Susanna and the children to go with Johanna to Ruth and Eli's. As they walked down the dirt lane that ran from one house to the other, Johanna was sure that this was God's plan for her. She and her children were happy; they were useful and loved. Surely, risking everything to marry Roland, or anyone else, would be the wrong choice. She'd been truly blessed by the Lord and expecting more of life would be selfish, not to mention foolhardy.

For a few seconds, Johanna felt a wave of sorrow, and the image of Roland's face as she'd seen it last Sunday afternoon formed in her mind. What if he *had* kissed her?

What then? What would she have done? But that was past and over. "I have to do what's right for my children," she murmured to Susanna.

"Ya," her little sister agreed with a wide smile.

"This is where I belong," Johanna said, clasping Susanna's chubby hand and squeezing it tight. "Home."

"Ya," Susanna repeated. "Home is *gut*."

A shiver ran through Johanna. "Home is best," she said. And then, she smiled at Susanna. "I love you, Susanna Banana."

Her sister giggled. "I love you too, Johanna. You are the *bestest* sister."

After such a large breakfast, dinner was light, and everyone was hungry again by suppertime. Eli and Charley had come over to help Irwin set up two long tables end-to-end on *Mam's* lawn. They carried out chairs and benches, and a big rocker for Ruth. She was getting so large with the babies that her back often ached, but she never complained. From her comfortable cushioned chair, Ruth could direct the setting of the table and help with organization.

Johanna had just carried out a large pitcher of lemonade when suddenly Susanna squealed and ran around the corner of the house. A minute later, she was back, walking hand in hand with her friend David.

"King David!" Susanna shouted breathlessly. "King David is here!"

Johanna looked questioningly at her mother. "I didn't know the Kings were coming. We'll have plenty of food, of course, but…"

Hannah shrugged. "I didn't know, either." She rose to

welcome David and his parents, but the only other person to round the house was Jonah, kicking his soccer ball.

Susanna tugged David across the lawn to where Hannah stood. "King David," she repeated. Susanna was smiling so hard that Johanna was afraid her face would crack. "My friend."

"It's good to see you, David," Johanna said. "Are your father and mother coming?"

"I *in-vited* him," Susanna said with emphasis. "I did. I said, come to visit."

"*Ne.* Not my *mam.* Not my *dat.* Just...just me." David grinned at Susanna. "Come to visit Sunday. Her." David wore his go-to-church black trousers, high-top black leather shoes, white shirt and black vest. Under his straw hat, Johanna could see the gold rim of his paper crown. David was so excited that his speech, never as clear as Susanna's, was difficult to understand, but it seemed that Susanna understood every word he said.

"King David and me," Susanna proclaimed. "We're walking. Us. Walking out."

"We can talk about that later," Hannah said gently, stepping between Susanna and David. "I think David is thirsty. You should get him something cold to drink."

"Want birch beer?" Susanna asked. "*Mam* makes good birch beer." She giggled, wrinkled her nose and shook her head. "Not beer beer. Soda-pop beer." When David nodded vigorously, they went in search of the soda.

Soon Miriam arrived with Anna and *Grossmama* and the children. Mae and Lori Ann had brought the rag dolls that Anna had sewn for them, complete with changes of clothing, white *Kapps* and small black bonnets. Katy was ecstatic when *Grossmama* pulled an identical doll out of her bag and presented it to her.

"I made the *Kapps*," Naomi said shyly. "*Grossmama* showed me how."

Soon, the three little girls had carried their dolls to the grape arbor to play house and *Grossmama* was seated under the tree near Ruth. Jonah was happily trailing after Samuel's twin sons, who were setting up a croquet game on the grass between the tables and the garden. Rebecca had found a copy of *Black Beauty* for Naomi, and she was happily reading on the back step, while Johanna and Ruth took turns holding baby Rose.

The boys had their game set up and were just starting to teach Jonah how to hit the wooden ball through the hoops when another visitor arrived. It was Nip Hilty, of all people.

"Who is that?" *Grossmama* called loudly. "I don't know him."

Aunt Jezzy leaped to her feet, fluttered her hands, and turned as red as a jar of pickled beets. She was so flustered that she just stood there, seemingly unable to greet her guest. *Mam* stepped into the breach, smiling and walking to meet him. "It's good to have you visit, Nip," she said.

Johanna glanced at Rebecca. Her sister shrugged, and behind them, Miriam twittered.

"Who do you think invited him?" Miriam whispered.

"She knows about Nip and Aunt Jezzy," Rebecca murmured to Johanna. "I'm telling you, it's scary. Nothing gets by *Mam*."

"I don't know you," *Grossmama* repeated from her chair. "Are you from Pennsylvania?" It was her standard question when she met someone she didn't recognize. "Do you know my son Jonas? He's milking the cows, but he'll be up in time for supper."

Nip was all smiles as he approached the other women. "You may not know me, but I know you. My late wife had a cousin in Ohio who's friends with your sister Ida. She said Lovina Yoder was the finest braid-rug maker she'd ever known and it was a crying shame that she moved to Delaware."

Grossmama blinked. "Ida. Your wife knows Ida?" *Grossmama's* eyes narrowed and she peered at Nip over her wire-frame glasses. "Ida makes rugs, but hers don't hold a candle to mine. I teach the Englishers at the Senior Center. I live with my son Jonah. That's his wife." She pointed at Ruth. "And this is my grandchild." She indicated Rose, now sleeping in Ruth's arms. "I'm going to show her how to braid rugs."

Nip sighed and hooked a thumb through his left suspender. "My wife would have been pleased to come to your classes, Lovina, but she died."

Grossmama was still taking him in. "Was she a faithful daughter to the church?"

"She was," Nip answered.

"Then she's in a better place." *Grossmama* seemed to then notice Aunt Jezzy's distress. "That's my sister," *Grossmama* pointed out. "But not Ida."

"Jezzy," Nip supplied. He glanced at Aunt Jezzy and smiled.

"Folks think she's odd," *Grossmama* continued in Pennsylvania *Deutch*. "Never married."

"I can't think why," Nip said, "as fine a woman as she is."

Grossmama tapped her forehead and whispered loudly. "*Narrisch.* Crazy."

"*Ne.*" Nip threw another admiring glance at the still-silent Aunt Jezzy. "*So schlau wie ein fuchs*—smart like a fox."

"I have to agree," came a man's voice from behind Johanna. She turned to see Roland standing there with J.J. on his shoulders.

"Roland?" Johanna said. "I didn't expect you today."

Roland grinned as he lowered his son to the grass. "Well, I'm here," he said. "Here and starving for some Yoder good cooking." He cut his eyes at Hannah, a sly smirk on his face now. "I guess she must have forgotten to mention that she invited us."

Chapter Eleven

Johanna threw her mother a questioning look, and a lump of emotion rose in Roland's throat. He was struck by how beautiful Johanna was, with her curling auburn hair tucked modestly beneath her *Kapp,* her apron crisp and white against the soft blue of her calf-length dress, and the dusting of golden freckles over her nose and cheeks.

"I invited J.J. and Roland," Hannah said, answering Johanna's unspoken question and flashing him a genuine smile. "It's been too long since they broke bread at our table."

Roland grinned. "She knew we'd be eating cheese-and-bologna sandwiches again tonight and took pity on us." Seeing Hannah, still so lively and rosy-cheeked in her middle age, made it easy to see why her daughters were all so attractive. *When Johanna is Hannah's age,* he thought, *she'll still be the loveliest* hausfrau *in the county.* But whether she would be his *frau* or not was yet to be seen.

"It's good to have you, Roland," Hannah continued. "Samuel tells me that you've been offered a contract with Windward Farms."

Johanna's eyes widened with interest. "A contract?" she asked. "I hadn't heard."

"Ya." Roland tried not to sound as though he was boasting. "You know Windward Farms? The big horse farm with the white fences on Fox Meadow Road? Their farrier is retiring, and John Hartman recommended me to take his place. I've been up there a couple of times, and I guess they liked my work."

"No reason why they shouldn't. Everyone says you're the best farrier in the county." Johanna smiled warmly at J.J. "Jonah and the big boys are playing croquet. I'm sure they'd like you to join them." And then to Roland, "I was just going inside to get the ice cream churn. We promised the children strawberry ice cream for dessert. Would you mind carrying it out for me?"

"Of course not." He lowered his son to the ground. "Go on," he said to J.J. "But stay out of mischief, and don't make a pest of yourself."

"I'm going that way. I'll go with you."

Hannah held out her hand and Roland watched them walk away. Raising a child on his own wasn't easy, and J.J. had been through more than most boys his age. His mother had always babied him, and losing her was a terrible blow. Now, acting as both mother and father, Roland never knew whether he was being too hard on the boy or too easy.

The elders quoted verses from the Bible that instructed a father not to spare the rod, but he was too soft to take a switch to J.J.'s tender skin. Johanna was a loving mother, and her children were well behaved, but spirited. If what he hoped for came to pass, and she did agree to become his wife, he was sure she'd be good for his son.

"Roland? The ice cream churn?"

Johanna had started back toward the house and he quickened his step to catch up. "I would have told you that we were coming, but I didn't see you after Hannah asked us." Johanna pushed open the gate and moved through it ahead of him, and his gaze fastened on the tiny russet curls at the nape of her neck. "Are you unhappy that we're here?" he asked, afraid of what she would say.

"Ne."

Relief seeped through him. "Are you glad?"

She ascended the back steps to the porch and then opened the screen door. Only then did she glance back at him over her shoulder. "You ask the strangest questions for a man," she observed. "Why wouldn't I be happy to have an old friend and his son visit us?"

He shook his head. "You aren't an easy woman to court, Johanna Yoder."

"Detweiler," she softly corrected. A wrinkle crinkled the smooth skin between her brows. "You forget Wilmer."

"I'd like to forget him," he agreed, standing at the bottom of the steps, looking up at her. "I wish he'd never come to Seven Poplars and that you'd never married him."

She gave a graceful shrug. "But then I wouldn't have Katy or Jonah. And they are the dearest things in this world to me."

"As they should be. I didn't mean it that way. They are wonderful children. Being a mother is part of who you are, but you'll always be one of the Yoder girls to me—the finest one."

A peach blush spread over her cheeks, but Roland could tell by the gleam in her eyes that she was pleased. Johanna hesitated, half in and half out of the doorway, her slim hands gripping the wooden frame of the screen door. She averted her gaze and then looked up at him from under thick lashes. "You shouldn't say such things."

"But lying is a sin." He placed a hand protectively over one of hers.

"And so is pride." She slid the captured hand out from under his, leaving him with the memory of her touch. "You'll tempt me to have foolish thoughts," she said.

"If there's a sin for saying what I believe, I'll pay the price."

She shook her head and tried to assume a disapproving expression, but he knew her too well. Johanna could never hide her feelings from him. "You always had the knack for saying the right things to all the girls," she said, as the corners of her mouth tugged upward into the hint of a smile. "Even to the ones who were...plain. And that was something I liked about you."

"Not you, Johanna. You were never plain."

She moved into the kitchen and again, he followed. It was warm in there. Not a breeze stirred the curtains through the open windows, but Roland could feel the buzz of tension between them, and he had the urge to kiss her. He remembered the sweet taste of her lips and the way she'd felt in his arms. An aching rose inside him. He wanted her to be his wife, and if he couldn't have her, he didn't know how he could face the rest of his life.

She turned to face him and recognition flickered in Johanna's eyes. He knew with certainty that she felt the same thrumming in the still air that he did. Her lips parted, and she uttered a small sigh as she took a step backward. "There," she said brusquely as she pointed to the wooden churn standing on the counter. "It's heavy. We've already packed the ice and salt around the barrel."

Roland took a moment to collect himself and then

lifted the churn off the counter. "It's not that heavy," he said. Beads of condensation gathered on the outside of the wooden container, soaking through his thin shirt and cooling his skin. "Is this the same one your *dat* used to make ice cream when we were kids?" He gazed intensely into Johanna's eyes. "I remember the afternoon he made blueberry ice cream and Charley and I went home with blue lips and tongues."

"*Ya.*" She chuckled. "The same one. A wheelwright built them in Lancaster back in the twenties. He did good work. The metal crank still turns as easily as it ever did."

"That was a *gut* day, when we had the blueberry ice cream. I remember that Jonas built a fire when it got dark and let us make popcorn and toast marshmallows on willow sticks."

"And we chased lightning bugs and put them in glass jars so they blinked on and off in the dark like lanterns. Remember? *Dat* made us let them all go before bedtime. He was so kind he didn't want to see even a lightning bug hurt needlessly." Johanna's face softened, and the years fell away so that he could see the laughing girl she'd been that night—teasing and merry, without a care in the world.

"We could do that again tonight," he said. "Catch lightning bugs. The children would like it. It seems as though there are a lot of them this summer. And early in the season to see so many."

"Children or lightning bugs?" she teased.

Roland grip tightened on the churn. He shivered as the cold seeped through to his chest. "Johanna..." His voice grew husky. "I want to—"

"*Mam!*" Katy's small voice came through the screen door. "*Mam,* are you in here?"

"Ya," Johanna answered. Her gaze shifted from the entrance back to meet his. "Here, Katy."

Roland saw the tautness go out of Johanna's shoulders, and he knew that she welcomed her daughter's interruption.

"We're coming," Johanna said with forced cheerfulness.

Roland fought a momentary feeling of disappointment. For a second there, things had been right between them...as easy and comfortable as it used to be. And, foolishly, he'd hoped...

She crossed the kitchen and opened the door. "Roland's going to make ice cream for us." He couldn't see the little girl, but he heard her excited giggles. "And tonight, when it gets dark, we're all going to catch lightning bugs. Would you like that?"

Johanna stepped back, pulling the door open even wider so that he could pass through. As he did, she smiled up at him. "Strawberry ice cream, this time. Will it taste as good as blueberry, do you think?"

His heartbeat quickened at the warm affection in her eyes, and hope flared in his chest. He scrambled to think of something to say that wouldn't take away from the moment. "At least it won't turn our lips blue," he managed, and was rewarded by the sound of her soft chuckle.

Whatever that feeling of warmth had been that had passed between Roland and Johanna in the kitchen changed everything. He had followed her into the house, afraid he didn't belong there, no matter how much he wanted to be. But when they rejoined the family, he slipped into his old place of years ago among the Yoders, just as easily as shaping a horseshoe at his own forge.

Susanna and her friend David were sitting at the end of the table, their heads close together, giggling and playing with a cat's cradle, a loop of yarn that first one and then the other would try to twist into different patterns. David's straw hat lay on the bench beside him, and his familiar paper crown hung precariously over one ear, but no one seemed to notice. Ruth, Hannah and Rebecca were admiring Anna's baby girl, cuddled in her mother's lap at the other end of the table, and J.J., face earnest, was trying desperately to drive a yellow ball through a series of hoops on the lawn while Jonah and Samuel's twins shouted advice.

Roland noted, to his surprise, that Nip Hilty and Johanna's Aunt Jezzy were seated together in the old porch swing that someone had carried out to the backyard. Nip was whittling a length of wood and talking a blue streak while she listened intently. He didn't know what they found so mutually interesting, but it was clear to him that both of them were enjoying the interlude. Johanna's grandmother was seated near them in a lawn chair, but she'd fallen asleep, her chin on her chest, snoring softly.

Charley, Samuel, Miriam and Eli were talking near the grape arbor. Roland heard snatches of their conversation. A discussion had arisen in the church as to whether a tractor with iron wheels could be used to power farm equipment, as some of the other Old Order Amish groups allowed. From what Roland could gather, Charley and Miriam favored the change, but Samuel didn't.

Later in the month, Roland knew he'd be called upon to vote on the question. Although women could be full members of the church, they weren't allowed to have a say in such matters, so Miriam's opinion didn't count, other than her influence on Charley or the male members of her family. Which was probably why she was the one talking the most. Roland hadn't made up his mind yet, but—in any case—the final decision would come from Bishop Atlee. The vote was only meant to help him make his decision. Whatever he decided would be part of the *Ordnung,* and the entire community would obey.

"Will this do?" Johanna asked, drawing Roland's attention back to the task at hand. She pointed to a small picnic table, one usually used for the children.

"Perfect," Roland answered. If she'd asked, he would have churned the ice cream while standing in the duck pond or balancing on top of the chicken house. What mattered was that he and Johanna were doing something together, something fun, without arguing.

She cleared the plates and glasses to one side and he placed the churn on the table and began to turn the crank. It usually took between twenty and thirty minutes to turn the milk, cream, sugar and strawberries into ice cream, and the cranking grew more difficult as the mixture hardened. Fortunately, the years of swinging a hammer in his craft as a farrier had given him strong arms. One of Samuel's twins brought a bucket of cracked ice and a box of salt, so they could stop and refill the outer chamber as the ice melted.

With Johanna there, the time went by all too fast. When the ice cream was ready, they packed the churn into a washtub, added the remaining ice and swaddled the whole thing in an old blanket. Then they stowed it in the shade under the grape arbor to freeze solid, and everyone gathered around the table for supper.

Hannah waved Roland to a place on the bench beside J.J. and Jonah, directly across the table from Johanna and Katy. The only thing better would have been to be seated beside Johanna. But that was rarely done in their community because the women had to get up and down to bring food from the kitchen or serve the guests and family.

Roland ate until he thought he would burst, and then he had two slices of Johanna's peach-and-rhubarb pie with strawberry ice cream on top. The children pronounced the ice cream the best they'd ever eaten, and Roland felt pleased that he'd been able to add something to the wonderful Sunday supper.

Afterward, the adults rested on blankets spread on the grass and the children played around them. The sun was already behind the trees, and twilight filled the Yoder farm with a delightful peacefulness. Susanna and David joined the youngsters at a final game of croquet before it got too dark to see the wire hoops, and the little girls crept under the table to play house with their dolls.

"I think I'll check on my bees," Johanna said to Roland. "Would you like to walk back to the hives with me?"

"I'd like that." He glanced at Hannah to see if she would object, but she was engaged in conversation with Anna and Ruth. Aunt Jezzy and Nip had claimed their seat on the swing again and, once more, Nip was talking and whittling while she provided a willing audience.

Johanna bent and peered under the table. "Katy, we're taking a walk. Do you want to come with us?"

"Ne, Mam," Roland heard a small voice reply. "Want to play babies with Mae and Lori Ann."

"All right." Johanna dropped the tablecloth. "If you need anything, go to Aunt Rebecca."

"Mam!" Jonah called. "When are we going to catch lightning bugs?"

"Soon," Johanna promised. "We have to wait until it

gets dark enough so that you can see them." She smiled at Roland as they walked away from the others and around the house. "It was a good idea," she said. "The kids are so excited. I can't believe we haven't thought to do it yet this summer."

"You're a busy woman," he said. "What with your bees, turkeys and sheep and quilts, I don't know anyone who works any harder."

Johanna shrugged. "Anna. I don't know where she gets her energy, and her with five older children *and* a new baby."

"She has Naomi to help her, and Rebecca. And I heard Samuel say one of his cousins was sending a daughter out to give Anna a hand in the house."

"Esther Mast. *Ya,* she is," Johanna agreed. "She's seventeen or eighteen. She was here visiting last summer, and she and Anna got on well. She's strong and willing and good with the children. *Mam's* offered to let her stay with us since Grace will be leaving us soon. That way Esther can have her own room."

"Not many young women would want to leave home to do chores at someone else's house. She must be good-natured."

"She comes from a big family and they live in a small community in Missouri. I think there are six or seven girls. Her mother thinks Anna's the perfect person to teach her how to run a house, and I think Esther wants to see a new part of the country before she settles down and gets married."

They crossed the barnyard and started down the lane that led to the orchard. Roland heard the bleat of a lamb in the sheepfold and the answering call of its mother. Overhead, wings fluttered as pigeons returned to their roosts in the attic of the granary. The smells were familiar and sweet, the scent of new-cut hay, horses and honeysuckle. For the first time in a long while, Roland felt content.

He glanced at Johanna, and when she smiled back at him, he reached out and took her hand. To his surprise, she didn't pull away or protest. They walked on without speaking, enjoying the quiet of the fading day, and Roland laced his fingers around hers and savored the warm feel of her hand in his.

When they reached the first of her beehives, long shadows of evening has already fallen over the white wooden boxes, and the bees were quiet except for a low, contented buzzing. She remained next to him, still very close, and Roland looked down at her. "They don't seem to be awake," he said.

"I didn't think they would be."

"Then why—"

Her chuckle was soft and light, and he found himself chuckling with her. "You've been dragged out here under false pretenses," she said.

"Does this mean we're courting?" he asked. His breath caught in his throat as he waited for her answer.

"Ne," she murmured. "I'm not ready for that yet, but I wanted to see what it would feel like—to have you hold my hand. It's been so long."

"Since Wilmer?"

She shook her head. He could no longer see the expression in her eyes because it was too dark, but he felt the sadness radiating from her. "I wasn't thinking of Wilmer," she admitted. "I was thinking of you and me. Wilmer wasn't that kind of man…he wasn't one to make a show of affection."

Roland was struck by the foolishness of the man, and

for a few seconds he allowed himself to pity Wilmer. "Not even with his wife?"

She sighed. "We need more time like this," she said, leaving his question unanswered. "You and I."

He threaded his fingers through hers. "And what would you have done if I hadn't tried to hold your hand?"

"I suppose I would have had to make the first move." And then, before he could think of something clever to say, she went on. "Jonah and Katy would love to go to the ocean. Do you think we might hire a driver and take them to the beach next weekend?"

"You want us to go together?"

She chuckled. "With the children. And J.J., of course. I thought to ask Aunt Jezzy to come along with us."

"I'm nearly thirty, both of us were married before and with children. Do we still need a chaperone?"

Her chuckle became a merry laugh. "Susanna would probably like to go with us, as well. But if you'd rather not—"

"We'll go," he said quickly. "Of course we'll go. And there's no need to wait until next Saturday. I don't have any farrier work to do Wednesday. Could we go Wednesday? All of us?"

"Susanna, too?"

"And your mother, if you like. I want to be with you, Johanna. Whatever it takes to get you to trust me again, I'll do."

"I think it would be good for us," she said. "It would be fun." She let go of his hand and turned back toward the house. "And now we have lightning bugs and children to chase."

"Johanna, wait." He caught hold of her and pulled her

into his arms. He felt her tremble in his arms as he lowered his mouth toward hers.

"Are you kissing?" Susanna's voice came out of the darkness. "No kissing, Johanna." She appeared out of the darkness, followed by a bulky shadow that could only be David. "*Mam* said, 'No kissing!' And if I can't kiss David, you can't kiss Roland."

And then they all laughed.

Chapter Twelve

"Towels. Don't forget towels. And make Jonah wear his hat on the beach," Hannah advised. "I put a bottle of sunscreen in your bag. I hope it will be enough for everyone."

"We'll be fine, *Mam,*" Johanna assured her. "I promise they won't come back the color of cranberries."

Hannah paused in the center of the kitchen, laundry basket in hand, and smiled at her. "I know they will both love the ocean," she said. "And you have such a pretty day for an outing." She looked as though she wanted to say something else, but was biting her tongue.

"What is it, *Mam?*" Johanna chuckled. "Out with it, before you burst."

"You have a good time, too. You and Roland. You deserve it."

Johanna pushed the canning jar full of ice deep into the cooler that was resting on the kitchen table. "We're not walking out if that's what you mean. Don't start counting celery stalks yet."

"So you're still unsure?" Hannah lowered the wicker basket to the floor. "Sunday night, when the two of you were chasing lightning bugs on the lawn...when you

tripped over that croquet hoop and Roland caught you...
it seemed like—"

"Like I was having a good time," Johanna finished
for her mother. "I was. It was a wonderful evening. Like
old times."

"Ne," Hannah said gently. "Not like old times. Neither of you are children anymore. You're a grown woman
with two children, and Roland is a father and a widower.
Maybe...new times?"

Johanna squeezed a quart of canned peaches into the
corner of the cooler. Roland had insisted on paying for
the van and driver, so she had insisted on packing lunch
for them all. The only difficult part was choosing foods
that would stay cool enough in the summer heat not to
spoil. She kept her menu simple: hard-boiled eggs, bread,
cheese, fruit, carrot strips and whoopie pies with marsh-
mallow filling that she and Susanna had made the previous night. She was taking plenty to drink, too—a gallon
of lemonade and another of fresh well water.

"Johanna?"

She sighed and looked up to meet her mother's shrewd
gaze. "I think I still care for Roland," she admitted, and
then corrected herself. "I know I do. But I'm afraid." She
opened her arms and let them fall to her sides. "I'm afraid
of making the wrong decision again and..."

"Afraid Roland will disappoint you as Wilmer did?"

"Ne." Johanna shook her head. "He's nothing like
Wilmer. I know Roland would never hurt me physically,
and he isn't sick in the head like poor Wilmer was. But it's
hard to forget what my bad choice brought upon me and
how much it hurt me. It's hard to consider placing myself
and my children in another man's hands. Even Roland's."

"Yet, our teachings bid us that the husband and father

must be the head of the family, and a good wife must listen to her husband's wishes."

She pushed aside the containers to make room for the sealed plastic container of whoopie pies, closed the cooler lid and latched it. "I know that, *Mam,*" she said. "But what if I can't be a good wife? What if it's better for all of us if I leave things as they are?" She didn't want to talk about this today, and especially not with *Mam.* It was too difficult. Just thinking about Roland was too difficult. Today was supposed to be fun, a day when she didn't have to be serious or make decisions that would change the rest of her life.

Hannah came close and hugged her. "You must follow your heart, my dear, dear child. And your head. But if you keep Roland waiting too long, he'll choose another— perhaps even that girl from Lancaster that Rebecca and Aunt Jezzy say is always talking to him at Spence's. Roland is a young man with responsibilities. He must take a wife and he must do it soon."

"If he wants to marry that silly Lancaster girl, let him do it and be done with it. I refuse to be pushed into a hasty decision that I might live to regret."

Hannah hugged her even tighter and whispered, "Do as you will, Johanna. You always have. No matter what, I'll always love you, and I'll always be here for you. But if this goes badly, just don't say that I didn't warn you." With a final squeeze, her mother let her go.

As you did about Wilmer? Johanna gritted her teeth and swallowed the sharp answer that rose in her throat. *Mam* wasn't one to say *I told you so.* She knew her mother had been right. She'd known it then and she knew it now. She'd married Wilmer—a man she hardly knew—

to salve the ache breaking up with Roland had caused her. *Mam* had warned her that Wilmer was too rigid.

"I'm sorry," Hannah murmured. "I'm an interfering woman. The Lord knows it's a fault I've struggled with all my life. I love my children, and I think I know best how they should solve their problems." She forced a chuckle. "The truth is that I don't, Johanna. I was wrong to speak so. You're old enough to know your own mind."

Johanna smiled back at her. "I should be," she said. "But it was a lot easier when I was a girl, and all I had to do was listen to you and *Dat* and do as I was told."

Hannah rolled her eyes. "As if that was ever so." Her laughter became genuine. "Oh, my sweet girl. You, I'm afraid, are too much like me. Too stubborn and willful for our own good. As my father always said, 'You, Hannah, are a trial to your parents, but a greater one to yourself. You'd cut off your own nose to spite your face.'"

The children were so excited when they tumbled out of the van at Delaware Seashore State Park that they were bouncing up and down like jumping jacks. "You look after the kids," Roland said, "and I'll get the coolers and the canopy."

Susanna and Aunt Jezzy ushered Jonah, Katy and J.J. out of the parking lot and onto the beach. Johanna handed each of them a towel and retied Katy's bonnet, which was in danger of blowing off. There was a brisk breeze off the ocean, and Johanna doubted that the boys' straw hats would stay on for long. Being bareheaded could be a real problem for Jonah with his fair skin. Both Katy and J.J. were better off, having a complexion that tanned rather than burned. Luckily, she had the sunscreen her mother had packed and she quickly applied it to their faces, arms and legs.

"Look, *Mam!*" Jonah pointed toward the inlet. "That man caught a fish!"

"And there's a big boat," J.J. chimed in. "I wish we could go on it."

Roland and the driver, Mike, unloaded the bag containing the canopy and carried it across the sand to a place about fifty feet from the water's edge. Johanna instructed the children to remove their shoes and stockings and then took them all down to play in the waves, while the two men set up the canopy and went back to the van for the coolers.

Roland had suggested they spend the day at the state park at Indian River rather than Rehoboth Beach because there would be fewer Englishers to stare and point at the quaint Amish. Johanna was glad that he had. The beach was nearly deserted: a young man was searching the dune area with a metal detector, and the couple sleeping on a blanket near the high-tide mark didn't even look up at the children's shouts of joy.

"Don't go out too far," Johanna warned.

Susanna echoed, "Too far!"

Soon, Johanna, Susanna and Aunt Jezzy joined the two boys in a game of Catch Me if You Can with the incoming waves, and Katy simply sat down on the damp sand and let the foamy salt water wash over her. Jonah and J.J. quickly became wet to their waists, and, as Johanna had feared, their hats flew off in the wind. Laughing, Susanna ran to chase them down, as Roland and the driver brought the last cooler down to the shade of the canopy.

"What did you pack in here?" Roland asked. "Rocks?"

"Food, silly," Susanna shouted back as she captured J.J.'s hat. Then, she squealed and pointed toward the parking lot.

A second van pulled up beside Mike's and the horn honked. The doors opened and more family poured out. Johanna recognized a waving Charley, Miriam and the identical red mops of Samuel's twins. 'Kota skipped along beside Miriam, but who was the other Amish man, seated in the front seat? It couldn't be Eli or Samuel. He wasn't tall enough.

Taking hold of Katy's hand and calling to J.J. and Jonah, Johanna walked back up the beach to meet the others. To her surprise, the man turned out to be Nip Hilty. Johanna turned back to see Aunt Jezzy splashing in the waves as she spun around three times and then reached down to grab handfuls of foam and toss them in the air. "Aunt Jezzy, look who it is," she called.

"I know." Her aunt giggled. "Nip said he was going to get a driver." And then, she turned away and began to walk down the beach picking up shells.

"Look! Look!" Susanna shrieked as one more person got out of the van. "It's my King David. He came! He came!"

"Not more food!" Roland exclaimed as they watched Charley and Rudy unload another cooler from their vehicle. "We'll never eat it all. We'll have to stay a week."

"We hope you don't mind," Miriam said as she came toward Johanna. "Nip invited us. It seemed like such a good idea, that Charley took the day off, and we sort of picked up a few more nephews on the way." Miriam reached into her bag and produced a blue pail full of plastic sand molds and a shovel. "This is for you, little Katydid," she said, handing them to her. "You're the only little girl here today so I think you deserve a special treat for putting up with all these boys."

"You know we're glad to have you." Johanna glanced down at Katy. "What do you say to Aunt Miriam for bringing you a present?"

"I'm not little. I'm big." She glanced up at her mother and realized her error. *"Danke,"* she said quickly.

"I've got a bucket, too," 'Kota declared. "Want to make a sand castle, Katy?"

"Don't you want to go in the water with the boys?" Johanna asked him.

'Kota shook his head. "Nope. Want to build a castle."

"Me, too," Katy agreed. "Build a…a…house!"

It seemed like chaos, but soon, the coolers were opened, cold lemonade and apples were handed around, and Susanna, David and the children all ran back to the water, supervised by Miriam, Charley, Aunt Jezzy and Nip. Katy and 'Kota settled down to construct a farm-yard and duck pond in the wet sand.

"If you dig a ditch and then a hole for your pond," Roland explained, "the waves will come in and fill it for you." He crouched down beside 'Kota and showed him where to begin his trench.

Katy dug furiously, piling sand to make her house, while Johanna brought buckets of seawater to wet the sand and make it easier to mold. It wasn't long before she and Roland were as wet as the children, much to the kids' delight. Roland rolled his pants to his knees, but then a big wave broke and splashed the entire front of his shirt and sent water rolling down his beard.

J.J. and Jonah soon joined the fun, expanding the canal to reach more hastily dug ponds. Soon, Nip discovered a small piece of driftwood and with his penknife quickly whittled a tiny boat, which he presented to Aunt Jezzy. She set it adrift in 'Kota's duck pond, to his and Katy's delight. After that, nothing would do but that he made boats for Jonah and J.J. as well, and there was a frantic search for more bits of suitable whittling material.

Jonah, expanding his canal, came upon a strange creature buried in the sand and called Johanna to see it. "What is it, *Mam?* Will it bite?"

She laughed. "It's a sand flea."

Katy wrinkled her nose. "Not a flea, *Mam.* Too big."

"It's little. Be gentle," Johanna cautioned. It began to wiggle and Jonah dropped it, and then shrieked with glee as it scurried away on spindly legs and began to tunnel down into the sand at the waterline.

The wind died down enough for the boys to put their hats back on, and Roland showed them how to look for bubbles in the wet sand and dig for clams. They didn't find any clams, but they did see a small fish, which swam back out to sea on the next wave. The boys howled in disappointment, but Katy laughed and clapped, shouting, "Swim away, fish. Swim away."

"When do we eat?" Charley asked. "I'm starving."

"You're always starving," Miriam teased.

"Me, too," David said. "Me!"

"All right," Johanna agreed. "Let's go have our lunch." Everyone trooped back to the canopy and dove into the contents of the two coolers. Roland and Nip poured cups of cold water all around and after a brief moment of silent prayer, they began to make short work of every bite that Miriam and Johanna had packed. Afterward, the women took the children up to the bathrooms, washed their hands and faces, and returned to join the others.

The children were all for returning to the ocean at

once, but the adults were adamant. No one could go back into the water until they'd rested for at least half an hour. Nip produced a pocket watch and became the official timekeeper. Katy curled up in Johanna's lap and fell asleep, one small hand still tightly clasping the handle of her blue shovel.

At last the thirty minutes was up, and the kids, all but a sleepy Katy, ran back toward the water, eager to get as wet and sandy as possible. Johanna got to her feet and was about to follow them, when Roland gestured to her. "Come walk with me," he said.

Johanna hesitated. She did want to walk on the beach, but she was responsible for her children. She glanced at Miriam. "Is it all right if…"

Miriam smiled. "Go on. Take some time for yourself. We'll watch the kids. Go. Have fun. You always loved the ocean. Enjoy it."

"Jonah doesn't always do what—"

Charley laughed. "It's fine, Johanna. Go with Roland. I think between us, we can handle a few small kids."

"If we don't get some practice, how will we know what to do with our own when God sends them?" Miriam asked.

Miriam could have passed for sixteen today. She hadn't worn a bonnet, but had braided her hair, pinned it up and covered it with a scarf. Somehow, she'd managed to lose the pins on one side, and that braid had tumbled down. Undaunted, Miriam had removed the bobby pins on the other side so that both braids hung down over her shoulders. She looked happy, Johanna thought, very happy. Who would have believed that Miriam would be so satisfied in her marriage to Charley, a boy she'd known all her life…a boy she'd told everyone was her best friend?

Why her and not me? Johanna wondered. How was Miriam so wise in picking a husband? Johanna had been certain that Miriam was going to choose John Hartman. If anyone was reckless enough to marry out of the church and leave the faith, she would have expected it to be Miriam, not Leah. *It's like* Grossmama *always says,* she mused. *Only God knows what's in another person's heart.*

"Johanna?" Roland held out a hand.

"Coming." She followed him, but didn't take his hand. He strode off in the direction of the inlet, and she matched him step for step, the wind tearing at her bonnet until she untied it and wrapped the ribbons around her fingers. Removing the heavy bonnet was a relief. She stopped, closed her eyes and inhaled deeply, savoring the taste of salt in the air. "I love the ocean," she said, opening her eyes again and looking up at Roland.

"I love you," he said. Or…she thought he said it.

Johanna felt her cheeks grow warm, despite the cool breeze. "You shouldn't say such things," she admonished. "It's not decent."

"What things?" He arched a brow mischievously. "What did I say?"

"That…that you…" She broke off and looked away. What if she were wrong? What if she'd imagined it? She'd already asked him to marry her. What if he hadn't said that at all and she called him on it? What kind of fast woman would she look like to suggest he'd…

"I'm teasing you, Johanna." His face crinkled in a grin. "Are you having a good time today?" He began walking again and she did the same.

Safer ground. "Ya," she answered. "A wonderful time. The best day ever. The children—"

"Not the children. *You.* Are *you* enjoying yourself?" he demanded.

"I am." She smiled back at him. "Thank you."

The sound of the tide rushing through the inlet grew louder the closer they got, and the air felt cooler. Roland reached out and took her hand, and this time she didn't protest. They reached the edge of the rocks, and he climbed up and helped her to a ledge where they had a better view of the dark, surging water. The giant boulder felt warm and solid beneath her, and she sat and curled her legs up under her skirt. Her dress was wrinkled but nearly dry.

They sat there, not speaking, her hand in his, with the sun on their faces and the powerful crash and curl of the inlet washing around them. It was Roland who finally broke the comfortable silence. "Well, Johanna Yoder. I'd say our courting is going pretty well, wouldn't you?"

She threw him a look. "Who says we're courting?"

"I do."

"And you're the judge of that?"

"I know you better than you think."

She sniffed. "You, Roland Byler, are entirely too fond of your own ideas."

"No argument. All I said was the truth. We're courting. Everyone knows it. Even your mother knows it. You're just too stubborn to admit when I'm right."

"You're saying I'm stubborn?"

He said nothing; he just looked at her.

She chuckled. "I suppose I am." Her eyes narrowed. "But courting doesn't mean marriage. I haven't made up my mind yet, and until I do—"

"It's because of what happened before, isn't it? Because of what I did in Pennsylvania when I almost got arrested? How many times do I have to tell you that I didn't intend to—"

"Ne." She pulled her hand out of his. "I don't want to talk about it. Not today. Don't spoil it for me. Please don't."

"I just want you to understand that I—"

She put a finger to her lips. "Shh. Not another word about what happened in Lancaster or you can sit on this rock by yourself."

"If you feel that way." His shoulders stiffened.

"I do. I came to have fun, not to remember bad times." She offered him a half smile. "We couldn't have done anything today that would have made me happier."

He nodded. "I'm glad."

His features remained strained and she knew that she'd hurt him. She hadn't wanted to…at least she hoped she hadn't. This time, she was the one who reached out a hand. "I do love you, Roland."

"Then you'll be my wife?"

She looked at their hands clasped together. "I don't know. I'm still trying to decide."

"How long? When will you know?"

She leaned forward and brushed her lips against his. "I can't say, Roland, but when I do decide, you'll be the first one I tell."

Chapter Thirteen

On Friday, Johanna sat on the grass by Roland's pond, with J.J. beside her. It was midmorning, and the day promised to be another hot one, with no sign of rain, which the crops and gardens could all use. The sun was shining, and white, lacy clouds drifted lazily across a robin's-egg-blue sky. Johanna and J.J. were watching the bees fly in and out of the new hive, while she shared some of the secrets of becoming a successful beekeeper.

Katy was spending the morning at Anna's, playing with her girls, and Jonah perched a few yards away on the bank of the pond. He held a homemade willow-branch fishing pole and was concentrating on his bobber. The cork danced tantalizingly, but whenever he snatched on the line, nothing came up but an empty hook. "They keep stealing my bait, *Mam*," Jonah protested. "I've only got two worms left." He sighed heavily. "I'll bet it's just sunnies. I don't think there are any big fish in here."

"*Ya*, there are," J.J. insisted. "*Dat* put baby bass in there a long time ago. Once he caught one this big!" He stretched his arms apart to show what Johanna thought must be an exaggerated size, even for a largemouth bass.

"I'm tired of fishing anyway." Jonah dropped the fishing pole onto the grass. "I'm thirsty."

"If you don't want to fish anymore today, put those worms back in the garden," Johanna instructed.

"*Mam,* I'm hot," Jonah whined. "They're just worms."

"The Lord made them as He made you," she said firmly, rising to her feet. "Wrap up your line and fasten that hook so you don't lose an eye. And take the worms back where you dug them. Now." She tugged the brim of her son's hat down. "And your hat will do you no good if it doesn't shade your face from the sun."

"Do we have to leave?" J.J. asked. "I like watching the bees."

"We do. I'm glad you're learning about the bees, but it's time we finished up our chores here and got back home."

Today wasn't Roland's regular day at the horse farm, but someone had stopped by and asked him to replace a shoe on a three-year-old that was scheduled to race. He'd brought J.J. to *Mam's* at 9:00 a.m. and asked Johanna if she could possibly watch J.J. for him. Naturally, she said she'd be glad to help. Roland was grateful, and it really was no trouble. She hadn't planned much for the day, other than to help prepare food for Sunday. And J.J. was a sweet child, not nearly as mischievous as her Jonah. Since she'd been coming to Roland's to tend this new hive, she'd been delighted to find J.J. so interested. She suspected that her earlier conclusions were true—Roland's boy had a real love for bees and a God-given gift for understanding them.

Even if J.J. hadn't shared her interest in bees, Johanna knew her heart would have gone out to him, as a poor motherless child. He had a father who loved him dearly, but the boy desperately missed his mother. He'd been young when Roland's wife had died of complications of diabetes, but he had been able to talk. Roland said that for months, his son had asked for his *mam* and cried out for her in his sleep.

Nighttime, according to Roland, was still a difficult time for them both. J.J., easy in daylight, became fearful and needy once the sun went down. He often woke screaming from nightmares that he couldn't remember. And now, by the way he followed her and clung to her skirt, J.J. was forming an attachment to her. She would have welcomed it, if she'd known for certain that she would become his mother. Another child would fit easily into her arms. But she was afraid that if she and Roland didn't wed, J.J. would be hurt again. And this time, who knew how deeply the boy would be affected.

Johanna never used to think about the complications of relationships. Maybe living with Wilmer and seeing the results of a troubled mind every day had made her more sympathetic to the emotional needs of her family and those around her. Before she'd married, she'd often been impatient with what she felt was weakness, and she'd been inclined to tell those afflicted to "just snap out of it." But, no more. J.J. was wounded. He didn't have a broken arm that could be seen and easily mended. He had suffered a blow to his spirit.

It was true that Katy and Jonah had both lost their father when Wilmer took his own life. But, although Katy had adored her father, there had always been a distance between Wilmer and Jonah. Her son had often been the victim of his father's outbursts, and no amount of persuading on her part had been able to soften Wilmer's verbal attacks on the boy. Strangely, Wilmer's death had caused Jonah's personality to blossom. In weeks, she'd seen her little boy gain self-confidence. He'd begun to speak up, to try new tasks. As perverse as it seemed, Wilmer's absence had brought happiness into Jonah's life. As for Katy, nothing could squelch her merry spirit. She accepted life as it came and enjoyed every moment of every day.

At first, Johanna had worried that having J.J. spend so much time with them, as he had been lately, might spark jealousy. She'd watched Jonah carefully, afraid that he might not like sharing his mother with another boy. But what she'd feared hadn't happened. Instead, Jonah fell into the role of big brother, and J.J. became the faithful pal.

There wasn't much difference in the boys' ages, but she'd tried to raise her children in the way that she'd been reared. Her parents had encouraged her and her sisters to be independent and to believe in their own ability to solve problems and be of help to the family. J.J.'s mother, Pauline, had kept him close, protecting—perhaps overprotecting—him and treating him as if he was younger than he really was. It had been a source of friction between Roland and his wife until her death, and something so obvious that others in the community, including Johanna and her sisters, had remarked on it.

Since Roland had become J.J.'s sole parent, both had had to make adjustments. As far as Johanna could see, Roland was a wonderful father, but it was obvious that he sometimes felt out of his depth. Children needed both a mother and a father. *Mam* was right. Roland needed to take another wife, and soon. She could be that wife... if only she could ease the uncertainty in her mind and her heart.

And she and Roland *were* courting.

He had pointed out the truth of that simple statement last Wednesday and, against her will, she'd had to admit that Roland was right. But she was still no closer to a decision on marriage. She'd enjoyed the day at the beach, even enjoyed kissing Roland more than she felt was decent, but she still felt so uncertain. Courting was a carefree time, a time for a boy and girl to learn more about each other and to learn to be at ease in each other's company. But Roland was no stranger to her. She knew his strengths and his weaknesses. And, more importantly, she knew her own. So their courting was something different. For her, it was about whether or not she wanted to marry again.

Once she made a choice to marry Roland or to remain a widow, she would live with it. She'd already proved with Wilmer that she was capable of dealing with even the most difficult situations. But did she want to? Wasn't it easier to simply step away from remarriage and build a life caring for her son and daughter, and helping her mother with dear Susanna? Wouldn't God approve of that sacrifice? Her sister Ruth had once believed that singleness was the path the Lord had planned for her. But what if it wasn't Ruth who was supposed to serve in that way? What if it was her?

Johanna had been praying for an answer every morning when she woke, and every night before she went to sleep. "Please, Lord, tell me what to do," she pleaded. "Tell me what's right for me, for Roland, for Katy and J.J. and Jonah. Give me the wisdom to know what you want of me."

"*Mam,* I'm hungry."

Jonah's voice interrupted her reverie. "We'll go to

Aunt Anna's," she said. "She asked us to take the noon meal with her. Fried chicken and biscuits."

"And blackberry pie," J.J. said, reaching up to clasp Johanna's hand. "Pie is my favorite."

Johanna nodded. Feeding hungry children was something she knew how to do. Johanna had made four loaves of raisin bread early that morning. She'd brought one loaf and a quart of *Mam's* chicken-corn soup and put them in Roland's refrigerator for them to have for that evening's supper. Whether or not she decided to become Roland's wife and J.J.'s mother, they still had to eat. Hadn't *Mam* taught her that looking after neighbors was the right thing to do? Even *Mam* couldn't suggest that she was leading Roland on by seeing that he and his son didn't go without. Or could she?

Johanna was still asking that same question on Sunday when she sat on the bench between Miriam and Aunt Jezzy, and Uncle Reuben asked everyone to stand for "'S Lobg-sang," a slow, traditional hymn that was always sung by the congregation at service. Her mind should have been on the song of praise, but instead, she kept thinking back over the past week.

Thursday night, Roland had come to take her for a drive. They'd left the three children with *Mam,* Rebecca, Grace and Susanna, and they'd gone for pizza and come home the long way. She and Roland had laughed and talked. He'd made no attempt to hold her hand again, and she hadn't tried to kiss him, but she had wondered if he wanted to kiss her. And if he hadn't wanted to… why not? Did it mean that he'd thought she was forward when she'd kissed him at the inlet?

If she leaned a little closer to Aunt Jezzy, she could

see Roland standing in the second row behind Anna's Samuel. He'd trimmed his beard that morning, but he needed a haircut. His hair hung over his eyes, and he kept brushing it out of the way. She wondered why his sister Mary hadn't said something about it. It was endless, the list of things that a man living alone with a small boy forgot to do for himself. Maybe she should offer to cut it for him.... She'd trimmed J.J.'s yesterday afternoon when she'd done Jonah's. But it wasn't really fitting for her to cut Roland's hair. That was a little too intimate for comfort. She would suggest that Mary or his mother cut it.

Johanna forced herself to look straight ahead, but she couldn't keep thoughts of Roland out of her head. She could pick out his rich baritone among all the other men. He had a good, strong singing voice, and he never slurred the words to the old songs as some of the younger fellows did. Roland knew all the lyrics, and he could carry the tune, no matter how slow.

She was listening so hard to Roland that she nearly missed a note herself. Miriam cut her eyes at her and suppressed a smile. Johanna averted her gaze, and when she looked up, saw that her aunt Martha, seated just in the next row, had turned to scowl at her. Was it that obvious to everyone that she hadn't been paying attention—that her mind had been on Roland instead of the service? Embarrassed, Johanna gripped the *Ausbund,* the hymnbook, tighter and let her voice blend with the women around her.

When the hymn ended and Preacher Perry began to tell how the Pharaoh's daughter sent her servants to fetch a floating basket from the river, Johanna forced herself to listen to the familiar story of Baby Moses and how he was saved and grew up in the palace as an Egyptian prince. It was a tale she'd always loved, and one Hannah had elaborated on when Johanna was small. *The princess loved the baby as her own, Mam* had said, *just as I love you, and you, and you...* pointing out each of them in turn.

Perry Hershberger was a good speaker and a much-loved preacher, but he suffered from poor health, and his voice was often weak. Today, he seemed better than he had been in many weeks, and Johanna had no trouble following his sermon. His sermons were never as wordy or as dull as Uncle Reuben's, and Preacher Perry usually recited the Bible passages in Low German, not the High German that most preachers favored. Usually, Johanna loved it when he spoke, but today, her mind kept wandering.

Lydia and Norman, this Sunday's hosts, had thrown open the windows to catch the breeze, and fresh air wafted in from outside, making the crowded rooms comfortable for a summer's day. The rest of the service passed quickly, and the next time the congregation rose for a hymn, Johanna kept herself from seeking out Roland Byler with her eyes and making a complete fool of herself.

Bishop Atlee finished with a prayer, and then Samuel, who was deacon, got to his feet to deliver the announcements for the week. Johanna's thoughts drifted again as the bishop asked for remembrance for those who were ill and reminded the community that the next service would be at Aunt Martha and Uncle Reuben's house. He asked for volunteers to paint the Coblentz barn, and then cleared his throat. "Banns are read for couples Menno Swartzentruber and Susie Raber. That's Susie Raber of Swan Creek, Missouri. I think some of you met the John Rabers last year when they came for Wilmer's funeral."

Johanna remembered Ethel Raber, John's wife, but which of her three daughters was Susie? Johanna hadn't heard that Menno was getting married, but that wasn't unusual. Many Amish couples preferred to keep their plans secret until the coming nuptials were announced in church.

She wondered when the bride-to-be and Menno had met and courted, or if theirs was an arranged marriage, as some were. It happened here occasionally, more so out in the Western states, but she'd heard that such unions, typically arranged by parents, usually turned out well. It certainly wouldn't have suited her. At least she'd known Wilmer and had no one else to blame for the disaster of her marriage but herself.

"And first banns called for Naphtali Hilty of District 4, here in Kent County, and our own Jezebel Miller."

Miriam elbowed Johanna as a wave of murmurs rippled through the congregation. Johanna blinked and mouthed silently to her sister, *What? Who?*

"Say that again, Samuel," Noodle Troyer urged from the far corner of the men's benches. "Did you say Jezebel Miller?"

Samuel reddened and cleared his throat again. "Banns called for Naphtali—that's *Nip* Hilty—and *Jezzy* Miller."

Johanna turned to stare at Aunt Jezzy. "Are you… You aren't…"

Aunt Jezzy didn't answer. She just sat primly on her seat, the faintest smile on her lips, one toe tapping the floor, and turned her hymnbook in a circle, very slowly, precisely three times.

"Can I drive you home?" Roland stood by the back porch, waiting as Johanna came down the steps with a market basket full of empty dishes in one hand. It was late afternoon, the Sunday communal meal had been served, the last prayers had been said and the women had cleaned up. Most of the families had already left to do their evening chores.

"The children and I came with *Mam* and Susanna and Rebecca, in our buggy," Johanna answered.

"I know, but J.J. and I want to take you home. He gets bored riding only with his *dat,* don't you, son?" He jiggled the brim of J.J.'s hat.

"Can we, *Mam?*" Katy asked, tugging on her skirt. "Can we ride with Roland and J.J.? Please, can we?"

Jonah had already gone ahead with Charley and Miriam. Charley had promised Jonah that he'd let him help feed the horses.

Roland looked at her expectantly, and she nodded. What did it matter if people saw them leaving together? Dorcas, *Grossmama* and two other women had already asked her after services if she and Roland were courting. It was being talked about all over the community. Grace called it the Amish Skype. How had Grace put it? *For people who don't have phones or internet service, you can pass news faster than NBC.* Johanna wasn't certain what Skype was or how it worked, but she wasn't about to admit that to Grace.

"J.J. and Katy can act as chaperones," Roland teased as Johanna climbed up into his buggy. Secretly, she was pleased that Roland had asked her to ride with him. You couldn't get much more respectable than riding home from services with a beau.

"Did you know about your aunt and Nip?" Roland flicked the leathers over his gelding's back. "Walk on," he ordered, and the standardbred started out at a brisk walk and then flowed smoothly into a steady pace.

"*Ne.* It was a total surprise to me. None of us expected her to ever marry."

"She'll make him a good wife. I imagine he's lonely. It's hard for a married man to suddenly be alone. A house feels empty without a woman's footsteps."

Behind them the two children giggled and wiggled, standing up to peer out at other buggies through the small window at the back of the vehicle.

"I'm sorry to hear about your brother-in-law," Roland continued. "Daniel."

The Saturday mail delivery had brought *Mam* a letter from Leah telling that her husband had suffered a relapse of the fever that had plagued him on and off during the rainy season. They had traveled to the city nearest to their mission, where Daniel had received first-rate care. He was expected to make a full recovery, but Leah had asked for prayers from her family. Samuel had taken the request further, and had asked the bishop to lead the congregation in prayer for Daniel's health.

"I worry about Leah, so far away with a baby. It could easily have been one of them who fell ill. Who knows what kinds of fever they have in the jungle? It was kind of Bishop Atlee to ask for everyone to remember Daniel in their devotions. Some bishops wouldn't be so understanding...since Leah left our faith to become Mennonite."

"Bishop Atlee is a kind man, one who truly walks in God's ways, as much as he can." Her hand rested on the bench seat, and Roland laid his lightly on top of it. "You must miss her a lot. I can't imagine being that far from Charley or Mary."

"I do miss her," Johanna agreed.

The buggy wheels and the horse's hooves made a comforting sound as they struck the road. *Sounds of home,* Johanna thought. And she wondered what strange sounds Leah heard in the Brazilian jungle.

"J.J. and I appreciated the soup and the raisin bread," Roland said. "Especially the raisin bread. We finished it up for breakfast this morning, all but three slices."

Johanna's eyes widened. "An entire loaf?"

"We were hungry, weren't we, son?"

"Ya, Dat," J.J. agreed. "We were hungry."

"When have you ever *not* been hungry?" Johanna teased. Tenseness drained out of her body, and she found that she was enjoying herself. When Roland wasn't pressing her to give him a decision, she loved being with him. It was almost like old times…maybe even better.

The journey home from Lydia and Norman's didn't take long, but when they came up the Yoder driveway and drove around to the farmyard, the first thing she saw was Charley's open buggy and Miriam's brown-and-white pony, Taffy, hitched to the rail.

"Why are Charley and Miriam here?" Johanna asked. "They didn't leave long before we did." The thought that something might have happened to Jonah occurred to her, and her stomach sank. "I hope—"

"Johanna!" Eli stepped out of the kitchen door. "Ruth's time. It's come."

Johanna was already scrambling down from the buggy. "Get Katy," she called over her shoulder to Roland. "Have you sent someone to call for the midwife?" Johanna asked her brother-in-law. "Where's Ruth? Is she—"

"In the house here," Eli answered. "My wife got it in her head that she wanted the babies to be born here, in the same room where she was born. Miriam's with her."

"Jonah?"

"In the barn. I thought it best to keep him out of the house, so I told him to feed the cows."

Johanna turned to Roland. "Thank you for bringing me home. I have to go to help Ruth." And then to Eli, "The midwife? Has someone sent for her?" Ruth had engaged the services of a midwife affiliated with an obstetrical practice in Dover. They'd planned a home birth from the beginning, but this was the first that Johanna had known that Ruth wanted to have the babies here at their childhood home.

"Charley," Eli answered, sounding a little lost. "Charley went to use the phone at the chair shop."

"How about if I take Jonah home with me?" Roland offered. "Eli's right. A birthing's no place for a young boy."

"Or a little girl." Johanna thought for a moment. "If you don't mind, take Katy to Fannie and Roman's."

Katy popped her head out of the buggy.

"Would you like that?" Johanna asked. "Would you like to go and play with Fannie's girls?"

"*Ya,*" Katy agreed. Fannie's youngest two were seven and nine, and Katy adored them.

"Don't worry about your children," Roland said. "I'll see to them."

Johanna nodded and hurried toward the house. Ruth had said she was tired that morning and that her back ached. *Mam* had rightfully advised her to stay home from services. "How is she?" Johanna asked Eli. "Is she certain it's her time?"

"She's certain," Eli said. "Her pains are coming regularly and her water broke about an hour ago."

"It sounds as though you're about to become a father," Johanna said, trying to sound cheerful. "I'd appreciate it if you'd see to our animals—the chickens, horses, cows—"

Eli nodded. "Glad to do it. Glad to have something useful to do."

Johanna smiled at him. "It will be all right, Eli. Women have been having babies since the beginning of time. Ruth is a strong woman, and she's in good health. Pray for her, and don't worry."

"I'll pray," Eli promised, "but don't expect me not to worry. That's my Ruth in there."

Chapter Fourteen

Leaving Roland to care for her children, Johanna entered the kitchen and found both Miriam and Ruth standing by the sink. Ruth was filling a teakettle. "Are you in labor?" Johanna asked. She took one look at Ruth's strained face and knew that the question was unnecessary. "How often are your contractions?"

"About ten minutes apart." Ruth set the kettle on the counter, leaned against the cabinets and closed her eyes. "They're strong," she admitted softly, "but nothing I can't deal with. I wouldn't have said anything yet if my water hadn't broken." She raised an eyebrow. "Eli's making a fuss for nothing. I'm not going to have these babies for hours."

"I tried to get her into bed." Miriam had her hands on her hips, an expression on her face that was exactly like *Mam's* when she was cross. "But Ruth wanted peppermint tea and insists on making it herself."

"I can't just sit around and wait. I've been waiting for months." Ruth exhaled slowly and her features relaxed. "There, better now. I'm not sick. I'm just having a baby... babies. *Mam* had seven of us, all born here at home." Her gaze locked with Johanna's, and Johanna saw a flicker of uncertainty. "I didn't want to go to the hospital—to have my babies come into the world in a strange room full of noise and Englishers. Do you think that's silly of me?"

Unconsciously, Ruth crumpled the corner of her apron between her fingers, a habit of hers when she was uncertain. As a young girl, Ruth had chewed the ends of her apron strings ragged, but thankfully, she seemed to have outgrown that. *Mam* had worried that she never would.

Ruth wasn't quite as brave as she lets on, Johanna decided, wondering if Ruth was concerned due to her own difficulty with Jonah's birth. Her son had come too early, and she'd nearly lost him. *"Ne,"* she said soothingly. "I think it makes sense, Ruth. Everything has gone well with you. And your midwife wouldn't have approved a home birth if she wasn't certain everything would go well." Ruth was always uneasy outside of her Amish community, and there was no reason for her to be in the hospital as long as the delivery went smoothly.

"Everyone says that twins come early, but these two are a week overdue. Linda said that if they weren't born soon, she would admit me and have Dr. Sharez induce labor." Ruth made a face. "I didn't want that. It seems unnatural. I always thought they would come in God's time."

"And so they have." Johanna removed her black bonnet and offered Ruth a comforting smile. "Well, I think tea is a good idea. We'd better make a big pot. *Mam,* Susanna and Rebecca will be home soon." She crossed the worn kitchen floor and touched Ruth's cheek. "You can do this, little sister. Look at our Leah. She gave birth to her baby in the jungle, with only Daniel to help her."

"And put it in a hammock," Miriam noted. "Everyone

in the house sleeps in a hammock. We did, too, when we were there visiting. You should have seen Charley trying to get the hang of it." She chuckled, and then went on. "Leah said she was afraid to put the baby in a cradle because there are giant ants." She grimaced. "At least Ruth doesn't have to worry about ants."

Ruth put the teakettle on the gas stove and lit the burner. "We sent Charley to call the midwife and I asked him to fetch Anna."

"That's another good reason for coming home to *Mam's* to deliver your precious babies," Johanna said. "*Mam's* house is a lot bigger than yours, and, counting her, the four of us and—"

"Five, counting Grace," Miriam corrected. "Don't forget Grace. She'll be home eventually."

"Five of us, plus Aunt Jezzy. And speaking of Aunt Jezzy…" In the excitement about Ruth's coming childbirth, Johanna had almost forgotten about Aunt Jezzy's surprise announcement. "You are never going to believe it, but Samuel called the banns for her and Nip after services and…"

Ruth chuckled. "Miriam told me. Good for her. I like Nip. He'll take good care of her." She reached up on a shelf and brought down an old tin box with Dutch flowers painted on it. "Peppermint all right with you?"

"I want chamomile," Miriam said and then went on in a rush, "I'm so excited for Aunt Jezzy. She's spent her whole life taking care of *Grossmama*. She deserves to be happy."

"I have to admit, I was shocked." Johanna dangled her bonnet by the strings. She hesitated, and then said what was foremost in her thoughts. "And being happy, if you're a woman, does it always mean marrying?" She sighed.

"Never mind me. Forget I asked that." She glanced at Ruth again. "This is a happy time for you, for all of us. Give me a few minutes to change out of my church clothes, and we'll all have that tea before you get too uncomfortable to enjoy it."

"Take your time," Ruth said as she put tea bags into mugs. Another contraction began and she gritted her teeth and rubbed the small of her back. "I'm not going anywhere."

The kitchen door opened and Eli poked his head in. "Ruth, are you all right? Why aren't you in bed?" He glanced at Johanna for confirmation. "Shouldn't she be—?"

"*Ne,* Eli." Ruth went to the door, and touched his hand lightly. "I'm fine," she assured him. "Stop worrying. Surely you must have animals to feed."

Johanna turned away, strangely touched by the tenderness between them. Among her people, public shows of affection, even between husband and wife, were rare. But Ruth and Eli were a lot like *Mam* and *Dat.* They didn't seem to care who saw that they loved each other.

"We'll take good care of her," Johanna called over her shoulder. She didn't want to intrude, but as she walked into the hallway that led to the parlor, she couldn't help hearing Eli's reply.

"I fed them. And I watered them all and forked down hay."

"Then go home and feed Charley's stock and our own," Ruth suggested. "This is no place for a man. This is women's work."

"But I want to do something."

"Pray for our babies," she said.

"And for you, Ruth. I—"

Johanna couldn't hear the rest of what Eli said, but the sense of his caring and his love for her sister brought a catch to her throat. Ruth had found a good man. He made her happy. And if she felt the restraint of being subject to her husband's will, Ruth had never hinted at it by word or action.

Would that Wilmer and I could have had such a relationship, she thought wistfully. He'd been away the night Jonah had come into the world, and he'd only come to the hospital twice, once to pick her up when she was released and again, weeks later, when their tiny son had finally been strong enough to come home. The Amish didn't believe in insurance, as the English did, feeling that paying outsiders to cover unexpected losses showed a lack of faith in the Lord. Her own C-section and Jonah's long stay in the neonatal care unit had saddled them with a heavy debt. And Wilmer had unconsciously blamed Jonah for the burden.

As she climbed the stairs, she reminded herself that life moves on. *Wilmer is dead, gone on to a better place, and God has blessed me with two healthy children.* Today, she had learned that her dear aunt was marrying, and Ruth—after waiting so long—was going to become a mother. Maybe her mother was right. Maybe it was time she put the past behind her and looked to the future…whatever that would be.

The sounds of Susanna's whoop of excitement, Jeremiah's high-pitched barking and the bustle of more people coming into the house quickened Johanna's step. She promised herself that she wouldn't wallow in her own concerns, but give herself wholeheartedly to Ruth's special day.

In her room, Johanna changed quickly into a clean,

everyday work dress and apron. And by the time she got back to the kitchen, she found not only Rebecca, *Mam* and Susanna there, but Anna, Aunt Jezzy and *Grossmama,* as well. Ruth was refilling the teakettle while Susanna fetched sugar, milk and lemon slices for their grandmother's tea.

"Marrying, at your age." *Grossmama* shook her finger at Aunt Jezzy. "And to a man old enough to be your grandfather. It's indecent."

Aunt Jezzy giggled, blushed and twirled her tea cup. "She doesn't think I'm old enough to get married," she said to Johanna.

Johanna tried not to show her amusement. Aunt Jezzy was *Grossmama's* younger sister but, still, a woman in her sixties. Her grandmother's mind often wandered these days, and her family was usually at odds as whether to laugh or cry at her stubborn declarations...especially the one where she believed *Dat, Grossmama's* only son, was still alive and in the barn milking.

"At fifteen?" *Grossmama* exclaimed, insisting that Aunt Jezzy was a teenage girl. "The bishop won't allow it. It's your duty to stay home and help your mother raise the younger children."

Johanna had learned that the easiest way to handle her grandmother was to agree with whatever she said and wait for her to move on to a new topic. The strangest thing was that for much of the time, she was perfectly lucid and had an excellent memory.

Johanna found a seat beside *Grossmama* and slipped an arm around her shoulders. "But Nip will be a good provider," she said. "People order his bridles and halters from all over the country." *Grossmama* frowned, and Johanna went on. "And you married young, yourself, *ne?*"

Grossmama snorted. "And lived to regret it. All those useless girls and only a single son to support me in my old age." She pointed at Anna. "My Jonas's wife. She's a good girl. She's given him two strong sons and this sweet baby girl." She waved a wrinkled finger at tiny Rose, who was now cradled in *Mam's* arms.

Johanna didn't try to explain that Anna was Jonas's daughter and stepmother to Samuel's two boys and three little girls. Baby Rose was Anna and Samuel's child. That part, at least, was true. "But your mother has other girls at home to help her," Johanna said, humoring her grandmother. "Better Jezzy marry her good harness maker before some other *meadle* snatches him up." Johanna hoped God would forgive her for encouraging her *Grossmama's* fancies, but arguing with her just made her worse. And there should be no strife here today with Ruth's babies coming so soon.

"True, true," *Grossmama* agreed. "Jezzy's nothing to look at, and her butter never firms up. I always made the best butter, sweet and salty and yellow as the sun, so my *Dat* always said."

"Your butter is the best," Aunt Jezzy agreed with a twinkle in her eye. "And our Ruthie takes after you." She patted her sister's hand and smiled at Johanna. "And I will be close by if you need anything, just next door."

Johanna tilted her head and her eyes widened in curiosity. "Next door?"

"Ya." Anna joined the conversation. "Nip has bought five acres from Samuel just across the road from our house. He wants to leave his harness shop and house for his second son, Joel, and build a new house for Aunt Jezzy. He thought it might be hard for her to change

church districts and leave all of us. So she and Nip will be our new neighbors."

"I never!" Aunt Martha and her daughter Dorcas stood in the open doorway, arms full. "You could have knocked me over with a feather when Samuel cried the banns for Aunt Jezzy and Nip. And him to build her a new house! If we have snow in midsummer or Rebecca married a Quaker, I'd not be more surprised."

"Just a little house." Aunt Jezzy hurried to take the pound cake from Aunt Martha's hands while Dorcas carried a heavy kettle of soup and set it on the stove. "The two of us don't need so much room and Joel will be wanting a wife soon. Best we leave him to it. He's a fine harness maker, Nip says, and walking out with a girl from Belleville. Easier for the young folk to make a start without old folks peering over their shoulders."

"I never," Aunt Martha repeated. "That's more words than I ever heard you string together at one time, and you quiet as mouse about courting Nip." She shook her head and took down a coffee cup. "We've come to help out," she said. "Had a vegetable beef soup warming on the back of the stove and said to Reuben, 'I'll just take that soup and that lemon pound cake to Hannah's. I've sat at many a birthing.'" She offered a tight smile to Ruth. "Sensible for you to have your little ones here. No need for English doctors and hospitals." She threw a glance at Dorcas. "You see that, daughter? Ruth found a good man, and her with red hair and freckles and a tongue in her mouth that won't stop. You could do the same if you'd put your mind to—"

"Am I too late?" Grace said, barely visible under a sliding tower of pizza boxes, as she came into the kitchen. "Ruth didn't have the babies—"

"Not yet." Ruth rose to her feet and extended her arms to catch a falling pizza. "Didn't you and John have a meeting with your preacher tonight? About your wedding?"

"Daniel's aunt got a call from her cousin Arnie Brown. Noodle Troyer said you were in labor. Pizza Tonight messed up the order for our adult evening Sunday-school class and brought us double. The minister said there'd be a lot of people here, and Hannah shouldn't have to cook and I should just bring the extra pizzas." Grace dumped four boxes on the counter. "Are you really going to have the babies here?" Grace demanded. "Tonight?" She looked around. "With all of us here?"

Ruth chuckled. "I hope we'll have them tonight. And this is just what I want. My family—"

A car horn sounded outside, and Johanna leaned back to push aside the curtain and peer out. A blue sedan with a stork decal on the door was just pulling up to the fence. "There's the midwife," Johanna said. "But there's another woman with her."

"That's the RN, Jennifer Bryant," Ruth answered. "She's... Ohhh." She gasped. "That's a strong one."

"Good." Johanna clasped her hands together. "I guess that means we're going to have these babies sooner rather than later."

As Johanna had predicted, Ruth's labor and delivery went as smoothly as possible. Red-haired Adam, six pounds and fourteen ounces, slid into the midwife's hands at 5:43 a.m., followed only twenty-one minutes later by blond and chubby Luke, who outweighed his older brother by five ounces. Both boys had dark blue eyes and fair complexions. Other than hair color, they seemed as identical and content as two peas in a pod as they stared with wide-eyed innocence as joyous women gathered to welcome them into the world.

By ten o'clock that morning, the nurse and the midwife had given final instructions and gone, promising to return several times over the coming week. Aunt Martha and Dorcas had driven *Grossmama,* Anna and Rose home, and Aunt Jezzy had gone to take a nap. Ruth and Eli were sharing tea and slices of blueberry pie at *Mam's* table while Irwin admired the new babies.

"They're so small," Irwin said. "They have little fingers and noses."

"Ya," Susanna agreed. "Little noses." She giggled. "King David and me. We're getting married. Having two babies." Her round face beamed. "Girl babies."

"Not anytime soon, I hope," *Mam* said. "Now, be a big help to me, and you and Irwin go feed the chickens."

Johanna sat in Aunt Jezzy's rocker with Luke while Eli cradled Adam in the crook of his arm. She looked down at Luke. Had her own felt this sweet in her arms... been this tiny and perfect? She knew that Jonah had been even smaller, but it was easy to forget the softness of a newborn's skin and the scent of a clean baby.

Adam was fast asleep, but Luke's eyes were open, his pink lips pursed and dribbling a few drops of milk. Ruth had dressed the boys in pale blue cotton gowns, long-sleeved, that tied at the bottom. White, tight-fitting caps covered their heads, but ringlets peeped out at the forehead and cheeks.

"I'm surprised they have so much hair," Eli said.

Ruth smiled and her weary but happy gaze met Johanna's. Ruth's face was pale, but other than the shadows under her eyes, she hardly looked like a woman who'd stayed awake all night and delivered twins. The nurse had urged her to try to get some sleep, but Ruth insisted on getting up and coming to the kitchen for breakfast.

Johanna had been concerned, but *Mam* wasn't.

"I was exactly the same way," *Mam* pronounced. "When the house quiets down and the excitement wears off, they can all three sleep."

"Mam!" Miriam called from the pantry. "Where's the detergent?" She and Rebecca had volunteered to do the Monday wash.

"There a new box behind... Never mind, I'll find it," *Mam* answered, rising to her feet. On her way out of the kitchen, she stopped to gaze down at the baby in Johanna's arms. "The Lord has blessed you and Eli," she said to Ruth. "Now comes the hard part, raising them to be men like Eli and my Jonas."

"We'll do our best," Ruth promised, stroking Adam's cheek. Then she glanced over at Johanna. "I can't believe they're here. I can't believe..."

"There was ever a time without them," Johanna finished for her. She tucked her index finger into Luke's hand and he tightened his grip around it. A flood of emotion brought tears to Johanna's eyes.

She gathered Luke in her arms and cradled him against her shoulder. He wiggled and made small baby noises that tugged at her heart. *I need another baby.* And suddenly, all the doubts about remarrying that had troubled her for months dissolved away into nothing. Family was what was important. And if she wanted more children, she would have to marry. "I have to go and see Roland," she said abruptly.

Ruth chuckled. "It's about time." She looked at Eli,

whose expression was blank. "Poor Roland. He doesn't know it, but his single days are numbered."

Eli glanced at Johanna. "You Yoder girls... Do you have any idea what's she's talking about?"

Johanna didn't answer. She passed sweet Luke to *Mam,* grabbed a scarf off the peg by the door and tied it over her hair as she hurried out the door.

"Where are you off to in such a hurry?" her mother called after her.

"Roland's!" Johanna's heart pounded in her chest. She crossed the yard, nearly colliding with Irwin, who was coming out of the barn. "Could you hitch Blackie for me?" she said. "To *Dat's* courting buggy."

"Now?" Irwin grimaced and reached up to scratch a mosquito bite on his arm. "Jonas's courting buggy? There's two bags of feed sitting in front of—"

"That's the carriage I want," she said. "I need the courting buggy. It's past time I found a husband."

Chapter Fifteen

Johanna drove Blackie at a fast trot down the lane toward the blacktop. She knew she was being impulsive, but she couldn't help herself. She'd always been that way; once she made up her mind on something, she had to do something about it. And she was going to do something about her and Roland.

She'd had enough courting. What woman her age courted, anyway? If Roland wanted to marry her, as he said he did, it was time. They were a well-matched couple. They had grown up with the same values and the same customs and friends. Despite what had happened before between them when they were teens, she knew the measure of Roland as a man. She could give herself entirely to the partnership with him without fear that he would be unkind to her children or fail to provide for them.

It had been difficult and had required many hours of prayer and many tears, but gradually, she had forgiven Wilmer for his weaknesses…for his illness. She was not so much locking the gate on that part of her life, but opening a window to let in the fresh air of spring after a long, dark winter. Wilmer was in God's care, and it was not her place to judge Wilmer or to speak ill to Jonas and Katy of their father. Instead, she had sought diligently for something honest she could tell them and found a gentle truth. *Wilmer was a man who spent his lifetime seeking God and struggling with his own human failures to live according to the faith.* That should give both her children a sense of satisfaction and hope that the Lord would consider his sickness and take pity on him.

"I'll not make the mistakes I made with Wilmer," Johanna said aloud. Blackie heard her and perked up his ears. She reined him to a halt as they neared the road and looked both ways to see that no traffic was coming. Then she flicked the leathers over his back to guide him out onto the shoulder that bordered the high-crowned blacktop.

"I'll curb my willful nature," she pronounced, more to herself than to the horse. Blackie tossed his head, but whether he agreed or disagreed or was simply shaking off a horsefly, she didn't know. Her thoughts were now flying in so many directions…life was so full of possibilities.

From the first day she exchanged vows with Roland, she would put aside her own selfish needs. She would be more like Anna, making an effort to curb her stubbornness and to remember that her husband was ordained by God to be the head of the family. Not that she wouldn't speak up, but she'd allow herself to be guided by her husband.

In return, she would have her own house again. J.J., Jonah and Katy would have both a mother and a father, and she and Roland could work together to teach all three of them, bringing them up to be good and productive members of the community. Her fears that she would be a burden on her mother would vanish, and she would have the pleasure of cleaning and reorganizing Roland's home from top to bottom. And, God willing, she and Roland would be blessed by more children...her own sweet babies to cuddle and care for.

By the time she turned into Roland's lane, Johanna's spirits were high. It had always been that way for her. She would struggle for days or weeks with a decision, but once it had been made, she threw herself into whatever it was wholeheartedly. "How do you like this barnyard?" she asked Blackie. "And the stable? It looks comfortable to me. Maybe you'll be living here soon." She couldn't help but smile at her own silliness in talking to a horse as if it understood. If anyone heard her, they'd think she'd been eating too much May butter and was addled.

It was a good place, this farm of Roland's. It pleased Johanna to see the buildings tidy, the roofs sound, the siding and concrete block walls painted red with white trim, the doors hanging straight, with no sagging. Likewise, the windmill—blades turning regularly in the wind—seemed as solid and substantial as the rest of the outbuildings. It was evident that Roland was a hard worker, a man who believed in keeping his barn and sheds and house in shape.

She reined in Blackie near the hitching rail and gave a sigh of relief to see that Roland's buggy was still in the open shed.

Her gaze fell on a bare patch at the back of the house. There was a low brick wall running around it, telling Johanna that someone had once planted flowers there. It would be a good spot for climbing roses, she thought. She'd always favored red roses, the old-fashioned kind that took the heat well and thrived with only a little care.

She could imagine the way the air would smell early in the morning, and decided that when she came to be the wife in this house, she would plant flowers everywhere.

At that instant, Jonah and J.J. came running around the chicken coop. Jonah was in front, and he had lengths of baling twine tied to each arm. J.J. was behind him, holding the strings as though they were reins. When he caught sight of her, J.J. stopped short and dropped the reins onto the ground.

Jonah snorted like a horse, jumped into the air, and then saw her and began to giggle. *"Mam!"* he cried and ran up and hugged her. "J.J. has a cart, like a wagon, but with two wheels. We were playing horse and…and… Are my baby cousins—did they come last night?"

"Early this morning." She squeezed him tightly. "Good morning, J.J.," she said with a smile, and then went on about the babies. "Two little boys, Adam and Luke, one with yellow hair and one with ginger."

"Like me!"

"Like you," she agreed. "It looks like you two are having fun. I hope you helped Roland with chores this morning." She looked around but didn't see him. "Is J.J.'s father in the house?"

The back door opened and Roland's sister Mary stepped out. "Morning!" she called. "Did everything go well with Ruth?"

"It did, God be thanked. The babies are healthy and Ruth is already up and on her feet." Johanna straightened Jonah's straw hat. "Go and play while you can," she said. "We'll be going home soon."

"I get to be the horse next," J.J. called.

"All right." Jonah nodded. "But first you have to catch

me!" With that, he darted off, J.J. shrieking merrily and scampering after him.

"I've just made a fresh pot of coffee," Mary said, "and corn muffins for the boys. Would you like to come in and have some? It seems so long since we've had time for a good chat."

Johanna hesitated. She liked Mary, considered her one of her good friends, and she always enjoyed visiting with her, but today... Johanna swallowed, trying to ease the tightness in her throat. "Actually," she admitted, "I've come to talk to Roland."

"He's not here," Mary answered. "I'm sorry, but he was called to his new job at Windward Farms. John Hartman picked him up early this morning. That's why I'm here with the boys." Mary's expression showed her concern. "I hope it's nothing bad," she said.

Johanna's stomach clenched. "He's not here? But I thought... I saw his buggy and..." Mary's words sank in. John had picked him up. *Roland wasn't here.* She'd gotten her nerve up and come to say her piece, and it was all for nothing.

"I hope whatever it is..." Mary brought a hand to her mouth, clearly torn between wanting to know what was so important between them and not wanting to seem nosy. "You two..." She took a deep breath and went on in a rush. "I hope that your courting...you know what I mean." She flushed. "I guess what I'm trying to say is that I'd love to have you as my sister...if..."

Johanna smiled. "You know I can think of no one I'd rather have for a new sister than you."

"Sorry you missed him. I don't know how long before he'll be home." She motioned toward the direction the boys had gone. "Anyway, J.J. and Jonah are having such a good time, would you care if your boy stayed here? I can get my driver to drop him off at the house when I go home. It was short notice." She chuckled. "Roland sent John for me this morning after he got word he was needed. It's a wonder John gets any vet business done, what with all his running around, driving the Amish."

Johanna felt the energy drain out of her. Suddenly, the strain of being up all night without sleep began to sink in. If she couldn't speak to Roland this morning, she wondered if she'd have the nerve to try again tomorrow. "You don't mind watching Jonah?" she asked. "Are you sure you don't mind?"

"Ne." Mary opened the screen door wider to let a striped tabby cat walk into the kitchen. "Not at all. Jonah is always good for me. Helpful and well mannered."

Johanna grimaced. "Better here than at home, I suppose. Sometimes, he can be a handful."

"Natural for boys," Mary said. "You should see some of my cousins' kids. But Jonah will be a help. I've got some string beans for them to snap after their lunch, and eggs to gather, but mostly they can play. J.J. gets lonely here all by himself. I'm glad he has a chance to be with Jonah today."

"If you're sure..." Johanna glanced back at the hitching rail where Blackie waited. "He's at Windward, you say. That isn't far. I think..." Suddenly, she remembered that she'd come away from the house in just her old blue scarf, not fitting to be seen by English or by strangers on the road. She didn't want to shame herself or Roland. But Mary was wearing her starched white *Kapp*...

"Mary? Could I borrow your prayer *Kapp* and bonnet?"

"My *Kapp* and bonnet? Of course, but...sure." She

went back into the house and returned in less than a minute with her black bonnet. "Why do you need it?" But she was already removing the pins that held her *Kapp* in place.

"I'm going to find Roland," Johanna said, trading her worn scarf for Mary's *Kapp* and bonnet. "What I need to say, I have to say now, and if it means following him to his work, I'll have to do it."

"If it's so important, you should go," Mary encouraged.

Johanna thought she read admiration mixed with curiosity in Mary's eyes. "Roland may be shocked to see me there, but I only need to talk to him for a few minutes," she said, more to convince herself than Mary. "It's just that this can't wait."

"Ya," Mary agreed. Then, impulsively, she hugged Johanna and kissed her cheek. "Be careful out on the roads among the English," she cautioned. "I can't have anything happen to my new sister-to-be."

Johanna tied Mary's bonnet over the white *Kapp* and hurried toward her buggy. She hoped Roland wouldn't be angry to see her at his place of work, but if his first reaction was disapproval, maybe he'd change his mind once he heard what she had to say. And now that she'd made up her mind, she had to get it out or burst.

Mary waved as Johanna untied Blackie, got into the buggy and turned around in the yard. "Good luck!" Mary called.

"Thanks," Johanna replied, heart racing. "I'll need it."

Roland, accompanied by John Hartman, approached one of the main paddocks at Windward Farms, where a trainer was working with a yearling colt. "That's Sea

You Later, out of Seaside Belle," John said, pointing to the bay colt Rodney Dale was lunging. "You wouldn't believe how much they paid for him."

"You're right," Roland agreed with a grin. "I probably wouldn't."

He liked John, and he was glad he'd been there today to ease the awkwardness of meeting the trainer and grooms that he hadn't had an opportunity to meet before. Usually, Roland was fine around the English, but horsemen could be difficult. He had to gain their respect by doing a good job with their animals. And some of the horses were worth more than he made in a year.

Still, horses were horses, and he knew horses. He'd learned his skills from an uncle, and he was still learning. John had been headed to Windward Farms to give some vaccinations, and he'd offered to give Roland a ride there, and promised to stop back later in the day to take him home.

John, a local veterinarian, was betrothed to Johanna's half sister Grace, and if his own marriage went off with Johanna, as Roland hoped, he and John would be brothers-in-law. For all his education, John didn't seem as English as the others did to Roland. Of course, John was Mennonite, and the Amish and the Mennonite shared history and beliefs. John might not have been born in Kent County, but he fit in well here, and was well liked by the Amish and English farmers and horsemen alike. Roland was pleased to count John as a friend, and John seemed to return the sentiment.

The trainer brought the young horse to a halt and waved Roland and John into the paddock. "I wanted you to check out his hooves," Rodney said. "I think there's a crack in—" He stopped and looked past the two men. "Don't see that often around here."

Roland turned to see Johanna in the Yoder buggy pull in front of the barn, and he walked quickly toward her. His first thought was that something had happened to J.J., and a band tightened around his chest. "Johanna?" he called. "Are the boys all right?" He went to her and placed a hand on the dashboard.

"Our boys are fine. With Mary," Johanna insisted. "And Ruth was delivered of two healthy sons. She's good, as well."

Confusion made his voice sharper than he intended. "Then why—"

"I know this is not the place," she said, glancing at the other men, then back at him. "But it is the time. And if I didn't come now, I might not have had the courage to say this again. Please, Roland." She clutched at his arm. "We need to talk. Privately."

"All right." He nodded and glanced back to where John and Rodney waited. "I'll just be a minute," he shouted to them.

John raised a hand in acknowledgment.

Roland cleared his throat. "Say what you've come to say, then, Johanna." His first thought was *I'm going to lose her*. He wanted to cover his ears and shout, anything to block out the words that would mean it was over between them. "But you do know that I love you," he managed. "That I've never stopped loving you."

"Roland…" she began.

"Ne." He held up a hand. "It's true, God help me. I married a good woman, respected her, cared for her, honored her. But secretly, in my heart, I've always held a place for you, Johanna." He swallowed, trying to rid

his mouth of the taste of ashes. "I promise you, if you'll give me the chance, you'll never find another man who will cherish and care for you and your children as I will."

"Will you stop talking for just one minute," she said, "and let me speak my piece?" Tears filled her eyes and spilled over, catching the sunlight and sparkling on her freckled cheeks. "I'm not breaking up with you, *dummkopf.* I want you to ask Samuel to read our banns at the next service. I've done all you asked of me, and I think we should stop all this game-playing and marry. As soon as permitted."

The ground shifted under him. He couldn't catch his breath. She wanted him—wanted to marry him. She loved him as he loved her. He wasn't losing her after all. "Johanna... I..." He looked into her eyes, and a chill seeped through his rising joy. "Marry now?" he asked.

"*Ya,* marry now, or stop seeing each other altogether." Her chin firmed. "If you want me to be your wife, you need to make a decision."

A part of him wanted to pull her out of the buggy and swing her in his arms. *They could be married!*

But a part of him was immediately suspicious. He knew Johanna well and this was not like her—to come here declaring her love. "Why now? Why are you saying this here...today?" he asked, searching her beautiful face. "Have your feelings about me changed from last time we talked about this?"

Her gaze shifted, no longer meeting his, and Roland felt his hopes sink. *Let it go. Take her hand, tell her you'll have the banns read next Sunday and be thankful for what you have.* But he couldn't do that.

"Do you love me, Johanna?" He leaned closer to her, looking up into her face. "Truly love me?"

She hesitated and when she spoke again, her voice took on a stubborn tone. "Why does that matter?"

"It matters to *me*."

She hesitated, then shifted her gaze to his again. "Do you want me to lie to you?" Now he heard anger in her voice. "I loved you once, and you broke my heart. I won't do that again, Roland. I can't. I'll marry you and give you all that's due a husband, but don't ask for love, Roland, because I don't have it to give."

Chapter Sixteen

Roland's face went gray, and for an instant, Johanna wished she could take back the words. She didn't want to cause him pain—but would it be fair to go into a marriage without being honest? "Roland," she began in a softer voice. "I don't—"

"Ne." His jawline went rigid. The lines of his face grew taut, and beneath his worn blue shirt, farrier's muscles knotted and strained against the thin fabric.

He needs someone to sew him a new shirt. The notion came swiftly and unbidden, even as the passion in his voice pierced her thoughts.

"Ne. It won't be like that," he said. "I won't allow your foolish pride to ruin what we could have together."

"Pride?" The sharpness of the accusation stung with a black wasp's venom. "I'll admit to a stubborn nature," she replied, looking down at him from her perch on the buggy seat, "but you can't accuse me of *Hochmut.*" The sin of pride was a major fault in the followers of her faith, and to have Roland think it of her—let alone speak it aloud—was an insult.

"I do accuse you of pride. And of being judgmental."

"I'm not," she protested, cheeks burning. "How can you say such a thing?"

"Who was the one who set her mind against Grace? Who refused to give her a chance—who didn't want to accept her as the sister she is to you now?"

A metallic taste spread across the roof of Johanna's mouth. *"Ya,"* she admitted grudgingly. "I was uncharitable toward Grace, at first, but it was to protect *Mam*."

Roland was quiet.

Her stomach clenched and she felt the sting of tears on the inside of her eyelids. Whether the tears were anger or regret, she didn't know. "I apologized to Grace, and told her I was wrong. I'm just slow to come around sometimes. Even Anna thinks we share *Grossmama* Yoder's stubborn streak."

Roland glanced toward the ring where the two men waited and then turned his attention back to her. "I never held your stubborn nature against you," he said. "I've always admired it. What I'm saying is that it's your pride that's the problem. And if you can't see it when it's staring you in the face, there's no chance for us."

Johanna recoiled. "How is it pride to remember that you betrayed me? Betrayed the promises we'd made to each other?"

A dark flush washed over his chiseled features. "We were young, Johanna. I was young and foolish, and I let Emma Mae Troyer kiss me." He threw up his hands. "I shouldn't have let it happen, but honestly—"

"I don't want to hear it." Johanna grabbed for the reins, but Roland was quicker. He clasped them tightly in one hand and seized her hand with the other. She tried to pull away, but he held on to her.

"You will listen," he said quietly, but firmly. "If you

never speak a word to me again, you will hear me out." His mouth tightened into a thin line, and his hard gaze penetrated hers.

Johanna felt goose bumps rise on her arms. Never in his life had Roland spoken to her in this tone. And yet, even as she wanted to contest what he was saying, she wasn't in the least frightened—not as she had been when Wilmer had been in one of his rages.

She began to wish she hadn't come here…that she hadn't given in to her impulsiveness. She should have just waited and approached Roland that evening at home. This certainly wasn't how she meant this to turn out.

"It was a harvest party. At Saul Beachy's farm."

"I've heard all I want to hear about you and Emma Mae Troyer—enough to last me a lifetime."

Roland released her hand. "You need to listen to me," he said. "Please listen."

She tucked her hand under her apron, trying to shake off the warmth of his touch, trying to deny that some small part of her had wanted him to go on holding her. She stared straight ahead. "I'm listening."

"Some of the older fellows, my cousin Al and some of his buddies, had bought beer," Roland said. "Two of the English girls were drinking, too. I didn't see any Amish girls drink alcohol, but you know how the young people are up there. Most of the Lancaster communities allow *Rumspringa*. Some kids behave badly before they settle down and join the church."

"And you?" she flung at him. "You didn't see that it was wrong?"

"I didn't drink any of the beer."

"But you didn't leave, either, did you? You knew we

were going to get married, but you didn't care if you shamed me by taking part in such a gathering?"

"It was just a barn frolic. We were bringing in shocks and husking corn. Al brought a radio and everyone was listening to the music." He swallowed, and she saw uncertainty cloud his eyes. "It was exciting," Roland admitted. "We were just joking around, having fun. Some people were dancing. I knew it wasn't something my father would approve of, but I didn't know how to get out of it and not feel embarrassed. I'd come with Al, and I knew that if I hitched a ride home to my uncle's, he'd want to know where Al was."

"So you knew it was wrong, but you went along with it anyway," she said.

Roland nodded. "I can't blame Al or anyone else. The fault was mine."

She felt her cheeks grow warm. "So you thought you might as well join in the fun and kiss Emma Mae?"

"Ne." Roland shook his head. "It wasn't like that. We were playing a game—shucking corn to see who was fastest. Emma Mae got the red ear of corn, and the other kids started shouting, 'Forfeit! Forfeit!'"

Johanna gritted her teeth.

"Al yelled for Emma Mae to kiss a guy for her forfeit, and everybody started clapping and stamping their feet. She picked me, and—"

"You didn't say no."

Roland shook his head. "I didn't say no."

Johanna turned her head away, but she couldn't keep the familiar ache from rising in her chest. It still hurt, after all this time.

"Emma Mae…wasn't a pretty girl. She was plain, really plain, with big teeth, and all I could think was that if I turned her down, everybody would laugh at her."

"You didn't care that it would hurt me."

He exhaled softly. "None of us thought the Pennsylvania State Police would bust into the barn with searchlights, bullhorns and half the church elders in Lancaster. Everyone went crazy. Kids were running in all directions, trying to get out of there. One of the guys threw his beer, and it splashed all over me. That's why the police thought I'd been drinking. Because I smelled like beer."

Johanna's eyes narrowed. "Go on."

"We were taken into the police station for alcohol breathalyzer tests."

"And you were unlucky enough to have some newspaper reporter take your picture as you were being loaded into the police van? The picture we all saw in the Englisher newspaper."

"*Ya,* I was," he said.

She considered his explanation. Roland had never lied to her. If he said that he hadn't intended to kiss Emma Mae, she had to take him at his word. But... She inhaled deeply, feeling almost dizzy. Was that really all that had happened? Had she really changed the outcome of her whole life...of *their* lives, for something so small?

"I passed the test, Johanna," Roland said. "The machine didn't register any alcohol on my breath. I *looked* guilty, but it proved that I was innocent, and they didn't press charges against me. I was never arrested for underage drinking."

Johanna remembered, with a sick feeling, that the opinions in the Amish community had been harsh after the incident. Sermons had been preached against evil and worldly behavior. The bishop had named Roland Byler as one of those who had shamed the faith, his parents and community. Even *Dat,* who rarely lost his temper, had been furious with what Roland had done.

"Johanna?"

"I don't know what to say, Roland."

"I'm not the stupid boy I was then. That one mistake cost me everything. You know that I repented and joined the church. Since then, I've tried to live our faith as best I can."

"So this is all my fault?"

"Doesn't the Bible teach us to forgive? If I wronged you—and I did—haven't I made up for it? It's time for you to forgive me. Truly forgive me. It's the only way we can go on from here."

She pressed her fingertips to her forehead. "Why didn't you come to me after it happened, Roland? I loved you then. It would have been so much easier if you—"

"But I *did* come," he insisted. "Don't you remember? As soon as I got home from Lancaster. I went to your house to explain, but Jonas turned me away."

"Dat?" She stared down at him in disbelief. *"Dat* kept you from speaking to me?"

"*Ya.* He said I was not the kind of man he wanted as a husband to you and a father to your children. He told me not to set foot on his land again."

She shook her head slowly. "He wouldn't have done that."

"I asked him if you felt the same way, and he said you did. He said I had nothing to say that you wanted to hear—that we were finished."

"I didn't know," she murmured, looking down, then back at him. "And you believed him? That I wouldn't want to talk face-to-face? Does that sound like me?"

He shrugged his broad shoulders. "Again, I was young. And embarrassed and feeling so guilty. I thought of Jonas as more than a friend, almost as a second father. Why wouldn't I have believed him?"

"So you went away."

"*Ya.* I left Delaware the following day, spent the summer harvesting grain in Kansas and Nebraska. And when I finally came home, Mary told me that you were promised to Wilmer Detweiler, and that you seemed happy. I didn't want to hurt you again… I thought it was too late for us."

The tears that had threatened were gone, replaced with an emptiness. Could *Dat* really have sent him away and never told her? She didn't want to believe it, but Roland had never lied to her…and *Dat* wasn't here to ask.

"You need to give me time to think," she said as she reached for the reins again. "This is a lot to think about."

This time, he placed the reins in her hands. "You can go, but you can't keep running from the truth. It's not what I did at that frolic that you've held against me all these years. It's that I embarrassed you. It's your pride that has kept us apart, Johanna. And it's your pride that keeps you from admitting that you still love me."

Anger flared in her chest and she lifted the reins. His words were so hurtful. "That's the way you feel?"

"It is."

"Then I'll take that as a refusal of my proposal. You can consider our courtship officially ended," she said, looking straight ahead. "You were right. It's too late for us, Roland. If I am so stubborn and full of pride, I'm not the woman you want as a wife."

All the way home from the horse farm, Johanna tried to hold herself together. She didn't dare shed a single tear;

she had to pick up Katy from Fannie and Roman's, and if she allowed herself to weaken, she'd fall apart. Having Fannie and her children or Katy see her cry wasn't something she wanted to do.

At Fannie's, Katy had come running, full of chatter about her visit and spilling over with questions about her aunt Ruth's new baby boys. Fannie and her girls had been just as excited, and Johanna had been forced to pretend a joyfulness she didn't feel at the moment. Not that she wasn't thrilled for Ruth and Eli, or that she didn't welcome the twins wholeheartedly. But the confrontation she'd had with Roland had her shaking inside.

When she and Katy had finally taken their leave of Fannie and driven home, Johanna had hoped to find a quiet corner where she could think. But there seemed to be none. Although Eli had taken Ruth and the boys home to sleep in their own beds, *Mam's* place was still teeming with family.

Rebecca had offered to keep Anna's children while she went to make supper for the new parents, and—much to Katy's delight—the three girls were running in and out of the house in a spirited game of tag, cheered on by Susanna. Irwin, Rudy, Peter and two of Irwin's cousins were playing ball in the pasture beside the barn. Aunt Jezzy and Nip Hilty were sitting on the front porch, snapping string beans. Johanna's hope that she could escape to solitude in the garden was dashed by Susanna's declaration that *Mam* and Miriam were in the garden setting out a row of zucchini plants.

The kitchen was no better. Aunt Martha and *Grossmama* were trying to teach Lydia Beachy a fancy stitch they were using to knit sweaters for Ruth's babies, and Dorcas was putting together a huge pan of blueberry crisp. As Katy scrambled to catch up with Anna's Lori Ann, Mae and Naomi, Rebecca came out of the pantry with a bucket and mop. She'd just finished scrubbing the floor and was about to do the same in the downstairs bathroom and front parlor.

Johanna tried to make small talk with her aunt and cousin, agreeing that, yes, Ruth's twins looked like Yoders, and no, her labor hadn't been long, all the while edging her way toward the far doorway. Johanna loved her family and she was used to having a lot of people around her. But she didn't want to look foolish by bursting into tears and she certainly didn't want to have to explain to Aunt Martha the reason for such outlandish behavior.

Aunt Martha's pointed questions about whether *Mam* had planted an unusual amount of celery this year, and if Johanna thought there might be any more surprise announcements at the next church meeting, was the final straw. "I have to go!" Johanna said and fled the kitchen.

By the time she reached the bottom of the steps, all Johanna's self-control was gone and she was sobbing with great noisy gasps. Almost blindly she raced up the steps, down the second-floor hallway and into her bedroom. She slammed the door behind her and flung herself across her neatly made bed.

Tears came in floods. She buried her face in her Star of Bethlehem quilt and wept until she could hardly catch her breath. She was still crying when a persistent rapping at the door broke through her misery.

"Go away," she said. "Leave me alone."

"Johanna? Are you all right?" It was Rebecca's voice.

"Please," she said. "I just want to…be…" Another sob. "Alone."

The door hinges squeaked, and Johanna heard footsteps on the pine floorboards. "What's wrong?" The mattress gave as Rebecca sank down on the bed beside her. She handed her the tissue box from the table beside the bed. "Tell me what's going on."

"Roland," Johanna rasped.

"Ah."

"We… He… I went to…"

Rebecca handed her a tissue. "Blow your nose," she ordered. "Did you and Roland argue?"

"Ya…ne…" Johanna sat up, blew her nose and used a clean tissue to wipe her eyes. She sniffed. "I went to find him, to tell him that we should stop with the courting and…" Somehow, although she hadn't meant to, everything spilled out. And Rebecca, in her quiet, comforting way, sat and listened patiently to her story.

"And the worst part was, he…he called me prideful," Johanna said.

Rebecca sighed. "And you denied it?"

Johanna nodded. "He said I haven't been able to forgive him for embarrassing me." She took a shuddering breath. "He said that when he came back from Lancaster, he came here to try to explain to me what had happened, but *Dat* sent him away."

"Which *Dat* did." Rebecca pushed a damp lock of hair off Johanna's forehead and searched her gaze. "But you didn't know?"

"I didn't know," Johanna whispered.

"Oh, dear." Rebecca sighed. "I thought you knew. Everyone in the family did. *Mam* was not happy with *Dat,* and they had words over it."

Johanna's looked at her sister in astonishment. "How do you know?"

Rebecca shrugged. "I heard them. I was eating grapes

on the far side of the arbor when *Mam* and *Dat* came into the backyard." A hint of mischief danced in her eyes. "I did what every young girl does when she hears adults quarreling. I listened."

Johanna closed her eyes for a moment. "This changes everything."

Rebecca shook her head. "No, it doesn't. What Roland did or didn't do at that frolic, what *Dat* said or didn't say, doesn't matter as much as what you're doing right now. Roland is right. You wouldn't forgive him, because he'd hurt your pride. I don't say this to hurt you, sister, but I always thought you married Wilmer to spite Roland. I thought you did it to show everyone that you could get a husband—a more Godly man than Roland Byler."

"Everyone always tells me that I'm stubborn, but it's not my greatest fault," Johanna mused aloud. "It's pride. How could I be so foolish?" She buried her face in her hands.

Rebecca rubbed her back. "I think maybe it's fear, too."

"Fear?" Johanna dabbed a tissue under her nose.

"You're afraid of loving him. Because you do."

"Because I do love him," Johanna whispered. The thought came to her with another flood of emotions. Of course she loved him. She'd always loved him. All these years. "I've ruined everything," she whispered to her sister.

"Nonsense. There's nothing you've said or done that can't be fixed if you're truly sorry."

More hot tears slipped down Johanna's cheeks. "You don't understand. I broke off our...our courtship. I knew what Roland said was true, but I wouldn't admit it. I told him I didn't want him for a husband."

"But do you?"

She looked up at Rebecca. "I do," she admitted. "I want to marry him because it's the right thing to do... but also because I love him."

"So go to him and tell him. If Roland truly loves you, and he does, he'll forgive you. You two can go back to courting and marry and make each other miserable for the rest of your lives."

Johanna pulled away from her sister. "Rebecca!"

"Just teasing you. Go on. Go to him." She chuckled. "But don't go until you've washed your face and made yourself pretty. You can't ask him to marry you with a red nose and swollen eyes and hair sticking out all over like a haystack. That's not how you persuade a man to do what you want him to do."

"Rebecca Yoder," Johanna exclaimed in astonishment, dabbing at her eyes with another tissue. "What would a modest *maedle* know about persuading men?"

Rebecca's chuckle became a merry giggle. "Some things, sister, a girl is just born knowing."

Chapter Seventeen

Deciding to go back to Roland and admit that she was wrong was easier said than done. First, there was the question as to whether or not he was still too angry to listen to reason. Second, there was the possibility that he would refuse her apology and tell her that marrying a prideful woman like her was the furthest thing from his mind. And third, maybe most important, was the when and how she should make her case to Roland. How was she going to make him believe that she truly did love him with all her heart? That what Rebecca said was true. That it was also fear that had made her behave the way she had.

As always, once she'd made up her mind, Johanna was eager to carry out her mission. But getting away from the house at suppertime was nearly impossible. There was the family to feed, the children to look after and a stream of visitors to welcome and share the good news about Ruth and Eli's babies. And as the eldest unmarried daughter, a good portion of the work fell to her.

Had she simply gone to *Mam* and told her how important it was for her to speak with Roland this evening, her mother would have insisted that she go at once. But *Mam* was rushing about, sixteen to a dozen. Rebecca's and Susanna's hands were busy looking after the Yoder children and those of their guests, keeping them from falling out of the hayloft, or climbing into the pigpen to cuddle one of the piglets that had been born two days earlier.

Of course, there were the usual evening chores that had to be done on even an ordinary summer day. Cows had to be fed and milked, horses turned into their stalls and given measures of grain. Turkeys had to be driven and penned for the night against the threat of stray dogs and foxes, and sheep had to be counted and driven into their fold.

With Irwin a part of the household, the care of the animals should have fallen to him, but so far he had proved more trouble than he was worth as a help around the farm. Susanna had more sense when it came to locking gates behind her, remembering to check to see if water troughs were filled, and knowing that cows could kick over milk buckets. It wasn't enough for *Mam* or Johanna to ask Irwin if the animals had been properly seen to. They had to ask about each task specifically. Otherwise, one cow might be forgotten, or the first person in the barn for morning milking might discover a lid off the feed barrel and a mouse feast in progress. Tonight, *Mam* was too busy receiving neighbors, so the task of managing Irwin fell to Johanna.

Once supper was cleared away and the animals content, Johanna might have slipped away, except for the arrival of Bishop Atlee and his wife with chicken potpies, a pound cake and a baked ham for Ruth and Eli.

"We'd not think of bothering them tonight," the bishop said, "or you. I'm sure everyone in Kent County has stopped by to offer their good wishes and prayers for your daughter and her sons, but I know one of your girls

won't mind just running these things over. No need for
Ruth to trouble herself by cooking."

"No need," *Mam* had echoed with hearty smile. And
no need for her to make less of the bishop's wife's con-
tributions by telling either of them that everyone who'd
come by today had brought food for the young household.

Buns and streusels, pies and tins of cookies shared the
pantry table and shelves with jars of pickles, chow-chow,
hard-boiled eggs pickled in beet juice, potato salad, mac-
aroni salad, spiced peaches, relish and blackberry jam.
There was a rice pudding sprinkled with nutmeg, a pan
of freshly made scrapple, three bowls of coleslaw, a jellied
veal loaf, a roasted duck, a German noodle ring and at least
one kettle of clam chowder and a second of split-pea soup.

Whether the new twins were to consume all this food
or Eli and the new mother, Johanna wasn't sure. But one
thing was for certain: the Yoders, the Masts, and Charley and Miriam would eat well for the next week, without any of the women having to cook. And every giver
would be thanked as sincerely as if they were the only
ones who'd been so thoughtful as to think of providing
a meal for Ruth and Eli's table.

As Bishop Atlee's buggy rolled out of the yard, Rebecca pulled Johanna aside. "Why haven't you gone
to Roland's yet?" she demanded. "Have you lost your
nerve?" She frowned. "If you wait until tomorrow, you'll
just make the situation worse."

"The children…"

"Grace and I will put Katy and Jonah to bed. Go."

Johanna glanced at her mother, who was standing on
the back porch watching them intently. "What does she
know?" Johanna whispered to her sister. "You didn't tell
her anything I told you, did you?"

"*Ne.* Shall I tell Irwin to hitch up Blackie?"

"If I take the buggy, *Mam* will ask why and I'll have to explain. I'll just walk over. It's not that far."

"Don't chicken out on me," Rebecca warned.

"What do you two have your heads together about?" Grace called from the porch, where she'd joined *Mam.* "I'm just going over to Ruth's to take this clam chowder. There's no more room in the refrigerator. If one of you comes with me, you can carry a bowl of sliced peaches."

Rebecca looked at Johanna.

"I'll go," Johanna called. And then to Rebecca, she whispered, "It's hardly any farther from Ruth's to Roland's. I'll just stay a minute, and that way *Mam* won't—"

"Know what you're up to," Rebecca finished. "Okay, but hurry, or your potential betrothed will be asleep before you tell him the good news."

As the two walked to Ruth's, Johanna filled Grace in on what had happened earlier in the day between her and Roland. "I don't know how I could have been so blind," she confessed as they crossed the field with their heavy containers of food. "Our church teaches us that pride is wrong, but all I could see was what Roland had done to me."

"It'll all work out," Grace said. "I know he's crazy about you."

Miriam pushed open the back door. "Come on in," she called to her sisters. "Adam is awake. Wait until you see those gorgeous eyes."

Johanna and Grace followed her into the house, and soon they were admiring the twins, chatting with a sleepy Ruth and inquiring as to how she felt. For a few minutes, Johanna was caught up in the excitement of the babies and her sister's happiness.

Just ten more minutes. Roland will still be up. It won't hurt to stay here with Ruth and my sisters a little while longer. It will be easier to talk to Roland if J.J.'s in bed when I get there. She'd almost convinced herself that she was worried for nothing, that the explanation and Roland's forgiveness would come easily, when Charley burst in with news.

"Roland's got company," Charley announced to the room. "And it means trouble." He fixed his gaze on Johanna.

"What are you talking about?" Miriam balanced Luke against her shoulder and patted his back. "What trouble?"

Charley shoved his hands into his pockets. "I just came from there."

"And?" Ruth asked. "You know you're going to explode if you don't tell us."

"Well, it's not like I haven't said this might happen," Charley went on, obviously pleased to be the center of attention. "You know that Lancaster girl, the one who works at the cheese shop at Spence's Market? The one who's had her eye on Roland?"

"She's at his house?" Grace asked. "The girl?"

"Not the girl," Charley answered. "Her father and two of his uncles, come all the way from Lancaster. They hired a driver and—"

"We don't care how they got here." Miriam passed the baby to Ruth. "What are they doing here? What do they want with Roland?"

"From what the driver said, her father's eager to find her a husband. She's got two younger sisters who've had offers, but can't marry until she does. And apparently, she's picky."

"But what does that have to do with Roland?" Johanna asked, all too certain that she already knew the answer.

"The driver said the girl has set her *Kapp* for Roland.

The father has already asked a lot of questions about Roland, and now they've come to look him over. The driver says they want to offer the girl to him as a wife—one that comes with one hundred acres of Lancaster farmland, a house and a stone barn as a dowry."

Eli let out a low whistle. "A hundred-acre farm. In Lancaster. Land up there is worth a fortune. It will be hard for Roland to pass up." He rolled his eyes innocently toward the ceiling. "Especially since things haven't worked out here for him. He might decide moving to Pennsylvania would be in his best interest."

"What do you mean they haven't *worked out?*" Ruth asked. "He's been courting Johanna. Who would throw Johanna over for a cheese girl and a stone barn in the middle of a cow pasture?"

"There's a herd of cows that comes with the pasture," Charley teased. "The driver says—"

Miriam silenced him with a look.

Grace turned to Johanna. "I suppose it's too late for you to make a counteroffer—to keep him from accepting these Lancaster people."

"If it was me," Miriam said, "I wouldn't have let Charley go without putting up a fight."

A smile teased at the corners of Grace's mouth. "I thought you Amish were against fighting."

"There's fighting and then there's fighting," Johanna answered softly. "And as *Dat* always said, it's never too late to pray for rain until the barn has already burned down."

Grace got out of the car and gave Johanna a hug. "It's really dark. Are you sure you don't want a flashlight? I've got one in the glove box. Or I could drive you up to the house."

"Ne," Johanna answered. "I can see well enough to walk up the lane. And I'd rather no one saw me coming."

"Good luck." Grace gave her a kiss on the cheek.

"Ya. I think I'll need it." Johanna turned away from the vehicle and started up the drive at a quick pace. She didn't know what she was going to do or say when she got to the house, but she couldn't stop now. If she hesitated, she might lose her nerve.

Roland's yard was dark. A soft glow from the kitchen and parlor propane lamps spilled through the open windows. Around her, lightning bugs flashed, and frogs and crickets chirped the melody of a muggy summer night.

The day that had begun so sunny had turned damp and there was the oppressive feel of approaching rain. In the distance, Johanna could hear the rumble of thunder. It was that way in Delaware. As the old folks were fond of saying, "If you don't like the weather, wait half an hour and it will change." She was glad she hadn't brought the buggy. She wasn't afraid of a storm, but Blackie was. Better to depend on her own two feet.

Feet that were now carrying her closer and closer to Roland and a situation that might be beyond her ability to make right. She was scared, scared to the bone. Her heart was racing, her thoughts were all in a jumble, and her stomach made her wish she hadn't eaten that cup of chowder earlier. What would she do if she walked into Roland's kitchen and threw up all over his shoes? That would be embarrassing, but not as devastating as finding out that Roland and the cheese girl's father had already come to an agreement, shaken hands on the deal and set a date for marriage banns to be read.

She had been a fool. She'd been stubborn, prideful and fearful, and she'd let the man the Lord had sent her slip through her fingers. How could she have been so concerned with a silly incident that had happened years ago? How could she have failed to see that she was throwing away her future happiness and security out of her own weaknesses? Not only was she ruining the chances of a happy marriage, she was spoiling everything for three innocent children.

Mam had told her; Ruth, Rebecca, Anna, Miriam and Grace had told her. Even Susanna had seemed to understand that Roland and J.J. were already part of the family.

"Please, God," Johanna prayed under her breath. "I know I don't deserve a second chance, but Katy and Jonah and J.J. do. Roland does. And if you please help me out of this jam, I promise I'll never…"

She stopped and exhaled softly, then sucked in lungs full of the humid air. "I'll try harder," she promised. "I'll do what I can to curb my pride and stubbornness. I promise I'll do everything I can to be the best wife any man could ever want."

She was nearing the house now. The black shadows of lilac bushes loomed on either side of the drive. Through the open windows, she heard Roland's sister Mary and the answering rumble of a man's voice. She listened for Roland, but didn't hear him. Then came a second voice, injecting something she couldn't make out. He spoke in Pennsylvania *Deutch,* his distinctly Lancaster accent giving a different lilt to his comment.

Johanna was tempted to creep close to the window to find out what was happening, if what Charley had said was true, but rejected that as too petty. No, she would have to confront her rivals head-on. With her father dead and no uncle she could count on to speak for her, she was on her own.

She moved on quiet feet, through the gloom, toward the back door. Blood pounded in her ears. Her fingers and toes felt numb. As the first drops of rain splattered on her face, she felt as if were wading through thick mud. "Just a few more steps," she muttered.

Abruptly, she slammed into something in the darkness. Not something—someone. A cry of fright rose from her throat to be cut off by the sensation of arms wrapping around her and strong fingers clapping over her mouth.

"Johanna," Roland whispered urgently. "Don't be scared. It's just me."

"Roland?" she mumbled.

He removed his hand. "Shh," he repeated. "They'll hear you."

Her heart settled back into her chest, but she was so light-headed that she swayed in his arms, nearly losing her balance. Roland's strong arms held her as a shimmering wave of rain enveloped them both.

"Come on," he urged. "We'll get soaked out here." He caught her hand and dashed away from the house back toward the barn. Not knowing what else to do, she ran with him.

When the barn loomed above, Roland flung open the door and pulled her inside. Instantly, she was enveloped in the warm, sweet smells of fresh-cut hay, molasses, oats and horses. "What are you doing out there in the dark?" she demanded.

"That was close," he said. "What are *you* doing here? I didn't know what was coming out of the dark. You scared me half—"

"*I* scared *you?* How do you think…" Suddenly, it struck her as funny. Roland's visitors were inside, and he was outside in the bushes. A snort of amusement bubbled up from the pit of her belly in her throat. "You were hiding from them," she declared.

"No, I wasn't."

"Yes, you were." The snort became a chuckle and then a peal of laughter. "Roland Byler, you are such a fibber."

"Shh, they'll hear you." He pulled her deeper into the familiar sanctuary of the barn. "What was I supposed to say to them?"

"'Hello. How can I help you?' That might be a start," she whispered with a giggle. He was still holding her hand, but she was no longer his captive…more his partner in crime. "If you didn't speak to them, how did you know who they were and why they've come?"

"Oh, I know why they're here. They got here first, but I met their driver at the end of the lane. Mary was still—" He broke off. "What were you doing hiding in my bushes?"

"I had to come. Charley told me they were here."

"My brother couldn't keep a secret if his crop depended on it. I didn't want you to know—"

"What?" She felt a little pang of fear. Maybe she *was* too late. "I was supposed to learn that you were marrying your Lancaster cheese peddler when the bishop cried your banns at next service?"

He pulled her into the circle of his arms, and she knew in her heart of hearts that she wasn't too late. She inhaled deeply of the damp, clean, male scent of him. *Safe. I feel safe here. This is where I belong.*

"Don't be *lecherich,* Johanna," Roland said. "How could I have two wives? I still intend to marry you, once you realize that I'm right, and that you love me, and that it was your stubborn pride—"

"That kept us apart," she finished. "And my fear…my

fear of loving you. Of knowing how much I've loved you all along." He brushed his fingertips across her cheek and joy blossomed inside her. "So you weren't going to accept the offer of a rich farm and a stone barn full of cows? Pretty *dumm* to take a sharp-tongued widow with only a few scraggly sheep and—"

"She has a stone barn and cows?" he interrupted.

She dug her fingers into his side and he laughed.

"Bees," he said. "You have lots of bees."

"And turkeys."

Roland lowered his head, the teasing gone from his voice. "I know you, Johanna. I knew when you left the horse farm that it was only a matter of time before you thought it through and realized—"

"That I love you," she finished, realizing she could hold nothing back from Roland. Not ever again.

"Almost as much as I love you."

His lips brushed hers in a tender kiss that sent all her fears flying into the night. For a long moment, she savored the feel of his mouth and the warmth of his arms before she stepped away. "Best that waits awhile longer," she whispered breathlessly. "Or…"

"Or we will both be on our knees in front of the congregation," he agreed.

For another moment or two, they remained bodies apart, but fingers still laced together. Johanna listened to the rain on the roof, the movement of the horses in their stalls, and the sound of Roland's breathing. "What now?" she asked him.

"Now I go in and thank our visitors for their kind offer," he said.

"That they haven't made yet. And…" She waited, certain he already knew what he would say that would make everything right.

"And I tell them that I'm honored that they'd think of me, but I've already spoken to my preacher about calling the banns for my wedding to the widow Johanna Detweiler."

"You would lie to them?"

This time it was Roland who laughed. "Johanna, my love. I've known you too long and faced your temper too many times. It burns fierce and hot, but in the end, your sense of fairness wins out. I knew that, sooner or later, you would come to tell me you were sorry and loved me more than bread and honey."

"You did not!" she accused, barely able to contain another burst of laughter.

"Ah, but I did. Ask him. John and I stopped by the bishop's house on the way home. After that, it was just a matter of waiting for you to come to your senses. The visitors from Lancaster nearly upset all my plans. What if you hadn't given in and come tonight? How could I have told them that I was already betrothed before I was?"

"But you could tell Bishop Atlee we were?"

"*Ne.* I simply asked him to cry the banns. I never said you had agreed to marry me."

"And if I'd said no?"

"But you said yes, didn't you? You and I will take our vows as soon as is decent, our children will have a mother and a father again, and the cheese seller's daughter will have to seek out another bridegroom."

And that was exactly the way it all happened....

Epilogue

Nine Months Later...

It was a wet March Saturday, too mild for a last blast of winter and too blustery for the coming spring. For two days, heavy rain had pelted the roofs and roads and fields of Seven Poplars, driven the livestock inside to seek shelter and sent Vs of wild geese flying north overhead, honking their plaintive cries.

The rain didn't trouble the Amish community, as a whole. The farmers and their wives welcomed the downpour because it filled their wells and soaked the newly plowed fields. Soon, seeds would go into the fertile earth, and the moisture would ensure lush crops of grain, vegetables and hay. The children, however, cooped up inside for days, yearned to have the chance to burn up their energy. They wanted to shout without being told to lower their voices, play ball, climb trees and cast the first baited hooks and bobbers into ponds.

But the rain continued to fall, and heavy, gray clouds offered no hint of sunshine and no chance to enjoy what should have been a fun-filled Saturday, after a week of school. Or so Jonah and J.J. thought.

They didn't know what their parents were up to. Enlisting Katy as a coconspirator, Johanna and Roland had made a plan for a great adventure. First, J.J. and Jonah were both blindfolded and led to the family buggy. Then, they were driven around—where, they didn't know, much to a giggling Katy's delight. The only hint as to what the adventure might be was the tantalizing smell of gingerbread, barbecued chicken, baked beans and *knabru*s that drifted from the back of the carriage.

"Where are we going?" J.J. asked for the tenth time.

Johanna chuckled. "We can't tell you. It's a surprise."

"It's a pic—" Katy squealed, covering her mouth with her hands. "A surprise," she repeated.

"But when will we get there?" Jonah demanded. "We've been driving for hours."

Roland laughed. "Hardly, but…" He reined in his roan and the buggy came to a stop. "We're almost there."

"Hurray!" both boys cried in unison.

"Hurray!" Katy shouted and then dissolved into giggles again.

Johanna waited until Roland had opened the double doors wide and then guided the horse and buggy inside the barn. "Don't take your blindfolds off yet," she warned. "You'll spoil the surprise." She knotted the leathers around the dashboard rail, climbed down and helped Katy out of the carriage.

Roland closed the doors behind them and lifted first Jonah and then J.J. down from the vehicle. "It *is* a picnic," he declared, "but a special one."

"How can you have a picnic in the rain?" J.J. asked, practically vibrating with excitement.

"Wait and see." Johanna took J.J.'s hand and led him to the base of the ladder that led to the hayloft, while Roland did the same for Jonah. "Now, take off your blindfolds."

Both whipped the bandanas off their faces.

"Aw, it's just our barn," Jonah said, turning around.

"*Ya,* just our barn," J.J. echoed, dejectedly.

"*Ne.*" Johanna chuckled. "That's what *you* think. It's our special picnic spot where no other boy in Seven Poplars has ever picnicked before."

"Up the ladder," Roland ordered as he removed the heavy baskets from the back of the buggy.

Soon Johanna and Katy, J.J., Jonah and Roland were all standing on the floor of the hayloft. This winter, this part of the loft had been used to store straw, and earlier today, Johanna had covered some of the bales with clean white sheets to make a table. There were plates and mugs and napkins, and standing beside the straw table was a shiny new bucket with thermoses of hot chocolate for everyone.

"*Wunderbar!*" Katy exclaimed. "A kitchen in the hayloft!"

"Who's hungry?" Johanna asked. In moments, Roland had brought up the picnic baskets from the buggy, and the bowls and pans of food were on the table. The family gathered around to hold hands and bow their heads for the moment of silent grace that signaled the beginning of every meal.

Katy's enthusiasm was catching, and soon the boys were having as much fun as she was. Everyone laughed and talked and ate until they were stuffed, and when the two boys begged for one last gingerbread man, Johanna couldn't help but allow them the additional treat. Afterward, she cleared away the dishes, tucked the containers back into the picnic baskets and Roland drew a deck of Dutch Blitz cards out of his pocket.

"Games!" J.J. cried. He loved games, especially Old Maid and Go Fish and checkers. Katy was just learning the rules, but J.J. was especially brotherly to her, helping her with her choices and cheering on her moves.

The family card game was followed by a story about a fishing trip that Roland had taken with their *Grossdaddi* Yoder, one that the boys loved because it always ended with *Mam* catching more fish than *Dat*.

After the last chuckle had faded, Johanna brought out the big children's Bible storybook that her mother had given her and read the story of Noah and the Flood. The rain beating against the cedar roof shingles made a perfect background for the old and familiar tale. They all listened in silence to Johanna's words and sighed with contentment at the end when Noah opened the doors of the Ark and the people saw green.

"This is the best picnic ever!" Jonah pronounced.

"The best," J.J. agreed.

Katy yawned and nodded her approval.

"Just one more thing," Johanna said, glancing at Roland. He nodded, rose and climbed back down the ladder.

After a few minutes, he returned to the barn and called up. "You children might want to come down. There's something here that I think belongs to you."

"What?" Jonah asked.

All three small heads leaned over the opening to the ladder.

"You'll have to come down. Katy first."

One by one, the children descended the ladder. Johanna watched from the hayloft as Roland reached into a feed barrel and lifted out a wriggling bundle of black-

and-white fur. Two black eyes peered out from under a fringe of hair, and a small, pink, puppy tongue licked at Katy's cheek.

"Es hundli!" she squealed. "Is it ours? To keep?"

"If you love him and care for him," Johanna called down. "He's a Bernese Mountain Dog, and he'll get a lot bigger."

After delivering a few instructions about how to handle the puppy, Roland left the children below and climbed back up the ladder to join Johanna. "That should keep them busy for a while," he said.

Johanna leaned close and kissed his cheek. "You are the best father any child could want," she said. "You spoil them."

"I hope not." He enfolded her hand in his and squeezed it gently. "I hope I raise them with love and care, so that they will grow to be good and faithful members of our church and community."

"I am proud of you."

His eyes lit with mischief. "Pride from the mother of my children? I thought you had put that all behind you when we took our vows."

She chuckled. "I am a work in progress, Roland Byler, and don't you forget it."

"But a good mother," he said, becoming serious, "and a good wife."

"I try. Every day, I open my eyes and thank God for you and our family, and I promise myself to work at being worthy of His blessings."

"You make me happy," he said, glancing deeper into the loft, then back at her. "But there's something…"

"Ya? What is it, Roland?"

"I've always wanted to take a pretty *frau* into the hay-loft and kiss her."

"Roland Byler, and you a married man," she teased, but she picked up a clean sheet and spread it over a pile of loose straw. "So what's keeping you from it?"

He put his arm around her and they sank into the soft and fragrant bed. For a long time, they lay together, her head on his shoulder, not speaking, listening to the sweet sounds of their children's voices and the rain on the roof before she spoke. "Is this what you wanted?"

"Ya." He sighed with contentment and kissed her cheek. "Exactly what I dreamed about. You, Johanna, no other, just you beside me."

"Not just me," she corrected. "Not exactly. There is another."

Puzzled, he glanced into her face. "Another?"

She laughed softly. "For an observant man, there is much you don't see, husband."

"What are you talking about?"

"Something I have wanted for a long time."

"What is it, Johanna? I'll give you whatever you wish, if I can…if I can afford it."

She lay back against him and snuggled close. "This, I think we can afford. I want you to place an order from Eli, at the chair shop."

"You want a chair?"

Johanna chuckled. *"Ne,* my love, not a chair. A cradle."

He sat bolt upright and stared at her. "A cradle? You mean you… We?"

She laughed again, raised her face and kissed him full on the mouth. "Is it so surprising that the Lord who could save Noah and all his people from the flood can't provide us with one small baby?" And then a doubt threw a shadow over her excitement. "You are happy, aren't you? To be a father again?"

But Roland didn't need to answer because the look in his eyes told her all she needed to know. And the tears that spilled down her cheeks were ones of pure joy.

* * * * *

PLAIN PROTECTOR

Alison Stone

To my daughter Kelsey. You are smart, kind
and beautiful. You work hard to reach your goals,
yet take everything in stride. This ability
amazes me and will take you far in life.
I am so proud of you. I love you.
And to Scott, Scotty, Alex and Leah.
Love you guys, always and forever.

But when I am afraid, I will put my trust in You.
—*Psalms* 56:3

Chapter One

⟨ornament⟩

Sarah Gardner never thought a master's degree in social work would mean she'd be sweeping the floor of the basement meeting room of the Apple Creek Community Church on a Sunday evening. No, she had thought she'd have her own office in a hospital or a private clinic, a family and maybe even a child by now.

But when Sarah was a promising young college student, she couldn't imagine the things her life would be lacking at the ripe old age of thirty. No decent job, no car, no close friends. All in an effort to maintain a low profile for fear her ex-boyfriend would find her.

Yes, her life was a mess because she'd chosen the wrong guy to date. She swept a little more vigorously than necessary, sending a cloud of dust into the air, making her cough.

A loud slam made Sarah jump. She spun around to find Mary Ruth Beiler with her hand on the closet door and an apologetic look on her face. Sometimes Sarah envied the young Amish girl who seemed to have her entire life mapped out for her in the insular Amish community of Apple Creek, New York. Mary Ruth's options had been pruned to the point that she didn't have much room to make bad choices.

But not having choices didn't mean freedom.

Sarah knew as much.

"Sarah," Mary Ruth said in a soft voice, "I put the folding chairs in the closet. Is there anything else you need help with before I go?"

"I think we're set." Sarah wanted to make a few notes from the group meeting tonight before her thoughts slipped away, much like the wisps of dreams from her childhood that vanished when she opened her eyes after a fitful night's sleep.

Sarah had set up a group meeting for primarily Amish youth, whose parents would rather they be attending the Sunday evening singings. But holding the meeting the same night as the bimonthly Sunday singings gave the teens an excuse to leave home without explaining where they were heading. They came to discuss the dangers of drinking and drugs—for some a reality, for others merely a temptation—and other worldly concerns. Sarah suspected some of their parents knew where their sons and daughters were really going and only pretended their offspring were enjoying the singings with hopes that soon they would be back within the fold. Other parents flat out forbade their children from associating with this *Englischer* who was surely giving them worldly ideas.

But if these same Amish parents knew the trouble their precious children were flirting with, they might remember Sarah in their prayers instead of regarding the outsider with a sideways glance and a cold shoulder.

Lord knew she could use their prayers.

"Yes, we're all set," Sarah said. "Thank you for your help." She dug into her jeans' pocket and handed the girl payment, payment she could ill afford if she had to remain holed up in Apple Creek much longer like she was some criminal on the run and not the victim that she was. The pastor of the church paid her a modest stipend to work with the youth in the community.

Having sweet Mary Ruth as an assistant was a bridge, however precarious, to the Amish youth, many of whom needed Sarah's services, but, like their parents, were leery of outsiders. Some kids had found their way to drugs and alcohol—just like the youth she used to work with back in Buffalo—and their peers knew it. Mary Ruth made the first few introductions. From there, word spread. The rumor mill among the teens in Amish country was no less efficient than their texting counterparts in the outside world.

Now, every two weeks, Mary Ruth helped Sarah set up the room and serve as a friendly face to newcomers and repeat visitors alike. The gatherings usually only had four or five members, but even if she only touched one person's life, it would be worth the effort.

Most Sundays, Mary Ruth then ran off to the Sunday singings. But not this week. This week she had stayed, a part of the group but separate. She seemed intrigued by the choices some of her peers had made, or choices they were courting.

Sarah hoped the youth kept her number one rule: what was said in this room, stayed in this room. She trusted Mary Ruth, but each newcomer was a risk. Despite their age difference, Sarah considered Mary Ruth a friend.

Perhaps her only friend in Apple Creek.

"Do you need my help at all during the week?" Mary Ruth lingered at the stairway leading to the exit.

"Yes, if you'd like. I was going to make a few home

visits to young, single mothers in town who might be in need of services." The women weren't Amish and often needed help understanding what services were available to them and their babies until they got back on their feet.

"These new mothers really need you, don't they?" Mary Ruth asked, as if she were just now coming to appreciate Sarah's work in the community.

"Some of them don't have anyone else."

"It's sad. Their future is uncertain." Mary Ruth played with the folds in her long dress, its hem brushing the tops of her black boots.

The irony that Sarah's future was probably the most precarious of them all was not lost on her, but she kept her thoughts to herself.

"I admire the work you do. Sometimes I wish Amish women could be independent like you."

Independent. Sarah outwardly appeared independent, but on the inside she was a trembling mess. "How old are you, Mary Ruth?"

"Eighteen?" Her answer sounded more like a question.

"Ah, you have your whole life in front of you."

"A life that has already been planned out." There was a faraway quality to her voice. "Most of my friends are hoping to get married soon."

"And you?"

Mary Ruth hitched a shoulder and her cheeks turned pink. The Amish didn't talk much about dating and courtship, at least not to her. Some successfully hid their wedding plans until the church published their engagement announcement only weeks before their actual wedding.

Sarah did know that Mary Ruth had been spending time with a young Amish man, Ruben Zook, who lived next door to the cottage Sarah rented. But she didn't dare inquire about Mary Ruth's plans, respecting the Amish ways.

Sarah waved her hand. "You're a smart girl. I'm sure you'll figure it out."

"Guten nacht," Mary Ruth said, in a singsong voice as she climbed the stairs, her mood seeming to lift. She very rarely spoke Pennsylvania Dutch to Sarah, except for when she said good-night. Sarah was still smiling when the outside door opened with a creak and then slammed shut.

Unease whispered at the back of Sarah's neck as a pronounced silence settled across the room. Her plan to sit at her desk in her tiny basement office and make notes no longer seemed like a smart idea. It had been a habit during her years of working in Buffalo. Make notes immediately so that one patient didn't blend in with the next. However, here in Apple Creek, her workload was lighter and she had no distractions at home.

Here, she didn't have a boyfriend pestering her to know what she was doing every minute of every day. Nor did she have to worry that she'd inadvertently provide the wrong answer. An answer that would send him into a blind rage.

Icy dread pooled in the pit of her stomach. *How did I allow myself to get tangled up with Jimmy Braeden?* She had always considered herself a smart girl.

Even smart girls made bad choices sometimes.

Letting out a long breath and wishing she could silence all the doubts and worries in her head, Sarah gathered up her papers and jammed them into her bag with shaky hands. She hated that Jimmy had made her afraid. Made her hide. Made her into someone even she couldn't heal.

A shadow crossed the basement floor and Sarah

glanced up at the narrow windows that faced the church parking lot. Nothing. Just the fading blue sky, which made her realize if she didn't hurry, she'd have to walk the mile home in the dark.

Sure, Jimmy didn't know where she was. *She hoped.* But that didn't mean it was wise to tempt fate as a single woman alone after dark on a deserted country road.

Sarah hoisted the strap of her bag over her shoulder and flipped off the light switch at the bottom of the stairs when a crashing sound exploded, disrupting the quiet night air. Shards of glass rained down over her head.

Sarah bit back a yelp and flattened herself against the wall of the basement under the broken window. Her pulse beat wildly in her ears as she fumbled in her bag. She was searching for a cell phone, when she remembered she didn't have one. It was one of the many things she had given up when she decided to disappear.

A cell phone was too easy to trace.

Sarah gingerly touched her head and her fingers came back sticky. She closed her eyes and muttered a silent prayer: *Dear Lord, please protect me.* If there was one thing she clung to through her turned-upside-down life, it was her faith. One constant in a crazy world.

Biting her lip, she glanced toward the stairs. Toward the exit. The unlocked door. Dread knotted her stomach. She stood, frozen, until her heart rate returned to normal. *Almost.* She figured her nerves wouldn't truly settle until she was safely at home, locked inside.

Her gaze landed on a large rock in the center of the room. Good thing she hadn't been struck by that or she might be unconscious.

Sarah couldn't stand here forever. She took a hesitant step toward the stairs.

Was someone waiting for her outside?

With a burst of courage—the same courage that had her leave her abusive ex—Sarah bolted up the stairs, clinging to her bag as if it could protect her. She pushed the door open and the still night air greeted her. Without a backward glance, she bolted as fast as her legs would carry her across the wide expanse of the parking lot to the pastor's house on the opposite side.

She pounded up the porch steps and lifted her fist and hammered on the door, immediately taking her back to another day, another time, when her boyfriend was chasing her. Promising he'd kill her if he caught her. Swallowing her dizzying panic, she glanced over her shoulder.

No one was chasing her now.

Just the shadows. And the haunting memories that refused to leave her alone.

When Deputy Sheriff Nick Jennings pulled up in front of the Apple Creek Diner, he had only two things on his mind: coffee and Flo's pie. His stomach growled as he considered his options. He was in the mood for some banana cream. As he pulled the door's release, his radio crackled to life. He listened intently, frowning when he heard there had been an incident at the church. Flo's pie would have to wait.

"I'm at the Apple Creek Diner," he said into the radio. "I can be at the church in three minutes." Nick flipped on the lights and pressed his foot to the floor, not necessary since he was only a few minutes out, but he missed the occasional adrenaline surge. Policing small-town Apple Creek didn't provide the same rush as serving in the army in times of war.

Not that he wanted to go back to war.

"The victim, a Miss Sarah Lynn, is at the pastor's residence," the dispatcher said. "The pastor's wife claims she's pretty shaken up."

Sarah Lynn? The name didn't register.

Nick tightened his grip on the steering wheel and as promised, made it to the parking lot of the church in under three minutes. Dusk had cloaked the area in the first hint of shadows, and his headlights arched across two people standing on the pastor's stoop. One was Miss Ellinor, the pastor's wife, the other was a petite woman he had noticed around town. That must be Sarah Lynn.

Nick had only been back in Apple Creek for a few months himself when this young woman arrived. Residents of a small town tended to notice new arrivals, even if they weren't petite and pretty, which this one certainly was. Flo at the diner, who had a habit of trying to fix him up, mentioned that this woman seemed to keep to herself most of the time, hadn't even offered up her name. A few speculated on why she had suddenly shown up in town—employment, low rent or maybe she was hiding from something—but mostly the residents of Apple Creek let her be. Nick assumed she probably did have her share of secrets. Having come off a bad breakup with a woman who was a master secret keeper, Nick figured he'd pass.

Nick climbed out of his cruiser and strode toward the pastor's neat, white-sided home. He tipped his hat toward the women. "Hello, Miss Ellinor." He thought it best if he waited for the young woman to introduce herself. That's when he noticed she was doing more than touching her forehead, she was holding a cloth to it.

"Are you injured?"

"I'm fine. My name is Sarah. Sarah Lynn…" The corners of her mouth turned down and the woman seemed to be studying her shoes. This woman was either afraid or hiding something. Perhaps both.

Apparently the residents of Apple Creek were collectively a pretty good judge of character.

"I'm Deputy Sheriff Nick Jennings. What happened here?"

Sarah shook her head, but it was Miss Ellinor who spoke first. "Someone smashed one of the basement windows of the church. I'm afraid Sarah has a pretty deep cut on her forehead. You'll probably have to call an ambulance. Is an ambulance coming?"

Sarah held up her hand, her eyes growing wide. "I don't need an ambulance. I'm fine." Her voice shook. She didn't sound fine.

"May I take a look?" Nick stepped toward Sarah and she took a half step back, hemmed in by the front door of the pastor's home behind her.

Sarah dropped her hand and her long hair fell over the wound. She stared up at him with a look of defiance, although he may have misinterpreted the emotion in the dim lighting.

Nick held up his hands in a nonthreatening gesture. "I don't need to look at it, but *someone* should."

"I'm fine, really." Sarah's repeated use of the word *fine* seemed forced. She bent and picked up a heavy-looking bag. When she straightened, all the color drained from her face. If he hadn't been watching her, he might not have seen the terror that flashed across her pretty features and then disappeared into the firm set of her mouth and her narrowed gaze.

He wasn't going to have her pass out on his watch. "Let me drive you to the hospital. Have someone take a look at that cut."

Sarah pressed the wadded-up paper towel to her fore-head and frowned. "I'm fine, really." There was that word again. "I just want to go home."

Miss Ellinor's features grew pinched. "Child, I know you like to put on a brave face, but if you don't get that cut checked out, you're going to end up with a big scar on your forehead. It would be a shame to mar that pretty face of yours. Wouldn't you agree, Deputy Jennings?"

Nick felt a corner of his mouth tugging into a grin, despite suspecting his amusement might annoy the young woman. Miss Ellinor, the pastor's wife, was a chatty soul who said whatever was on her mind. Being a woman of a certain age and position, no one seemed to call her on it. "A scar on that pretty face would be a shame."

Sarah squared her shoulders, apparently unsure of how to take his compliment.

Nick tipped his head toward his patrol vehicle. "I'll take you to the emergency room."

"Is this really necessary?" Sarah skirted past him and clearly had no intention of getting into his car.

"Would you rather I call an ambulance?"

Sarah sighed heavily. "I do *not* need an ambulance."

Nick decided to change his line of questioning. "Any idea who might have tossed a rock through the window?"

Miss Ellinor shook her head. "Bored kids causing trouble, I suppose."

Nick thought he noticed Sarah blanch. "I'm a social worker, and every other Sunday, to coincide with the Amish Sunday-night singings, I run a group meeting for Amish youth who may have alcohol or drug issues. Or other concerns."

"Really?"

Sarah slowly turned, her sneaker pivoting on the

gravel. "Is there something wrong with that? This community is an underserved area. For some Amish youth, the years leading up to their baptism can be stressful. It's a huge decision, which can lead to unhealthy behaviors to deal with stress. Because of their insular life, they are often ill equipped to handle the temptation of drugs and alcohol." Despite the cool bite to her tone, she sounded rehearsed, like she was reading from a brochure.

"No, ma'am. I didn't mean to imply that what you're doing is wrong. Do you have reason to believe someone from your meeting tonight took issue with you? Or something that was said?"

Sarah adjusted the paper towel on her forehead. "I'm a social worker. Unfortunately, being…" she seemed to be searching for the right word "…*harassed* on occasion is one of the challenges of the job." She cut her gaze toward him, making a show of running her eyes the length of his deputy sheriff's uniform. "You can understand that." Unfortunately, in today's climate, he could.

"I'm issued a gun. What do you have for protection?" His pulse ticked in his jaw, anger growing in his gut. If some punk was messing with a social worker who was trying to help him, Nick would have to set him straight.

"Oh my, we've never had trouble here before." Miss Ellinor's hands fluttered at the collar of her floral shirt. Her white hair seemed to glow under the bright porch light.

Sarah reached for Miss Ellinor's hand and squeezed it. "It's okay. I wouldn't know what to do with a gun. And," she said, lowering her voice, "I don't think someone would be receptive to my help if I had a gun strapped to my body."

"Any self-defense classes then?" Nick didn't understand why he was so interested in this woman. He was here to answer a call about a broken window. See that she receive medical attention. That's it.

"I took a few self-defense classes back when I was in college. But, I do my best to avoid conflict. Beats getting my head trapped in a headlock." Half her mouth quirked up. Nick could tell she was trying to defuse the situation with humor, but what happened here tonight wasn't funny.

Sarah cleared her throat and pulled the paper towel away from her forehead and suddenly seemed impatient to leave.

"Wait by the vehicle. I need to check out the broken window. I won't be but a minute."

Sarah nodded.

"Make sure she gets that cut looked at, Nick," Miss Ellinor hollered after him.

He waved and smiled. "Sure thing." He had a feeling that was going to be a difficult promise to keep.

Nick checked out the broken window, then went inside and assessed the damage. A large rock sat in the middle of the room. *Punks.*

When he returned to his vehicle, he found Sarah standing alone. "Miss Ellinor had to go in. She's babysitting her granddaughter. The pastor's not home. I told her I'd clean up the mess tomorrow."

Nick nodded, but didn't say anything. Sarah looked tiny standing next to his cruiser, one hand pressed to her forehead, the other arm wrapped around her middle. A large bag resting on her hip. He opened his passenger door and she cut him a cynical gaze. "Not going to make me ride in the back?"

"Are you a criminal?" He arched an eyebrow.

Without answering, she slipped into his car. "I'm not going to the hospital. You can take me directly home."

Despite Sarah's firm tone, her hands shook under the dome light as she fastened her seatbelt. She looked like a deer frozen in headlights, uncertain if safety existed a few steps away or if annihilation under the massive weight of an eighteen-wheeler bearing down on her was inevitable.

The familiar sight of the interior of the patrol vehicle, with all its lights, displays and gadgets made Sarah suck in a breath, only to inhale the distinct police-car smell: part antiseptic, part vinyl, part whoever had been transported in the backseat. And the crackle of the radio sent Sarah reeling back to another time.

Sarah threaded her trembling hands, trying to maintain her composure. Trying to stay in the here and now. *I will* not *have a panic attack. I will not give this man a reason to question me any more than he already has. I can do this.*

Breathe...

"Any idea which of your clients could have thrown a rock through the church window? Anyone particularly angry or rude this evening?"

Sarah shook her head, not trusting her voice. "I'd just be guessing." *Or lying.* Did she really believe it was one of the Amish men or women from her meeting tonight? "If you don't mind, I'm tired. Can you please take me home?"

"I promised Miss Ellinor I'd get that cut on your head looked after. I'm not a man who goes back on a promise."

Sarah sighed heavily. She wasn't up for all this chivalrous stuff. She had been conned by the biggest con man himself, and she didn't trust herself when it came to reading people's—no, scratch that—men's true intentions.

Act tougher than you are. Don't let him take control.

Sarah shifted in her seat and squared her shoulders. "Truth be told, I don't have any insurance, and as you might have guessed, living in Apple Creek, working as a social worker, I'm not in a position to be forking out money for unnecessary medical expenses. As it is, I'll have a tough time paying my rent this month." She figured God would forgive her this little lie. She did have medical insurance, but she didn't dare use it. Just one more way for her former boyfriend to track her down. Everything she had Googled about vanishing had said to wipe her digital blueprint clean.

In today's modern world, that was tougher than ever.

Checking into a hospital with all the paperwork and computer records would likely raise a red flag if her former boyfriend was still looking for her. *If.* Inwardly she rolled her eyes. Of course he was still looking for her. Jimmy Braeden didn't give up a fight easily.

Sarah turned her head slowly, keenly aware of the man studying her in the confined space of his patrol vehicle. Her heartbeat kicked up a notch, but surprisingly not out of fear, but out of uncertainty. How was she going to convince him to take her home?

She forced a smile. "Please, take me home." She tried once again for the direct approach.

He smiled back, revealing perfectly even white teeth. "I can't do that." Under other circumstances, Sarah would have immediately put up her defenses. She had vowed she'd never let a man control her like Jimmy had. Yet, Deputy Jennings seemed to give off a different vibe than her macho ex. There was something soft around his hard edges.

But her hunches had been wrong before. Just the fact that she was in this situation proved her point. She couldn't let her guard down because a handsome man smiled at her.

"I have a place I can take you." Deputy Jennings shifted the vehicle into drive and her stomach lurched.

"No, please. Take me home."

He cut her a sideways glance and his eyebrow twitched. Had he sensed her growing panic? If he had, he didn't say as much.

"You can call me Nick."

"*Nick*, take me home." Frustration bubbled up inside her. The thought of pulling the door handle while they cruised at forty-five miles per hour down the country road entered her mind and left just as quickly. She had tried that once before, and Jimmy had grabbed her ponytail and yanked her back in, promising he'd snap her neck if she ever tried that again.

Nick didn't look like the kind of man who would lay a hand on a woman.

Jimmy didn't look like that kind of man, either. Not initially.

"Please, I need to go home."

A look of confusion flickered across Nick's face before he focused on the road in front of him again. "It's okay. I won't take you to the hospital. My sister runs a small health-care clinic on the edge of town. It won't cost you anything. If we hurry, we can catch her before she closes up for the night. She usually works late. She can stitch you up right quick."

When Sarah gasped, Nick added, "It won't be bad, I've had plenty of stitches over the years, much to the dismay of my nanny. My sister'll do it as a favor to me. Don't worry about the cost."

"Oh, I can't." Sarah's head throbbed. She really, *really* wanted to go home and forget this miserable day. She couldn't take free services that were meant for someone who really needed them. And they'd ask for her name. Details that could get her killed.

Her anxiety spiked. If she freaked out now, Deputy Jennings—Nick—would think she had a screw loose. Best to remain calm and not raise any more suspicions.

The yellow dash on the country road mesmerized Sarah. She had gotten used to hoofing it these past six months. A car required a license, registration, a digital footprint. Again, all things that would reveal her location, only sixty miles away from her stalker. She'd run away, but not too far. She needed to be able to reach her sick mother in Buffalo in an emergency. But for now, she stayed away, prayed for her mother's health and maintained a low profile.

"How come we've never officially met before?" Nick asked, as if reading her thoughts.

"I haven't been in town long." *Be vague.*

"What brought you to Apple Creek?" He cut a sideways glance before returning his attention to what was in front of him and the equally spaced cat's eyes dotting the edge of the dark road. His question sounded innocent enough, but how could she be sure?

"I'm a social worker working with individuals who are either addicted or susceptible to drug or alcohol addiction. I also work with single mothers—not necessarily Amish—to help them access programs and—"

"You mentioned that before. But why here? Why Apple Creek?" Nick glanced at her quickly, then back at the road.

"Why not?" Her words came out clipped despite her efforts to keep her tone even.

"Seems like a remote place. Most newcomers to Apple Creek nowadays are the Amish folk. Do you have ties to the area? Family?"

She crossed her ankles, then uncrossed them when she thought about the possibility of being in an accident and having her legs pinned against the dash in a contorted position. Sarah had a knack for worrying about everything.

She cleared her throat. "The Amish are an underserved area. Many young adults are afraid to reveal their problems, substance abuse or otherwise, to their own community for fear of punishment from the church. At least with me, I can help them work through their issues without the added burden of feeling like they've let down their parents or the church. My hope is to help my clients be the best person they can be, whether they decide to stay in the community or not. No judgment on my part."

"How does that go over with the Amish community?" His tone reminded her of when people asked, "How's that working for ya?" when it obviously wasn't working at all.

"I want to believe most Amish people appreciate my efforts, even if they won't publicly acknowledge what I'm doing. I can respect that. The Amish are a humble people who prefer to remain true to their own community." She wanted, no she *needed*, to work under the radar. Nick didn't need to know that. The fewer people who knew her predicament, the less likely she'd be discovered. "If I can help someone who is struggling with drugs or alcohol, everyone benefits." Sarah let out a long sigh. Her own father had been killed by a drunk driver. Sarah had heard more than once that social workers tended to come out of the ranks of individuals who needed some fixing in their own lives. If only the person who'd decided to drink and drive the day her father had been killed had chosen a different path. Had chosen to get help. How different her life might have been.

"Do you think the person who threw the rock tonight was someone from your group meeting? Or maybe an angry family member who doesn't appreciate what they might consider outside interference?"

"I don't want to believe one of the people I'm trying to help did this." A chill skittered up her spine. *Actually, Deputy Jennings, I think it was my crazy ex-boyfriend, but I don't know how he would have found me.* Sarah had taken tremendous pains to keep her location secret. The only ones who knew her background were the pastor and his wife. And Sarah trusted them completely.

Of course, her mom back in Buffalo knew where her daughter was, but was careful to only contact her through her pastor, who would relay the message to Pastor Mike here in Apple Creek.

Sarah's life had become a tangled web of carefully crafted half-truths and secrets. The more she talked, the greater chance she had of being discovered. That's why outside of work she had primarily kept to herself since she arrived in Apple Creek six months ago.

"Most of my clients' names are kept confidential." Even as the words slipped from her mouth, she knew that wasn't foolproof for confidentiality. Trust was the foundation of her group meetings. She couldn't control what clients revealed about themselves or others once they left.

Being a social worker, regardless of the community, had inherent risks: unstable patients, angry relatives and venturing into unsavory neighborhoods. But her need to help others—provide hope—trumped any threat to her personal safety. She took precautions. She wasn't stupid.

Nick made a noncommittal sound and slowed the vehicle, turning into the parking lot of a nondescript building. A lonely sedan with a dent in the back panel sat in the parking lot. "Good, we caught her."

Her, no doubt, being his sister. The physician.

Sarah's mouth went dry. "I can't. I won't get out of the car."

"My sister's a great doctor. Don't worry."

Sarah glanced around the empty parking lot. The lonely country road beyond that. Her stomach knotted.

Suddenly, she was irrationally angry at this man who, on the surface, only wanted to help her.

"You shouldn't have brought me here," she bit out.

Under the white glow from the spotlights illuminating the building and parking lot, a flash of something raced across his features. For the second time since she had met him earlier tonight, she noticed the vulnerability in his face. He turned to her, a look of apology in his eyes. "Let my sister take a look. Just a look. If after that you want to go home, I'll take you. No questions asked." He cracked his door and the dome light popped on.

Nodding, Sarah squinted against the brightness. Her stomach felt queasy.

The first rule of disappearing—her personal rule—was not to get involved with anyone. Nick Jennings looked a lot like someone who might be worth breaking a rule for.

If only he weren't a police officer.

Sarah knew more than anyone that sometimes even the guys who were supposed to be good weren't.

Jimmy Braeden, her stalker ex-boyfriend, was a prime

example. Her ex was a cop. And if tonight was any indication, he may have finally found her.

Goose bumps raced across her arms and she shuddered. She turned and saw her hollow eyes in the reflection of the passenger window.

"Okay," she said, part agreement, part sigh, "I'll let
your sister take a look." Her acquiescence was mostly to
get inside, out of the open. Away from the crosshairs of
an abusive man who threatened he'd kill her before he'd
ever let her go.

Chapter Two

Sarah's vision narrowed tunnellike as she climbed out of the deputy's vehicle in the parking lot of the health-care clinic. In a flash, Nick moved next to her and grabbed her arm. Her first instinct was to pull away.

Run.

She blinked up at him.

"Are you okay? Here, sit." His words sounded distant, jumbled in her ears. She was only partially aware of him yanking open the car door she had just slammed shut and ushering her to a seated position inside his vehicle. He crouched down in front of her and studied her eyes. "Are you dizzy?"

"I stood up too fast." She had learned to make excuses to cover her panic attacks. It was less embarrassing this way. Her feelings were irrational, self-created, yet she couldn't always control them.

"You've had a head injury."

Sarah absentmindedly reached up and touched her head and pulled her fingers away, sticky with her own blood. Her stomach lurched and she shoved back a million memories of another time her head had been bleeding. Back then, the man with her hadn't offered to help. No, it took several hours and a heaping dose of remorse before he came back to her, pleading for forgiveness with a promise to never lift a hand to her again.

Until the next time.

"Do you think you can make it into the clinic? If not, I can get a wheelchair from inside."

Embarrassment edged out her feelings of anxiety, two emotions that twined around her lungs and made it difficult to breathe. "I can walk in." One thing her ex-boyfriend had taught her was to pretend to be tough.

She had gotten good at pretending. At a lot of things.

Sarah stood and the officer hung close by her side, holding her elbow. He obviously wasn't convinced. When they reached the door of the health-care clinic, it was locked. He buzzed the intercom and a crackling voice responded. "Who is it?"

"Christina, it's Nick. I have a patient for you to examine." He was talking into the intercom but his intense brown eyes were locked on hers, unnerving her.

"Urgent?" came his sister's one word response.

"No, a few stitches."

"Not a good idea," Sarah muttered. She tried to pull away, but Nick gripped her arm tighter. She winced and he eased his hold, but not completely. She must have appeared as unsteady as she felt.

"I'm not going to let you go home with a head wound. I don't want to get a call that you ended up dying in your sleep."

Sarah wasn't sure if his words were an exaggeration to wear down her resistance or a flat-out lie. She hardly thought her injury was that serious. "I was cut by glass, not hit by the rock." She lifted her eyebrows and could feel the stiffness of the dried blood on her forehead.

The annoying buzzer released the lock on the door. As the deputy pulled it open, he whispered, "I'm trying to help you. Are you going to fight me every step of the way?"

She shrugged. She imagined she'd thank him one day for insisting she be treated for the cut on her head, sparing her from a lifetime of explaining how she got the scar, but today wasn't that day.

They reached the dated waiting room. Dark stains—including a now-black piece of bubblegum—marred the bluish-gray carpet. Nick didn't ask her to sit down on one of the blue plastic chairs, something her pounding head definitely would have appreciated. Instead he guided her through the office with a gentle hand on her waist and found his sister on the phone in the back.

The attractive woman, her long dark hair pulled up into a messy bun, mouthed without making a sound, "Give me a minute." Her gaze traveled the length of Sarah, a scrutiny Sarah had tried to avoid at all costs since she had moved into the small cottage in Apple Creek and set up her quiet practice through the church.

Sarah's face heated and the urge to flee nearly overwhelmed her. *Don't have a panic attack. Don't have a panic attack.*

The physician pointed at the open door of an adjacent examination room. Nick understood the silent directive and led Sarah into the room. At his insistence, she sat on the exam table, the white, protective paper crinkling as she scooted back. Nick stood sentinel at her side, and an awkward silence joined the steady hum of an air conditioner. Sarah was grateful for the cool air blowing across her skin.

The doctor's appearance in the doorway was never more welcomed. Her gaze went from her brother to Sarah and back to her brother.

"Sarah was cut by broken glass. Someone threw a rock through the basement window of the church."

If Sarah hadn't been watching the doctor's face, she might have missed the slight flinch. "The church, huh? Is nothing sacred?"

Sarah lifted a shoulder, finding it difficult to respond.

"I don't have insurance," Sarah repeated her lie. "I can pay over time if that's okay?"

"We treat a lot of patients without insurance. We'll figure something out. First things first." The physician grabbed a clipboard. "Do you mind filling out this form?"

Sarah took the clipboard in her shaky hands and stared at it. Her pulse rushed in her head and the letters forming the words *Name*, *Address*, *Phone number* scrambled in her field of vision. She placed the clipboard down on the crinkly white paper and slid off the table.

Nick gently touched her elbow.

The world shifted around Sarah, and she grabbed the smooth vinyl edge of the table to steady herself. "This was a mistake. I shouldn't have come here."

"You need to have that cut looked at." Nick, in his crisp sheriff's uniform, loomed over her, his commanding voice vibrating through her. The walls grew close. Too close.

Sarah pushed past him. "I don't *have* to do anything."

"Wait," the physician said. Instinctively, Sarah stopped in her tracks. "You." The physician pointed at her brother.

"Wait outside." She turned to Sarah. "And you. Please, let me look at your injuries."

A small smile touched the attractive doctor's face. "You don't have to fill out any paperwork."

Sarah let out a long sigh, and without meeting Nick's gaze, she returned to the exam table. The deputy slipped outside and closed the door.

The physician examined her in silence. The young doctor smelled like flowers and coconut lotion. She brushed a damp gauze pad across Sarah's wound. "I'd feel better if we put a few stitches in this cut. I'd hate for you to have a huge scar."

"Do you really think that's necessary, Dr. Jennings?" Sarah didn't notice a wedding ring on her finger, and since she was the deputy's sister, she made the leap that her last name was the same as Nick's.

"Yes, I do. And feel free to call me Christina. If I wanted to be Dr. Jennings I would have stayed at the big research hospital where I did my residency before I opened this clinic."

Christina got out her instruments, and Sarah found herself wrapping her fingers around the edge of the table as another wave of panic crested below the surface.

"Perhaps you should lie down. I'd hate for you to pass out while I'm working on you." With her hand to Sarah's shoulder, Christina guided her patient to a supine position.

Christina cleaned the wound with a cool swab. "I'm glad you caught me. I was about to close up for the night." The doctor ran the back of her protective glove across her forehead. "It's been a long day, and the paperwork is endless."

As Christina leaned in close to examine Sarah's

wound, Sarah noticed creases lined the physician's pretty brown eyes, making her a few years older than Sarah first would have guessed.

"Thank you. I appreciate you taking the time. I had tried to tell your brother I didn't need medical attention."

Christina made a sound with her lips pressed together, a cross between an "I see" and "let me make that decision." Sarah didn't ask what she meant by that because she figured it didn't matter. If she got these stitches maybe Nick would leave her alone and she'd resume her quiet life. God willing.

Unless Jimmy had found her...

Sarah swallowed back her nausea, fearing if she let her worries take root, she'd have a full-blown anxiety attack.

Dear Lord, protect me and please, please, please keep me safe from Jimmy.

They fell into silence as Christina focused on the task of suturing Sarah's wound. After Christina finished, she placed a small bandage across Sarah's forehead near her hairline. Christina smiled at her work. "I think that should heal nicely. My father once suggested I go into plastic surgery, but my heart had more humble goals." Christina's brown eyes met Sarah's as if to say, "So, here I am in this small-town health-care clinic."

Christina held Sarah's hand and helped her swing around to a seated position. The physician tipped her head and met Sarah's eyes. "You feel okay?"

Sarah nodded. *As good as I'm going to feel under the circumstances.* But she kept that thought to herself. She had learned to keep a lot of things to herself over the past six months. And even before that.

Christina turned her back to Sarah and put a few instruments onto a tray. "Is there anything you'd like to share with me?"

Emotion rose in Sarah's throat, and she cut her gaze toward the door. The need for escape was strong. "I don't know what you mean."

Christina turned around slowly. "I've seen a lot working in a rural health-care clinic." She tipped her chin toward the discarded clipboard. "You didn't want to share any personal information. What or *who* are you hiding from?"

Sarah's cheeks flared hot. "I'm…" The lie died on her lips. She had mentally trained herself to deny, deny, deny even though deceit went against her Christian upbringing. White lies were a matter of self-preservation. She prayed God would understand.

Sarah looked at the closed door. Christina was bound by doctor-patient confidentiality. Sarah closed her eyes and made a decision. She'd confide in Christina.

Sarah swallowed around the lump in her throat. "I came to Apple Creek to get away from my ex-boyfriend."

"He's abusive."

"Yes. I feared if I stayed in Buffalo, he'd kill me."

Christina reached out and squeezed Sarah's hand. "I'm sorry." She narrowed her gaze. "Do you think he found you? Do you think he could have been the one to throw the rock through the window? To scare you?"

"No, no. No one knows where I am." Sarah hoped saying the words out loud would make them true.

"No one?"

"Only the pastor and his wife. And our pastor back home. My mother also knows where I am. It gives her some peace to know."

Christina flattened her lips and nodded, as if giving it some thought.

"And my brother?"

Sarah shook her head, her eyes flaring wide. "No, I just met your brother tonight."

"My brother's a deputy. He can protect you."

"My ex-boyfriend's a cop. He's on the force in Orchard Gardens, a suburb of Buffalo." Sarah's voice grew soft, dejected. "He didn't protect me."

Christina twisted her lips. "My brother's a good guy."

Sarah gingerly touched the bandage on her forehead. "A lot of people think Officer Jimmy Braeden is a good guy. Do you know how hard it is to file a police report when his brothers in blue think he's such a great guy?" All the old hurt and pain twisted in her gut. "No thanks."

"I think you'd be safer if someone in law enforcement here in Apple Creek knew to be on the lookout for him. Where do you live?"

A little voice in the back of Sarah's head was growing louder and louder: *Don't tell her. Don't let her in. He'll find you.*

"I rented the cottage on the Zook's property." A knot in her chest eased a fraction. It felt good to confide in someone. Was Christina right? Should she let Nick in on her secret?

"I don't want anyone else to know what I'm running away from. I'm safer this way," Sarah blurted before she changed her mind.

"What about tonight? Do you think he found you?"

The heat of anxiety rippled across Sarah's skin. "Tonight was just some kids."

"But you don't *know* that."

"There's no way Jimmy knows where I am."

"Are you sure?" The tone of the doctor's voice sent cold shards shooting through Sarah's veins.

Sarah shoved back her shoulders, trying to muster a confidence she didn't feel. "I have stayed off the radar for six months. No car. No credit card purchases. I've been careful about contact with anyone from my past. There's no way he can know I'm here." And if Jimmy had found her, he wouldn't have simply thrown a rock through the window and fled. He would have stayed, stormed into the basement and killed her.

Unless he wanted to terrorize her first. Make a game of it. Jimmy loved nothing more than playing games. Games that were stacked in his favor.

Sarah shook her head both to answer Christina's question and to shake away her constant irrational thoughts. *This* is what Jimmy had done to her. Not just the physical abuse, he had made her question her own sanity.

She had to flee Buffalo to save herself physically, emotionally and professionally. Jimmy was able to poke so many holes in her accusations that her job as a social worker for the county had been in jeopardy.

Christina ran a hand across her chin. "If you're running away, why only go an hour from Buffalo? You could have gone anywhere. The other side of the country."

"It's twofold really. The pastor of my old church had a connection here in Apple Creek. They needed a social worker. And my mother still lives in the area."

"You realize it's dangerous to contact your mother. Your boyfriend—"

"*Ex*-boyfriend."

"Well, he's probably keeping tabs on your mother in case you make contact."

"I haven't. Only through the pastors have we kept in

touch. Through letters." Loss and nostalgia clogged her throat. "My mom's sick. I need updates, and I need to be able to run home in an emergency."

Christina bit her lower lip and nodded. Sarah appreciated that Christina didn't question her need to be near her mom. Just in case.

"If even one person knows where you are, you're in jeopardy," Christina added.

Sarah was about to say something when a quiet knock sounded on the door.

Christina lowered her voice so Nick wouldn't overhear through the door. "If you're not going to leave Apple Creek, I strongly encourage you to confide in my brother. He can protect you," she repeated.

A stark reality weighed heavily on Sarah. If Jimmy Braeden found her, no one could protect her.

"A deputy sheriff's escort to my home is more than enough. You don't have to walk me to the door, *Officer* Jennings." Sarah slowed at the bottom step of her rented cottage and turned to face him, obviously trying her best to put her protective shield back in place. Nick could see it in her eyes. She was refusing his help every step of the way.

What secret was she hiding?

"You were attacked this evening, and whoever did it is still out there."

"I was hardly attacked. Someone threw a rock through a window, and I got in the way. It was probably kids fooling around."

Nick raised an eyebrow. "May I make sure your property's secure?" He framed it as a question, but he wasn't leaving until he made sure she was safe.

"Only in a small town." Sarah shrugged and smiled, an attempt to sound light and breezy, but she wasn't fooling him.

"I'll check the doors and windows."

"Okay." Sarah sounded exhausted.

His cell phone chirped, and he glanced at it and held up his finger.

"Deputy Sheriff Jennings."

"Hey, Nick." It was Lila, the dispatcher. "Sheriff Maxwell caught some kids lurking around behind the general store. They were throwing empty liquor bottles against the wall."

"Any of them confess to shattering the church window?"

"Not yet, but I imagine once we get some of their fathers in here, they'll straighten right quick."

"Amish?"

"Three of the five. Two are townies."

"Are they being held?"

"Yes, at the station. If you want to put the fear of God in them, you should come in quick. I don't imagine they'll be there long."

"Okay." Nick clicked End and looked at Sarah.

"They caught some kids breaking glass bottles behind the general store. No one claims to have thrown a rock through the church window, but it's possible."

An overwhelming need to protect Sarah filled him. What was it about her? Her petite stature? Her vulnerability? Or was he drawn to Sarah's fiery attitude that emerged every time he suggested something she didn't like.

His mind flashed to his sister Christina. She seemed to have her life together now—she lived and breathed the health-care clinic—but there was a time when she, too, had been vulnerable and he hadn't been there to help her. His stomach twisted at the thought of what might have happened if she hadn't gotten away the night she was attacked on campus. His head told him he couldn't be everywhere, but the pain in his heart told him he needed to try. It made him want to be a better officer.

They stood in silence for a minute before Sarah turned and inserted the key into the lock. Most people in Apple Creek didn't lock their doors, but he supposed a single woman living out here all alone wasn't like *most* people.

And enough bad things had happened, even here in Apple Creek, that eventually everyone would realize they're not immune to evil.

Sarah pushed open the door and propped the screen door open with her hip. She turned to face him. "Since they picked up the kids breaking bottles, I'm fine out here." There was a hint of a question in her tone.

"Hold on, you're not slipping away from me that easily."

Sarah narrowed her eyes. He couldn't seem to reach her, and he wasn't sure why he was striking out.

"I'm going to call Sheriff Maxwell and get their names, and you can tell me if you know any of them from your meetings."

Sarah leaned on the doorframe and held the screen door open a fraction with the palm of her hand, apparently still hesitant to allow him into her home.

Once Nick gave the names, Sarah frowned. "Ruben and Ephram Zook live next door." She stretched out her arm and pointed to the well-tended home across the field. "I'm surprised they'd get caught up in such foolishness. I'm renting the house from their parents. Their father is rather strict. However, I suppose saying an Amish father is strict is redundant." The tight set of her mouth relaxed into an all-too-fleeting smile. "But neither boy has been to one of my meetings. I've never heard of them having issues with alcohol or drugs. Or being otherwise wild during *rumspringa*."

"What about the other names?"

Sarah shook her head. "Not familiar to me."

"I'll have to talk to each of them. See if they'd been near the church first."

"Please don't tell anyone you asked if the young Amish men had been to one of my meetings. My work is based on trust. They'll be afraid to come if they think I'll rat them out."

Trust.

Nick nodded. Strange word for a woman who seemed afraid to trust him. She was obviously harboring secrets.

"You going to be okay out here?"

"Yes, I'm fine."

Nick hesitated a fraction before pivoting on his heel and stomping down the porch steps.

Sarah Lynn had secrets. Unless her secrets drew the attention of the Apple Creek sheriff's department, Nick decided he'd let her be.

The last thing he needed was to get caught up with someone like Sarah. It would be easy to do. But Nick had already been burned by a woman with her share of secrets.

Once in a man's lifetime was enough.

Sarah walked through the small cottage she rented—cash only—from the Amish family next door without turning on any lights. The downstairs windows lacked curtains, and she hadn't remedied the situation because she had to be conservative with her money. Make it last. But she hated the lack of privacy. A woman who had a stalker didn't relish the notion of being in a lit-up fish tank. So most nights, she retired to her upstairs bedroom to read in privacy.

How long can I keep hiding? Delaying my life because I'm afraid of one man?

Sarah reached the kitchen. The white moonlight slanted across the neat and functional cabinets and stove. *Englischers*, as the Amish called people like her, had lived here and when they moved away, Amos Zook had purchased the house adjacent to his land for future use by one of his children. Therefore, the house had modern amenities, such as they were, that would have to be torn out once one of the sons and his new bride moved into the house. Perhaps when Ruben, their second-eldest son, married Mary Ruth. If the rumor mill was to be believed. When Sarah first heard the plans for the house, she found it amusing. Updating a home by removing modern conveniences.

Sarah opened a cabinet closest to the sink and got a glass for water. As the cool liquid slid down her throat, her mind drifted to her mother. Alone in the only home Sarah had ever known.

She and her mother had been exchanging letters through their pastors. Her mother's were always filled with cheery accounts of what she had been up to depending on the day and the weather.

"Weeded the garden today. You should see your father's rosebushes." Her father had been dead twenty years, but his rosebushes kept thriving.

"Wow, had to shovel the walkway three times today. I don't think spring is ever going to get here."

Or...

"It's been so hot that I've had to turn on the fan at night. You know how I hate to sleep with that fan."

Despite her mother's lung cancer diagnosis almost a year ago, Sarah rarely ever heard her mother complain about her health. And when it came time to flee Buffalo because of Jimmy, her mother encouraged her to go and live her life, happy and healthy and away from that domineering man.

Her mother made it sound like her last wish: that her daughter live a happy life. Perhaps the kind of life that had eluded her mother after she lost her husband in a drunk-driving accident.

Pinpricks of tears bit at the back of her eyes. Losing a dad as a little kid did that to a person. Her poor dad had gone out for ice cream when some drunk teenager T-boned him at an intersection. Sarah inhaled through her nose and exhaled through her mouth, a trick she had learned to calm her anxiety. It worked maybe half the time.

Sarah glanced around the dark kitchen, and her cheeks flushed. Her mother had been widowed when Sarah was only ten. She raised Sarah to be a confident, independent woman. It shamed Sarah that she had fallen for a man who was able to control her.

Instead of following her mother's lead, Sarah had grown up fearful, cautious, contained.

Now she'd have to spend the rest of her days hiding. And pray she'd get to visit her mother again in person before the horrible disease took its toll.

A rush of nostalgia overwhelmed her, and the sudden urge to call her mother nearly brought her to tears. Sarah moved to the kitchen hutch in the darkness and opened the middle drawer. It opened with a creak, sending shivers up and down her spine. Sarah hated that she had grown fearful of her own shadow. Yet, she had turned Nick away when he volunteered to check her house. Such was the conundrum of being stalked by a cop.

Afraid, but too afraid to call the police.

Glancing around the darkened space of her current home, she convinced herself she was alone. Safe, but alone. She laughed, an awkward sound in the silence.

Boy, am I ever alone.

Leaning down, she stretched her arm to the back of the drawer. There, she found the disposable phone and a pre-paid card with one hundred minutes. Items she had purchased—*with cash*—in a moment of weakness, but then never used. Sometimes just knowing she had a phone, a way to reach out, made her feel less lonely.

Tonight she had reached her breaking point. No one could trace the call, she reasoned. She needed her mom. What girl didn't? She needed to hear her mother's reassuring voice. Tonight of all nights.

Sarah flipped on a light. Her hands shook with the knowledge of what she was about to do. Sarah fumbled with the packaging until she freed the phone. It fell and clattered against the pine table in her kitchen. She scooped it up and held it close to her beating heart, feeling as if she were doing something criminal.

The tiny hairs on her arms stood on edge and she couldn't shake that feeling that someone was watching her. She lifted her head and stared toward the back window, her reflection caught in the glass. Beyond that, the yard was pitch-black. A surge of icy dread coursed through her veins. She'd have to save up for curtains. Sitting here like a duck on a target stand with a big red bull's-eye over her head didn't do anything for her nerves.

She gathered up the phone's instructions and turned off the lamp. She hurried into the downstairs bathroom, closed the door and turned on the light to read the instructions. In short order—after installing the battery and activating the phone—she was calling the familiar phone number of her childhood home. The same phone number Sarah had since the time she could reach her mother's rotary phone mounted on the wall in the kitchen. The phone had been updated, but little else had in her mother's cozy home.

Yeah, the Gardners didn't have the fanciest gadgets, but they did have each other. Sort of.

With shaky fingers, Sarah pressed the last digit of her home phone number and held her breath. Silence stretched across the phone for a long time. Sarah pulled it away from her ear and glanced at it, wondering if it actually worked. A distant ringing sounded in the quiet space, and Sarah quickly pressed the phone to her ear. It was getting late, but she knew her mother didn't sleep much nowadays.

...Three, four, five...

She counted the rings.

"Come on, Mom, answer the phone."

She imagined her mother pushing off the recliner—maybe asleep in front of whatever show happened to be on right now—muttering about the nerve of someone calling so late. No matter how many times she told her mother to keep the portable phone by her side, her mother insisted on placing it in the charger.

Every. Time.

...Eight, nine...

Sarah's body hummed with impatience.

"Hello," came her mother's curt greeting, startling Sarah who had all but given up hope that she'd reach her mom tonight.

Sarah swallowed a knot of emotion. "Mom." The word came out high-pitched and tight.

"Sarah…" her mother said her name on a hopeful sigh.

"Yeah, it's me."

Her mother's tone shifted from surprised delight to concern. "Is everything okay?"

Sarah touched the bandage on her head. "Yeah, yeah, I just missed you and needed to hear your voice."

Her mother made an indecipherable sound and started to cough, a wet, popping noise. Her mother tried to talk, but the racking cough consumed her.

Sadness, helplessness and terror seized Sarah's heart.

She envisioned her mother reaching for a tissue and holding it in a tight fist against her mouth as her pale face grew red from the exertion of coughing. Her eyes watering. A loud gasp sounded across the line as her mom struggled to catch her breath.

Sarah muttered a curse against Jimmy. She should be there caring for her mother. Not hiding an hour away, alone in someone else's house.

After a moment, when the coughing slowed, Sarah asked, "Are you okay?"

Her mother seemed to have collected herself. "I think I'm coming down with a cold."

Her poor, sweet mother, always trying to protect her only daughter. Sarah hadn't magically forgotten that her mother had lung cancer.

"Have you been keeping up with your doctor's appointments?"

"Yes. There's just so many. Sometimes I'll have a coughing jag when I'm driving…" Her mother forced a cheery tone. "Now, don't worry about me. I'm as tough as they come. Now tell me about you. I thought we were only supposed to write letters. Safer that way."

"I called on a disposable phone."

Silence stretched across the line. "Jimmy came here the other day."

Sarah's heart jackhammered in her chest. "What did he want?" *You, stupid, stupid girl!* Suddenly the phone felt like a hot coal in her hand. What if he tracked her down here? How? It was a disposable phone.

Jimmy was resourceful.

She looked up at the lavender walls of the small downstairs half bath. She'd have to run again. This time farther away. Away from her mother.

"Jimmy acted like he was checking up on me, seeing if I needed anything—boy, that man could charm a lollipop from a baby—but I knew better. He was fishing around to see if I knew where you were. Same as he's done the other times he's swung by the house on the guise of checking up on me."

Sarah pressed the phone tighter to her ear, her racing pulse making it more difficult to hear. "What did you tell him?" Sarah's mouth grew dry as she anticipated her mother's answer. They had rehearsed before Sarah left as to what her mother should say or do, but Sarah constantly worried that her mother's illness, medication or just a plain old slip of the tongue would jeopardize her location.

Sarah knew she was being irrational, but having someone mess with your mind for two years straight had forced an otherwise sane girl to consider every crazy scenario.

Her mother started coughing again, but regained her composure more quickly this time. "I told him what we agreed upon. *Again.* That you had a job opportunity in California. Lord, forgive me for lying, but I do it to keep you safe."

"I imagine he's pressing you for an address. A phone number."

"I told him it was best if he moved on now."

Sarah could imagine Jimmy's reaction when he was told to give up on something. Jimmy Braeden wasn't a quitter. Or one who liked to lose. And losing Sarah had come as a huge blow to his ego.

"Mom, there's no way Jimmy believes I moved to California for a job. Not when you're not feeling well." *Not feeling well.* That was an understatement. "He's going to keep pushing." Maybe they should have come up with a different story.

Jimmy would never stop looking for her. That much she knew for sure. Knees feeling weak, Sarah grabbed the towel bar and lowered herself onto the closed toilet lid. She reached forward and turned the lock on the bathroom door.

One swift nudge with a strong shoulder would send the door into splinters. How pitiful. She had locked herself into the bathroom of the home where she lived alone.

"I'm sorry I'm not there for you." Sarah fought to keep the tears from her voice.

"I'm managing fine."

Sarah cleared her throat. "What did the doctor say last time you were there?"

She envisioned her mom waving her hand in dismissal.

"Oh, the same as always. If I believed everything they told me, I'd be buried next to your father already."

Cold dread pooled in Sarah's stomach. She feared her mother would never tell her the truth when it came to her prognosis.

Sarah traced the round edge of the brass door handle. "Maybe it's time I came home."

"I'm fine." Her mother's forced cheeriness sounded shrill. They both knew Sarah returning to Buffalo would only add more stress to her mother's already stressed life. And they both knew Jimmy was a violent man who had the backing of his brothers in uniform—both in Orchard Gardens where he worked and his fellow cops in nearby Buffalo. All the cops seemed to know each other. Yet, Sarah couldn't fault the men. Jimmy was a great liar and friend, when he wasn't beating up his girlfriend. She didn't blame his fellow cops for being deceived. Hadn't she been? When Sarah tried to make a report, Jimmy's own mother gave him an alibi. Then the rumors began when Sarah showed up at the station with a black eye.

Sarah had been out drinking and picked up the wrong guy. Now to save face, she's trying to blame it on Officer Braeden because they just went through a bad breakup.

It was then that she knew she'd never get justice. And if she valued her life and her mother's peace of mind, she had to leave.

Sarah pulled off a strip of toilet paper and wiped her nose. "Maybe you and I can go off somewhere. Somewhere where Jimmy can't find us."

"Sarah… Sarah…" her mother said, in her familiar soothing voice that made Sarah's chest ache with nostalgia. "We've been through all this. I need to stay close to my doctors. And I like my home. Tending the garden." *I want to be in my own bed when I die*. Her mother didn't say it, but it was implied.

Sarah swallowed around the knot of emotion in her throat.

"Have you made any friends where you are? Someone you can trust?"

Nick's kind smile floated to mind. "It's hard, Mom. I don't know who I can trust." However, Sarah *had* confided in Nick's sister, but Christina was bound by doctor-patient confidentiality. And sweet, Amish Mary Ruth would never understand her new friend's predicament.

And Sarah didn't trust her own decision-making skills. She had been wrong—so very wrong—before.

"You need to stay safe," her mom said, her voice cracking. "*Please*, I love you."

"I love you, too, Mom. I'll stay here."

"That's my girl. Go and save the world." Her mother liked to tout that her only daughter was always looking for ways to help people. Too bad Sarah didn't know how to help herself.

Chapter Three

The next morning, Nick grabbed two large coffees—one black, one double cream, double sugar—and headed to his sister's clinic. When he arrived, the first rays of sun were poking over the full foliage of the trees. He could already tell it was going to be a scorcher today. They were in the dog days of summer, and in a few short months, everyone would be grumbling about the snow and cold.

He glanced at the clock on his dash. The clinic didn't open for another thirty minutes, but he knew his sister would already be doing paperwork and preparing for the day. Both he and his sister were workaholics in jobs that served the public. Nick always figured that had a lot to do with their upbringing, the children of two entrepreneurs who made and lost their first fortune before they were thirty-five and made it again by forty. The second time was a keeper.

All the children could have gone into the family business—only their younger sister Kelly had—and continued to live a life of privilege, but instead Christina and Nick seemed determined to save the world. Their parents, although wealthy and living lives unimaginable by most, had been philanthropists and had made things like Christina's health-care clinic possible. Linda and John Jennings were well respected in Apple Creek even though they only touched down at their home base once or twice a year.

Nick went around back to the alley and found his sister's car parked next to the back door. He tried the handle, but found it locked. He was relieved. Christina was a smart, compassionate doctor and street savvy. Even in small towns, addicts and other low-life criminals sought out drugs from whatever source they could find them. He was glad his sister took her safety seriously.

Juggling the stacked coffees in one hand, he pulled out his cell phone and texted Christina.

At back door

A few seconds later the door opened. Christina initially looked like she was going to scold him for bothering her this early, but when her eyes landed on the coffee, a bright smile crossed her features.

Christina was his little sister, younger by three years. The two of them grew up in Apple Creek and mostly only had each other and Kelly as playmates on their parents' sprawling estate. Their mom and dad, both self-employed, could work from anywhere, and when Nick, Christina and Kelly were young, they decided the tranquility of Apple Creek was as good a place as any to build a home.

"Double cream, double sugar?" Christina reached out with the look of a woman in need of a caffeine fix.

"Of course. First coffee of the day?"

"Yes, I usually wait until the office staff comes in to start the coffeemaker."

Christina stepped back, allowing her brother entry into the clinic. She peeled back the brown lid from the take-out coffee and inhaled the scent.

"You really love that stuff."

Christina laughed. "Love is a strong word." She took a long sip with her eyes closed, then lifted them to study him. "What brings you here bright and early, big brother?" She held up her hand. "Oh, let me guess. Does it have anything to do with a pretty, petite blonde who got three stitches in her forehead last night?"

"Am I that transparent?" A corner of his mouth quirked up.

"I'm your sister. You've always worn your heart on your sleeve."

"This has nothing to do with my heart."

Christina arched a skeptical brow. "Really?" She put the coffee down and sat on the corner of her desk and crossed her arms over her chest.

"I know you can't break doctor-patient confidentiality."

"But you're hoping I might?"

"No, but is there something I need to know? To protect her."

Christina laughed. "Right. You're looking for an excuse to talk to her again. I don't blame you. It's been, what…a year or so since you and Amber went your separate ways."

Just the mention of the name Amber sent Nick's mood spiraling into the depths of the foulest garbage dump. He and Amber had met five years ago at a Christmas party at his parents' home. They hit it off and had been inseparable until Nick was deployed. Turned out, Amber wasn't the kind to wait. Turned out, Amber and some-one—Troy or Trey or something like that—were secretly dating behind his back.

Amber sent him a Dear John letter while he was still deployed. It was like getting punched while dodging IEDs.

"Yeah, do me a favor, don't mention Amber." Nick hadn't dated anyone seriously since. He didn't trust his instincts. He had thought Amber was the one. Turns out so did Troy/Trey. They were married a few months ago at the country club. Their wedding had been featured prominently on the front page of the LifeStyle section of the newspaper. Nick suspected Amber loved money more than him, and when she realized he wasn't going to follow in his parents' footsteps, she decided she had better find another meal ticket.

The coffee roiled in his gut. *How had he not seen through Amber?*

Christina pushed off her desk and turned around to fumble with some neatly stacked papers. He knew his sister well enough to know she was struggling to decide how much to tell him about Sarah.

Nick respected her job, the need for confidentiality. But he'd also hate to ignore his instincts on this one. Sure, his dating instincts were terrible, but his law enforcement instincts were usually spot-on.

Sarah was afraid of something. More than a rock thrown through the basement window.

Christina picked up a clipboard and held it close to her chest. "You might want to pay Sarah a visit. You could tell her you're following up from last night. I think she needs someone to talk to."

He studied his sister closely.

"And hey, maybe you could ask her out for dinner."

Nick's head jerked back. "I'm done with women with secrets."

Christina pinned him with her gaze. "You're going to have to get over Amber."

"I'm over her."

Christina didn't say anything, suggesting she doubted him. "Then, go out and visit Sarah. Maybe you'll surprise yourself."

"I don't make a habit of asking crime victims out on a date."

Christina touched his arm. "Will you please get over yourself? We live in a small town. If an attractive young woman happens to move here, there's nothing wrong with asking her out on a date."

Nick felt flustered in only the way a little sister could fluster a big brother. "I didn't come out here to ask you for dating advice. I came as a sheriff's deputy to ask you if there's something I should know about our newest resident."

Christina frowned. "And you know full well I couldn't tell you." With both her hands planted on his chest, she shoved him playfully toward the door. He put one hand on the lid of his coffee to prevent it from spilling.

Nick stepped out onto the pavement of the back alley, the sun now above the trees. Christina held the door open with her shoulder. She tapped the metal trim on the bottom of the door with her black loafers. "Sarah could use a friend."

Nick studied his sister's face. Christina was the only one who truly got him. He smiled. "Go finish your coffee before it gets cold."

A shrill buzz sounded from inside the clinic. Someone was at the front door. "Looks like duty calls."

"Have a good day, little sis."

"You, too. Be safe."

Nick waved and watched as the door slammed shut. Instinctively he tested the lock, making sure his sister was secure in the clinic. He knew he couldn't protect everyone at all times…but he'd sure try.

The image of Sarah's pretty face filled his mind. His gut told him she was in need of protecting.

Sarah flipped back the covers on her purple-and-pink bedspread with oversize tulips and gazed around her childhood bedroom. She glanced down at her favorite Holly Hobbie nightgown and ran her hand along its soft fabric. Even in her dream, Sarah knew she was dreaming. *She turned her gaze to the corner. Her dolly was tucked under a quilt her mother had made in a crib her father had taken special pride in crafting.*

Sarah had had a charmed childhood. Until that fateful day…

Sarah's dreaming self flipped her legs over the edge of the bed and swung them, trying to take it all in. Trying to memorize every detail of this dream. Hoping her father would come in to kiss her goodnight. To say their evening prayers together.

Feelings of warmth and nostalgia made her smile.

Sarah stretched her legs and curled her toes into the shag rug shaped in the form of a rainbow. She loved that rug. She had spent countless hours with her dollies on that rug pretending they lived in a retro 70s apartment.

Bang! Bang!

Still dreaming, Sarah snapped her attention to the closed bedroom door.

Thud…thud…thud.

Sarah rolled over, consciousness seeping into her dream world. She cracked her eyes open a slit, and a stream of sunshine slipped in through the edge of the white roller shades. Her Amish-made quilt was pretty, but not the same as her childhood favorite. The quilt had slid off the edge of her bed during her fitful dreams. She blinked a few times, trying to recall the last one. The warm fuzziness of it. The return to her childhood.

She smiled and stretched. Talking to her mom last night had made for some vivid dreams. She was surprised she had even slept. She had tossed and turned for hours, until finally getting up around four in the morning. She had gone downstairs, got a glass of water and written in her journal a bit. Her journal kept her sanity, allowing her to empty her mind of her worst fears and worries. Allowing her mind to quiet so she could drift off to sleep.

Sighing, Sarah swung her legs over the edge of the bed. Her toes touched the smooth wood of the pine floor. Nothing to curl her toes into. Maybe she'd buy herself an area rug. Undoubtedly the Apple Creek General Store probably didn't carry what she was looking for. The market for 70s shag here in Apple Creek was slim to nonexistent.

A distant thought niggled at her brain. Had something woken her up? A sound? Sarah rolled her shoulders. She was probably still spooked from the incident last night at the church. Lifting her hand, she touched the bandage on her forehead and groaned.

She'd get lots of questions today from her clients.

She'd mention the broken window, but play it off. She preferred to keep the focus on them. Not her.

Sarah quickly got ready for the day and twirled her hair into a ponytail. Living out here in the country, she had come to enjoy jeans, a T-shirt, no makeup and no-fuss hair. In many ways it was freeing.

Jimmy preferred it when she was all made up.

Sarah jogged down the stairs and froze with her hand on the railing. The front door stood ajar. She took a step back and lost her balance, landing on her backside on the stairs. She pulled herself up by the railing. Her heart beat wildly in her ears. She bent and leaned over the railing, trying to see if someone had come into her house. She hadn't left the door open last night.

Or unlocked.

And her house was secure when she had gotten up in the middle of the night.

She bit her lower lip, and her legs went to Jell-O.

Had Jimmy found her after all? Picked the lock? Had it been a coincidence that some boys had been caught smashing bottles against an alley wall near the church where a window was broken?

Cautiously, she descended the remaining stairs, listening for any out-of-place creak, voice, breath…anything that would indicate she wasn't alone. She inhaled deeply through her nose, wondering if she could detect Jimmy's cologne, a scent that often lingered in a room long after he had left.

Nothing.

Leaving the door open—it would serve as a quick escape if she needed it—Sarah tiptoed through the sitting room and into the kitchen. She stiffened in the doorway, panic sending ripples of goose bumps racing across her flesh.

Her hand flew to her mouth to cover a silent scream. There on the table were the remains of a thick snake, its head cut off and placed on top of the phone she had used last night. The phone she had carefully tucked back into the center drawer of the hutch. Her diary sat on the edge of the table where she had left it.

Nerves on edge, she backed up.

Get out! Get out!

A solid chest and firm hands on her arms stopped her backward progression.

A scream ripped from her throat.

Chapter Four

"It's okay. It's me." Nick released his grasp on Sarah's arms and stepped around in front of her so she could see him. "It's Nick Jennings. You're okay."

Sarah clamped her mouth shut and a hint of embarrassment touched the corners of her eyes.

Nick's gaze drifted from her frightened face to the tableau on Sarah's kitchen table. "What happened here?" He quickly glanced around the room.

"Do you think I honestly know?" Her voice held more than an edge of annoyance. "I came downstairs and found this." She jabbed her index finger at the coiled-up snake on her kitchen table. She picked up a small book on the edge of the table and slipped it into the hutch.

"Was your front door open when you came downstairs?" He made the logical leap, having found the door yawning open upon his arrival.

"Yes." She rubbed her forehead and winced when she made contact with the bandage. "I don't understand. I locked up last night after you left."

"You didn't hear anything?"

Sarah shook her head; all the color had drained from her already pale face.

"I came down around four in the morning to get a glass of water. There was nothing on the table then—I'm sure of it. I mean, other than my notebook." With a shaky hand, she pointed toward the hutch where she had just put the book. "Whoever did this, did it in the early-morning hours."

Nick tipped his head, looking out the back kitchen window. From here, he could see a couple Amish boys doing chores at the neighboring barn. "Maybe someone next door saw something. I'll go pay them a visit."

"Ephram and Ruben Zook were picked up last night for smashing bottles, remember? I don't think they're going to want to talk to you." Sarah pulled out a chair and sat down heavily. She moved as if to put her elbows on the table when she grimaced at the proximity of the snake and slumped against the tall wooden back of the chair and crossed her arms. Every muscle in her body seemed to be trembling.

"Did they admit to throwing the rock through the church window?" Sarah looked up at Nick with a hint of hope in her eyes that he didn't understand.

"No. Only a few bottles were smashed. They hadn't meant any harm and promised to clean it up today. Apparently, they were returning home after the Sunday singings when they ran into some of their *Englisch* friends." He lifted his palms. "Might have been a case of hanging out with the wrong crowd."

Sarah rubbed the back of her neck. "Let's leave them out of this then. I don't want to stir up any more trouble."

"That ship has sailed. Between last night and this morning, it seems you have poked a hornet's nest."

She looked up at him with an unreadable expression.

He leaned in closer to examine a cell phone under a severed snake's head. *Gruesome.* He frowned. "I have a hard time believing the same person who threw a rock through the window did this." He winced at the putrid smell. "Dismembering animals? That's sick." He shook his head. "Not to mention breaking and entering."

Sarah rubbed the back of her neck but didn't say anything.

"Is there anything else you might want to share with me?" Nick thought of the vague reference his sister had made. Did Sarah have dark secrets that put her in jeopardy? Or had some punks thought it would be great fun to harass a single woman living out in the country on her own?

Sarah's weary gaze shifted to the badge on his uniform, then up to his face. The brief moment of vulnerability disappeared and was replaced by an inscrutable expression. "No. I don't know who did this."

"What are you hiding?" Nick's job always had him pushing for the truth from people who often weren't willing to offer it.

Was she a fugitive?

The unlikely scenario flitted from his brain when footsteps sounded on the front porch. "Hello," called a woman with the lilt he recognized as belonging to the Amish.

Nick moved to the front door. Sarah followed close behind.

Nick stepped into the doorway and was greeted by an Amish woman with a young Amish girl by her side. Sarah slipped next to him and paused in the doorway. Standing this close to her emphasized how petite and vulnerable she was.

"Good morning, Temperance," Sarah greeted the Amish woman, then her gaze dropped to the little girl, no more than seven or eight years old, holding her mother's hand. "Morning, Patience."

Temperance fidgeted with the apron on her dress. "Is everything okay? We noticed you had law enforcement over here. I know my boys got in some trouble last night. This doesn't have anything to do with that, does it? They said they weren't near the church." The Amish woman's gaze drifted from Nick to the bandage on her neighbor's head. "My boys are *gut*. They wouldn't have damaged a church."

Sarah lifted her hand and touched the bandage gingerly. "I know. Ruben and Ephram have been nothing but helpful to me."

"Is everything okay this morning?" Temperance asked.

Sarah waved her hand in dismissal. "I'm fine. Deputy Jennings was checking up on me." Nick had never actually told her why he had shown up this morning. Checking in on her was part of it. The other was to see if she was in any real danger. Based on the circumstances, he'd have to go with yes.

As if reading his mind, Sarah squared her shoulders and stepped onto the porch. Was she trying to block the view into her home to make sure her neighbor's young daughter wasn't frightened by the dead snake on the table? Nick doubted they'd be able to see all the way into the kitchen. To be sure, Nick joined her and pulled the door closed behind him. "Hate to let bugs into the house."

"Everything's okay." Sarah smiled at the child. "You want to come over later and we'll read more of Laura Ingalls Wilder?"

The little girl smiled brightly, but her mother took her

by the shoulders and guided her toward the porch steps. "Patience has a few chores to do. I don't know if she'll have time for stories."

Sarah's shoulders sagged, and the small smile slid from her lips. "Okay." The single word held so much disappointment.

Temperance brushed at an imaginary spot on her cape. "We wanted to make sure everything was *gut* over here. That's all. We have a lot to do on the farm."

The two guests said their goodbyes, and Sarah's eyes followed the pair as they crossed the yard to their home next door.

"Temperance is usually friendlier to me," Sarah said, almost as if musing to herself. "She must be upset that I got her boys into trouble."

"You didn't get her boys into trouble. They made their own decision when they smashed the bottles. Besides, the Amish aren't partial to law enforcement. Maybe once they knew you were okay, they were eager to leave because of me." Nick wanted to run the back of his fingers across the porcelain skin of her cheek and give her the "it's not you, it's me" speech, but he knew better. She was a stranger, really. Prior to last night, he had only passed her with little more than a "Hello" or "Goodbye" in small-town Apple Creek.

Sarah sat down on the top step of the porch. Her pink toes curved around the edge of the step. "What brought you out here this morning, *Deputy* Jennings?" She emphasized his title, as if it were a bad thing. "Did your sister talk to you?"

Walking over to the railing, he rubbed the back of his neck. He leaned back against the railing so that they were almost back-to-back. He turned to study her serious profile. It was as if she didn't want to make eye contact. "It's not what you think. My sister always respects doctor-patient confidentiality."

"But you suspected something more was going on than a rock through a church window?"

Nick let the silence stretch between them. A gust of wind rustled up and bent the corn stalks growing in the fields next to her house.

Sarah ran a hand down her long ponytail and shifted to face him, a serious expression in her bright blue eyes. "I'm afraid he's found me." Her shoulders drew up, then came down on a heavy sigh.

Nick jerked his head back, and he pushed off the railing. He slipped past her on the steps and turned around to face her so he could look into her eyes. "Who found you?" Nick didn't understand the protective urge he felt for this woman. He hardly knew her.

Sarah gave him a cynical look and no longer seemed to want to talk to him.

"You know the person who broke into your house? Do you think he also threw the rock last night?"

He studied her. Her blond bangs framed her face, hiding most of the bandage covering her stitches. "I'm afraid I do."

Frustration grew in his belly. "Stop being coy and start talking if you want me to help you."

"I didn't ask for your help." She stared at him, anger flashing in her eyes, before she looked away.

"My job is to help you." Then he softened his tone. "Who has an ax to grind with you?"

"I'm a social worker. I'm sure I have lots of enemies." Was she suddenly backpedalling?

Nick tilted his head and tried to coax her to look at

him, but she seemed more focused on the street behind him. "You said you thought you knew who did this."

Sarah bowed her head and threaded her fingers behind her neck. "My ex-boyfriend found me. Now he's going to toy with me until I go running back home. Where he can protect me." Cynicism and defeat laced her tone. "It's the only explanation." She narrowed her gaze but still didn't look at him. "He must really think I'm stupid."

"You ran away from your ex-boyfriend?" Hot blood pumped through his veins.

Her head snapped up, and she directed her fiery gaze at him. "It's not like I had a choice."

"I didn't…" Nick forced his hands to relax, and he sat down on the step next to her. "I'm sorry, I didn't mean to sound accusatory. I have zero tolerance for men who hit women…"

"That makes two of us." She laughed, a brittle sound. "I put up with him for longer than I should have." She shook her head slowly. "I couldn't believe I had turned into one of those women who lets men—" she seemed to be struggling for the right word "—control them. My mother raised me better." The summer sunlight shimmered in unshed tears. He resisted the urge to pull her into an embrace.

"You did nothing wrong," he said, trying to comfort her with his words, all he had a right to offer.

"I didn't have a choice."

"What about the police?"

"He is the police." Sarah studied him as he absorbed that piece of information.

"Where?"

"In a small town right outside of Buffalo. Orchard Gardens." She sounded resigned, sad. "I lived in Buffalo, but he knew a lot of guys on the force there, too. I didn't know who to trust."

"Why didn't you tell me this last night?"

Her gaze locked on the badge on his chest. Then she lifted her wounded eyes to meet his.

"Do you think we belong to one big fraternity? That we'll protect each other no matter what?"

"That's what happened at home. Jimmy can be persuasive. He concocted some story that was so convincing that the other officers thought I was crazy. That I had a drinking problem and was using him to cover it up."

"I'm sorry."

He caught her hiking a skeptical eyebrow.

"You can trust me." The words sounded strange on his lips. Here he was telling her she could trust him, when he had his own trust issues.

"I don't know who to trust anymore. So few people know where I am, I don't know how he found me."

"We don't know that for sure."

"It seems like the only logical answer."

He watched myriad emotions play across her face. He wished he knew her—the situation—well enough to offer her solid advice. Instead he asked, "What do you plan to do now?"

"I don't know." She ran a finger along the tender skin under her eye. "I guess I'll have to move. Again."

Six months.

Six. Short. Months. Apparently that's the expiration date on keeping secrets. It took six months for Officer Jimmy Braeden to find Sarah. Now she'd have to move. Again.

But for now, she had to sit. Focus. Figure out her next step.

Life seemed surreal sitting on her front porch next to Deputy Jennings. She had a hard time thinking of him as simply Nick. He really seemed to care about her well-being, but was his interest genuine?

What if he knows Jimmy? Buffalo isn't that far away, and law enforcement is one big boys' club. Dread pooled in her stomach. *Has Jimmy asked him to keep tabs on me? Or am I being overly dramatic?* Seeing a dead snake sliced up on her table could do that to a girl living alone.

Or maybe this was how small-town cops operated. Making personal visits to the victim the next morning. No nefarious intent.

Sarah blinked and refocused her eyes on the stalks of corn swaying in the morning breeze in the field across the street. There was a sense of timelessness about sitting out here on the farmhouse steps, where a farmer and his family once lived over a hundred years ago.

"Maybe the Amish are on to something?" Sarah's gaze drifted to the farm next door.

"What's that?" Nick's smooth, deep voice had a soothing quality. He turned and they locked gazes. Half his mouth crooked into a wry grin. If she was being truthful, she'd admit to herself how handsome he was. Longish wavy dark hair swept off his face and behind his ears, the ends brushing against his collar. A neatly trimmed goatee on his chin.

A breeze picked up, and a hint of aloe and soap mingled with the corn and freshly chopped hay. She quickly dismissed her keen sense of awareness of him. She had been alone too long. She refocused her attention on the farm next door. Her Amish neighbors made their life off the land, dependent on no one, save for the small rent she paid on this house.

"The Amish live a quiet life. Each generation following in the steps of the one before them. Very little changing." She thought of Mary Ruth, her young Amish friend, who liked to chat about her future. She seemed so full of hope. Sarah didn't know what hope felt like anymore. Didn't know if she'd ever have hope again. Would she forever have to hide from Jimmy?

Sarah ran a hand down her bare arm. The heat from the sun was already strong, beating down on her. If she sat here much longer, she'd be sunburned. She laughed to herself. That was the least of her worries.

She reached up and grabbed the railing and pulled herself to her feet. She swiped the dust of the porch from the back of her pants.

"I have a meeting with a client later today."

"An Amish client?"

"Not today." But it wasn't unusual to see Amish clients. Not all was right within the Amish world. The young adults seemed to struggle the most as the temptations of the outside world crept into their insular lifestyle, tainting it. "It's with a single mom. I can't cancel the meeting. Not at the last minute."

Sarah decided she'd explain to her client that a personal matter had come up and she wouldn't be able to make future meetings. A tiny piece of her heart broke. How long would it be before another social worker took her place? She sighed. Maybe never. "I'll have to come up with a plan for my next move."

Nick stood and faced her. "Do you think that's a good idea?"

"Deputy Jennings—"

"Call me Nick," he said again. She was trying to avoid

calling him by his given name, believing the formality would keep a wall between them.

"As long as we're talking names, my full name is Sarah Lynn Gardner. I've used Sarah Lynn to protect my identity. But I suppose that's not relevant anymore."

Sarah gazed at him warily. "I left my sick mother in Buffalo to hide here in Apple Creek. Apparently, I wasn't adept at staying under the radar." She shrugged. "Maybe my next move should be home. Since Jimmy's going to find me anyway…" The sound of her mother's breathless gasps over the phone broke her heart. "I'm afraid my mother won't be around much longer."

"I'm sorry about your mother."

"Me, too." She paused with her hand on the doorknob. "I'm beginning to think that no matter what I do, it won't be the right thing. I have to be able to live with myself. And right now, I'm thinking I'll live with regret for the rest of my life if my mother dies when I'm not there."

"How would your mother feel if your ex-boyfriend killed you?"

Sarah spun around, anger pumping through her veins. "Low blow."

"Your ex must be violent if you're hiding here."

She nodded, a lump clogging her throat. Jimmy was capable of doing almost anything. She had promised her mother she'd stay safe. Running back to Jimmy's home turf wasn't staying safe. Putting herself in jeopardy would be going against her mother's wishes.

And wouldn't she be putting her mother in jeopardy, too?

And how could Sarah abandon her clients here? It was unlikely another social worker would move to Apple

Creek anytime soon. Sarah pressed her fingers to her temple, a headache forming behind her eyes.

"Are you okay?" Nick asked, his voice low and full of concern. "I didn't mean to be so blunt." If she hadn't sworn off all men, he'd be someone she'd be drawn to. Too bad she wasn't interested in starting a relationship. And especially not with another cop.

"I'm getting a headache."

"You said earlier that social workers are often the target of disgruntled clients."

"Yeah…" she replied, wondering what he was getting at.

"Before you uproot your entire life here in Apple Creek, let me do some investigating. Maybe those boys caught throwing bottles in town last night really do know something about this." Nick pointed at her front door, indicating the dismembered snake inside.

Sarah rubbed her arms. A flicker of hope blossomed in her belly. Some angry Amish boys seemed a whole lot less threatening than six-foot-four Jimmy Braeden. However, the dismembered snake head placed on her phone—the one she had used for the first time to call her mom—sent renewed dread pulsing through her heart.

It had to be Jimmy.

It had to be.

"I'm going to talk to Ephram and Ruben Zook. They were part of the group last night." Nick slowed at the bottom of the porch steps.

Sarah paused with her hand on the doorknob. Closing her eyes briefly, her shoulders sagged. "They're good boys. Perhaps just caught up with the wrong kids last night."

"Maybe they can shed some light on what happened."

"Like I said before, they're not going to want to talk to you."

"I'll play nice."

"Temperance's sons don't strike me as the kind to get into trouble. Ruben has been courting Mary Ruth Beiler, one of the Amish girls who I've grown fond of." Sarah scratched her head.

"It's not unusual for the Amish to blow off some steam after the Sunday-night singings. They *are* teenagers after all." Sarah touched her bandage and winced. "Maybe it's not such a good idea for you to go over there. I don't want to cause any trouble. Amos, their father, has been kind enough to rent me this house. Temperance brings me vegetables from their garden. I don't want to stir up trouble for them."

Climbing the steps to close the distance between them, Nick held up his palms. "Ruben and Ephram are young adults. I have to check to see if they know something. Or maybe they saw something. You think the snake was left in the early morning hours?"

"It wasn't there when I came down during the night for a glass of water." Sarah got a faraway look in her eyes, and he thought he detected a shudder. "What if whoever left the snake was already in the house watching me get a glass of water? Writing in my journal?"

Nick placed a hand on her arm and had to admit he was surprised when she didn't pull away. "You're fine. I won't let anything happen to you."

"You can't promise that."

"I'll start by finding you someplace else to stay."

Sarah stuck out her lower lip and blew her bangs off her forehead. "I—" she ran her fingers through her bangs

"—I haven't decided what I'm going to do." Indecision flashed in her eyes.

Nick tipped his head at Sarah and lifted an eyebrow. "Do you feel safe staying here?"

"Maybe it was a foolish prank." Sarah's voice didn't hold any conviction.

"I wouldn't feel comfortable letting you stay here alone in this house."

"Letting me?" A fiery look descended into her eyes. She shook her head in disgust despite the flicker of fear that swept across her features. This was a woman who had been badly hurt and had trust issues bigger than his.

Nick decided to extend a peace offering for his misstep. "Would you mind coming next door with me? They might be more receptive to talking if I brought along a friendly face." Nick lifted a pleading eyebrow.

"Yeah, throw me under the bus." She pointed to her forehead. "Remember, I'm the reason they got hauled in last night."

"Technically, they were picked up for breaking bottles in the alley." He watched Sarah carefully, waiting for her hard expression to soften.

"At the very least, the Zooks should know that someone broke into your house. They are your neighbors and your landlord. They need to take precautions, too."

"Let's go then. But my money is on Jimmy."

Nick followed Sarah across the lawn to the neighbor's property. A couple young men, their heads covered by straw hats, worked near the barn. Sarah pointed at the closer man. "That's Ephram. And Ruben's over there."

Ephram stopped what he was doing as they approached. Ruben seemed determined to finish his morning chores without interruption.

Nick had been warned when he had started this job about a year ago when he returned from his military service that the Amish were good people, but they didn't take kindly to law enforcement. They liked to handle things within their own community. Having grown up here, Nick already understood this, but he had never worked in the capacity of law enforcement and been directly impacted by their misgivings until recently.

"Morning, men," Nick called, trying to sound friendly. "Could Miss Gardner and I have a word with you?"

"Hello, boys." Sarah smiled. "Ephram, Ruben, this is Deputy Jennings." Ephram and Ruben both looked to be in their late teens, twenty at most.

Ruben stepped forward and crossed his arms, tucking his fingers under his armpits. His eyes moved to the bandage on Sarah's head. "Real sorry to hear you're injured. Good thing Mary Ruth wasn't there. She could have been injured, too." Something about the tight set of his mouth suggested he wasn't happy about Mary Ruth working with Sarah. But Nick couldn't be sure.

"Do you know who was horsing around outside the church? Who might have thrown the rock?"

"We went to the singing," Ruben said. "Mary Ruth was supposed to be there." A hint of annoyance laced his tone. "We were foolish and broke some bottles in the alley. That's all. We weren't near the church."

"Listen," Nick spoke up, "Miss Gardner had more trouble in the early morning hours. Right here at the house on your property."

Ephram stopped shoveling slop into the pigs' troughs and stared at him. "What kind of trouble?" Nick tried to determine if his question was genuine or an act.

Sarah opened her mouth, but before she had a chance

to say anything, Nick help up his hand. He didn't want her to give away details of the crime. Not yet.

"Someone broke into Sarah's house between the hours of four and eight a.m. Did you see anything?"

Ephram glanced down and pushed the dirt around with the toe of his boot. *"Neh."*

"What about you, Ruben?" Sarah asked.

Ruben took off his hat and scrubbed his hand across his blunt-cut hair. His face was clean shaven now, but once he got married, Nick wondered if he'd have enough facial hair to grow a beard. "I overslept this morning."

"And I had to do his chores until he got his sorry self down here."

"No sign of anyone lurking on the porch? Running across the yard? Anything?"

"Neh," they said in unison.

Out of the corner of his eye, Nick noticed their mother crossing the yard to them. "Can we help you?" Temperance seemed more standoffish than she had when she made her way over to Sarah's porch just a little while ago.

"We're trying to determine if your sons saw anything suspicious around my house in the early-morning hours."

Temperance snapped her attention to her nearly grown sons. "This morning? Something happened at the house this morning? Why didn't you tell me when I came over?"

"I didn't want to worry little Patience," Sarah said.

Temperance's lips thinned into a line. "Apple Creek sure has had its share of incidences over the past few years. If you boys saw something, you need to speak up."

"Neh, Mem, we didn't see anything," Ruben said.

Temperance smiled tightly at her neighbor. "My boys are *gut* boys. They both have plans to prepare for baptism, and I don't want anything to derail that. Nothing," she added for emphasis. "It makes me wonder if renting that place to an *Englischer* was such a good idea."

All the color seemed to drain from Sarah's face.

Temperance adjusted her bonnet and straightened her shoulders. "I like you, Sarah, and I understand you've fallen on hard times. But my husband decided to rent the house next door against his better wishes. He warned me this was one step closer to inviting the outside world in." She fussed with her apron, obviously uncomfortable with the direction of the conversation. "I had to convince my husband to rent the home to you. Miss Ellinor has always been kind to me. It was a favor. Please don't make me regret my decision."

Out of the corner of his eye, Nick could see Sarah squirming. She was obviously a woman who didn't like conflict.

"That's not my intent," Sarah said, tucking a loose strand of hair behind her ear. "I'm sorry. We'll let you get back to work."

"Sarah," Temperance called, "I know you're doing the work you feel you need to do, but the Amish like to keep things within their own community."

"I understand and respect that," Sarah said. "However, if someone chooses to come to me for help, I will not turn them away. And my intent is not to encourage them to leave the Amish faith, but rather heal within themselves so they can be the best person they can be, whether they choose to be baptized Amish or not."

Temperance seemed to wince. "I like you. I really do. I enjoy having you as a neighbor. But please be careful how you interact with the Amish."

"Do you know something, Mrs. Zook?" Nick asked.

Something in her nervous mannerisms made him grow suspicious.

"*Neh.* Not at all. Our family could use the extra finances from the rent, and I'd hate to see Sarah leave… or worse, get hurt."

"I'll see that she's kept safe," Nick said.

Sarah bowed her head, and red splotches appeared on her face.

Suddenly, Mrs. Zook's face lit up. "Perhaps we can let our dog come stay at the house. He makes a pretty good guard dog." The woman was obviously ready to change the subject. "He'd probably lick an attacker to death, but at least his bark would alert you."

"That's not a bad idea." But Nick still felt it advisable for Sarah to move out. She was too isolated out here, even with the Zooks next door. Several hundred feet across a vast field afforded a potential attacker the time and seclusion he needed to do whatever he desired.

Nick tipped his head toward the boys working near the barn. "If your boys remember anything, you'll let me know?" He realized he was grasping at straws. No way would Mrs. Zook contact him.

"They're *gut*," she repeated.

"Even the strongest kids have fallen prey to peer pressure," Nick said evenly.

"Peer pressure out here on the farm is different than whatever you experienced growing up in that big estate on Apple Creek Bluff. You can't relate." She hesitated a fraction. "Nor do we expect you to."

Nick forced a weary smile, deciding he'd catch the boys another time. Perhaps when he noticed them in town, away from the watchful eye of their parents. "If you see anything suspicious on your property, please let me know."

Temperance lifted her chin and gave him a subtle nod.

When they returned to Sarah's yard, she turned to Nick. "What did Temperance mean about you not being able to relate because of where you grew up?"

He rubbed the back of his neck, debating how much to tell her. Who he was and where he grew up weren't secrets, but it seemed that once people found out he was one of the Jennings who grew up in the huge home sitting on the escarpment in Apple Creek, well, it colored their perception of him. Made them believe he was some rich boy playing at being a cop.

He dropped his arm and smiled. If he wanted Sarah to trust him, he'd have to trust her. "My parents own Jennings Enterprises. They have a lot of money." He left it at that. "I grew up pretty comfortable."

She studied him for a second, then shrugged. "No shame in that, but I can see some people might take issue with it."

"Mostly because they believe I can't relate because I've never struggled with money issues." He supported himself now. He was an adult, but he definitely had a leg up on getting to where he was today.

"What do you make of our conversation with the Zooks?" Nick changed the subject.

"The Zooks are a good family. I'm sure if they saw something, they would have told us." Sarah slowed by the porch. "Temperance is feeling particularly vulnerable. Her sons are right at the age where they'll be making the decision to be baptized and marry and join the Amish community for life. She's undoubtedly afraid they'll get caught up in something that might delay their entrance into the baptismal preparation classes."

Nick rocked back on his heels. "You've picked up on the local customs rather quickly. How long have you been in town?" He felt a smile pulling at the corners of his mouth.

"Six months." She smiled. Her whole face changed when she smiled. He didn't think she could be more attractive. "My job sometimes involves counseling the Amish. Knowing about their culture helps me help them."

Nick nodded.

"I hate dragging a good family into my mess. I don't want to put them in danger." Sarah bit her lip, indecision darkening her eyes.

"They might know something."

"Maybe." She sounded doubtful.

"You really think it's your old boyfriend."

"I'm worried."

"Let me protect you."

"I'd hardly think it's appropriate for me to move in with you. Perhaps I'll take Temperance up on her offer and have their dog keep me company."

It was Nick's turn to smile.

"Let me make a few phone calls. I can send extra patrols out here. What time will you be done with work today?"

"Late afternoon."

"Meet me at the diner for dinner? We can come up with a plan."

"A plan other than packing up and moving again doesn't sound practical." She tipped her head from side to side as if easing out the kinks. "I don't think so."

"You can't keep running."

"I can if I want to live."

Chapter Five

The memory of the smell of guts and decay made Sarah want to puke. Thankfully, Nick had donned yellow latex kitchen gloves and disposed of the snake before he left.

Gross, gross, triple gross, ran over and over in her head as she scrubbed her kitchen table one more time for good measure, using almost a whole roll of paper towel. She took the garbage and tied it up in a plastic bag. Holding the bag as far away from her body as she could, she pushed through the screen door. She went around the side of the house, dumped it into the trash can. After securing the lid, she glanced around. Awareness prickled her skin.

Relax, you're okay. Even Sarah knew that Jimmy was too much of a coward to attack her in broad daylight. The hallmark of his abuse included keeping it a secret and making everyone question her story. Not his.

She strode back into the house and turned the lock on the door all the same. She said a silent prayer that this lock would be enough. Nick had found one of her windows unlocked, and they assumed this had been the point of entry. Now that it was secured, she should be safe.

Please, Lord, let me be safe.

After Nick had cleaned up the snake, he had bagged the phone for prints. Sarah doubted uncovering the intruder would be that easy.

A little voice in her head, no doubt planted by Jimmy's relentless barbs, told her she had brought all this upon herself. She should have never called her mom last night.

But what about the incident at the church prior to that? What had she done to bring that on?

Nothing. She had done nothing. But she knew what she had to do now. She washed her hands, changed her clothes and headed out on the walk to the center of town to Apple Creek Community Church.

Normally she enjoyed the peaceful stroll along the quiet country road, the solace of it, but today it was too quiet. The wind rustling through the cornstalks lining both sides of the road unnerved her. Nick had told her to call him for a ride, but she needed to do this one thing before she lost her nerve.

And she didn't want Nick to be any more involved than he already was.

She'd have to resign her position at the church and leave Apple Creek.

Run away.

Again.

The memory of the phone call with her mother reverberated in her mind. She couldn't go too far. Her mother wasn't doing well, despite her protests.

The gravel on the berm of the road crunched under her tennis shoes as Sarah picked up her pace. The occasional truck and horse and buggy passed her, but mostly she was alone out here. She hated the feelings of being out of control. Afraid. Unprotected with only cornfields on either side of the road.

Running away to Apple Creek had sent Sarah into a downward spiral, but now—even after all the precautions she had taken—it seemed Jimmy had found her. She fought off the pit of despair that tried to consume her.

The dark emotions reminded her of when her father died. Her world had swirled out of control. Her father had been her protector. Her hero. And then he was gone.

Leaving her and her mother as an incomplete family of two.

After her father's death, she had spent her early adulthood picking the wrong men. Perhaps looking for a father figure. Someone to love her. Someone to protect her. She thought she had found that in Jimmy Braeden. He had been so attentive. Affectionate.

Abusive.

But she didn't realize the latter until it was far too late. Until Jimmy had her in his clutches and wouldn't let go.

The midmorning sun beat hot and steady on her head. She wished she had grabbed a hat before heading out the door. She ran a hand across her forehead. Don't think about it. Keep walking.

It had been next to impossible to leave Buffalo the first time. Now it would be difficult to move again. Sarah had grown accustomed to the quiet, and she'd miss her new friends, however few.

The six months she lived in Apple Creek had been tranquil.

Until yesterday.

Now, with the events of the past twenty-four hours weighing on her shoulders, she arrived at the church. She jogged the last fifty feet, as if a burst of decisiveness wanted to outrun her indecision. And she longed for the wall of air-conditioning she knew would hit her as soon as she opened the door to the church basement.

When Sarah reached the door handle, it made her think of home base in hide-and-seek, a game she had played with the neighborhood kids as a child. They'd run as fast as they could until they threw themselves at the tree, front porch or a square in the cement. Whatever arbitrary location the players had chosen as safe. And then they'd flop over, exhausted, relieved, knowing they were safe and some other sap would be "it." But as an adult, she realized she no longer had a home base.

No place was safe.

Not anymore.

Sarah yanked on the door handle, and the heavy blue door swung open. Pastor Mike had said they were a welcoming church. Locked doors would only create barriers to those who wanted to get closer to God. Or those who were seeking…something.

She slipped inside, and the door slammed behind her and her nerves hummed to life. Anyone could be in the basement meeting room of the church. Yet another reason she had to leave. She'd gather a few of her personal things from her office and then tell Pastor Mike her plans.

Sarah tried not to look at the plywood covering the broken window—had it been some reckless teenagers?

Oh, but what about the snake on my kitchen table?

Either way, she was grateful that someone had cleaned up the mess. She had already dealt with too much this morning. Sarah scrunched her nose, trying to dispel the horrid smell of the dead animal that still lingered, even if only in her memory. Focusing on the task at hand, she emptied a box of hymnals, figuring the pastor wouldn't mind if she used the empty box to pack. She stacked the books neatly on a corner table. As she gathered her personal items, she heard the door open and then after a long silence, click closed. Sarah froze. Her decision to return without her personal protector suddenly didn't seem like a good idea. What would they call her in one of those movies? Too stupid to live?

"Hello."

Sarah's heart soared. Miss Ellinor's voice had never sounded sweeter. "You're in the office early today. I noticed you jogging across the parking lot as if a wild hog was chasing you through the fields. Is everything okay?" Her words floated down the staircase as the older woman gripped the railing and descended each step gingerly.

When she reached the bottom step, Miss Ellinor planted a fist on her hip. "Everything isn't okay. What's going on?"

Sarah stopped putting items into the box. "I was hoping to talk to you and Pastor Mike at the same time."

"He's visiting a church member in the hospital. Poor Mrs. Mann fell and broke a hip."

"I'm sorry to hear that." Sarah admired how the pastor and his wife devoted their lives to their ministry. Helping people as a social worker was the best part of Sarah's job, but lately she wondered how much more she could give to other people before she lost herself entirely.

A pang of guilt pinged her insides. She felt selfish. People in Apple Creek had begun to count on her, and she was ready to run again, leaving them without an advocate when it came to receiving the services they required and deserved.

Let someone else do it. I have my own problems.

Selfish! But dying wasn't going to help anyone.

Miss Ellinor lowered herself into one of the rickety old

wooden folding chairs that were probably manufactured circa 1960 and were ubiquitous in church basements. "You're leaving us." It was a statement, not a question.

The look of disappointment on the older woman's face slammed Sarah in the heart. Sarah grabbed a chair and propped it open. She sat next to Miss Ellinor. "I can't thank you and the pastor enough for taking me in. For finding me a place to live. But I'm afraid—" she paused, unwilling to utter his name "—*he* knows where I am. I have to leave. I can't risk anyone getting hurt on account of me."

Miss Ellinor folded her hands in her lap. "I thought the police found a few young men misbehaving in town?"

"They did." Sarah scratched her head and blinked away the image of the snake.

Miss Ellinor pressed her palms together as if she were praying. "Then, there's nothing to worry about. And now that you've gotten to know that nice handsome officer, he can protect you."

Sarah smiled, unwilling to be rude to the woman who had been so kind to her. She didn't want to remind her that her last boyfriend—her current stalker—had been a police officer. And Nick was a deputy sheriff.

"I'm not interested in dating."

Miss Ellinor squared her shoulders and pressed her lips together, the face she often made before she was ready to regale her with a story. "Now, that would be a shame. Nick is such a nice man, and his last girlfriend treated him like dirt. Broke his heart. I'd love to see a girl like you end up with a strong, handsome man like him. A man who treats you right." She quickly shook her head, as if reading Sarah's mind. "He's tough on the outside, but that man has a heart of gold. Do you know his parents are the wealthy folks who have that fancy house up on the hill?" Nick had mentioned something about his parents' wealth.

"Nick could have walked right into his father's business," the pastor's wife continued, "and have a fancy car and all, but he chose to first serve his country and then join the sheriff's department here. Nothing glamorous about that," she added, as if thinking aloud. "Only a good man would make a choice like that when he could have had almost anything he wanted."

Sarah could feel heat and shame pulsing through her veins. Part of her wanted to stop the woman from invading Nick's privacy, the other half—the curious part—wanted to pepper her with a million questions.

Someone broke Nick's heart?

Why didn't he go into the family business?

And he's still single?

Sarah shook the silly thoughts aside. It was totally none of her business, and poor Nick would probably be embarrassed if he knew Miss Ellinor was spilling his secrets.

A cool knot twisted in her stomach. Had Miss Ellinor ever shared Sarah's secrets? Secrets that could jeopardize her safety?

"I'm not looking for a boyfriend," Sarah said, her common sense winning out over her curiosity. Certainly not one who is a cop. "I don't imagine Nick would like us talking about him."

Miss Ellinor waved her hand. "Oh, I'm not being gossipy. All of Apple Creek knows what happened to Nick. That girl was a fool for cheating on him. *And* when he was serving our country. Can you imagine that girl's nerve? Some of the younger generation are so self-involved."

Miss Ellinor leaned forward and pulled Sarah's hands in hers. Tears bit at the back of Sarah's eyes as she stared at their clasped hands. She hadn't realized how separate she had held herself here in Apple Creek. She had missed the simple comforts of a deep friendship. Of course, Sarah had become friendly with Mary Ruth, but out of necessity, Sarah kept a certain distance between them. A tear slipped out of the corner of Sarah's eye and rolled down her cheek.

"Oh, honey, it's okay. Don't cry. What can I do for you?" Miss Ellinor patted her hand.

"I'm a grown woman and I'm crying because I miss my mom." Her nose tingled and she had to swallow back a knot of emotion. "It's silly, I know."

Miss Ellinor stood and bent over, hugging Sarah. "You aren't silly at all. You've had a rough time of it. Of course you miss your mother. How does she seem in her letters?"

"Her letters are all cheery. She's putting on a brave face." Sarah decided not to get into the prohibited phone call she had made last night. "I'm worried."

"We'll keep her in our prayers." Miss Ellinor patted her back and straightened. "Please don't go. Apple Creek needs you."

Sarah bit her lip, considering. A little part of her wondered if Miss Ellinor had only said that out of pity.

"I do like my work here." She traced the flat edge of the rickety wooden folding chair.

"Then stay." Miss Ellinor held herself with an air of determination. "You're running before you know what's going on. Can you stay until you know you're really in danger from that evil man?" She gave her a knowing glance.

"Even if it's not my former boyfriend, someone's harassing me."

The pastor's wife planted a fist on her hip. "Every time you run into conflict, you're going to run away?" The older woman shook her head. She pursed her lips, but she had a twinkle in her eye, obviously knowing she was slowly chipping away at Sarah's resolve.

Miss Ellinor pointed to the stairway. "We'll add security features here at the church. We'll lock the doors and make sure you have an escort back and forth from your home."

"But what about the pastor's open-door policy?"

Miss Ellinor waved her hand. "Never hurt a person to knock or ring the bell. Your safety is more important than anything." The older woman patted Sarah's shoulder.

Sarah gave her a sad smile. As much as she appreciated everything Miss Ellinor was willing to do to keep her safe, nothing and no one could protect her from Jimmy if he had a mind to hurt her.

Sarah collapsed into an oversize leather chair in her tiny office in the church basement after her only client for the day left. The hum of the AC unit in the window kept her company. She traced the six-inch tear in the black leather, and her mind drifted.

The client who had just left—she wasn't Amish—had two young children, and although she wouldn't admit it, Sarah suspected she was in an abusive relationship. The young woman wanted to get a divorce, but had no means of support. Sarah promised her that if she really wanted to leave, Sarah would find resources for her.

This was the reason she needed to stay. But could she?

"Are you okay?"

Sarah bolted upright in the chair and swung around. She pressed a hand to her beating chest. "You scared about ten years off my life."

"Sorry, I thought you heard me come in." Mary Ruth smiled sheepishly.

Sarah stood and turned off the AC unit, sending the room into silence, save for Sarah's still-racing heart. She waved her hand. "It's okay."

Her Amish friend turned around and pointed to the box Sarah had left outside her small office. "Are you going somewhere?"

"I was thinking about it."

A thin line creased the young woman's forehead. "Because of what happened here last night?" Mary Ruth leaned back and looked at the boarded-up window. "I feel bad that I wasn't here when it happened."

Sarah shrugged. She was growing tired of being the center of attention. The one thing she enjoyed about Apple Creek was the anonymity. Someone wasn't asking her questions every other minute. Until now.

"It's fine." Then feeling a little embarrassed that she hadn't thought about how this mess had affected Mary Ruth, she asked, "How's Ruben? I hope he's not in too much trouble with his father."

Mary Ruth cocked her head and drew a hand down the long string of her bonnet. "I wouldn't know."

Sarah watched the emotions play across her friend's face. "Aren't you and Ruben getting along?"

Mary Ruth tapped her boot nervously on the doorframe. "I called things off with Ruben."

Sarah made an effort to hide her surprise. "I didn't

know." Did last night have something to do with it? Smashing bottles seemed like a minor offense. "Why?"

"It wonders me if I'm not cut out for married life."

Sarah ran her hand over her mouth and gave her next words careful consideration. "Marriage is a huge part of Amish life. If not Ruben, maybe someone else."

Mary Ruth simply raised her shoulders and let them fall. "Maybe."

Sarah thought back to the past few months. Mary Ruth had been spending more and more time helping her. "I appreciate your help here, but maybe it's interfering with your plans to live the Amish way. Maybe you shouldn't have skipped the Sunday singings this past week. You enjoy that time."

"It was easier than facing Ruben," Mary Ruth said, frustration evident in her voice. "He can be very persistent."

Alarm bells clamored in Sarah's head. "He hasn't hurt you, has he?"

Mary Ruth lowered her gaze and shook her head adamantly. *"Neh, neh..."* She slipped into her Pennsylvania Dutch. "He still wants to court me."

"He hasn't accepted the breakup?" Sarah searched the young girl's face.

"He will. He just wants to save face. We hadn't been officially published, nor had he talked to the bishop about marriage, but—" she shrugged again "—people start getting ideas. People talk."

"Do you think it's just a matter of time and he'll move on?" Something about Mary Ruth's hesitation unnerved Sarah. Or maybe she was overly sensitive to boy-girl relationships gone bad.

"Yes, that's it. It's a matter of time."

"Please let me know if I can do anything." Sarah lifted her hands, indicating her small office. "This is my job."

It was Mary Ruth's turn to wave her hand. "It's nothing as serious as that. Ruben needs to move on. That's all."

Sarah pressed her hands together and studied Mary Ruth. "What are your plans?"

"I admire the work you do. I'd love to be able to help people."

Education beyond the eighth grade was frowned upon in the Amish community. On the farm, there was no need for education beyond the basics. A highly educated Amish person might get ideas. So, it wasn't like Mary Ruth could go to college to become a social worker.

Sarah's pulse beat low and steady in her ears. She swallowed hard. "Are you thinking of leaving the Amish?" Mary Ruth's parents would be devastated, having already lost a son to the outside world. Sarah also realized if her closest Amish friend left the church, it might make Sarah's work in helping the Amish more difficult. Already she was considered an interloper, and if Mary Ruth left, the worst fears of the Amish would be realized.

She was a negative influence.

Sarah shook away the thought. Besides being selfish, did it really matter? Hadn't Sarah decided to leave Apple Creek, anyway?

As if reading her mind, Mary Ruth said, "I have no plans to leave the Amish." She leaned her hip against the doorframe. "But maybe, somehow, I can find a way to help people."

Sarah subconsciously ran a hand across her bandage. "I'm glad you told me. I'll do whatever I can to help you."

Mary Ruth tipped her head toward the box again.

"Where are you going?" A frown pulled at the corner of her mouth.

"There's a lot going on right now, and I really don't know what I'm doing."

Mary Ruth levered off the doorframe. "I'm here if you need someone to talk to, too." She smiled.

"Thank you."

"I stopped by to see if you needed help cleaning up the mess, but I see someone already has." Mary Ruth looked around.

"I appreciate it."

"Well, I better go, then. My *mem* needs help with my little sisters so she can run some errands. I told her I'd hurry back. Last time I didn't arrive home on time my *dat* got mad. I don't want him to start telling me I can't come here." Mary Ruth's father worked at a nearby business that manufactured outdoor play sets, allowing—much to his dismay—more freedom for his family to do things away from the farm. Like Mary Ruth helping Sarah. Or like his son getting in with the wrong gang.

"Go then. I'll see you soon."

"Of course." Mary Ruth spun around, her long dress twirling about her.

Sarah leaned back in her large chair and listened to Mary Ruth's footsteps up the stairs. *Why didn't I know Mary Ruth and Ruben were no longer courting?* Sarah must have misread Mary Ruth's hope for the future all wrong. Mary Ruth hadn't been excited about settling into marriage. She had been excited by other possibilities.

Sarah smiled to herself.

Perhaps it was Sarah's turn to learn something from the young Amish girl.

Excited by the possibilities.

Then another thought struck her like a freight train. Mary Ruth's boyfriend suddenly had motive to make Sarah's life miserable.

No, Ruben was a good guy. He had always been pleasant around her. Helpful, even. Well, until his aloofness this morning. But that's to be expected. He was probably still angry about having to go down to the sheriff's station after smashing the bottles.

All indications showed Ruben was a solid young man, intent on living in the Amish way.

Mary Ruth's family might not be too happy with Sarah, either. Her stomach pitched.

Sarah was grasping at straws. It was Jimmy who was harassing her. It had to be. *Right?* Sarah winced at the headache forming behind her eyes.

How could she ever trust herself again to be a good judge of character?

Outside the church, the late afternoon sun beat down on Nick. He drew in a deep breath. After serving overseas in times of war, he'd never again take for granted the clean scent of country air, even with its manure undertones. But fortunately this afternoon, he only caught a whiff of bundled hay and fresh-cut grass.

Miss Ellinor had called him at the station, encouraging him to check on Sarah when he got out of work. The pastor's wife had insisted it wasn't an emergency, but that the "sweet thing" looked like she could use a friend. Miss Ellinor's phone call had been serendipitous because Sarah had been reluctant to agree to meet him at the diner to discuss the next course of action. Now he had an excuse to see her. He had made a few phone calls today to a friend in Buffalo, and Sarah's story didn't seem to add up.

Nick didn't like secrets.

He slammed his truck door shut and spun around at the sound of gravel crunching under footsteps. He wasn't partial to surprises, either.

Miss Ellinor lifted a picnic basket by the handle and smiled, by way of explanation. "I had some leftovers, and I thought you and Sarah might like a nice picnic. Down by the lake maybe?"

Nick shook his head and smiled. "You're incorrigible. I'm guessing Sarah didn't really look like she could use a friend."

"Oh, no, she looks like she could use a friend, especially a handsome young friend like yourself." She smiled coyly and without a hint of apology.

"I'm not as young as you might think." He ran a hand across his scratchy beard.

"All the more reason to get you settled down."

Nick slowly shook his head but couldn't stop the smile from spreading across his face. He wasn't interested in getting involved with someone. Especially not with someone who seemed to be harboring as many secrets as the last woman he had gotten involved with. He had seen firsthand the destruction secrets had on a solid relationship. Never mind trying to build a relationship on the shaky foundation of skeletons in a closet.

The side door of the church swung open and Sarah stepped out clutching her large bag. She seemed to startle a minute when her gaze landed on Nick. She composed herself and made her way over to where he and Miss Ellinor stood.

"Um…" Her gaze drifted from Nick to the picnic basket in Miss Ellinor's hand and back to Nick. "Did we have plans?"

"I'll leave this picnic basket here," Miss Ellinor said as she placed it in the bed of Nick's truck. "I went through a lot of effort, I wouldn't want it to go to waste."

"Thank you." Nick didn't take his eyes off Sarah, who narrowed her gaze.

"What's this about?"

"Miss Ellinor called me and told me to come check on you."

Sarah raised a skeptical eyebrow.

"But apparently it was a ruse to send us off on a picnic." Nick walked around to the back of his pickup truck and lifted one side of the picnic basket. The items were neatly secured, but he could smell the fresh bread and a hint of egg and onion. "Oh, man, I think she made us her famous potato salad." Nick wasn't the kind to attend church, but as a deputy sheriff, he had the occasion to sample Miss Ellinor's cooking at the annual church outing. Most of the town attended, even the Amish, so he never felt out of place despite his lack of Sunday church attendance.

"Potato salad?" Sarah shook her head, smiling. "I suppose it would be a shame to let it go to waste."

"We need to eat, right?"

"We do." Sarah surprisingly seemed downright agreeable. Or maybe she was hungry.

Once they were settled in his truck, Nick turned to her. "Should we have a picnic by the lake?"

Sarah shoved her oversize bag down next to her legs. "That's fine."

He turned out onto the road and decided he needed

to get a few things off his chest before they reached the lake. Maybe then they could relax and enjoy their meal.

"I made a few phone calls this morning."

"Phone calls?" He could hear the trepidation in her tone. "In regards to me?"

"I have a friend who's a private investigator in Buffalo."

"What did you do?" Her voice was barely above a whisper, but it held tremendous restraint. "I've been hiding in Apple Creek for six months, keeping all my communication with my mother carefully orchestrated, and then I meet you. Now, you up and call a friend? An investigator whose questions will likely raise more questions. About me!" Her voice grew high-pitched. "Take me home."

"Please, we need to talk." A muscle worked in his jaw.

Sarah shifted in her seat and said what was really on her mind, "What if the two incidents weren't Jimmy? Now you've drawn him a map to my front door. He'll find me for sure."

"My friend can be trusted."

"I need to know everything you said. I need to know who he talked to." Sarah turned to face him, and he gave her a sideways glance. The distrust in her eyes cut him to the core.

Sarah watched the cornfields roll by as Nick drove along the country road. She clamped her jaw shut, seething at his audacity at calling a private investigator about her situation.

"I asked him to quietly look into Jimmy Braeden," Nick said, his voice holding a hint of an apology. "Check out his work schedule. See if he could find out what the man was up to without drawing any attention to himself…or more importantly, *you*."

"You shouldn't have." Sarah closed her eyes and sank into the seat. Nick had no right to contact anyone in Buffalo on her behalf. She could only imagine what Nick had said about her. Her ears grew hot at the thought of people talking about her, discussing her situation.

"By all accounts, Officer Braeden is a good guy." Nick's comment was like a knife to the heart.

"Do you think I'm lying?"

"I'm trying to uncover the truth."

"I don't lie." Sarah fisted her hands in her lap as he slowed the truck and turned into a gravel lot. "Why would I make up a story about an abusive boyfriend?"

Nick cut her a sideways glance. "You have no reason to."

Sarah wasn't sure if he meant it or if he was saying it to appease her. *Why had she agreed to come on a picnic with him?*

"Can we please enjoy this meal Miss Ellinor made for us? Call a truce for the next hour?" Nick sounded so sincere.

Sarah turned and looked out over the water. The afternoon sun was glittering on the lake. It was beautiful. She found some of the anxiety ebbing away. Not all of it, but some. She figured just enough to allow her to hold a civil conversation and maybe enjoy the picnic Miss Ellinor had taken the time to prepare.

Without waiting for an answer, Nick hopped out of the vehicle and went around and opened the door for her. Jimmy had long ago stopped making her feel special by performing simple courtesies. Like opening a car door.

Nick smiled at her, one that seemed to be asking for

forgiveness. She wished it was as easy as that and this was simply a nice first date between two single people in Apple Creek, but her life had taken too many twists and turns over the years to let her guard down.

Besides, she wasn't staying in Apple Creek. Not long term anyway.

And she wasn't interested in dating. Not a cop. Not Nick.

He grabbed the picnic basket and headed toward the water's edge. She was surprised no one else was out enjoying the park.

He set the basket down and opened one side and pulled out a red-and-white-checkered blanket.

"Looks like Miss Ellinor thought of everything," Nick said as he spread the blanket on the grass. He plopped down on it and seemed unconcerned that Sarah was standing there watching him.

"She's a wonderful cook."

Nick laughed. "And apparently a matchmaker." He shrugged. "I suppose it's not that unusual. As a pastor's wife, she must meet a lot of people who have things in common."

"Do we?" Sarah asked, unable to keep the sarcasm from her tone.

He pulled out a cold bottle of water and handed it to her. "I'd like to think so." He squinted up at her and smiled, a smile that reached his warm brown eyes. She accepted the bottle and dropped to her knees on the blanket.

Nick pulled out potato salad in two plastic containers, a bag of chips and individually wrapped sandwiches.

Sarah's stomach growled. "I've been so busy all day, I didn't realize how hungry I was." She pulled back the plastic wrap covering hers and took a bite of the chicken-salad sandwich. "Wow, this is really good."

They ate in silence for a few minutes until Nick spoke. "Now about those phone calls I made…"

Sarah's adrenaline spiked, and she lowered her sandwich. "Has it already been an hour? Remember our truce?"

Nick lifted an eyebrow as if to say, "You didn't actually think we could avoid the elephant in the room?"

Sarah maneuvered her legs from a kneeling position to a more comfortable sitting position. Her feet tingled from lack of circulation. "You know how to ruin a girl's appetite." She held her breath, waiting, anxious to know if his phone calls had uncovered anything.

"Matt, the private investigator, and I served together in the army."

Sarah moved her potato salad around with her fork. "Jimmy has a lot of friends, and he's *very* convincing." Already she felt defensive.

"You're right. Jimmy claims you were fired from your last job and were forced to move away."

"He's lying."

"I know." Nick reached across and touched her knee. She was too weary to pull away.

"What if your friend's inquiries cause me more problems?"

"We can trust my friend Matt. He's a good guy. He's smart. He won't say anything to put you in jeopardy."

Sarah bowed her head and studied the blanket.

"Can you trust me on this?"

She slowly looked up, and a pang of regret zinged her heart when she saw the despondent look on his face.

"I hardly know you."

"Hear me out. Matt made a call to one of his friends at Orchard Gardens police headquarters and discreetly checked the work rosters. James Braeden was working last night."

Her mouth immediately went dry. "Jimmy normally works the day shift."

"He apparently worked a few doubles recently. Maybe there's something going on at work?"

"Are you saying he couldn't have been harassing me because he was at work?" She felt the knot easing between her shoulder blades.

"It would seem that way."

Sarah nodded, letting what he said sink in. "That means someone else smashed the window and left the snake on my kitchen table." But for some strange reason, a stranger harassing her seemed less threatening than Jimmy.

Sarah bowed her head and tucked a strand of hair behind her ear. "That jibes with something else I learned today." She looked up and met his encouraging gaze. "Mary Ruth told me she broke up with Ruben. Maybe he blames my influence for the demise of his relationship."

Nick nodded. "Maybe. What about her family? They would be upset, too. Baptism and marriage are important milestones in the Amish community. I understand Mary Ruth's older brother recently moved away."

Sarah had yet to meet Mary Ruth's family. It was almost like the young woman was working hard to keep the parts of her life separate. Considering their different backgrounds, Sarah understood that, but did that also mean she had a very angry family member at home who might blame Sarah for the perceived influence she had over Mary Ruth, especially in light of her brother jumping the fence?

Sarah dragged her fingers through her hair. "I wish my job came with a training manual, sometimes."

Nick wiped his mouth with a napkin. "I'll do some digging."

Sarah reached out and clasped his wrist. "Don't make it obvious. I have a tough enough time getting the few Amish who do come to me for help to trust me. I don't want them to think they no longer can."

"I understand." He tilted his head to look deeply in her eyes. "Can *you* trust *me*?"

Sarah nodded. She could. She had to.

"There's something else." Nick bent his knee in front of him and rested his elbow on it and stared over the lake, giving Sarah the opportunity to study his strong profile.

If only they had met under different circumstances...

"I had Matt do a welfare check on your mother."

Sarah's heart skipped a beat. She was unsure if she should be mad or grateful. Right now, she chose to be grateful.

"How is she?" The world seemed to slow down as she held her breath and waited for a response.

Nick slowly turned to look at her. "He's never met your mom before, but he thought perhaps she wasn't doing well. The house was a mess and—"

"My mother always kept a meticulous house." Suddenly the chicken sandwich didn't sit so well in her stomach. Her mind drifted to the conversation last night. Her mother's persistent cough. All Sarah's doubts and regrets overwhelmed her.

Maybe Sarah shouldn't have left Buffalo.

Sarah closed her eyes. "What am I going to do?"

"I'll help you. However I can." Nick's compassionate words washed over her. "But I don't know if it's safe to visit her. That's what you're thinking, right?"

Tears burned the back of her eyes, and she struggled to find the words. What could she say? "You have to understand how hard it is to be away from my mom at this time."

His intense scrutiny unnerved her, so she redirected the conversation. "Are you close with your parents?"

Nick laughed. "Well, my parents are a little different. They're entrepreneurs and they travel the world. Work has always been their first priority, but they always made sure we had everything we needed. And they're very generous in the community."

Curiosity piqued her interest. "How did both you and your sister end up in Apple Creek?"

"When we were little, my parents wanted to get away from the city. They needed a quiet place to think. Since they owned their own business…well, *businesses* now, they could live anywhere. We moved from Buffalo to Apple Creek when I was around seven."

"You didn't follow them into the family business?"

Nick shook his head. "It never appealed to me. I wanted to do something more concrete. To help people."

"And your sister became a doctor in a health-care clinic. Interesting."

"Yes, and my parents see to it that the clinic is fully funded."

"Wow." Sarah took a sip of water. The soft breeze against her skin felt wonderful.

"Oh, but I have another sister. She went to school for accounting and she's very successful, running one arm of the family business." Nick got a faraway look in his eyes. "The lifestyle never interested me. My parents were always gone. I was raised more by the nanny than my parents." He waved his hand in dismissal.

"Trust me, growing up with a lot of money in a big house in the country wasn't a hardship. But when the time came, I wanted to go in a different direction career-wise. My parents were always supportive in the way they knew how. They paid for my college and they support the clinic." There was something lonely in his eyes that Sarah could relate to.

Sarah took another long drink of water. "What am I going to do about my mom? I'm hiding in Apple Creek to stay safe, but I won't be able to live with myself if my mom dies alone." Her voice cracked over the word *dies*.

Nick reached out and covered her hand. "Then I think *we* should pay her a visit."

Fear washed over her, and her anxiety made her stomach knot. "I promised my mother I'd stay safe."

"I'll keep you safe." The conviction and sincerity in his eyes warmed her heart. "You can't run away."

"I don't know..."

"*Can* you trust me?" He asked her yet again. He squeezed her hand.

Sarah had no reason not to trust him, but she had been wrong in her assessment of people before.

But what choice did she have? She nodded and turned to face him. They locked gazes. Sarah found herself hypnotized by his kind eyes. Before her brain engaged and she nipped her heart's impulse, she leaned in at the same time Nick did. His soft lips covered hers, a fleeting kiss full of promise. He pulled away and a light glistened in his eyes.

"I won't let you down." A small smile played on his lips.

A million emotions tangled inside her. Sarah shifted and turned her focus to the sparkling lake and let out a long sigh.

Dear Lord, I need Your guidance on this one. Can I trust this man?

Chapter Six

On the drive home from their picnic at the lake, Sarah tried to sift through her conflicted feelings of despair, uncertainty and a new emotion: hope. Could she trust Nick to protect her secret? To protect her? Could they really go visit her mom?

Her swirling thoughts created overwhelming anxiety that nearly consumed her by the time they reached her house. Sarah was about to tell Nick to forget their plans of checking on her mother in Buffalo—it was too risky—when she noticed Mary Ruth sitting on her front porch. Her bonneted head leaned in close to a dog, a golden retriever. He must belong to the Zooks. Mary Ruth stroked his soft fur and seemed to be lost in thought.

Nick noticed the Amish girl at the same time Sarah did. "Mary Ruth, right?"

"Yeah, she usually visits me at the church. I wonder why she's here. I saw her earlier today."

"Do you want me to come with you to talk to her?"

Sarah slowly shook her head. "No, if something's wrong, she's more likely to open up to me when I'm alone." She cut a sideways glance to Nick. "No offense."

"None taken." Sarah was still trying to adjust to his easy manner. "Think about that trip to Buffalo. I could take you later this week."

"Are you sure that's a good idea?" Sarah's stomach dropped. *Can I really visit my mom?*

"Yes. You'll be fine. You can wear something nondescript," Nick continued. "Do you have a baseball cap?"

She couldn't help but smile. Nick sounded like he was planning a bank heist. Not a trip to her childhood home. "I might be able to find a cap."

"Great." Nick turned to face her, and a light twinkled in his eyes. He reached out and covered her hand with his, and the warmth spread up her arm and coiled around her heart.

Heat warmed her cheeks, and once again she wished their circumstances had been different. She couldn't allow herself to be caught up with another charming guy.

Especially not another cop.

Sarah might be willing to trust Nick to keep her safe, *for now*. But she couldn't trust her heart to him.

Then why did I kiss him by the lake?

Sarah pulled her hand out from under his. "Later this week we'll go to Buffalo. Visit my mom. But we can't tell her ahead of time. I'd hate for her to tell someone in her excitement." She forced a confidence into her voice that she didn't feel. She climbed out of the truck and walked slowly toward the front porch. Mary Ruth didn't get up to greet her; instead she seemed to be holding tighter onto the dog's collar as his tail whacked the young girl's shoulder when it stood and barked, enthusiastically greeting Sarah.

"Is this my guard dog the Zooks promised?"

"Yes, Mrs. Zook walked him over while I was waiting for you. I didn't have the heart to tell her you were leaving. And she didn't seem to want to stick around to talk to me."

"Temperance knows about you and Ruben?"

"I suppose *everyone* knows about me and Ruben."

"Word really does spread quickly in a small town." Sarah leaned a hip on the porch railing. She studied Mary Ruth. While most girls her age back home were experimenting with makeup and fashion, Mary Ruth looked fresh and cute in her bonnet and makeup-free face.

Such innocence. Yet underneath lay such turmoil.

"I had to come by. I couldn't get the fact that you're leaving out of my head. I hope you'll reconsider." Mary Ruth swiped at a tear. "You can't run away like my brother."

Sarah bit her tongue, not wanting to disappoint her friend further, but also unable to lie. Sarah had no idea how much longer she could stay in Apple Creek.

"Mary Ruth, you're stronger than you think." The young woman needed to know that, for many reasons. Mary Ruth needed the confidence to face her parents, Ruben, the bishop, her community if she hoped to find peace in her life.

Mary Ruth hitched a shoulder. The dog licked the Amish girl's cheek, sensing her need for comfort.

The conversation Sarah and Nick had had by the lake flitted in her brain like a fly trying to make its escape out the closed window and bouncing off the screen. "Does your family know you've called off your courtship with Ruben?"

"*Yah*, my *dat* was asking a lot of questions about if I'd be joining the next baptismal class." An Amish person was baptized prior to marriage.

Sarah sat next to her young friend. She wanted to put her hand on her back, but she didn't know how well it would be received. The Amish weren't big on outward displays of affection.

"I have all these decisions to make, and I'm scared and confused," Mary Ruth whispered. "My parents expect so much of me since my brother left. They're worried. It's every Amish parent's wish that their children stay in the community."

Sarah knew that overwhelmingly, the young Amish did remain, which explained the growing numbers of Amish. Sarah supposed it was easier to commit to the familiar than make the bold move to leave home, often forever.

The dog walked over Mary Ruth's lap and wedged himself between the two women and put his head down on Sarah's lap. She ran her hand absentmindedly down the smooth fur of his head.

"Take it as it comes. You're young. You have time to figure it out. If you don't join the next baptismal class, you can join the one after that." It would be worse if Mary Ruth were baptized and then decided to leave. Baptism was a forever commitment. If she left after baptism, she'd be shunned.

"They're worried I'll be a negative influence on my siblings. They want me to hurry up and commit for fear I won't ever."

The stalks of corn rustled in the wind in the nearby field. All these months Sarah had gotten to know Mary Ruth, she thought the young girl was steadfast in her determination to be baptized into the Amish community and then be married. Turned out no one ever knows what was truly in another person's heart.

"Did something else happen? Besides your brother leaving?" Sarah pivoted, and the dog shoved his snout under Sarah's chin and she couldn't help but smile and pat his head. *Some guard dog.* "You know, your brother may find his way back. Don't give up hope. And please, don't make a lifetime decision because you're afraid of disappointing your parents. You have to reach in deep and do what you feel God is calling you to in your heart." Sarah had always been careful not to sway an Amish person against their way of life, but she sensed Mary Ruth's struggle was real. The poor girl had to find her place in the world.

A pink flush crept up Mary Ruth's face. "You think differently than I've been taught. The Amish are more community driven. It's not supposed to be about what I want."

Sarah grabbed the railing and stood. The dog jumped up, perhaps thinking they were going for a walk. "I'd never try and convince you to leave the Amish community. I'm just asking that you dig deep and try to envision the life that's best suited for you."

Mary Ruth stood and swiped at the back of her long skirt. "Please don't leave Apple Creek."

Sarah hated to disappoint her friend, but she couldn't lie to her, either. She didn't know what her next step was.

Sarah rubbed the dog's head, and he leaned into her leg. She laughed, shaking her head. "Do the Zooks really think this dog—what's his name? Buddy?—will make a good guard dog?"

Mary Ruth laughed. "He barks every time a stranger comes up. What more do you need?"

"Can you do me a favor?" Sarah asked as she stroked the dog's fur. "Can you take the dog back over to the

Zooks? Tell them I'll be happy to have him come back, maybe in a few days." She didn't want to worry about Buddy when she and Nick took their trip into Buffalo.

Mary Ruth's mouth formed into a perfect O.

"You can't keep avoiding Ruben. It's a small town." And maybe some of the hard feelings would go away if Ruben and Mary Ruth had a chance to talk.

The image of the dismembered snake flashed in her mind. Could Ruben be that angry? No, that had all the markings of Jimmy. Mary Ruth stomped down the steps, her posture resigned. At the bottom of the steps, she turned around and faced Sarah. "You always give me advice, but can I give you some?"

Sarah raised her eyebrows and held out her hand as if to say, "Go ahead."

"You deserve happiness, too."

Not sure what to say, Sarah plastered on a false smile. Sarah made her life's work about helping others without revealing much about herself.

"You help people like me, but you seem sad and lonely." Mary Ruth absentmindedly reached for Buddy as he jumped around the folds of her long dress, eager for attention, lightening the mood.

Sarah smiled. "Buddy wants to play."

Mary Ruth crouched down and patted the dog's head. "He makes it hard to have a serious discussion."

"I know." Sarah crossed her arms and grew solemn. "I can't share why I'm in Apple Creek, but I'm learning to trust Nick." She wasn't sure why she shared this information, but she supposed she didn't want her young Amish friend to worry.

It was Mary Ruth's turn to raise her eyebrows. "So,

it's Nick now." She beamed. "You're not leaving?" Her hopeful tone buoyed Sarah.

"Not yet."

"Gut." Mary Ruth said.

"And Mary Ruth… Don't feel you need someone else to make you happy. Find happiness within yourself." This had been a mantra Sarah repeated to herself often. She understood the Amish way wasn't to pursue personal goals, but rather work for the community, but she wanted her friend to make this very serious choice about baptism and marriage from a place of strength and not out of desperation, need or loneliness.

"I'll do my best."

Sarah watched Mary Ruth cross the yard. Sarah's heart started pounding when she noticed Ruben cutting across the property to meet her at the fence. Sarah lifted her hand to wave, but he turned his back to her without waving back. He must not have seen her.

Or maybe he really was angry with her.

The fluttery feelings in Sarah's stomach had only intensified over the past few days, a mixture of excitement and pure dread. Now the day had come, and she and Nick were headed to Buffalo to visit her mom. All had been quiet in Apple Creek since the snake incident—perhaps the increased sheriff's patrols by her rented house had been a deterrent—but Sarah couldn't help but feel like going to Buffalo was poking a hornet's nest.

"You haven't been home in six months?" Nick merged the sleek compact car onto the road after stopping at her mother's favorite bakery to pick up some pastry hearts. He had borrowed it from his parents' fleet of executive vehicles that were registered in Buffalo, not Apple Creek, one of the many precautions they had taken. The other was leaving after nightfall.

"No, I haven't been back." Sarah threaded her fingers and twisted her hands. "At the next light turn right." At this hour, she envisioned her mother sitting in her favorite recliner watching whatever police drama was running on cable. She had tried to show her mother how to use Netflix so she could binge-watch her favorite shows whenever she wanted, but all the controls and choices were too much for her. Her mother liked things simple.

Sarah laughed to herself. Her mother had always made the best of things, until cancer and Jimmy Braeden infected their lives. Some things were too hard to overcome. Sarah hoped her surprise visit didn't negatively affect her mom, making it even harder for her mom once she had left again.

Oh, maybe this isn't a good idea.

As they approached her old neighborhood in Buffalo, Sarah's nerves vibrated with anticipation. She longed to see Mom, but she couldn't shake the foreboding that something bad was going to happen—*really* bad. Ever since Sarah's panic attacks started, she struggled to separate real danger from perceived danger.

She sent up a silent prayer that her fight-or-flight response was off-kilter considering she was home for the first time in half a year.

"I live—my mom lives," she corrected herself, "on this street about ten houses in on the left."

Nick must have sensed her unease. "Everything is going to be all right. This car is registered to my parents' company, which has a Buffalo address. It would take a huge leap to connect it to Apple Creek and you, for that matter."

"So, remind me of this great plan." Sarah's tone came off as sarcastic, but inside she was trembling and nauseous. She prayed she'd be strong for Mom. And she prayed her mom was doing better than Nick's friend had led her to believe. Matt didn't know her mother, so what basis did he have to make that call?

That's the lie she had been telling herself since Nick had suggested they visit her mom. And what she was quickly learning about Nick, when he made a decision, he didn't waste time putting it into action.

"We'll park on the street a house away so as not to draw attention."

"What if someone sees me?" Sarah's legs started to shake, and she couldn't stop them.

"Did you bring a hat?"

Sarah nodded and pulled out a university baseball cap. It had her college logo on it, a large public university where she'd earned her master's degree. She couldn't recall ever having worn it. She looked goofy in hats.

"Tuck your hair up in it."

Sarah did as Nick had instructed as he came to a stop at the light at the corner of her street. Nostalgia bit at her insides when she remembered how many times she used to ride her bike around the block in this neighborhood. How she and her friends would make a hopscotch board with chalk or play on the shuffleboard court painted on her best friend's driveway.

All a lifetime ago.

The light turned green, and the car in front of them proceeded through the intersection, allowing Nick to turn right onto her street.

Sarah's heart plummeted and her mouth went dry. Rescue vehicles were parked near the house. Sarah couldn't find any words. *Are they here for my mom? No, no, no...*

Nick reached across and touched her hand, sensing her unease. He parked across the street and down two houses. Sarah stared at the fire truck on the street and the ambulance in her mother's driveway. Her stomach knotted, and she feared she was going to throw up.

"My mom," she whispered, her voice hoarse with emotion. She pushed open the door and climbed out, her legs unsteady under her.

Nick scrambled out of the car and jogged around to her side and grabbed her elbow. "It's okay. Let's go in and see what's going on."

Unable to speak around the lump in her throat, Sarah nodded. *Please don't be dead. Please don't be dead.* Then she closed her eyes and prayed in earnest. *Dear Lord, watch over my mom. Let her be okay. Let me be able to see her again.*

"Are you okay?" Sarah opened her eyes to find Nick close to her, studying her face.

"I need to see my mom."

"Come on. I'll be right there with you." He took her elbow. Sarah turned toward the house and noticed the outline of a man in her mother's doorway.

Broad shoulders. Thick chest. Flat buzz cut.

Jimmy.

It couldn't be.

It had to be. She'd recognize his stance anywhere.

Sarah yanked away from Nick's touch, her world tipping off its axis. She flattened her hand against the cool metal of the passenger window and ducked her head.

"It's him," Sarah whispered. "Jimmy Braeden is standing in my mother's foyer."

* * *

At the alarmed expression on Sarah's face, Nick's gaze snapped to the front door. A tall, broad-shouldered police officer stood in the doorway. Nick couldn't be certain if the man was watching them or the EMTs loading the ambulance.

"Are you sure it's him?"

From her semicrouched position, Sarah glanced over the roof of the car. "Yes." She visibly shuddered. "It's him. I'm sure. I don't know why he's here. He's not a Buffalo cop. He's in a neighboring suburb."

Nick gently took Sarah's trembling hand. His heart shattered for her. "You're safe. I'm here." She looked up at him, and her eyes glistened under the white glow of the moonlight. Sarah nodded slightly. Unsure. He hated that a man had done this to her. Made her afraid. He tamped down his anger. He had to keep calm if he didn't want to raise any red flags.

"Get inside the car and lock the doors. Stay low. I'll be right back."

Sarah stared at him, uncertainty flickering across her face. "Don't leave me here on the street. Alone."

"It'll be okay. Lock the doors," he repeated. "We need to see what's going on with your mom."

Sarah spun around and clutched his arm. "Let's follow the ambulance to the hospital. Don't waste time talking to him."

"Sarah, trust me." Nick brushed his thumb across her cheek, and she leaned into his touch. "I won't jeopardize your safety."

Sarah nodded slightly and slipped into the car. Nick handed her the keys. "Stay in the car. Don't get out no matter what. And if things go south, drive away."

She opened her mouth to protest. Nick locked gazes with her. *Trust me.*

Wide-eyed, Sarah nodded in silent agreement. He trusted she wouldn't leave the car. He straightened and placed a hand on the doorframe. "Hand me the bakery bag."

Sarah twisted around and grabbed the bag from the floor in the back of the car.

Nick watched the man still standing in the doorway. "What church does your mom belong to?"

"Saint Al's?" Sarah answered, a question in her voice.

"Okay…now lock the doors as soon as I close the door."

Sarah nodded ever so slightly. Nick closed the door and heard the click of the automatic locks. He crossed the street with the bakery bag in hand. He glanced over his shoulder at the car. In the darkness, Sarah wasn't visible inside. Nick made a straight line toward the ambulance, but the man who had been standing in the doorway strode out to the driveway and cut him off.

The man matched the image of Officer James Braeden that Nick had pulled up on the Orchard Gardens Police website.

"Can I help you?" Jimmy asked, his eyes piercing and dark. Anger and entitlement rolled off him in waves.

Nick tamped down his growing dislike for the man, afraid it would show on his face. He relaxed his shoulders and tried to act like he wasn't former military or current law enforcement. Nonthreatening.

"Is that Mrs. Gardner? Is she okay?" Nick put on an air of concern consistent with being a long-time friend.

"And you are?" Jimmy asked, not offering any information. Nick wondered why he was here when he wasn't a Buffalo cop.

"Oh, I'm sorry." Nick held out his free hand, offering to shake the man's hand. "I'm Nick—" he purposely didn't give a last name, even a fake one. Harder for the officer to catch him in a lie. "My mother and Mrs. Gardner are friends from St. Al's. My mother wanted Mrs. Gardner to have these baked goods." Nick lifted up the bag as evidence. "Thought they'd cheer her up. But now I see she's taken a turn for the worse." Nick turned toward the street and noticed the taillights of the ambulance disappear. He knew Sarah must be going out of her mind stuck inside the car, wondering what was going on with her mother.

With Jimmy.

Nick hoped she took comfort in seeing the ambulance didn't have on its lights and siren. That had to be an encouraging sign.

Unless she suspected there was no longer any sense of urgency.

Nick turned back around and found Jimmy staring at him, the two men squaring off eye to eye. "As you can see, Mrs. Gardner has been taken to the hospital."

"Did she call the ambulance?" Nick asked, trying to glean some information to share with Sarah.

"A neighbor did. Happened to stop by to check on her. When Mrs. Gardner didn't answer, she peered through the window and found the old lady flat on the floor. Unconscious." Jimmy looked past him to his vehicle parked in the street. Nick had purposely made sure he didn't park under a streetlamp so as not to draw attention to the details of the car. Now, he was especially glad because Sarah was nothing more than a shadow.

"My mother's a friend. She'll be concerned. Is there any news I can give her?"

"They're taking her to Buffalo Mercy."

"Did she regain consciousness?"

"Yes, but she's confused." Jimmy turned his focus to Nick's car. "Is someone waiting in the car?"

Nick lifted a hand, he tried to act casual, but he was on high alert. "My wife. We're on our way out tonight. Once she saw the ambulance, we knew we wouldn't be visiting with Mrs. Gardner." Nick frowned. "I suppose I won't be leaving these baked goods. Any chance anyone else in the house would enjoy them?"

"If you knew Mrs. Gardner, then you'd know she only has one daughter. She's currently out of town." The tight set of Jimmy's mouth must have been his "I'm annoyed with the world" tell.

"It's my mother who likes to visit with her friends after church. Me, I'm more a get in and get out and I'm good for another week." Nick shrugged. "Just hope lightning doesn't strike me dead while I'm there."

Behind Jimmy in the house, Nick heard a Buffalo police officer instructing another officer to make sure the house was secure before they left.

"It's a shame her daughter is out of town. Has someone contacted her? Let her know her mother has fallen ill?" Nick let the question hang out there.

Jimmy scrubbed a hand across his cropped hair as he studied Nick. Nick had to resist the urge not to put this guy in his place. He didn't want to trigger Jimmy's temper.

"Someone from our department will be sure to track her down," the Buffalo cop said.

Nick nodded curtly. "Night." Nick made eye contact

with the Buffalo cop and then Jimmy. Nick turned and jogged across the lawn. He waited until Jimmy climbed into a large SUV parked in front of Mrs. Gardner's house and pulled away. He didn't want to open the car door and allow the dome light to reveal his passenger.

In the briefest of seconds before he pulled his door shut and the dome light went dark, he saw tears shining on Sarah's pretty face. His heart went out to her.

Given a chance, he'd punch old Jimmy in the jaw. No man had the right to treat a woman as poorly as he had treated Sarah. Now she had lost time with her mother.

He hoped they weren't too late.

Undoubtedly, Sarah would insist they go to the hospital to check on her mother. Given the circumstances, he couldn't deny her.

He only hoped he could protect her.

Chapter Seven

Sarah and Nick waited two hours and then entered the hospital through the emergency-room doors. Under normal circumstances, Sarah would have never hoped for a busy ER when her mother was somewhere inside awaiting treatment. The crowded waiting room allowed her and Nick to slip in relatively unnoticed by the busy medical staff once Nick and she got past security with a flick of his badge. The wait was excruciating, but they had hoped the initial chaos of her mother's arrival—and the chance of running into Jimmy—had gone down exponentially.

Sarah had worked at this hospital a few years back as an intern in social work. She was familiar with the layout of the ER. She showed Nick a photo from her wallet of her mother. Separately, they each traveled down each side of the long hallway of examination rooms. When she spotted her mom in the last room, her heart stopped and her vision narrowed.

Sarah stared at her mother through the glass on the top half of the door. Her mother looked old and frail under the white sheet. Her face sunken. Her skin papery white.

Her eyes closed. Tears blurred Sarah's vision, and she quickly swiped at them. She had to be strong.

Sarah glanced over at Nick, and he had just turned from looking in the last room on his side of the hallway. She nodded to him. Concern flashed in his eyes. He hustled across the hall to her and put a comforting hand on the small of her back. He didn't say anything. He didn't have to.

"I wonder if a doctor can answer any of our questions?" Sarah whispered.

"I'll find one. You go in and see your mother."

She nodded, suddenly feeling like the little girl who visited her dad one last time in the emergency room the night of his accident. She shoved the thought aside and pushed open the door. Her mother didn't move. Cold fear pulsed through her veins. What if this was the end?

Dear Lord, please don't let this be the end. I'm not ready. I need more time. Please watch over her.

Sarah moved to her mother's side. She took off her baseball cap and set it down on the edge of the bed, letting her long blond hair cascade over her shoulders. She felt ridiculous in the cap, but understood she needed to hide her identity.

As an afterthought, she glanced around the room, hoping there weren't security cameras and then decided for once she was going to put Jimmy out of her mind.

Dismissing her plight—she felt selfish at times—she took her mother's smooth, cool hand in her own. She studied her mother's wedding rings, something she hadn't taken off even though she had been a widow longer than she had been married.

"Mom," she whispered, emotion clogging her throat, "I love you."

"Love you, too," came her mother's quiet, raspy reply.

Sarah's eyes flashed to her mother's face. Her eyes were still closed, but her mother squeezed her daughter's hand. A faint squeeze, but a response all the same. A tear trickled down Sarah's face.

"How do you feel, Mom?" Sarah glanced toward the door, hoping Nick would reappear with a doctor or nurse to answer her questions.

Her mother pried her eyes open a slant. "Oh, the light is bright."

Sarah glanced around, but didn't see a switch. Since this was the ER and not a private room, she figured her mother would have to deal with the lights. "I'm sorry." She smoothed her mother's hair off her forehead. "What happened?"

Her mother's forehead creased. "I don't remember..."

"Don't worry. You're getting care now."

"How did you know I was in the hospital? Who called you?"

Sarah smiled. "Even sick, you don't miss a beat, do you, Mom?"

A thin smile curved her mother's lips.

"I snuck back home to see you. Good thing, too."

"I didn't mean to worry you. Is it safe for you to be here?" Her mother examined Sarah and noticed the bandage. "Your forehead? What happened?"

"Mom, you're in the ER and you're worried about me?" Sarah leaned over her mom and kissed her cheek, the smell of coconut lotion immediately making her homesick. "Just a little cut. I'm fine."

"I'm fine, too. I must have forgotten to eat and passed out."

A realization rolled over Sarah. "You can't go back home. You shouldn't be alone. You need help."

"I've never needed help." Her voice sounded sleepy, confused. Yet determined. "I can take care of myself. You need to live your own life."

Loud voices sounded in the hall. Cold dread pooled in Sarah's gut even before she heard Nick practically shouting his greeting to "Officer Jimmy Braeden."

Sarah glanced around the room. A door to a small bathroom stood ajar. She pressed a kiss to her mother's cheek. "Mom, a friend of mine may be coming into the room. He's protecting me. His name's Nick Jennings." She glanced at the door, her heart jackhammering in her chest. "If he says you know his mother from church, go along with it." She rushed to get all the information out.

Her mother opened her eyes wide for the first time. "I'll never understand you, Sarah Lynn."

"Pretend you know him, Mom. And don't say anything about me being here."

Her mother lifted her hand slightly, then let it drop.

Through the glass of the door, she saw the back of Nick's head. She knew he was holding off Jimmy to give her time to hide. She ran to the bathroom and slid behind the door, pushing it almost closed, leaving a narrow view of the room through the crack. All she could see was a portion of her mother's face and the water jug on the side table.

The door to the room swooshed open. Nick's was the first voice she heard. "Hello, Mrs. Gardner. How are you?"

Her mother's gaze drifted to the bathroom.

No, Mom, don't look at me!

"I've had better days."

Her mother lifted a hand to her hair, as if to fluff it up. Despite Sarah's racing heart and dry mouth, she couldn't help but smile. Her mother always flirted with the handsome men. And Nick was definitely handsome.

"This man claims you know his mother." The voice of Jimmy had Sarah closing her eyes. She tried to imagine herself invisible behind the bathroom door. Pinpricks of panic raced across her scalp.

"Of course I know his mother. From church."

Good, Mom.

"I appreciate your looking out for me, Jimmy, but I'm very tired. I could use some rest."

"Of course. I'll check in on you tomorrow morning. Need anything?"

Sarah gathered the courage to peek, and her mother shook her head. "Jimmy, you don't need to fuss over me. I know you and my Sarah are no longer together. You don't owe me anything."

"You're no trouble at all, Mrs. Gardner. I like to keep tabs on those I care about." The tightness in his voice made Sarah's blood turn cold in her veins. "Whose baseball cap is this?"

Sarah sucked in a breath and pressed her back against the wall, wishing she could melt into it. How had she been so careless as to leave her cap?

"Baseball cap?" Her mother sounded confused.

"Yeah, same college as Sarah's."

Her mother didn't say anything.

"Have you seen Sarah recently, Mrs. Gardner? She'd want to know you're in the hospital. I could contact her for you?"

Her mother made a sound Sarah couldn't decipher. "I'm fine. I don't need anyone to make a fuss over me."

"I'd be happy to check in on you," Nick said. "My mother's already planning your menu for the week. I hope you like chicken noodle soup."

Sarah closed her eyes. If she didn't know Nick was lying, she would have believed every word he was saying.

"Sounds lovely." Her mother's voice grew weaker.

"We should be going," Nick said, his voice full of authority.

Sarah couldn't see Jimmy or Nick from her hiding place, but she sensed Nick was ushering Jimmy out the door. She feared Jimmy wasn't going to take kindly to being forced out.

"Good night, Mrs. Gardner. Please know my mother sends her best."

"Thank you." Her mother stared straight ahead. "Good night, Jimmy."

After a few moments, her mother turned toward the bathroom where she was hiding. "They're gone."

Sarah slipped out of the bathroom, keeping her eye on the door to the hallway. Pressing her hand to her chest, she heaved a heavy sigh. "That was too close."

"I hate seeing you like this," her mother whispered, as if afraid to make the admission.

"I hate it, too, but Jimmy's dangerous." Sarah touched her throat, remembering the time Jimmy held her against the wall with one hand around her neck. She pressed charges the next day.

That's when Jimmy's smear campaign started in earnest. When the battle seemed insurmountable, she fled town.

Her mother gestured toward her. "Let me hold your hand."

Sarah gave her a shaky smile.

"There's something I haven't told you." There was a clarity in her mother's eyes she hadn't noticed before.

A cold, icy knot tightened in Sarah's belly.

"There's nothing more the doctors can do."

For her cancer?

All the appropriate phrases slammed into Sarah's brain:

No, there has to be something.

Are you sure?

No, no, no!

But instead Sarah bent down and buried her nose in her mother's hair and cried. "I'm sorry."

Sarah pulled back so she could read her mother's expression. "I know. I know. Don't cry."

Sarah sniffed, trying to pull it together and forgetting for once to look over her shoulder for fear the man who threatened to kill her would make good on his promise.

Nick couldn't bear to listen to Sarah's quiet sobs in the passenger seat as they headed back to Apple Creek after visiting Mrs. Gardner. He hardly knew this woman sitting next to him, but his heart broke for both her and her mother.

After escorting Jimmy out of Mrs. Gardner's room, Nick had waited in the car near the ER entrance, ever vigilant that Jimmy could return at any moment. Nick didn't let down his guard until Sarah had returned to the car after saying goodbye to her mother.

They switched back to his truck at one of his father's offices about forty-five minutes outside of Apple Creek. Nick's heartache for Sarah morphed into renewed anger against Jimmy. Why did some men feel the need to control women? Hot anger pulsed through his veins. Jimmy had already cost Sarah her job in Buffalo. Her home. Was

Nick going to allow Jimmy to make her miss being with her mother in her time of need?

Nick glanced over to his passenger and noticed her head was dipping at an awkward angle. She was exhausted. "Sarah," he whispered. "Sarah?"

She didn't answer. He dug the phone out of his pocket and dialed his sister's number. He didn't want to use his Bluetooth connection for fear the voice booming over the speaker would wake Sarah.

His sister Christina answered after the second ring. "Hey there, sister."

"Something wrong?" she asked, worry lacing her tone.

"Why do you think something has to be wrong for me to call my baby sister?"

Nick could imagine her "give me more credit than that" look with her fisted hand planted on her narrow waist.

"It's late. I know. I'm sorry. Sarah's mom needs hospice care." Sarah told Nick the devastating news that the doctors had exhausted treatment options for her mother. He glanced over as they passed under a streetlight, and he caught a flicker of Sarah's peaceful face, even if her neck was cricked at an awkward angle.

"You want to know if I can provide care if you bring Mrs. Gardner to Apple Creek to live with Sarah."

"Whoever said you weren't smart…" He felt a smile pulling at his lips. Bringing Mrs. Gardner to Apple Creek would solve a lot of his concerns. Sarah could be with her mom, and Nick could protect Sarah.

"Who said I wasn't smart?" Christina said playfully, then she grew quiet. "That's too bad about her mom. How's Sarah taking it?"

"As well as can be expected."

"Does Sarah plan to stay in Apple Creek? And is her mom willing to come here?"

Nick turned toward the driver's side window and whispered in a low voice. "It's yet to be determined. But I wanted to explore all options before I make any suggestions."

A long silence stretched across the line. "Nick, this woman's important to you, isn't she?"

Nick didn't dare look to see if Sarah was awake. Mostly, he was glad she couldn't hear his sister's end of the conversation. "Yeah."

"She's right there, isn't she?"

"Yeah," he said, ever more cryptic. "Can you meet us at the house in ten minutes? Bring stuff to stay over? I don't think she should be alone."

"I'll do whatever I can to help you, Sarah and her mother. I love you, big brother."

"I love you, too." Nick ended the call and set the phone on the middle console.

"I'm sorry I'm not very good company," Sarah said in a sleepy voice.

"You must be exhausted."

"I am."

"You've had a rough—"

"Couple years."

Nick slowed and turned up the bumpy driveway to her rented cottage. He glanced up at the darkened home. Only a small light glowed from the Zooks' home next door. "I don't like you staying here all by yourself."

Sarah tipped her head back on the seat and sighed heavily. She pressed the heels of her hands into her eyes. "I'm too tired to think. Who were you talking to?"

"My sister."

"Hmm," Sarah said, still dreamily. "You guys are close."

"Yes, we are."

"I was an only child." There was a wistful quality to her tone. "Did you tell her she had to stay at the house with me?"

"Listen, Sarah," Nick shifted in his seat to face her more fully. "I have an idea."

Sarah yawned. "Can we get out of the car and talk about it? I need to walk. Get some blood circulating before I fall asleep again."

"Sure." Nick climbed out of the truck and went around and opened Sarah's door. She squinted against the glow of the dome light. He couldn't help but notice that her eyes were red from the combination of tears and exhaustion.

"It's a nice night." Nick reached for her hand and helped her. Her hand felt cool and delicate in his. *What was it about this woman?* Was he drawn to her or the need to protect her?

Or both.

When they reached the steps, she pulled her hand out of his, as if just now realizing they were walking hand in hand. "What is it you wanted to talk about?"

"Why don't you bring your mother here?"

Sarah jerked her head back. "To Apple Creek?"

"Yes, my sister agreed to monitor your mother's health while she's here. Since…" He stopped himself, not wanting to remind her of what she'd likely never forget. Mrs. Gardner's condition was beyond treatment. Mostly likely, she'd be given medications for pain and maintenance.

"You've been too kind." She brushed a hand across his cheek. "But I don't think my mom would leave her house." She worked her lower lip. "I'm going to have to seriously consider leaving Apple Creek. My mom needs me back in Buffalo."

"Please, give my suggestion some thought." Nick wanted to be the one to protect Sarah. He couldn't do that if she moved an hour away. And especially not if she moved back near Jimmy. "Talk to your mom about it."

Sarah laughed. "You don't know my mom. She's pretty stubborn."

"Like mother like daughter."

Sarah rewarded him with a quiet laugh. "Then you should know better than to argue with me." She reached for the handle on the screen door. "Good night, Nick."

"Hold up. My sister is on the way over to stay with you."

Sarah's eyes widened. "Oh, I can't put her out."

"She doesn't mind." Nick brushed a tear from her cheek with the back of his fingers. "Besides, I'm sure she'll ask me for a really big favor down the road." He tried to lighten the mood. "That's what family is for, right?"

The sound of tires on gravel had him turn toward the road. He recognized his sister's sedan. "She's here. You wouldn't want her to have come all this way for nothing."

Nick reached out and squeezed Sarah's hand. "It's going to be okay."

"You really shouldn't have asked her…" Sarah stood with a hand on her hip and the other palm flattened against the propped open screen door. When she realized this was really happening, she finally agreed.

"Glad to hear reason has won out." Nick glanced over to his sister's car. She was talking on her phone. "Let me check the house, then I'll help my sister."

Nick checked the house, then went back outside.

Christina had climbed out of her car and was standing next to her open trunk. Nick crossed the yard, kissed his sister's cheek, then grabbed her duffel bag. "Thanks. I owe you."

"Of course you do," Christina said and playfully tapped him on the arm. Then she lowered her voice. "What did she think about bringing her mother here?"

"She's not convinced. She believes her mother will be more comfortable in her own home."

"We'll convince her mom," Christina said in the easy manner of someone who confidently dealt in life-and-death situations on a regular basis.

Once inside the house, Christina admired the space. "How cozy. I've been looking for a little place myself." His sister had been so busy trying to save the world, she hadn't really settled anywhere. Ever since she had returned to Apple Creek a few years ago, she had been renting one half of a duplex near Main Street. The only furnishings as far as he knew were the ones the landlord had provided.

"You could move into mother and father's house. I don't think they've been home from Europe since Christmas," Nick said.

"Do you really see me living in mom and dad's house? I need to be able to connect to my patients. Living there would send the wrong message."

Sarah stepped out of the small half bath patting her face with a pink hand towel. She forced a bright smile that didn't reach her sad eyes. "Nick shouldn't have called you. I hate to put you out. I'm fine here."

Christina touched Sarah's arm. "I'm sorry about your mom."

Sarah pressed her lips together and nodded. "Thanks." Her lips parted, as if she wanted to say more, but didn't.

"Well, it's been a long day," Nick said, "I'll let you get settled."

Sarah looked up and they locked gazes. "Thank you. If it weren't for you, I wouldn't have been there for my mom today." Her voice broke over the word *today*.

Nick hooked his thumbs in his jeans pockets, not knowing how to comfort her. Not knowing what was appropriate. Christina pulled Sarah into an embrace. Something he wanted to do, but felt it wasn't his place.

His sister pulled away and held Sarah at arm's length. Sarah met his gaze and her cheeks turned pink. "I'm a mess. I'm sorry."

"No need to apologize." Nick shifted his stance.

"I suggest you take Nick and me up on our offer to help care for your mother here in Apple Creek," Christina said. "You'll both feel better being around one another."

"I'm afraid Jimmy already knows where I am."

"What if he doesn't? We should be careful anyway," Christina said. "I can work with you and the hospital to have your mom released to a sister in Florida."

Sarah's eyebrows arched. "My aunt does live in Florida."

"Well, we'll contact her to make sure she's in on the ruse in case your ex tries to verify this. He'll run into a dead end."

"Assuming Jimmy hasn't already found me." Sarah kept coming back to this point. She pushed her bangs off her forehead. A beige bandage still covered her stitches. She looked like she wanted to argue, but she settled on a simple, "I don't think my mom will go for it."

"You won't know until you ask." Christina glanced

around the room. "I'm sorry to hear the doctors no longer feel they can treat your mother's cancer. But I can help make the time she has left comfortable. You have enough room here if you need to bring a hospital bed in."

Sarah pressed a hand to her cheek and wrapped the other arm around her thin waist. She nodded in agreement.

Sarah pressed her trembling lips together as a silent tear slipped down her cheek. "Can we really do this?"

"There's no reason we can't."

Hope blossomed in Nick's heart. He felt a little selfish because this also meant Sarah wouldn't be going anywhere.

"Between the two of us, we can make sure your mom is well cared for."

Sarah bowed her head and dragged her wet cheek across her shoulder. "I... I..."

"Ask your mom. You owe her and *yourself* that much," Nick said.

"She can't be alone and I'm her only daughter." Her voice shook.

An unreadable expression flashed across Sarah's face. "But what about Jimmy or whoever is harassing me? I don't want my mom harassed during her...final days." She closed her eyes briefly. "Oh, but he'd harass us for sure in Buffalo." Her words dripped with the agony of her impossible situation.

"If your mom decides to move in here, I'll set up a cot in the back room near the door." The idea struck Nick two seconds before he suggested it. *Was he crazy?* "Just until we catch whoever is harassing you," he quickly added.

"Do you think it's Jimmy? Your friend said he was working Sunday night."

"Doesn't mean he didn't sneak down to Apple Creek. But, I don't know...seems a little too juvenile for a mean guy like Jimmy. I've known guys like him. Controlling. Just plain mean. I think if it were him, he wouldn't have stopped with a threat. He would have..." he let his words trail off, realizing he was frightening her. Sarah appeared to be trembling. Christina must have sensed it at the same time. She took Sarah's elbow and guided her to the couch.

"I'll get you some water." Christina hustled into the kitchen.

"Jimmy liked to toy with me. Going in for the kill right away wasn't sporting of him," Sarah said in a mocking voice.

"I'll keep you safe."

"How? You can't be with me all the time."

Nick's stomach dropped. She was right.

"I can try."

"Oh, I don't know..." Sarah had a wary look in her eyes. "What would that look like? You staying here?"

"Your mom can be your chaperone," Christina said cheerily as she returned with Sarah's water. "Until then, I'll stay with you."

"My mom loves her house. Her friends at church..."

"You could think of all the reasons why it wouldn't work, or you can just have a little faith." Nick slipped in and sat next to her.

Sarah nodded slowly.

"It's late. Why don't you get some sleep?" He pushed to his feet. He kissed his sister's cheek. "Thank you." Then he turned to face Sarah. "We'll go back to Buffalo in the morning and invite your mom to come home with you."

Sarah's brow creased. "Don't you have to work?"

"I have the day off."

"Oh, okay." She seemed hesitant, almost disappointed that she had run out of excuses. "But it won't be her home." Sarah's voice was racked with worry.

"I have a feeling your mom will consider home anywhere you are."

Sarah stood and touched his arm. "You're a good man, Nick. Thank you."

Chapter Eight

A few days after Christina's suggestion that Sarah's mom move to Apple Creek, she had. Now, Sarah's mother had been here almost a week and seemed to be settling in, and Christina graciously managed her care. Sarah tried not to think of the reality of her mother's situation and instead cherished each day.

Tears burned the back of Sarah's eyes. Wasn't this what faith was all about? Trusting in God's plan? Sarah collected the dishes from the kitchen table. She dumped the cereal from her mother's partially eaten breakfast down the disposal.

Nick kept watch every evening, usually arriving close to dark and leaving at dawn. Sarah guessed he didn't want to impose on her time with her mother.

Through the window above the sink, she watched Mary Ruth take Sarah's mother by the elbow and help guide her down the back steps. Her mother had everyone, including Sarah, calling her Maggie, and Sarah was seeing a side to her mother that she never had. Her mother—*Maggie*—had interests that extended beyond being Sarah's mother. It shouldn't have surprised Sarah,

Her mother stopped and turned to face her. "Don't go feeling sorry for yourself since Jimmy turned out to be a no-good creep." Her mother grabbed Sarah's arm and gently shook her. "It's not your fault."

Sarah pressed her lips together, afraid to speak. Afraid her voice would tremble. Afraid she'd start crying and never stop. And she was tired of every conversation gravitating back to her. This was about Mary Ruth.

"Have you ever considered getting your GED?" Sarah asked. "It's the equivalent of a high school diploma."

"I'm not sure I'm book smart." A soft smile curved the corners of Mary Ruth's mouth. "Not like you."

Sarah shook her head. "Don't dismiss yourself."

"I'm not," Mary Ruth said assuredly, then she got a gleam in her eye. "I'm glad you came to Apple Creek. I'm sorry it was under these circumstances."

Impulsively, Sarah reached over and gave Mary Ruth a hug. The young Amish girl stiffened, then returned the embrace. Sarah was the first to pull away. "I didn't mean to make you uncomfortable."

Mary Ruth waved her hand. "The Amish aren't big on displays of affection."

Both Mary Ruth and Sarah turned when they heard her mother laugh. "Sarah was never the most affectionate person, either." She chuckled again, a delightful sound.

They reached a bench at the far corner of the yard where the Zooks' property ended at the creek. The water wound along the edge of a path bordering thick foliage. Nick had been kind enough to build the bench, specifically so Maggie could rest during her walks. Sarah's heart warmed at the simple kindness of this man. A man she had grown to learn was filled with much kindness and compassion, a far cry from her ex.

Her mother sat and ran her hands down the thighs of her jeans. "I feel rejuvenated here." She looked up with radiant eyes and reached for Sarah's hand and pulled her down next to her. "I'll never regret my coming to Apple Creek. I had held onto the house in Buffalo because it was my house with your father, but I can't turn back the hands of time. Your father's been gone a long time, and without you there, it didn't feel like home."

Sarah bowed her head, afraid to let her mother see the tears in her eyes. "You shouldn't have had to leave your home, especially not now."

"You shouldn't have had to leave your home, either. But you're doing well here in Apple Creek. Helping people. And I feel like I'm on a vacation. I don't have to look around the house and feel bad about all the things I can no longer do—gardening, cleaning, cooking. I'm enjoying my time here. All those chores left me feeling exhausted." Her voice cracked over the last words. Her mother lifted her hand and cupped Sarah's cheek. "We're blessed to have this time together. Never regret that."

Sarah lifted her eyes to meet her mother's gaze. They both had tears in their eyes. Sarah hugged her mom and held on tight, memorizing this moment. "I love you."

"I love you, too."

Sarah turned to see Mary Ruth had tears in her eyes, too. Sarah laughed. "Look at us, a sorry bunch."

Mary Ruth shrugged and glanced over her shoulder toward the barn next door. "Your mom said she'd like to see the horses."

Her mother nodded. "City girl that I am, I can count on one hand how many times I've come up close and personal with a horse."

"Really?" Mary Ruth said, not hiding the surprise from her voice.

"It must sound strange from someone who lives on the farm and uses them for transportation."

"It's funny. When I was younger, I used to watch cars go whizzing down the street and wonder where they were going. I'd daydream about the world outside. But that's not the Amish way," she quickly added.

"We all wonder about the what-ifs…" her mother's voice had a distant quality to it. "But—" Maggie's voice brightened "—I don't want my Sarah to ever wonder *what if* she had taken a chance on that handsome Deputy Jennings."

"Mom!" Sarah admonished playfully, suddenly envisioning Nick's warm brown eyes, his broad shoulders, his unshaven jaw. "He's just being nice." She tried to shake the image.

"You could use someone nice." Her mother grabbed the arm of the bench and pushed herself to a standing position. Sarah resisted the urge to jump up and help every time her mother did something. She knew her mother wouldn't want to be fussed over every second.

"Deputy Jennings *is* a very nice man. I've noticed him drive by quite often when he's working."

"He's doing his job, making sure I'm safe. I appreciate that he left his truck here in case we need transportation."

"You can make all the excuses you want, Sarah Lynn. But don't let your past dictate your future."

Sarah smiled, but didn't say anything.

"Can I see those horses?" her mother asked Mary Ruth.

"Sure. I saw little Patience playing by the barn. She'd be happy to show you her family's animals." It went without saying that Mary Ruth hoped she wouldn't run into Ruben.

"If you don't mind, I'm going to go in and do some paperwork."

Her mother waved her hand. "Go, go. We'll be fine."

Sarah watched her mother walk slowly next to Mary Ruth. She took comfort in knowing that her mother did seem content, despite her health and relocation.

Thank You, Lord.

Sometimes the simplest prayer was one of gratitude. *Thank You.*

When Sarah reached the back door, she heard her cell phone ringing. Nick had insisted she have one. He had registered it in his name and only a few trusted people had her number. She ran up the steps and into the house and grabbed the phone off the kitchen counter. She didn't recognize the number.

"Hello?"

"Hello," came the quiet voice, "is this Sarah Lynn?" Not everyone knew her full name.

"Yes?"

"Hi, I got your name from the pastor at Apple Creek Community Church. He told me you might be able to help me…" The woman's voice trailed off, and Sarah thought she heard her sniffle.

"Is everything okay?"

"No, I'm afraid my baby and I can't afford food, and I'm worried."

"The church has a food pantry."

"I don't have a car, and I've reached my wit's end."

Sarah paced the kitchen, and as the woman explained her dire situation, Nick's truck parked in the driveway came to mind.

"What's your name?"

A long pause stretched over the line. "I'm Jade Johnston. I live on the old farm on Route 62 out past the Troyers' garden nursery."

"Do you have food for your baby for today?"

Sarah thought she heard a child cry in the background, but she couldn't be sure.

"I'm so stupid. I don't know how I got myself in this situation. The baby's always hungry."

"Is the baby still on formula?" Sarah's mind raced.

"No, no. The baby's two."

"Okay." Sarah thought about calling Nick, but he was working and he had done so much for her already.

What could it hurt to help this woman? It would only take a few minutes, and she had the truck. She wouldn't be walking along the road, exposed.

"I'll bring some groceries to you today. And then we'll have to fill out some paperwork to make sure you and your baby have services until you get on your feet again."

"Oh, that would be great. Thank you."

Sarah ended the call, and something uneasy banded around her lungs. As she wrote a note to her mother and Mary Ruth and then climbed into Nick's truck, she assured herself her feelings of unease stemmed from the woman's desperate call and not her apprehension of driving out to an unfamiliar house alone.

Sarah turned the key in the ignition, dismissing her anxiety as one of the hazards of being a social worker. Always cautious.

Nick always looked forward to his lunch break at the Apple Creek Diner. He parked his cruiser along the curb and strolled inside. He tipped his hat at the couple sitting in the booth by the window. The elderly pair seemed to have claimed that table as their own.

Nick had grown up in Apple Creek. Despite his parents' wealth, they had insisted on public education through high school. After he graduated, he joined the service. His parents, who understood the need to follow one's passion, didn't dissuade him from going into law enforcement, although they would have preferred a safer path.

Nick had been back in Apple Creek a year, and he was still trying to get accustomed to the fact that everyone seemed to think they knew him. When most of them only knew that he was one of the Jennings' kids who grew up in the big house on the escarpment. They didn't truly know him.

Anonymity didn't exist in small towns.

"Hello there, Nick." Flo the waitress strolled over to his table. *Point made.* "We have chocolate cream pie and lemon meringue today."

"Oh, tough choice. Let me have a BLT for now, and I'll give my dessert choice some careful consideration." A slow smile crept across his face.

Flo put in his order, then made her way back over to him. "I was surprised to see you pull up. I thought you might have had the day off or something."

Nick cocked his head in curiosity.

"I saw your truck go by not more than ten minutes ago. Thought maybe you were headed out for another picnic with that pretty social worker I've heard you've been spending time with."

Nick blinked slowly and laughed. Truly nothing got past the residents of Apple Creek.

"Shame about her mother. Curious that her mom

would come to Apple Creek and Sarah didn't move back to Buffalo to help her while she's ill."

Apparently some rumors didn't get circulated. Namely, the one about Sarah being stalked by her ex-boyfriend. "I left her the truck in case she wanted to go somewhere with her mom."

Flo patted his shoulder. "You really are a good guy—" she leaned in conspiratorially "—despite what some people say."

Nick shook his head. "I can only imagine what *some* people say."

"I think it's a good thing you're doing. Helping her. Before you came along she seemed lost."

The cook dinged the bell. Flo strolled over to get his sandwich and returned, sliding the plate in front of him. "Have you decided on the pie?"

Nick twisted his lips, as if it were a hardship to decide. "I'm feeling chocolate cream today."

"Sounds good. I'll bring you a slice after you finish your sandwich."

The bells on the door chimed, and Flo walked away to seat a couple young men who were most likely taking summer classes on the nearby campus.

Alone with his sandwich and his thoughts, Nick couldn't help but wonder where Sarah was headed in his truck. She had seemed reluctant for him to leave it there, but he had insisted. He didn't like the idea of her isolated with a sick mother and a potential stalker around. Even though that hadn't been his intent, Sarah had told him she'd only use it in a true emergency.

Nick's heart sank. *Had something happened?*

Nick grabbed his cell phone from his utility belt and stared at it a minute before dialing. He didn't want Sarah to feel uncomfortable about using his truck—even if it was to do a grocery run—but a little voice in the back of his head nudged him to check in with her. To make sure she and her mother were okay. Sure, everything had been quiet recently, but that didn't mean Jimmy wasn't lying in wait.

The thought sent renewed anger pulsing through his veins. He put down his sandwich and dialed Sarah's number. He held his breath, waiting for her to answer.

She answered, sounding like she had run to the phone. "Where are you?"

Sarah gave her location before she paused midsentence and let out a bloodcurdling scream.

"Sarah! Sarah!" he yelled into the phone, but his pleas were only met with silence.

Chapter Nine

Sarah slowed the truck as it climbed the crest on Route 62. She'd passed the Troyers' nursery about a half mile back and knew the farm where the woman called from for assistance had to be just ahead. Sarah wasn't used to driving such a big vehicle and worried if she'd be able to navigate it up the driveway over a small wooden bridge over a ditch lining the country road. Many a drunk driver had ended up in a ditch along country roads in the dark of night.

Why did most of her nervousness surrounding driving always have to circle around to her dad's tragic accident? *Accident?* The man that had chosen to drink and then drive had killed her dad. That was no accident. He had acted willingly. Foolishly. Recklessly.

Sarah shoved the thought aside and focused instead on this good deed. This was how she had gotten through life. Refocus all her negative energy on good deeds. Helping others.

Her mother was right about her need to become a social worker. *Worker, heal thyself.*

If only.

She turned up the driveway and gripped the steering wheel tightly as the weight of the truck made the wooden slats of the makeshift bridge over the ditch groan. Calling to tell Nick he could retrieve his truck from a trench wasn't on her list of things she wanted to do. He had already gone too far out of his way for her.

Not to mention her strong desire *not* to be stranded in the middle of nowhere. She glanced over at her purse on the passenger seat, grateful she had a phone.

Sarah parked the truck alongside a broken-down home with gray siding that probably hadn't seen the underside of a paintbrush in fifty years. An abandoned Amish buggy sat unused and broken next to a barn farther back on the property. She had automatically assumed the caller was not Amish and figured that still might be the case, considering it wasn't unusual for the Amish to sell their homes to the *Englisch* and vice versa. She squinted through the windshield. Someone lived here? A child, no less?

Unease and goose bumps swept across her skin. Maybe it hadn't been a good idea to venture out here alone.

Before she lost her nerve, Sarah pushed open the truck's door and stepped out. Renewed determination to help this small family urged her forward. If she didn't help them, it was likely no one would.

Sarah grabbed the two bags of groceries she had picked up at the store, not wanting to take the time to visit the food pantry at church. God forgive her, but there was no such thing as a quick visit to the church with the pastor's wife there. She was a talker.

Sarah grabbed the handles of the plastic bags and strode toward the door. Dappled light filtered through the branches onto the pathway, stepping stones littered with brown pine needles. The word *isolated* popped into her mind. She pushed her shoulders back, much as she had done when approaching a new client's house, especially in a tough neighborhood.

Never let them see you sweat.

Sarah knocked on the door, and much to her surprise, it swung open on creaky hinges.

"Hello?" She poked her head in. The room was sparse with garbage gathered in the corners. A stroller parked in the middle of the room was the only indication someone with a child lived here.

"Hello?" Pulse pounding in her ears, Sarah stepped into the room. A baby blanket was bunched up in the stroller with a stuffed animal. A bottle was abandoned in the pile. Sarah picked it up and sniffed it. The milk wasn't spoiled, so someone had been here recently with a baby.

Her heart sank when she thought of a baby living in this squalor. A stale, dusty scent tickled her nose.

"Hello," she called again, her voice squeaky. All her training taught her to wait outside, make herself aware of her surroundings. Yet here she was standing in the middle of a seemingly deserted house.

All alone.

A breeze lifted the torn lacy curtain covering the window, and a shiver raced down Sarah's spine.

Sarah spun around and ran out of the house the way she had come in, suddenly feeling vulnerable. When she stepped outside, a breeze whispered across her damp skin.

Her ears perked when she heard a dog barking around back. Relief washed over her. *They must have stepped outside and didn't hear me at the front door.*

Adjusting the grocery bags in her grip, she made her way to the back, watching her step on the uneven ground. When she reached the other side of the house, abandoned toys from a yellow dump truck to a red plastic wagon littered the yard. On closer inspection, it seemed someone had used the neglected Amish buggy as a climbing toy. A child had left a small car on the seat.

Sarah set the groceries on a shaded patch under a large tree in the yard. Rubbing her palms together, she spun around to listen for the dog again. Maybe it had been a neighbor's pet.

Then she heard it. The barking sounded like it was coming from inside the barn. The barn—in a state of disrepair much like the house—sat in a strip of sun, making it seem less ominous. The barking grew frantic now, and Sarah wondered what was wrong. Perhaps the young woman who had called her had been hurt.

What about her baby?

Breaking into a jog, Sarah reached the open barn door. It took her eyes a minute to adjust to the heavy shadows broken up by sunlight slipping in through wooden slats, shrunken over time. The barking seemed to be coming from above her. That's when she saw him. A fluffy white dog standing on the ledge of the loft barking at her.

Sarah glanced around. Other than a few rusted tools, the barn, like the house, seemed to be uninhabited.

"How'd you get up there?" she said to the dog while approaching the loft. A ladder rested against the edge, and her confused mind wondered if the dog had climbed the ladder.

That wasn't possible, was it?

Sarah knew she couldn't leave the dog up there. If no one came for it, he'd die of thirst.

But how did he get up there?

Sarah grabbed her phone out of her purse and stuffed it into the back pocket of her jeans, feeling better about having it with her. She put her purse down on the straw-covered ground and grabbed a rung of the ladder. She shook it, trying to determine if it would hold her weight. It seemed pretty solid, and she didn't weigh that much.

The dog barked frantically down at her. The urge to rescue the dog and get back home was suddenly overwhelming.

Cautiously, she climbed the first few rungs of the ladder. The third rung creaked under her weight. Afraid she'd lose her nerve, she rushed to the top. When she reached the edge of the loft, the furry dog licked her face. "Hold on." Sarah scrunched up her face against the onslaught of kisses. "Back up so I don't fall." She laughed at the dog's enthusiasm. "How did you get up here anyway?" She grabbed on to the top of the ladder with one hand and held the dog back with the other. She debated for a minute how she was going to tuck the dog under her arm and navigate the ladder.

Holding on tight, she glanced down at the ground. From up here, it seemed much farther than when she was at the bottom looking up. Her knees grew weak.

This was so not a good idea. Didn't fire departments rescue animals? The phone she had stuffed into the back pocket of her jeans rang. She grabbed it with the hand that she had been holding the dog's collar with, and the furry animal took the opportunity to lick her squarely on the cheek. "Cut it out," she said before answering the call.

"Hello."

"Hey, where are you?"

"I'm at a farm on Route 62 just past the Troyers' nursery. I got a call from…" Out of the corner of her eye she saw a shadow explode out of the dark corner and bear down on her. A scream ripped from her throat as she dropped the cell phone.

She watched it smash against the barn floor in disbelief.

Panic had her scrambling down the ladder before she lost her balance and tumbled to the ground.

And then nothing.

Nick tossed money on the table, more than enough to cover his meal and tip, even though the diner offered those in law enforcement a meal for free. He jogged out to his patrol vehicle and flipped on the lights and headed toward Route 62 and the Troyers' nursery.

Strangely, he found himself saying a quick prayer for Sarah's safety. He hadn't said a prayer since he had been in a war-torn country, where the constant battles, death and destruction wore on him, making him question why he even bothered.

Just past the nursery, he slowed and glanced at each farm as he passed by. There weren't too many, but then he saw his truck parked in front of an old house and he couldn't help but mutter, "Thank You, Lord."

His relief was short lived when he noticed the windshield of his truck was smashed. Nick glanced around, but didn't see any sign of Sarah.

"Sarah!" he called.

No answer.

He jogged up to the house and found the front door ajar. "Sheriff's deputy," he announced as he strode into the abandoned house. It appeared as if a squatter lived here. Yet, a relatively new-looking stroller sat in the middle of the room.

Had Sarah come here to help a young mother?

Where are you, Sarah?

Nick made his way out the back door where he heard a dog barking from the rundown barn. With his hand hovering over his weapon, he moved quickly to the barn. He flattened himself against the exterior barn wall and leaned around to peer into the barn, not wanting to make himself a target.

It took his eyes a minute to adjust to the heavy shadows. His attention was drawn to the loft, where a dog was barking frantically. Then his gaze dropped. Sarah lay on the ground, unconscious.

Nick quickly scanned the barn, and except for the barking dog and the back of the loft where he couldn't see, the place seemed deserted.

He crouched by Sarah's side and brushed her hair out of her face. A steady pulse beat in her throat, and once again he thought, *Thank You, Lord.*

"Sarah, Sarah… It's Nick. Wake up."

Sarah's face scrunched up, and then she opened her eyes and winced. "Oh…what happened?"

She tried to push up on an elbow, and Nick told her to relax. Stay put.

"I was hoping you could tell me what happened."

"I was called out here by a young mom who needed assistance. When she wasn't home—" Sarah seemed to be struggling to piece together her memory of events "—I heard the dog." Her gaze drifted to the loft. "He's still up there. Someone else was up there." Her pale face grew whiter. "I was trying to get away and fell."

"Who? Did you see his face?"

She winced. "No."

"Stay put."

He aimed his gun toward the loft as he climbed the ladder slowly, hoping not to make a sound. To gain the advantage. Otherwise he was going to be in some serious trouble if someone appeared in the loft pointing a gun down at him.

The dog's barking grew frantic. *That* wasn't going to help him.

When Nick reached the top, he stared into the far reaches of the loft. The heavy shadows made it hard to discern if someone was lurking there. When nothing moved, he pulled himself onto the loft and tested his weight on the aged beams. Trusting that it was going to hold him, he moved swiftly to check each corner of the loft.

Empty.

Whoever had been waiting for Sarah was gone.

His stomach dropped. Sarah was alone on the floor of the barn. He moved to the edge of the loft and breathed a sigh of relief when he saw Sarah sitting against a support beam.

"I thought I told you to stay put."

She lifted her palms. "I did. I think I sprained my ankle. I hope it's not broken." Thankfully, she had made it half way down the ladder before she fell.

Nick scooped up the dog under his arm and backed down the ladder. He put the fur ball down on the ground, and the dog promptly ran to Sarah and licked her.

A beautiful smile graced her face as she playfully tried to fend the rambunctious dog off. "Friendly little thing." She felt around his furry neck. "No collar."

"I want to get you to the health-care clinic. Check you

out." Nick crouched next to Sarah and plucked a strand of hay out of her hair.

Her smile grew serious. "Jimmy's not going to stop, is he?"

"We don't know that it's him." Nick knew he was grasping at straws. They had to find a way to trap this guy.

"Who else would do this?" Sarah glanced up at the loft. "He wants to hurt me. He's mad that I left, and now he's toying with me. Making me suffer."

"Who called you out here?"

"A young woman. She said her name was Jade Johnston." She frowned and rubbed her forehead.

"We'll have to find her. Get her to answer some questions. But that can wait. Can you stand?" Nick asked, eager to get her safely home.

"On one foot." She scooted forward, and Nick wrapped his arm around her waist and pulled her up. Her hair smelled of flowers and hay, and a warmness surrounded his heart.

If only they had met under different circumstances. She wasn't in a relationship frame of mind, and he had been burned himself. But that wasn't something to think about now.

The dog barked at their feet.

Nick supported Sarah, and she tried to hop walk. She groaned as she leaned heavily on him. Suddenly, Nick had an urge to get out of here, fast.

"I'm going to carry you."

Before she had a chance to protest, he swept her off her feet. In an effort to lighten the mood, he grumbled, pretending she was heavy.

She playfully tapped his chest. "Thanks a lot." She

pointed back to the fluffy little white dog. "We can't leave him here."

"Come on, girl," Nick said and the dog ran at his heels while he strode out of the barn, determined to tuck Sarah safely in his vehicle and get her away from this deserted place.

Immediately.

Sarah wrapped her arm around Nick's neck and tried to support her own weight. But each time she put weight on her one ankle, pain shot up her leg.

She appreciated his help, but she felt more than a little foolish when Nick lifted her, as if he were carrying a bride on her wedding day. With her aching ankle, she didn't have much choice. She just prayed it wasn't broken.

She was embarrassed that she had come out here alone and allowed herself to be a target.

Sarah hadn't exactly had a good year.

As Nick rounded the dilapidated house carrying her, Sarah's mind immediately went to the stroller she had found inside. But all thoughts of that disappeared when she saw his truck.

"Oh, your truck." The windshield was smashed. She felt sick to her stomach. "That's something Jimmy would do," she whispered. "He probably thinks we're dating, and he wants to destroy your truck." If he was watching her house he would have seen it parked there. He might have gotten the wrong idea.

Nick didn't slow his pace. When he reached his patrol vehicle, he put her down. Sarah supported herself on one foot on the hard-packed dirt. "I'm sorry."

"Lean against the car."

She did as she was told, and he unlocked the front passenger door and held it open for her. "Get in."

Nick helped guide her inside, then leaned across her to buckle her in. He smelled clean, like soap and aloe. She hated that she was causing so many problems for this sweet man.

He opened the back door for the dog and she hopped right in. "I'll swing back later and see if I can locate the owners."

Once he climbed in his side, he said, "Don't worry about my truck. That can be fixed."

Sarah tried to move her ankle and groaned. "I'm sure my ankle can be fixed, too."

Nick shifted in the driver's seat to face her. "We have to catch this guy. You shouldn't have to live like this, always looking over your shoulder."

Sarah's heart sank. "Maybe it's time for me to move."

A shadow crossed the depths of his eyes, eliciting an emotion she couldn't quite name. "Do you think running will solve your problems?"

Tears burned the back of her eyes. "Mom's sick. I can't subject her to this."

"And moving will be a good thing?"

"Of course not." Guilt and fear were her steady companions.

"You're safer in Apple Creek with me to protect you." As long as she stayed home.

Renewed anger boiled in her gut. She wasn't a violent person, but the way she felt right now, she could wring Jimmy's neck.

Without waiting for her reply, Nick started the car and turned around to get out of the driveway. "I'll have a tow truck pick up my truck later. We need to get you checked out at the clinic."

Sarah shifted in her seat, trying to get comfortable.

"I don't know what I'd do if I hadn't met you."

Sometimes God puts people in your path when you need them most.

Nick gave her a quick, sideways glance. "I'm glad you didn't have to find out."

Chapter Ten

The next few days were quiet as Sarah recuperated from her sprained ankle. Thankfully, it was just a sprained ankle. Her mother and she had caught up with a few episodes of their favorite show on Netflix. Their dog, who they named Lola, seemed content, like she had belonged to them all her life. Nick had tried to find her owner without success. Sarah was happy for the little fur ball.

Nick spent nights at her home, hoping to catch Jimmy—or whoever it was—in the act of harassing her, but mostly Sarah supposed Nick only caught a crick in his neck and bags under his eyes.

Nick still slipped in after dark and left just after the sun rose. It seemed he wanted to protect her, but not intrude on her life.

The phone number of the young woman who had called to lure Sarah to the abandoned barn had been a dead end. And according to county records, the house had been abandoned for three years. Jade Johnston didn't exist. Someone had been very careful.

"Hello," Mary Ruth called from the back door. "I brought dinner."

Sarah aimed the remote at the TV, and the screen went dark. She tried to respect Mary Ruth by keeping TV and other worldly things at a minimum when she was around. And lately, she had been a huge help, providing meals and companionship as Sarah recovered from a concussion and a sprain.

Sarah's mother was the first to get up from the couch. "Oh, Mary Ruth, you shouldn't have." Her mother lifted the lid on the dish and drew in a deep breath. "But we're so glad you did." Her mother set the dish on the table and grabbed three plates from the cabinet.

Leaning heavily on the arm of the couch, Sarah stood and carefully checked her weight on the sprain. It was definitely getting better. A tiny headache pulsed behind her eyes. Christina had said that was to be expected with a concussion. Sarah was also supposed to limit screen time, but staring at a blank wall was driving her crazy. When the TV started to bother her, she'd shut her eyes.

Mary Ruth strolled back to the door as if to leave.

"You have to join us," Sarah's mother said. "We enjoy your company."

Mary Ruth lifted her hand. "I really shouldn't."

"Do you have plans?" Sarah grabbed a few forks out of the drawer.

"No, but…"

"No, but nothing. Join us. My mother and I love your company."

Mary Ruth's face lit up. "I enjoy spending time with you, too." Then her voice grew soft. "I've been arguing a lot with my parents lately. It's easier for me to stay away because when I'm home, they're pestering me about talking to the bishop about baptismal classes." She tugged at her bonnet strings. "They question my choice in friends." Mary Ruth met Sarah's gaze.

Sarah's heart sank. "I wish they didn't feel that way. But I understand. Please let them know I respect your Amish ways and would do nothing to offend you."

Mary Ruth waved her hand and laughed. "Sometimes they think the Amish can do no wrong. But you and I know better." Sarah and Mary Ruth locked eyes. They had heard a lot at the group meetings from some of the Amish youth. Many things that would make the bishop question if they'd ever be ready for baptismal classes.

"All people make mistakes. All people deserve the opportunity to turn their lives around." Something niggled at the back of Sarah's brain. "In order to help people, we have to make sure what they tell us is kept in confidence."

Mary Ruth's face flushed bright red against her white bonnet. "I would never gossip about what goes on at the meetings at the church."

"I know you wouldn't." Sarah softened her tone. "But sometimes we don't think much of telling one person, who then tells another." She shrugged. "You know how it goes."

Mary Ruth got a worried look in her eyes that made Sarah uneasy.

"Is everything okay?" Sarah asked, feeling the tips of her fingers tingle.

"*Yah*, fine." Mary Ruth opened the cabinet and got out glasses. She had spent a lot of time here lately. "I worry that my parents will forbid me to continue helping you."

"What do you want to do, honey?" Maggie asked.

"I enjoy helping Sarah. Some of the Amish might not come to the meetings if I wasn't there. They'd be intimidated, or maybe think they were doing something wrong."

"Try to talk to your parents, and ultimately, you're an adult. Do what you feel is right," Sarah said, knowing that wasn't being truly fair. The Amish weren't brought up to do what they felt was right for themselves. They were taught to live with the community in mind.

With the final dinner preparations complete, they gathered around the table and said a silent prayer. Sarah took a bite of mashed potatoes and smiled. "I don't know what you put in these potatoes, but they're wonderful."

"They sure are," her mother said. "It makes me miss cooking." Her mother made a thoughtful expression, which meant she was up to something.

"What is it, Mom?"

"Wouldn't it be nice to host a picnic? I'd love to have corn on the cob, grilled chicken, fresh salad."

"You need to rest, Mom."

Her mother waved her hand in dismissal. "I feel great. I don't know if it's the country air or just knowing I don't have the burden of taking care of my home. I have the energy. I want to do this. Now, while I can. It would be a nice way to thank Mary Ruth and our neighbors for all their thoughtfulness while you've been laid up."

Sarah slowly flexed her ankle, testing to see if it still hurt. She had been a good patient and had been resting it. "I can help."

"I don't need help." Her mother smiled, transforming her face. "Let's do this."

Maggie's enthusiasm was contagious. As a social worker, Sarah knew that having a goal and something to look forward to often helped patients to maintain a positive outlook. A sense of shared enthusiasm had her grinning. "Okay, let's do this."

Her mother leaned over and planted a kiss on Sarah's forehead. "I'm so excited." She beamed, and Sarah tried to memorize the moment.

"Now, tell me, where can I find pen and paper? I want to make a list."

Sarah patted her mother's hand. "First, eat."

Mary Ruth lifted her glass in a quasi toast. "I can help with the picnic, too."

Nick came to the house earlier than usual that night, and he and Sarah went out onto the porch to talk.

"I'm not sure this picnic is such a good idea," Nick said, watching the sun dip low over the horizon. At times like this, he understood why his parents left the city and moved to the country. Nature could be spectacular.

Sarah leaned her head back on the rocking chair and sighed heavily. "My mom's excited. I don't want to take this away from her."

"We don't know what Jimmy's up to or if he's paid someone to harass you." Nick had contacted his friend who was doing him a favor by keeping tabs on Jimmy, and he reported back that Jimmy hadn't left the Buffalo area. The obvious answer was that Jimmy had paid someone to harass Sarah. Or, even more perplexing, someone altogether different had it out for her. Neither Sarah nor Nick wanted to believe their Amish friends would go to such lengths to hurt her.

Sarah leaned forward and glanced back at the house. Lowering her voice, she said, "I'm not going to let Jimmy take every little bit of joy out of our lives. My mother's time is limited. We're not going to stay locked up in the house for fear that Jimmy might or might not show up."

Nick ran his hands back and forth across the arms of the wooden rocker. She had a point.

"You'll be there, right?" Sarah angled her head up at him and smiled. "You'll protect us." The way she said the words—half serious, half dreamy—warmed his heart.

Nick couldn't help but smile at her eager face. He reached out and ran the back of his knuckle across her soft cheek. Her face flushed a soft pink. He pulled his hand away. "I'm sorry."

Sarah surprised him and reached out and touched his hand. "I'm not." She lifted her hand and touched his face. She grew serious.

Nick's heart raced, and he leaned forward and brushed a kiss across her soft lips. He pulled away and studied her face. She blinked slowly, then a small smile graced her lips. He immediately wanted to kiss her again, but used restraint.

"So," she said playfully, "does this mean we're going to have a picnic?"

He raised an eyebrow. How could he say no to Sarah?

The day of the picnic was one of those glorious days in Western New York that made up for the months and months of winter with its cold temperatures and gigantic parking-lot snow piles. The sunshine and low humidity made living in this part of the country totally worth it.

Sarah stood in the doorway, holding a casserole dish she had just taken out of the oven. They couldn't have asked for a better day weather-wise. Her mother sat, head tipped in conversation with Miss Ellinor and Pastor Mike, on the wicker set they had moved from the front porch onto a patch of shaded lawn in the back. Maggie had a purple bandanna wrapped around her head. Her hair was slowly growing back now that she had stopped doing chemo.

Don't think about cancer today. Today is a celebration of summer. Of life.

The hiss of meat hitting the hot grill snapped her attention toward Nick, who stood at the fire with a fork in his hand. He looked comfortable at his station, as if he belonged there. At this house. With her. Neither had discussed their second kiss over a week ago, and it seemed like he was trying to avoid her. His last girlfriend must have really done a number on him.

Yet, he still came to her home late at night and left early in the morning, spending the night on the lumpy cot in the small room off the kitchen.

Her protector.

A warm breeze kicked up and blew a strand of hair across Sarah's face and tickled her nose. She didn't have a free hand to tug it away.

"Here, let me get that for you." Nick had put aside his grilling fork and took the casserole dish from her. Their fingers brushed in the exchange, and the memory of their kiss made her skin flush.

"Thank you."

Nick placed the dish on the table with the rest of the food. "The chicken's almost done."

"Great," Sarah said, suddenly not sure what to do with herself.

"Hey, I'm starving," Maggie called from across the yard. "What are you slowpokes doing?"

Sarah's heart filled with joy. Her mother really seemed to be doing well today. On days like this, she really missed her father. He should have been allowed to grow old and been there for his family.

Nick took the chicken off the grill and set it on the table, buffet style. The brothers, Ruben and Ephram, had lugged the long table from their barn. The Amish were well practiced at hosting a lot of people for meals. Every other week, one Amish family hosted the Sunday service and a meal afterward.

Christina and Mary Ruth strolled over to the table and sat down. The Zook family, minus their father, Amos, who was away at an auction, played a powder-puff game of volleyball. Temperance and Ephram against the younger siblings, Ruben and Patience. Mostly it seemed to be about letting Patience win. Sarah smiled, realizing some things were universal regardless of the cultural differences.

Sarah hoped that maybe Ruben and Mary Ruth could learn to be cordial, friends even. It was a small town, yet she hadn't noticed them talking. It was more a game of sticking to opposite sides of the yard.

"Does anyone need a fresh drink before we sit to eat?" Nick called. Before Sarah had a chance to take over, Nick walked away to collect the orders. Christina looked up at Sarah from the other side of the table. "I've never seen my brother look so happy."

Sarah tried to keep from smiling like the fool she was and sat down on the bench across from Nick's sister. "I was thinking the same thing about my mother." Instinctively, she changed the subject, uncertain of how to respond to what Christina had said. It didn't seem right that she could possibly make a man like Nick happy. He could have had any woman and certainly someone with far less baggage than she carried around.

"Your mother does seem happy." Christina lowered her voice and cut her gaze toward Maggie, who was still happily entertaining the pastor and his wife. Lola sat at her feet and enjoyed pats on the head from all of their guests. "Please don't hesitate to contact me if she gets uncomfortable. We can adjust her meds. There's a lot that can be done to make sure she remains pain-free."

Sarah nodded, unable to find the words. Every time she thought of her mother's illness taking over her body, a hollowness expanded inside her chest and crushed her lungs.

"I'm sorry, I shouldn't have brought that up right now." Christina reached between the tray of chicken and Miss Ellinor's famous potato salad and took Sarah's hand. "And don't think I didn't notice how you deflected the topic of my brother."

Sarah furrowed her brow in mock confusion.

"My brother really likes you. Don't do anything to hurt him, okay?" Christina's breezy tone held a hint of warning.

A knot twisted in Sarah's stomach. "I would never do that. Not intentionally. But you know my situation. I may have to leave Apple Creek." And Nick.

"My brother would never tell you this, but his last girlfriend broke his heart. *Really* broke his heart." Sarah knew more than she should have thanks to Miss Ellinor.

Sarah tracked Nick as he walked across the yard, stopping to talk to her mother. He seemed at ease and comfortable in jeans and a golf shirt. *Man, he is handsome.*

"I have a hard time believing someone would do that to a guy like Nick." Sarah's gaze snapped to Christina's, and heat flooded her face, wondering why she kept talking.

"He has a good heart. Sometimes I think women want

the bad boy. Outwardly, he may look like a bad boy, but he's not." She shrugged. "Amber broke up with him when he was overseas. Talk about low. Before he left, he had told me he could see being with her long-term." Christina pulled her hand away and brushed her bangs out of her eyes. "Anyway, I probably shouldn't tell you all his business. It's his story to tell. But he's my big brother and I love him and I see how he looks at you…"

Sarah ran her hand across the back of her neck, suddenly aware of every inch of her skin. Before she had a chance to say anything, Nick strolled over to them and handed each of them a soda. His gaze slid from his sister and then to Sarah. "What? Did I interrupt something?"

"Um…" Sarah let the word trail off.

Christina spoke up. "Sarah was saying how nice it was to have a man cook dinner for her."

Nick crossed his arms over his broad chest. "I wasn't cooking. I was manning the grill."

Sarah hitched an eyebrow. "Either way, the chicken looks great."

Nick's focus drifted to his sister. "I thought maybe you'd bring a date. Isn't it about time?"

Christina had been in the middle of taking a long swig of her soda, and she nearly spitted it out. "Way to get right to the point, big brother." Sarah had never seen the confident doctor blush before.

"Can't let one bad relationship stop you from finding another," Nick said, watching his sister carefully.

"Nice to know you take your own advice." Christina gave her big brother a wicked grin, then turned to wink at Sarah.

"See, this is what she does. When she doesn't want to

discuss her lack of social life, she turns it around on me."
Nick playfully tugged a loose strand of his sister's hair.

"You asked for it."

Sarah smiled at the exchange. Growing up an only child had some advantages, such as having the sole attention of her parents, but she never enjoyed the camaraderie of a sibling. A sibling would be a wonderful asset right now as she dealt with her mother's health crisis.

Dread whispered across her brain. *When Mom dies, I'll be all alone.*

Just as Sarah's thoughts were traveling down a dark path, she noticed Patience tearing across the grass toward her home, her long dress flapping around her legs. "*Dat*'s home. *Dat*'s home!" Across the field, Amos climbed out of his wagon, and he seemed to be looking—glowering actually—in her direction.

Sarah stood and called to Ruben, who was still standing near the volleyball net. "Invite your father over. There's plenty of food."

All the color seemed to drain from Temperance's face. "It wonders me if it's not time we went home. Amos must be tired from his day, and he'll be looking for a quiet meal."

Maggie's face fell. "Oh, don't run off. We have all this food."

"I'm afraid we must." Something in Temperance's tone and rushed movements unnerved Sarah.

"Is everything okay?" Sarah asked, her attention shifting back to Amos, who worked with jerky movements to unhitch their horse from the wagon.

Temperance studied the ground for a moment before looking up. "Amos isn't very social. He likes to eat at home."

"That's a shame," Maggie said, her tone resigned.

Sarah smiled at her mother, feeling her disappointment. But Sarah also understood Temperance. She and Amos had a traditional Amish relationship where the wife deferred to the husband. Of course, every Amish relationship wasn't the same, but theirs was very traditional.

"May the children stay and eat?" Maggie asked, hope radiating from her bright eyes.

Temperance bit her lower lip. Ephram stepped forward and tipped his straw hat. "Thank you for your hospitality, but I'm afraid we should go."

Sarah felt Nick's hand on the small of her back and did her best not to lean into him. As much as she wanted to.

Sarah's gaze drifted to Mary Ruth, who sat quietly eating with a blank expression on her face. It was a shame Mary Ruth and Ruben didn't have much time to reconcile, even if only for friendship's sake.

The glorious afternoon had definitely shifted in mood.

"Who's going to have some of my potato salad?" Miss Ellinor walked over to the table and grabbed a sturdy disposable plate. God love Miss Ellinor.

"You know I'll have some." Pastor Mike accepted the plate his wife offered him.

Sarah looked up at Nick and fought back the tears. Her mother had been so excited about hosting a big picnic, and here it was falling apart.

A soft breeze picked up and the tiny hairs on her arms prickled to life. A horrible sense of foreboding weighed on Sarah's heart. A foreboding that seemed far too unreasonable for a picnic cut short.

Chapter Eleven

Nick carried a tray of dishes into the house and set them down on the counter next to the sink.

"Thanks." Sarah grabbed a dish and submerged it in the soapy water.

The sounds of a sitcom floated in from the other room. Nick poked his head in to see Maggie on the couch with her feet up on an ottoman. "Great picnic, Maggie."

She gave him a tired smile. "It was too bad the Zooks had to leave so soon, but I had a wonderful time all the same. Your sister is such a lovely girl. I'm blessed that a doctor of her caliber is right here in Apple Creek. She takes good care of me."

Nick smiled. "Christina is very good at her job, and you are a wonderful patient."

Maggie's cheeks colored. He had noticed a change in her since her first day in Apple Creek. She seemed relaxed. At peace. Nick tipped his head toward the kitchen. "I'm going to grab a few more trays from the yard."

Maggie shifted in her seat, as if to get up, when Nick waved his hand. "There's only a few things. I've got it."

Maggie smiled and sank back into the couch. "If you insist."

Sarah glanced over her shoulder at Nick. She lowered her voice. "This was a great day for my mom. She needed something like this." She turned on the water and rinsed the suds from the glass and placed it upside down in the drying rack. "It's too bad our neighbors couldn't stay. I haven't been able to shake this horrible feeling since they left. I'm not sure why."

"You wanted everything perfect for your mom. But she seems content. The picnic was, by all accounts, a success."

"Miss Ellinor is lively conversation. And your sister seemed to connect with Mary Ruth." She shook her head as if deep in thought. "I worry about Mary Ruth. She's at a fork in the road. Sometimes I worry—despite my best attempts—that I'm a negative influence."

Nick jerked his chin back. "I can't imagine."

"I worry that she longs to live a different kind of life. One with TVs and careers."

"That's her choice."

Sarah leaned her hip against the counter and crossed her arms. "I know, but when I came here, I vowed to help the Amish without interfering in their way of life." She shrugged. "Maybe that was an unrealistic goal. Just by being here, I'm interfering."

"You're too hard on yourself."

Sarah turned back around and grabbed another dish out of the soapy water and began to scrub. "I had no idea that Amos kept such a tight rein on the family."

"The Amish are different."

Sarah grabbed a pair of glasses from the counter and placed them into the hot, soapy water. "Oh, I know. It's just that Temperance almost seemed frightened. Like a teenager who had done something wrong. I would have never invited them to the picnic if I had known it was going to be a problem."

Nick placed his hand on her arm. "You did nothing wrong. I know lots of Amish and *Englisch* who call each other friends and dine together." He frowned, realizing he could no longer delay telling her what had been on his mind.

"How did Mr. Zook feel about renting this house to you?"

Sarah slipped the dish towel from the oven handle and dried her hands. She leaned back on the counter, her forehead scrunched in concentration. "I hardly know the man. It has always been his wife, Temperance, and their children who I see. Temperance told me they decided to rent out the house for the extra money." She lifted a shoulder. "I don't suppose the breadwinner of the family would feel too good about his wife thinking he wasn't making enough."

"My thoughts exactly."

"You're not suggesting that Mr. Zook has been behind these…incidents," she said, apparently for lack of a better word.

Nick leaned against the counter next to Sarah, a clunky white drawer handle between them. "I don't think it's likely, but it's worth making note of."

"It has to be Jimmy. Or someone Jimmy hired."

"Unless," Nick said, truly grasping at straws, "Mr. Zook found my presence here to be yet another bad influence for his impressionable children, even though my presence is completely innocent."

Sarah crossed her arms and nodded. He detected a hint of pink creeping up her neck.

She pushed off the counter and pulled out a kitchen

chair, the legs scraping loudly against the wood floor. She flopped down in it and stared at the dirty food trays stacked on the table. She bowed her head, and her long blond hair fell forward. He wanted nothing more than to take her into his arms and comfort her.

He pulled out a second chair and sat in front of her, their knees pressed against each other. "I didn't bring this up to stress you. Rather, I think we need to be vigilant. Maybe danger is closer than we thought."

Sarah tucked a long strand of hair behind her ear. "You think I attract this many crazies?"

A smile tugged at the corners of his mouth. "Do you think I'm crazy?"

She ran a hand through her hair and laughed. "You're the craziest of them all."

The next morning, Sarah still couldn't get Nick's concern regarding Amos Zook out of her head. She watched from the front window until she noticed him leave in his buggy. She had cleaned Temperance's tray—the one she had used to bring fresh corn to the picnic—and decided she'd return it as an excuse to stop over and chat.

Sarah told her mother she'd be right back and slipped out the door. Unease knotted her insides as she strode across the yard. Despite the heat, she chose to wear khakis and a long-sleeved top instead of shorts and a tank. If Amos happened to come home, she didn't want to give him more reason to be annoyed with her.

If he was annoyed with her. Maybe both she and Nick had read too much into the Zook family's quick departure from the picnic last night. Maybe it was simply as Temperance had suggested—her husband liked a quiet meal at home with his family.

She lifted her hand to knock when the door swung open. Ruben stood in the doorway holding his little sister's hand. His eyebrows lifted in surprise. "I didn't know you were there."

Sarah laughed, but she felt like the joke was on her. "I hadn't had a chance to knock yet. I was bringing your mother's tray home." She lifted her arm and offered him the tray.

"I'll take that." Patience reached up and grabbed the dish. She spun around and ran toward the kitchen.

"Thank you. Is there anything else?" Ruben asked, a curious light in his dark eyes.

"I'm sorry things didn't work out with Mary Ruth."

Ruben immediately looked down and tapped the door-frame with his worn boot. He shrugged shyly. "I'll find someone else. But Mary Ruth is going to have a hard time." He looked up under the fringe of his bowl-cut hair. "Word's gotten around that she's spending too much time with outsiders."

Sarah's pulse kicked up a notch. "Are you referring to me?"

"You're not Amish, are you?"

Sarah jerked back her head, rather stunned. She hadn't expected such direct, rather rude, comments.

"Mary Ruth isn't doing anything wrong." Not that Sarah would guess. "She's been working with me. Honest work."

"The time for that has passed. She was supposed to be preparing for baptism and our marriage."

Sarah pressed her lips together as she struggled for the right thing to say. Had she always been conditioned to search for the right thing to say? To smooth things over?

"It's unfortunate that you feel that way. But—" it was

Sarah's turn to shrug "—like you said, you'll find someone else. Mary Ruth will be fine." Sarah felt a sudden need to defend her sweet friend.

Ruben twisted his lips, and a flicker of something flashed in his eyes. Sarah was about to ask him if she had somehow offended him when his mother appeared behind him.

Temperance's gaze moved to the road and then back to Sarah as if she was worried her husband would return.

Sarah pointed toward the kitchen. "I returned your dish. Patience put it away."

"Denki." Temperance lifted her eyebrows in expectation. "Is there something else? I have chores to do, and Ruben was going to take Patience into town for errands."

"Could I talk to you in private?"

A thin line creased Temperance's forehead. "Is something wrong?"

"I'll take Patience." Ruben disappeared into the house, and Temperance stepped onto the porch and closed the door behind her.

The floorboards of the front porch creaked under Sarah's steps. "I hope we didn't cause any trouble by inviting you to the picnic yesterday."

Temperance jerked her head back. *"Neh,* Amos was tired after his day at the auction. Our calves didn't fetch as much as he had hoped, so he was grumpy. Actually, the rent you pay helps tremendously right now."

"Are you sure everything is okay?" Sarah struggled to read the woman's guarded expression.

"Yah, everything is fine." Temperance reached for the door handle. "I'm sorry, but I have a lot of chores to do this morning. Please don't give it another thought."

"Okay." Sarah lingered for a moment before realizing Temperance wasn't going to open up to her. "Have a good day, then."

The Amish woman nodded and slipped back into the house. Sarah strolled across the yard, disappointed the meeting hadn't gone as she had hoped. Sarah stopped when she reached her porch and glanced back at her neighbor's home. She had the unnerving feeling that someone was watching her.

Insisting that Sarah not be without a vehicle while his truck was being fixed, Nick rented one for her. Initially, she resisted. He had already done so much for her. But now she was grateful. She had to run out for groceries. Her mother seemed especially tired this afternoon, and Sarah didn't want to leave her alone for long.

Sarah drove into the neighboring town and stocked up on groceries from a superstore. Tired yet relieved to have someone like Nick in her corner, Sarah made the drive back to her little home in the country.

The longer she was away from the house, the more she had a growing sense that something was wrong. She sent up a quick prayer that her mother was okay. Sarah hadn't left her mother alone for more than a few minutes here and there since she had moved in with her in Apple Creek. She prayed that nothing had happened to her in the two hours she was gone.

Sarah parked in front of the house and popped open the trunk. She grabbed the bags and headed toward the front door. She fumbled for the key, but something told her to try the handle. The door swung open.

Her heart dropped. She had distinctly locked it before she left. Maybe her mother had come outside to sit on the porch and then forgot to lock it again.

"Hello, Mom," Sarah called.

Silence except for the muffled sounds of barking.

She stepped into the room. Long shadows lingered in the corners. An episode of a familiar home-improvement show flickered on the corner TV set. Her mother was sitting in her recliner, her head angled in an awkward position.

Icy dread pulsed through Sarah's veins. She set the bags down on the floor and untwisted her hands from the wound-up plastic handles. "Mom?" she called again, hating the fear strangling her voice.

Sarah touched her mother's throat and said a prayer of thanks when she felt a steady pulse.

"She won't be up for a while."

Sarah's head snapped up. Jimmy stood in the doorway leading to the kitchen. Sarah backed up and tripped over the grocery bags and landed with an oomph.

Despite the sharp pain that shot up her spine, Sarah scrambled toward the door. Jimmy reached it first and slammed his hand against it. "Where do you think you're going?"

Her vision narrowed, a dark tunnel focused on his face. His mean, angry face. *How had I ever been attracted to this man? His ugliness radiates from his soul.*

"Don't do this, Jimmy. Let me go," Sarah pleaded, hating that she couldn't mask the fear in her voice.

"Are you going to leave your dear precious mother? And what about that rat of a dog I locked up in the bathroom? You know what I'm capable of."

"Please, leave us alone." She fought to keep the panic from her voice.

"Your mother was thirsty, so I ground up an extra dose of pain killers in her water. Now we can talk without being interrupted."

"I don't want to talk." Sarah jutted her chin out in a display of confidence she didn't feel.

Jimmy tilted his head. "That's obvious, since you took off without saying goodbye."

Sarah crossed her arms over her chest. Jimmy let his hot gaze travel the length of her.

"What? No thanks for looking out for your mother while you were gone and she was alone in Buffalo?"

Jimmy had stopped by to see her mother multiple times under the guise of checking up on her, but Sarah knew it was a ruse to find out where his former girl-friend was hiding.

"How did you find me?"

He stepped closer to her. "I'm a cop. It's what I do."

"You give cops a bad name." She blinked slowly, the rage building inside her. "Leave me and my mother alone. She deserves to spend her days in peace."

"If you didn't rip her away from one of the top treat-ment facilities, she wouldn't be counting down her last days. *Some* daughter you are." She could smell the al-cohol on his breath. "Nice try, but I didn't believe your mother went to Florida for a minute. Keep asking enough questions, someone finally slips up. You can thank a new nurse who thinks I'm rather handsome."

Sarah's stomach knotted.

There it was, Jimmy doing what Jimmy did best. Per-suading people. Trying to guilt her. But he wasn't going to succeed this time.

Her sole focus was to get rid of him. *Now.*

"Since you're standing next to the door, I suggest you leave," she bit out, trying to keep her jaw from trembling.

"Or what?" he asked in a tone Sarah suspected he

first began to hone during his bullying days back in junior high.

Once a bully, always a bully.

"Jimmy, I don't want to be with you. There's no reason for you to be here."

He lifted his index finger and jabbed it in her face. "You humiliated me with my department."

Sarah squared off her shoulders. "*You lied*. You cost me my job. My friends. My home."

"You did it to yourself…" He took a step closer, his solid frame looming over her. "You can't be happy here in the sticks. Come home." His voice intended to be smooth, silky, convincing. Instead she heard it as grating, pathetic, annoying.

"I *am* home."

Hope sparked in her racing heart. *She's home.*

Jimmy let out a rough laugh. "Who's the guy?"

"There's no guy." The words rushed out before Sarah could think things through. Mean Jimmy was bad enough. Jealous Jimmy was ruthless.

"Don't lie to me. I saw his overnight kit in the bathroom." He lifted an eyebrow. "Unless you or your mother have taken to using a man's razor and aftershave."

Her mother stirred in the chair. Sarah struggled to look past Jimmy, but he grabbed her cheeks. "Look at me while I'm talking."

Sarah batted his hand away. Her jaw trembled, and she feared she wouldn't be able to get the words out. "He's here to protect me and my mother."

"From what?" Contempt dripped from his voice.

"You!" she screamed, losing patience. "From you! I'm sick of you terrorizing me." She charged him and shoved at his solid chest. He didn't budge. "Get. Out. Now."

Jimmy reached up and clutched her arms and set her aside, as if she were a rag doll. "What do you mean? Terrorizing you?"

"You've been hounding me for weeks."

Jimmy smiled, mocking her. "I have no idea what you're talking about. I didn't find your address until that dear, sweet nurse on your mother's hospital floor blurted out where you were. Must have been the uniform that convinced her to tell me." The smile slid from his face. Evil radiated from his eyes.

"I don't believe you. You've been harassing me and my mother."

"I only wanted to make sure your mother was okay. What, with you running off and all."

Sarah's pulse beat steadily in her ears. "Please leave," she said, defeat edging her plea.

"Nope, don't want to." Jimmy plopped down on the couch as if he owned the place. "Why don't you make me and your mother something to eat. I'm hungry. And get me a beer while you're at it."

Sarah slipped past him into the kitchen, not bothering to tell him she didn't have any beer.

"Don't try to call anyone or get any ideas. You might get away, but your mom won't."

Sarah pulled out a pot and filled it with water; her movements were on autopilot. She had no idea what she was going to make. Or how she was going to get out of this mess.

But one thing she knew for sure, she couldn't leave her mother alone with Jimmy. He'd likely kill her just to prove a point.

Chapter Twelve

Nick was debating whether he should head to the diner for something to eat or risk showing up at Sarah's with an empty belly. He never wanted to presume he was a *regular* houseguest. He had a purpose. A job. To protect Sarah and her mother.

All indications pointed back to Jimmy. But until Jimmy messed up, Nick would have to keep doing his job. He had made a habit of arriving at Sarah's later in the evening so as not to intrude on her time with Maggie.

He didn't mind being her protector even if it involved sleeping on a lumpy cot in what must have once been a large pantry off the kitchen. He had caught a few z's in far rougher accommodations.

Nick was still undecided on what he was going to do now that his shift was over when his cell phone rang. He pulled it out and frowned. It was Matt, his friend who was keeping tabs on Jimmy.

"Yeah," Nick said, curtly.

"I have bad news. Jimmy's gone."

A knot twisted in his stomach. "What do you mean, he's gone?"

"Jimmy arrived for work. He's been on second shift recently. He parked behind the station and went in. I figured with the start of his shift, it was pretty safe to run and grab a bite to eat. When I came back, I noticed his truck was gone. I called one of my contacts at the station, and they said he went home sick." The private investigator's words seemed to be traveling through a long tunnel, getting further and further away.

"Let me guess. His truck's not at his house."

"No. I checked every location he's known to frequent. He's gone."

A muscle ticked in Nick's jaw. "Thanks for the heads-up. Call me if you find him." Nick ended the call and pressed his foot on the accelerator. There was no longer a question as to where he was headed.

When he reached Sarah's house, he pulled around back, scanning the landscape. That's when he saw it. The sun glinting off a piece of metal, the hood of a truck parked partially hidden by the barn. He shut off the ignition and climbed out.

Hand poised above his gun, he strode to the back porch. Nick poked his head around and saw a pot of water boiling on the stove.

He yanked open the screen door and cringed when it sent out a loud screech.

Jimmy stepped into the kitchen with an obnoxious smile on his face.

"What do we have here?" Jimmy asked, his words slurred. He glanced over his shoulder at something Nick couldn't see. "Your boyfriend's home."

"Jimmy, please, just leave." Sarah appeared behind Jimmy, a haggard expression on her face.

"Are you okay?" Nick asked, his hand lingering near his gun.

She blinked slowly, but didn't say anything.

Jimmy's gaze dropped to Nick's right hand. "What are you going to do, shoot me?" Jimmy rolled his eyes. His cheeks were flushed from drinking.

"The lady asked you to leave. I suggest you leave."

Jimmy twisted his lips. "I'll leave when I'm good and ready."

"I say you leave now." Nick took a step toward Sarah's former boyfriend. Jimmy blinked slowly, assessing the situation.

Jimmy smirked and sauntered toward the door. "I'm leaving." He pointed a finger in Sarah's face. "But I'll be back."

Jimmy pushed out the screen door, and it slammed shut behind him. Nick watched as the man crossed the yard and got into his truck. The tires spit out gravel as he tore out of the driveway.

"Are you okay?" Nick asked, pulling a trembling Sarah into his embrace.

With her head against his chest, she nodded. Then she pushed him away and ran to her mother. She bent down and patted Maggie's hand. "Mom, Mom?"

The older woman stirred, but didn't open her eyes.

Sarah glanced over her shoulder at him, worry lines creasing the corners of her eyes. "We need to call Christina. Jimmy drugged my mom. She's been out of it since I arrived home."

Nick dialed his sister's number and spoke to Sarah while he waited for Christina to pick up. "Jimmy was here waiting for you?"

"Yeah," she said on a shaky breath.

Nick nodded and then spoke to his sister when she got on the line. Assured she'd be right over, he hung up and called the dispatch to pick up Jimmy. He didn't seem to be in any condition to drive.

"Mom?" Sarah called again.

Her mother turned her head and half opened her eyes. Certainly a good sign.

"How do you feel, Mom?"

"So…so…tired."

"Christina's on her way."

"That would be nice." Maggie was still groggy, but at least she was coming around.

Nick paced next to Sarah. "What did Jimmy say?"

"Same old story. He wants me to come home. I kept asking him to leave."

"I should have been here," he scolded himself.

Sarah touched his arm. "I'm okay. You came when it counted." Then she cocked her head. "How did you know?"

"Matt called me when he realized Jimmy was missing." Nick rubbed his jaw. "Did Jimmy tell you how he found you?"

"Yes, but it can't be the whole truth. He claimed he got the info that my mom was here with me from a nurse at the hospital. But he knew I was here all along."

She shook her head, a distant look in her eyes. "He's been harassing me well before my mother ended up in the hospital."

"He's a known liar."

"I know. I learned that the hard way." She dragged a hand across her hair. "Am I going to have to move with my mother?" Her gaze drifted over to Maggie.

Nick's heart sank. He couldn't ask her to stay on account of him. But, then again, he couldn't protect her if she moved away from Apple Creek.

Sarah could finally breathe again when Christina showed up and assured her that Maggie would be fine. Groggy, but fine. Sarah and Christina helped Maggie into bed. Lola climbed in next to her. It seemed they both needed reassurance after their stressful day.

The rest of them returned to the sitting room. Tension rolled off Nick as he paced the small space, making and taking phone calls. It seemed that all his fellow officers were on the lookout for Jimmy's truck.

Nick was like a caged animal, ready to strike but confined to this place to protect Sarah in case Jimmy made his way back here as he had promised.

Jimmy's angry face was seared in her memory. He had left drunk and in a blind rage.

Nick opened his mouth to say something when his phone rang again. He held up a finger, then turned his back to take the call. Sarah listened—her heart thudding in her chest—as Nick gave a series of quick, one-word answers. When he turned back around, all the color had drained from his face.

Sarah's blood turned icy cold in her veins. She wanted to ask him what was wrong, but the words got tangled in a knot of emotion.

"That was Sheriff Maxwell."

"What's going on, Nick?" Christina spoke up for both of them.

"There's been an accident."

Pinpricks of panic raced across Sarah's flesh. She lowered herself onto the arm of the couch. "Jimmy?" The single word squeaked out. "Did he hurt someone?"

Nick crouched down in front of her and pulled her hands into his. Sarah lifted her gaze to Christina, who had a hand pressed to her mouth. Sarah met Nick's gaze and pleaded with her eyes to tell her what was going on.

"He crashed into a tree. Barely missed Ruben Zook in his wagon on the way back from town."

"Oh, no," Sarah breathed.

Nick squeezed her hands. "Ruben's fine." They locked gazes, and Sarah knew what he had to say before he said it.

"Jimmy's dead."

The walls swayed, and sweat broke out on her brow. Sarah pushed to her feet and felt lightheaded. She touched the back of her mother's recliner to steady herself. "Are they sure?"

"Yes."

A myriad of emotions playing out on Nick's handsome face. But most of all she saw compassion.

Sarah lifted her hand to cover her heart. "God forgive me, but I feel relieved. Is my nightmare finally over?"

A sad smile slanted the corners of Nick's mouth. "Jimmy Braeden won't be causing anyone any more trouble ever again."

Chapter Thirteen

Sarah brought her mother tea out on the front porch, where she sat in a rocker. "How do you feel this morning?" She set the tea down on the small side table. A few days had passed since Jimmy's fatal accident, and Sarah was still trying to get her head around it.

Her mother's chest expanded. "I don't know what it is about the country air, but I feel good." She covered her mouth and coughed. She leaned over and took a sip of the tea and waved her hand, apparently registering the concern on her daughter's face. "I'm fine. Just a little tickle in my throat."

They both knew it was more than a tickle, but her mother seemed to be enjoying her respite in the country.

"This place sure is quiet without Nick here," her mother said, changing the subject.

"Well, with Jimmy…" Sarah struggled to acknowledge his death. He had been a dark cloud hanging over her for so long.

Jimmy was really gone. Dead.

"Now that Jimmy can't hurt me, Nick doesn't have to protect us."

She traced the rim of her teacup. "Nick'll be missed. He's a good guy."

Sarah recalled the few phone calls Nick had made to her since Jimmy had driven his truck into a tree. Their conversations had been cordial, but always skirted around what was now at the forefront of her mind—could she and Nick have a future?

Why? What's the point? She'd be leaving Apple Creek soon.

"I've been thinking," her mother said.

"Sounds like trouble." Sarah laughed as she sat down next to her. There was a certain sadness in her heart knowing that Jimmy had lost his life. He had been a miserable man, but he was still someone's son and brother. Needless to say, she didn't go to the funeral or make contact with his family. They would feel nothing toward her but blame.

Even though her rational side told her he had brought this downfall upon himself. Her soft heart couldn't help but feel she had been partially responsible.

She knew it was ridiculous. She hoped time could heal all wounds, as they said.

"Are you going to tell me what you're thinking about?" Sarah asked.

"Staying here." Her mother tapped the arms of the rocking chair. "Right here."

Sarah made a funny face. "On the front porch?"

"You are a funny girl. No, right here in Apple Creek. It's peaceful. I feel good out here. The old house back home reminds me too much of all the sadness in our lives. This place feels fresh. Like new possibilities." A smile tugged at the corner of her mother's mouth. "Or maybe it's the fresh-cut grass I smell." She tilted her head and glanced at the farm next door. "I love watching the Amish family work. It's fascinating. It beats watching the soap operas and Mr. Davidson next door to the old house walk that yappy dog of his." Lola lifted her head as if she knew what they were talking about, then settled back down.

"Oh, Trinket—" Mr. Davidson's Jack Russell terrier "—wouldn't hurt a fly."

"I know. But that old man didn't do the dog any favors by not training him." Mostly her mother didn't appreciate Mr. Davidson not cleaning up after the small dog. Sarah couldn't blame her. "So, what do you think? Should we stay in Apple Creek for a little bit longer? Maybe until winter?"

Sarah thought of the poor clients in the rural countryside, the young struggling Amish and Nick. A spark of hope blossomed in her heart. "It's something we could consider," she said noncommittally when her heart was thumping, *yes, yes, yes.*

Sarah closed her eyes and tipped her head, resting it against the rocker. The sun warmed her face. She started to doze, then startled awake. She blinked a few times as the cornfield swayed in her line of vision. She no longer had anything to fear.

Jimmy was gone.

Yet a whisper of dread tickled her brain. *What if Jimmy hadn't been the only one harassing me?* She shook away the thought, figuring a person couldn't live under the constant threat of harm for so long without suffering negative aftereffects.

Jimmy's gone. Relax.

A few days later, Sarah said goodbye to the last young Amish man from her Sunday-night meeting in the church basement, then turned to Mary Ruth. "Let's leave the sweeping for another day."

Mary Ruth set the broom aside and smiled. "Sounds good."

"Come here, sit down."

Mary Ruth's eyes widened and her cheeks grew flushed as if she had done something wrong.

Sarah smiled. "I want to talk. So much has gone on, and I wanted to make sure you're okay."

Mary Ruth's hand flew to her chest. "You want to make sure I'm doing okay?" She angled her head in disbelief. "How are *you*?"

Sarah paused and gave her answer thoughtful consideration. "I'm doing well. I've done a lot of praying about Jimmy and realize he made his own choices."

"And how is Deputy Nick Jennings?"

Sarah reached over and playfully tugged on Mary Ruth's dress, the long fabric draping over her legs. "You've been talking to my mother."

"I love visiting with your mother. You're lucky to have her. My *mem* has been giving me what you'd call the cold shoulder since I called things off with Ruben. I suppose she assumes there are…what is the expression?…no more fish in the sea."

Mary Ruth's joke didn't mask the sadness radiating off her.

Sarah looked her young Amish friend in the eye. "Don't feel pressure to do anything you don't want to do."

Mary Ruth laughed, a shy awkward noise. "You sound like you're talking to the group about drugs or alcohol."

"I suppose that advice holds true for a lot of things. If you're not sure about your future, give it some prayerful consideration."

"Amish life isn't like *Englisch* life. Most of my friends are married. One is expecting a baby already." Sarah thought she detected a whiff of longing in Mary Ruth's voice.

"Is that what you want?"

"Someday, sure. But—" Mary Ruth shrugged "—I'm not sure. It seems my parents are harder on me ever since my brother left Apple Creek."

"Tell me, how would your life be different if your brother had stayed?"

"For one, my parents wouldn't be so focused on me all the time. I'm their second-oldest kid. I think they're having nightmares about how bad it will reflect on them if another one of their kids leaves."

Sarah reached out and caught Mary Ruth's hands. "Stop worrying about everyone else. What do you want to do?"

Mary Ruth blinked slowly. "I don't know."

"And that's okay." Sarah squeezed her hands. "Give yourself time."

Mary Ruth pulled her hands away and swiped at her long dress in a self-conscious gesture.

"Is that what you're doing?" Mary Ruth asked, her voice barely a whisper.

"What do you mean?"

"Giving yourself time to figure things out? Deputy Jennings sure seems to be sweet on you."

It was Sarah's turn to squirm in her chair. "My focus is on my mom."

"I've talked to your mom. She'd like you to channel some of that focus on something else."

Sarah laughed. "I guess I've been a bit of a hoverer."

"Like I said, you and your mom are lucky to have one another."

"You'd think she'd be bored at the house all day, but she enjoys being out in the country."

"Didn't you guys used to do some crafts? Maybe you could do that."

Excitement bubbled up in Sarah's chest. "That's a great idea. I should collect some of the flowers growing by the creek, and we could dry them out and make a wreath for the door."

"Sounds like fun. I could also teach your mom how to quilt."

Sarah nodded. "Sounds like a great idea." She tilted her head toward the door. "Should we call it a night?"

"Yah," Mary Ruth said, her Pennsylvania Dutch slipping through.

They climbed the stairs and pushed the door open, stepping out onto the church parking lot. Sarah turned the key in the door.

"Want a ride home?" Sarah asked. She had picked up a secondhand car recently. Reliable and affordable.

"I better walk. I don't want to give Mem or Dat a reason to scold me tonight."

Sarah lifted her hand and waved to the pastor's wife standing in the window with the curtain pulled back.

Turning her attention back to Mary Ruth, Sarah said, "Honoring your father and mother is a good thing, a very good thing. But you need to pray on your own future. God wants you to be happy, too."

Mary Ruth tipped her head shyly. "The *Englischers'* ways are so very different than Amish ways."

"I know, and I could never understand what it means to be Amish. So, please, consider that when you weigh my advice." Sarah lifted her eyebrows to emphasize the point.

"I hope you're praying on your future, too."

"Prayer is my constant companion," Sarah muttered.

"Then I think you're not listening too hard, because there's no way God would bring a man like Deputy Jennings into your life and expect you not to grab hold and start a new future." Mary Ruth lifted her eyebrows, mimicking Sarah.

"I'm the trained professional." Sarah forced a laugh, referring to her degree in social work.

"Fancy college degrees aren't necessary when it comes to affairs of the heart." It was Mary Ruth's turn to tip her head and study her friend closely.

Sarah shook her head and walked over to her car. The sun was hanging low on the horizon. "You'll want to hurry home before it gets dark."

Mary Ruth waved and strode across the parking lot toward the dark country road leading to her family's farm. Sarah started the car and pulled up alongside her. "Are you sure you don't want a ride?"

Mary Ruth hesitated for a moment, then scrunched up her face. "*Neh*, best if I hurry along."

Sarah sat in the car and watched her friend. Guilt rankled her for allowing the girl to walk home alone. But then again, it wasn't Sarah's choice. The young woman had a lot of choices to make for herself. Difficult ones that her Amish family may or may not agree with—depending on the road she took.

Another thought whispered across Sarah's brain. *Maybe I really am needed in Apple Creek.* One thing she knew for sure: when she left Apple Creek, she'd really miss it.

* * *

Nick's sister claimed the low-tire-pressure indicator kept popping on in her car's dash despite having put more air in the tire last night. Now, she needed a ride to check on Maggie. Nick suspected her car troubles were Christina's sly attempt at matchmaking.

Nick didn't mind. He hadn't seen Sarah in a few days, and time was slipping away. He couldn't help but fear Sarah and her mother would be moving back to Buffalo soon.

When Nick stepped through the front door behind his sister, he noticed Sarah look up from her book on the couch, a smile brightening her face.

His heart stuttered in his chest. *Man, he had missed her.*

"Good afternoon," Christina said cheerfully. "How is everyone doing?"

Sarah placed her book facedown on the side table to hold her page. "Hello. Fine, thanks. I didn't realize it had gotten so late." She blinked a few times as if trying to focus after being lost in a good book for a long time.

Maggie sat next to Mary Ruth at a large piece of fabric stretched across a wood frame. "We're doing great. Mary Ruth is teaching me how to quilt. By hand!" Maggie raised the thread and needle eye level and smiled. "Not with one of those fancy machines my friend Barbara is always going on about. The workmanship in this is incredible." She beamed with pride.

Nick leaned in to study the fabric. "Nice. Very nice." His gaze drifted to Sarah, and she glanced away.

Christina put her medical bag down on the table and studied her patient. "You do look well. The question is, how do you feel?"

"It feels great to be away from the hospital and all the treatments." She slipped the needle through the fabric to keep it in place. She set her hands in her lap. "You don't have to run out here. I promise I'll call if I'm not feeling well."

Suddenly realizing what she had said, Maggie threw up her hands. "Of course, we'd love to have either of the Jenningses visit us at any time, but it doesn't have to be an official visit."

Sarah drifted into the kitchen while Christina and Maggie chatted about her health. Nick followed her.

Sarah turned on the faucet and filled half the sink with soapy water. She set a few dishes in the water and turned around.

Nick held up his hand toward the sitting room. "My sister needed a ride."

"That was nice of you."

"I haven't seen you in town lately."

Sarah pulled her hair into a ponytail and wrapped an elastic band around it. She slumped back against the counter. "I've been seeing a few clients, but mostly I've been spending time with Mom."

"I'm glad you can enjoy this time in peace."

Sarah bowed her head and wiped at a tear that had trailed down her face. She pressed her lips together. Nick wanted to pull her into an embrace. To tell her everything was going to be okay. But it wasn't his place.

And it wasn't a promise he could make.

"I've spent so long running away from Jimmy that I missed precious time with my mom."

Nick swallowed hard, his heart breaking for her. "What's important is the time you have now."

Sarah looked up, her eyes shiny with tears. "It's hard. I still can't seem to totally let my guard down."

Nick cleared his throat. "How long do you plan to stay in Apple Creek?" He finally asked the question that had been heavy on his mind.

"Until the weather gets bad. My mom likes it here."

"It's not a bad place." Nick ran the back of his knuckles across her cheek.

Her face flushed.

"My parents were in town for a few days. They come home every so often to recharge, as they like to say."

Sarah brushed past him and sat down at the kitchen table. "Where are they now?"

"Jetted off to Paris." He waved his hand. "Or some other international city. They're semiretired now, so most of their travel they claim is for leisure. But knowing my parents, they've got their hands in different business ventures."

"I would have liked to meet them." She dragged her hand down her ponytail. "How did two wealthy entrepreneurs raise a police officer?"

"What about my sister the small-town doctor?"

Sarah raised her eyebrows. "But she's still a doctor." She laughed and shook her head.

"You need to meet our little sister, Kelly," Christina wandered into the kitchen. "Smarter than both of us combined."

Nick laughed. "Thanks, sis."

Christina smirked. "Hey, if Sarah hasn't already realized what a numskull you are, then…well, then I underestimated her."

Sarah rubbed the back of her neck, obviously feeling self-conscious.

"Ready to go?" Christina asked Nick.

He nodded, then turned to Sarah. "Hope to see you again soon."

Sarah stood. "Thanks for taking such good care of my mom. We both appreciate it."

"You're welcome." Christina squeezed Sarah's arm. "Make sure you take care of yourself, too."

Christina turned and grabbed her brother's arm. "Let's go."

Once they got outside and into his car, Christina didn't give him a chance to start the car before she started in on him. "If you let Sarah Gardner go, you're a bigger idiot than—"

"Sisterly love," he muttered.

Nick turned the key in the ignition and headed out onto the country road.

"Sarah's not Amber. You need to move past her."

Nick cut her a sideways glance. "You think I'm still pining away for Amber?" Forced disgust edged his tone.

"No, she wasn't right for you. But I think you're afraid of taking a chance. Amber said she'd wait for you when you were deployed. But she didn't. Now you're afraid to make a commitment to Sarah because you're…oh, I know…you're afraid she's going to leave."

"She *is* going to leave." Nick ran a hand over his jaw. "Besides, she's had her fill of cops."

"You're not like her former boyfriend. Any more than she's like your former girlfriend."

Nick tapped his fingers on the steering wheel. "It's not going to work."

"You know best," his sister said in the way little sisters talked to big brothers. "Like always." Sarcasm dripped

from her voice. "But relationships—solid relationships—
don't come around that often."

"Perhaps you should work on your own personal life,"
Nick said, feeling defensive.

"When I'm not saving the world," Christina replied
in a mocking tone. "When I'm not saving the world."

Chapter Fourteen

After enjoying a late dinner of take-out pizza, Mary Ruth and Sarah's mother went back to quilting. "Wow, you guys are determined." Sarah ran a finger over the delicate stitching.

"It's relaxing. You should try it," Maggie suggested. "Besides, what better thing to do on a rainy day?" The past few days had been rainy, and the two women had made a lot of progress on their quilt.

Mary Ruth looked up. "I'm enjoying this single life. If I were married, my husband would be looking for dinner and I'd probably be doing dishes—" she got a faraway look "—chasing after a toddler."

Maggie made a tsk-tsk sound. "Marriage is more than cooking dinner and doing dishes." She shook her head briefly as if stopping herself from saying more. "Just you wait until you meet the right man. A man who makes your heart go pitter-patter." Her mother met Sarah's gaze and lifted an eyebrow.

"Really now, Mom. Can we have one night where you guys aren't hounding me about Nick?"

"So, he *does* make your heart go pitter-patter." Mary

Ruth broke down in a laughing fit, her porcelain cheeks turning a bright red.

"You guys joke all you want. I'm going to stretch my legs. I need to work off all that pizza. Anyone want to join me?"

"This quilt's not going to make itself." Her mother tilted her head back and looked at the stitching through her readers.

"I'll be back shortly. The rain's let up for now."

Sarah slipped on a light jacket, and Lola jumped at her feet, eager to go outside. Once on the back porch, Sarah admired the magnificent view. Instead of walking along the country road—she had spent enough time doing that during the months she was trying to stay under Jimmy's radar—she decided to take a walk along the property's edge and farther along the creek. Maybe she'd find some of those wildflowers she promised to get so her mom could make a wreath. She hoped it wasn't too wet. Either way, she'd collect a nice bouquet of flowers.

Lola enjoyed exploring every inch of the path. The creek was babbling and racing downstream like Sarah had never seen it before. There were talks of floods in the next county.

As the long grass tickled the back of her legs, she tuned in to her strong muscles. Having lived with her mother these past few weeks made her appreciate every moment. Every full breath.

Pushing her shoulders back, Sarah strode farther along the edge of the creek. The rush of the water filled her ears. She understood why her mother was so at peace here.

Can I stay in Apple Creek?

Apprehension and a bubble of excitement swirled in her belly.

Should she take the risk?

The creek edged the back of the Zooks' property and disappeared through the woods. She had never ventured this far, but she was enjoying being alone with her thoughts and was curious where the path led. She decided she'd follow it a little way until the bugs got to be too much.

As she followed the trail along the creek, she swatted at a few insects swarming around her head. "Maybe we should turn back," she said to the dog. "It's awfully buggy out here."

A twig snapped behind her, and she spun around and came up short. Ruben was standing in her path. The way he stared at her made her skin crawl, far more than any bugs flitting around her face.

"You should have turned back a long time ago," he said, his voice even. Lola yapped at his feet.

"I'm…" Her head swirled in confusion. "What do you need, Ruben?"

Ruben pushed the dog aside with his foot, and Sarah opened her mouth to protest when he took a step toward her. Instinctively, Sarah took a step back. A million crushing moments flashed through her brain. Moments when Jimmy had intimidated her. Had kept her in her place. Had chased her away.

But Jimmy was dead.

And here another man made the same horrible feeling snake up her spine.

"I'm walking on my property," Ruben answered with a snarl.

Panic bit her fingertips and raced up her arms. Lola's

incessant barking amped up her alarm. "Excuse me. I have to get back." She attempted to brush past Ruben when his arm snaked out and caught her wrist.

"You should have left a long time ago."

Sarah yanked her arm, but Ruben tightened his grip.

"Let go!" she demanded. She forced a confidence in her voice that she didn't feel.

"*No*. You should have left Apple Creek a long time ago. What does it take?" He gritted his teeth. "I've tried everything. A dead snake. Pushing you off the ladder."

Sarah gasped and tried desperately to wrench out of his grasp.

"*Yah*, well…you're going now." Ruben took his other hand and shoved her shoulder and let go of her wrist at the same time. Sarah lost her footing and tumbled into the swollen creek. The last thing she saw before the black water swallowed her up was Ruben's icy gaze.

Nick had been thinking nonstop about Sarah these past few days. When he arrived home and glanced around, he had a startling realization: he had a house. It had everything he needed to live, but it never felt like home.

When do I most feel at home?

The answer hit him like a bullet between his eyes. He felt like home with Sarah. He dropped into the oversize chair parked in front of the television and picked up the remote, but he didn't turn it on. That's all he did when he was home. Watch TV. He supposed it was his way of avoiding the loneliness.

Nick leaned over and opened the drawer in the side table. He pulled out a framed photo of him and Amber that had been taken at the airport, him in his army fatigues, Amber in her skinny jeans and sweater, an expensive handbag hanging over her arm.

He had cared for her, but even before he got a Dear John letter from her when he was hunkered down in a tent in the middle of the desert, he had sensed it was over. Sure, the way she had done it tore his heart out.

What kind of woman broke up with her boyfriend when he was on a tour of duty? And it reinforced some trust issues.

But Sarah wasn't Amber.

Nick had been blinded by the type of women he met in his parents' affluent circles. But Sarah was the kind of woman he could fall in love with...

Fall in love...

Nick tossed the framed photo back in the table drawer and slammed it shut. He got to his feet, hurried to change his clothes, then grabbed his car keys from the table.

Nick had to tell her how he felt before she left Apple Creek for good.

For a man who claimed to have nerves of steel under a stressful situation, Nick Jennings thought his heart was going to race out of his chest as he stood on Sarah's porch with a bouquet of wildflowers in his hand.

He knocked and Mary Ruth answered. Her eyes dropped to the flowers in his hand and amusement danced in her eyes. "Hello, Deputy Jennings."

"Hello. Is Sarah here?"

"Who's here?" Maggie called from inside the house.

"It's Deputy Jennings. I think he's sweet on our Sarah."

Maggie appeared behind Mary Ruth, a colorful bandanna wrapped around her head. "Well, it's about time."

She smiled and reached around Mary Ruth to squeeze his arm. "Sarah went for a walk. I expect her back any minute." Maggie waved her arm. "Come in. Wait for her."

Nick rolled up on the balls of his feet. He couldn't wait inside. He'd go stir-crazy. "Where does she normally walk?" He hadn't noticed Sarah walking along the road on his drive over.

Mary Ruth smiled and pointed with her thumb toward the back of the house. "I believe she took a walk along the creek."

"Thanks. I'll be right back."

"Be good to my daughter," Maggie hollered after Nick as he pivoted on his heel and jogged down the steps, still holding on to the flowers. He figured the flowers would be an icebreaker when the right words wouldn't come. Besides, he didn't want an audience, even if it was in the form of sweet Maggie and Mary Ruth. What he had to say was between him and Sarah.

A nervous bubble exploded in his gut, and he picked up his pace before he lost his nerve.

Some tough guy.

He jogged around to the back of the house and followed the path until he reached the woods. He swatted at the mosquitos buzzing around his head.

In the distance he could hear barking.

Alarm spiked his pulse.

Nick wanted to call out to Sarah, but something kept him silent. He tossed the bouquet of flowers aside and ran. Something in his gut told him Sarah was in danger. Lola wouldn't be barking like that otherwise.

The gray shadows of dusk hovered over the path. The creek churned on his right, angry from the constant rains of the past few days.

Around the first bend, an Amish man in a straw hat held a long branch in his hands and was beating at something in the creek.

Instinctively, Nick's hand hovered over the gun he always carried on his belt, even when he was off duty. "What's going on?"

The man turned his head, and Nick recognized him. Ruben Zook. He lived on the neighboring farm. Nick's posture relaxed, but then a trickle of unease wound its way up his spine when he tuned in to Ruben's angry gaze. Lola barked frantically at something in the creek.

"Get out of here." Ruben lunged toward Nick.

With one hand on his gun and the other out in front of him, Nick shouted, "Step back."

A bloodcurdling scream ripped from down below, along the steep edge of the creek.

"What's going on?" Nick repeated, easing his gun out of the holster and pointing it at the young Amish man.

"She ruined my life by putting stupid ideas in Mary Ruth's head."

Nick's finger twitched, millimeters from the trigger. He didn't have to ask who *she* was. His heart pulsing in his ear, Nick grabbed Ruben's stick and shoved the Amish man, making him land on his backside. Nick tossed the stick aside and handcuffed Ruben to get him out of the way.

Nick jabbed his finger in his face. "Don't move."

Nick proceeded to the edge of the creek near Lola, careful that the earth didn't crumble underneath his footing. "Sarah!" he called, but all he saw in the gathering dark was the churning waters.

"Sarah!"

With trembling hands he flicked on the flashlight on

his cell phone and scanned the waters. He glanced over his shoulder at Ruben, who was sniveling under his straw hat.

"Did she go into the creek?"

"Good riddance," Ruben muttered.

"Sarah!" The swollen creek could have carried her a long way down. But instead of running downstream, something kept him there. He moved the beam of the flashlight along the tangle of tree branches lining the edge, and that's when he saw her.

Sarah was caught up in the branches. Her face pale. Her eyes closed. Her lips blue.

His heart sank.

Dear Lord, please give me the strength to save her. Let her be okay.

Nick slid down the embankment. Holding on to a root, he leaned precariously over the raging creek toward Sarah. With all his strength, he pulled her toward him and out of the water. "I gotcha. I gotcha."

Help me, Lord.

He put Sarah over his shoulder in a fireman's hold and used the branch to pull himself back up to the pathway. He laid her down gently and smoothed her wet hair out of her eyes.

Nick gave Ruben a quick glance. He had the good sense to stay seated. Anger heated Nick's wet skin.

He checked her airway. Clear.

He watched the quiet rise and fall of her chest.

He felt Sarah's neck for a pulse. It beat steady.

Thank You, Lord.

Nick leaned in close to the woman he had grown to love. "Sarah… Sarah…"

She groaned. The most beautiful sound he had ever

heard. She struggled, then pushed up on her elbow and hung her head, sputtering and coughing.

"Ruben…"

"I know. He's not going anywhere."

Sarah tried to sit up, and Nick wrapped his arm around her to help her to a seated position. Her body trembled despite the humid evening. "Why are you here?" She lifted her eyes to meet his.

"I came here to talk to you." The reason could wait.

Sarah lifted her hand and patted his cheek. "Good thing for me…"

"No—" he ran the pad of his thumb across her wet cheek "—good thing for me." Nick bent down and scooped her up. "Let's get you to the house."

"I can walk."

"I know. But let me do this for you."

Sarah nodded and rested her head on his shoulder.

Nick barked out orders to Ruben to stand and follow them. Nick wasn't in the mood for nonsense.

And good thing for Ruben, he followed Nick's instructions.

Lola ran ahead to the house.

When they reached the back porch, Nick ordered Ruben to sit on the lawn. He carried Sarah up the porch steps and kicked the door to get Mary Ruth or Maggie's attention.

Mary Ruth appeared at the door. "What happened?" She pushed open the door, and Nick slipped in with Sarah in his arms. Lola scooted in and curled up on the couch.

Mary Ruth grabbed a quilt from the back of the couch. Nick put Sarah down, and the young Amish girl wrapped the quilt around Sarah's shoulders.

Sarah looked up at Nick, her lips quivering. "I need to change and get out of these wet clothes."

"Are you okay? Should I call my sister?"

"I'm fine. Thanks to you." She pulled the quilt tighter around her neck and a shiver shook her body. She turned to Mary Ruth. "It was Ruben. He tried to chase me out of town."

Mary Ruth's face grew pale, and she shook her head slowly. "Ruben's been harassing you?" Her lips trembled. "I'm sorry."

Sarah touched her friend's arm. "It's not your fault. We all have to take responsibility for our own actions."

Nick smiled. Seemed Sarah had finally realized she wasn't responsible for Jimmy's horrendous behavior.

"What brought you out to the path?"

"Go change and then I'll tell you."

Sarah smiled and tossed the quilt down on the couch and with Mary Ruth's assistance, went for dry clothes.

Maggie approached Nick, wide-eyed. "What happened?"

"Turns out it was Ruben Zook who has been harassing Sarah."

"Harassing her? Why? He pushed her into the creek?" The questions flowed out one after the other without waiting for an answer.

"He blames her for losing Mary Ruth." Nick squeezed Maggie's hand. "Sarah's fine."

"Thanks to you."

"I need to call the sheriff's station. Have someone take Ruben in." Nick looked through the screen door. Ruben sat with his head bowed. He seemed truly deflated.

Chapter Fifteen

After Sarah changed into warm, dry clothes, she found Mary Ruth sitting between Nick and her mother on the couch. Lola curled up on Maggie's lap. Sarah lingered in the doorway watching Mary Ruth bent over, sobbing, her face in her hands.

Her mother patted the Amish girl's back, and Nick seemed uncomfortable. Sarah shifted her feet and caught Nick's eye. He stood and held out his arm, gesturing for her to have his seat on the couch.

As she brushed past him, Nick placed his hand on the small of her back and whispered, "You look much better. You doing okay?"

Warmth coiled around her heart. "Yes, thanks to you." She kept her voice low, feeling a little disrespectful with Mary Ruth in tears on the couch. "I can't thank you enough."

Nick glanced over at Mary Ruth as Sarah's mother handed her a tissue. "I'm glad God put me in the right place at the right time."

"I am, too." Then Sarah looked around, suddenly concerned. "Where's Ruben?"

"The sheriff picked him up. When you're ready, we can go to the station and file a report."

Sarah nodded and joined Mary Ruth on the couch. Sarah leaned close to her friend's ear. "Everything's going to be okay."

Mary Ruth straightened and drew in a shuddering breath. "Ruben wasn't the right man for me, but I never thought he was evil."

"Sometimes people become unhinged when they love someone." Sarah's thoughts went to Jimmy. "Let me rephrase that: they do crazy things for what they think is love. That's not love. You were smart to kick him to the curb."

Mary Ruth swiped at her tears. "My family didn't think so."

"Your parents want you to live your life in the Amish community. They thought Ruben was your future. But they couldn't have known he had…issues," she said, for lack of a better word. "I'm sure you and your family will reconcile and eventually you'll meet another nice Amish boy."

Mary Ruth wiped her nose. Her whole body shook from a mix of laughter and tears. "I'm not getting any younger. Where will I meet someone?"

"There's nothing wrong with spending a little time getting to know yourself." Sarah looked up and met Nick's gaze and then quickly dropped it to Mary Ruth's trembling hands. "You've had a terrible shock today. Give it time. Have faith."

Mary Ruth reached out and clutched Sarah's hand. "Look at me bawling like a fool. You're the one who nearly drowned. How can you ever forgive me for putting you in this position?"

"It's not your fault. You didn't do these things to me. Ruben did." A little voice niggled at the back of her head.

All this time she had been bashing herself for all her bad choices and how she had ruined her life. But her only mistake had been trusting Jimmy. From there, his bad choices had been his own.

Sarah closed her eyes and breathed in deeply. Despite the horrible day, she felt like a weight had been lifted. Just like she had told Mary Ruth to let it go and move on, to not blame herself, Sarah had to do the same.

Sarah was only responsible for her own choices. Her eyes lifted and she met Nick's gaze. And in the scheme of life, she had made some wonderful choices.

Nick drove Mary Ruth home. When they reached her house, he offered to go in and explain the circumstances surrounding Ruben's arrest.

Mary Ruth shook her bonneted head. "*Neh*, it's time that I spoke to my parents. Really spoke to them. There's been a lot of tension since I called things off with Ruben. If I bring law enforcement in, it won't set the right tone." She hesitated a moment. "I'm sorry."

"No, don't be. I understand."

Mary Ruth nodded and pulled the handle, and the dome light popped on. "The benefit of the rumor mill in Apple Creek is that I probably won't have to tell them much. I'm sure they've already heard." She shook her head. "Well, they've probably heard a version of the truth."

Nick turned around in the driveway and as promised, headed back to Sarah's house. He had left her to chat with her mother. They both needed reassurance after what happened tonight. Ostensibly, he needed to bring her to the station for her official statement, but more important, he needed to tell Sarah what had brought him to her home earlier tonight in the first place.

When he arrived at her house, he was surprised to find Sarah sitting in the front-porch rocker. Nick climbed out of his car and strolled toward her. The moonlight glinted in the whites of her eyes. He placed his foot on the bottom step and rested his elbow on the railing.

"Mom was tired. She went to bed." Sarah answered the unasked question.

"Good. I'm sure she'll sleep well."

Sarah lifted her eyebrows. "I know I will."

"The first time I came over tonight—" Nick shifted the conversation, eager to say what he had been waiting to say all night "—I had a bouquet of wildflowers in my hand."

She rocked the chair by pushing her bare toes on the wood slats. "Likely story."

"Really. I did. But then I had to rescue someone."

"Someone? Really? So, you're a hero?" She pushed to her feet and crossed over to him. Nick climbed another step. She stopped at the top step looking down at him.

"I wouldn't call myself a hero."

"I would." She reached out and cupped his cheek, her warm fingers sending tingles of awareness through him. "How can I possibly thank you for being there for me tonight?" Sarah's voice cracked over the last words. "I don't want to think what could have…" she shook her head, and a shudder traveled through her body.

"Are you cold? Maybe you should go inside."

Sarah shook her head again. "It's a beautiful evening."

Nick wrapped his hand around her wrist and kissed the palm of her hand. She smelled fresh and clean from the shower after her dip in the creek.

Nick led her to the wicker love seat at the far end of the porch.

He tracked the lines on the palm of her hand. "I came over earlier tonight to tell you how much I cared about you. How I hoped you'd stay in Apple Creek. How I hoped we could make a serious go at—" he flicked his fingers in the air between them "—whatever this is between us. I mean, I've had trust issues. My last girlfriend..." Suddenly, he found himself rambling.

He had finally realized he couldn't let the hurt from his past relationship with Amber influence his future happiness. Sarah was nothing like Amber.

The pulse in his ears grew louder, drowning out his words. *Why isn't she saying anything?* Maybe it was too soon. Maybe he was...

Sarah leaned closer and brushed a kiss across his lips. She pulled back and stared deeply into his eyes. "I promised myself I'd never date another cop."

"I—"

Sarah pressed her index finger against his lips and smiled. "When I made that promise, I didn't know you." She pulled away her hand and traced his jawline with her thumb. "I have never met someone as caring as you. I would love to take the time to get to know you better." Her eyes lingered on his. "You can trust me."

"I know." A weight lifted from Nick's heart. "Does that mean you'll be staying in Apple Creek?"

Sarah glanced toward the door. "My mom loves it here. And full-confession mode—" she smiled brightly "—I do, too."

Nick took Sarah's face in both his hands and gave her a proper kiss. "I love you." He kissed her again, and he felt her lips curve against his into a smile.

Sarah wrapped both her hands around his wrists and beamed up at him. "I love you, too."

Epilogue

14 months later...

Nick arrived home from work and strode through the empty house. He reached the back door, and his heart lifted. His beautiful wife sat under the shade of the oak tree in their backyard of a newly renovated home in Apple Creek. It was probably one of the last few warm days before the weather would turn cold and snowy.

Nick still couldn't believe they had been married almost a year now.

Major life decisions took on new meaning when time was no longer a luxury.

Mary Ruth sat on the blanket with Sarah. His mother-in-law sat in a lawn chair looking lovingly at her granddaughter in her daughter's arms.

Nick's heart nearly burst with joy.

Things could have gone far differently if God hadn't been watching out for Sarah when Ruben had decided she was the root of his problems.

Turns out, Miss Ellinor, the pastor's wife, had confided in Ruben's mother about Sarah's need to get away from an abusive boyfriend. Her intentions had been innocent enough; Miss Ellinor was looking for a rental for Sarah. However, Ruben had eavesdropped. And when Mary Ruth had broken up with him, he used the information to try to scare Sarah. To make her think her ex had found her. Ruben had hoped to get Sarah away from Mary Ruth, whom he felt was unduly influenced by the evil *Englischer.*

Ruben confessed to everything, from throwing the rock through the church window to luring Sarah to the empty house and pushing her off the ladder. He never revealed whom he paid to make the phone call, but the young girl probably didn't realize what Ruben's true intentions were.

Thankfully, Ruben wasn't internet savvy, or he may have tracked down Jimmy himself and sent him after Sarah earlier. Nick prayed Ruben would change during his three-year stint in prison.

Nick needed to shove those memories aside, but he found they made him profoundly grateful.

He pushed open the back door and strolled across the lawn. "Hello. Did my little princess nap for you today?" He studied his wife's face. She was tired, but she always assured him it was tired in the very best possible way.

Sarah shook her head and planted a kiss on her daughter's forehead. "I had help, though, so I was able to take a little nap." She handed their daughter over to Maggie and adjusted the blanket around the baby.

Sarah came to him and wrapped her arms around his waist. He cherished the easy nature of their relationship. Sarah took pleasure in the little things. She had been through so much and seemed to share in his feelings of gratitude. He kissed her forehead, impressed with how well the scar from the broken glass had healed.

A lot of scars had healed over the past year.

The baby let out a little cry and Sarah spun around, ready to take their daughter into her arms.

Maggie held up one hand. "I've got this under control. Did you forget who raised you?" Maggie smiled, her thin hair a soft halo around her head. She had defied all the doctors' expectations for life expectancy. Through both the Gardner women, Nick had learned to take each day as it came. Sarah's family was different from his, who were always looking for the next achievement. The next goal. The next honor.

Nick loved the family that he was born into, but he loved the contentedness and satisfaction he felt with his new family: Sarah and little Emma May.

Sarah reluctantly pulled out of Nick's embrace. Every time he came home from work—*every time* he entered a room—a flush of warm emotions wrapped around her heart.

Her life had been a nightmare when she first moved to Apple Creek; now it was more than she could have ever hoped. She glanced over her shoulder at her mother and Mary Ruth cooing over her fussing baby—*Nick's and her* baby.

"I better start dinner." Sarah moved toward the house.

"Oh, no, let me do it." Mary Ruth stood and swatted at the back of her long dress. Sarah waved her off.

"I enjoy cooking, especially if Emma May is content with her auntie Mary Ruth and Grammy."

Mary Ruth beamed. "I'm really going to miss you all."

A thin line creased Nick's brow. "Miss us?"

Mary Ruth shook her bonneted head. "I've decided to spend some time in Florida."

"Florida?" Nick asked, obviously only able to get one or two words out at a time.

Sarah placed her hand on her husband's forearm. "Mary Ruth is going to spend some time with her grandmother in an Amish community in Florida."

"It'll be a nice change of pace." Mary Ruth ran her hand down Emma May's soft head. "But I'll visit." She lifted a shoulder. "The community is in affiliation with Apple Creek. I'll be free to come back if I wish. I have to figure out what I want to do."

Marriage was a well-respected institution among the Amish, and it had become apparent that Mary Ruth felt alone among all her married or soon-to-be married friends.

"I've made some money selling my quilts to buy a bus ticket. I leave next week."

"Well," Nick said, "we'll miss you, too."

"Absolutely. Well…dinner isn't going to make itself." Sarah went into the kitchen and opened the refrigerator.

Nick came up behind her and wrapped his arms around her waist and nuzzled her neck. "You smell nice."

Sarah turned around in his embrace and hugged him back. "What did I ever do to deserve you?"

Nick whispered in her ear, "You've deserved only good things all along. I'm just glad I was here when you finally realized it."

* * * * *

WE HOPE YOU ENJOYED THESE
LOVE INSPIRED®
AND
LOVE INSPIRED®
SUSPENSE
BOOKS.

Whether you prefer heartwarming contemporary romance or heart-pounding suspense, Love Inspired® books has it all!

Look for 6 new titles available every month from both Love Inspired® and Love Inspired® Suspense.

Love Inspired

Save $1.00

on the purchase of any
Love Inspired®,
Love Inspired® Suspense or
Love Inspired® Historical book.

Available wherever books are sold, including
most bookstores, supermarkets, drugstores
and discount stores.

Save $1.00

on the purchase of any Love Inspired®, Love Inspired® Suspense
or Love Inspired® Historical book.

Coupon valid until October 31, 2017. Redeemable at participating retail outlets in
the U.S. and Canada only. Limit one coupon per customer.

Canadian Retailers: Harlequin Enterprises Limited will pay the face value of this coupon plus 10.25¢ if submitted by customer for this product only. Any other use constitutes fraud. Coupon is nonassignable. Void if taxed, prohibited or restricted by law. Consumer must pay any government taxes. Void if copied. Inmar Promotional Services ("IPS") customers submit coupons and proof of sales to Harlequin Enterprises Limited, P.O. Box 3000, Saint John, NB E2L 4L3, Canada. Non-IPS retailer—for reimbursement submit coupons and proof of sales directly to Harlequin Enterprises Limited, Retail Marketing Department, 225 Duncan Mill Rd., Don Mills, ON M3B 3K9, Canada.

U.S. Retailers: Harlequin Enterprises Limited will pay the face value of this coupon plus 8¢ if submitted by customer for this product only. Any other use constitutes fraud. Coupon is nonassignable. Void if taxed, prohibited or restricted by law. Consumer must pay any government taxes. Void if copied. For reimbursement submit coupons and proof of sales directly to Harlequin Enterprises, Ltd 482, NCH Marketing Services, P.O. Box 880001, El Paso, TX 88588-0001, U.S.A. Cash value 1/100 cents.

52614981

5 65373 00076 2   (8100)0 12295

® and ™ are trademarks owned and used by the trademark owner and/or its licensee.

© 2017 Harlequin Enterprises Limited

LIINCICOUP0717

Ruby Plank comes to Seven Poplars to find a husband and soon literally stumbles into the arms of Joseph Brenneman. But will a secret threaten to keep them apart?

Read on for a sneak preview of
A GROOM FOR RUBY by **Emma Miller,**
available August 2017 from Love Inspired!

A young woman lay stretched out on a blanket, apparently lost in a book. But the most startling thing to Joseph was her hair. The woman's hair wasn't pinned up under a *kapp* or covered with a scarf. It rippled in a thick, shimmering mane down the back of her neck and over her shoulders nearly to her waist.

Joseph's mouth gaped. He clutched the bouquet of flowers so tightly between his hands that he distinctly heard several stems snap. He swallowed, unable to stop staring at her beautiful hair. It was brown, but brown in so many shades…tawny and russet, the color of shiny acorns in winter and the hue of ripe wheat. He'd intruded on a private moment, seen what he shouldn't. He should turn and walk away. But he couldn't.

"Hello," he stammered. "I'm sorry, I was looking for—"

"Ach!" The young woman rose on one elbow and twisted to face him. It was Ruby. Her eyes widened in surprise. "Joseph?"

"*Ya.* It's me."

Ruby sat up, dropping her paperback onto the blanket, pulling her knees up and tucking her feet under her skirt. "I was drying my hair," she said. "I washed it. I still had mud in it from last night."

Joseph grimaced. "Sorry."

"Everyone else went to Byler's store." She blushed. "But I stayed home. To wash my hair. What must you think of me without my *kapp*?"

She had a merry laugh, Joseph thought, a laugh as beautiful as she was. She was regarding him with definite interest. Her eyes were the shade of cinnamon splashed with swirls of chocolate. His mouth went dry.

She smiled encouragingly.

A dozen thoughts tumbled in his mind, but nothing seemed like the right thing to say. "I…I never know what to say to pretty girls," he admitted as he tore his gaze away from hers. "You must think I'm thickheaded." He shuffled his feet. "I'll come back another time when—"

"Who are those flowers for?" Ruby asked. "Did you bring them for Sara?"

"*Ne*, not Sara." Joseph's face grew hot. He tried to say, "I brought them for you," but again the words stuck in his throat. Dumbly, he held them out to her. It took every ounce of his courage not to turn and run.

Don't miss
A GROOM FOR RUBY
by Emma Miller, available August 2017 wherever
Love Inspired® books and ebooks are sold.

www.LoveInspired.com

Inspirational Romance to Warm Your Heart and Soul

Join our social communities to connect with other readers who share your love!

Sign up for the Love Inspired newsletter at **www.LoveInspired.com** to be the first to find out about upcoming titles, special promotions and exclusive content.

CONNECT WITH US AT:

Harlequin.com/Community

 Facebook.com/LoveInspiredBooks

 Twitter.com/LoveInspiredBks

LISOCIAL2017